HIS TRUE *North*

A. M. KUSI

Published by A. M. Kusi 2021

amkusinovels@gmail.com

Visit our website at www.amkusi.com

Editor: Anna Bishop of CREATING ink

Sensitivity Edit: Renita McKinney of A Book A Day

Proofreader: Judy's Proofreading

Cover Design: Regina Wamba of ReginaWamba.com

ISBN: 978-1949781199

OTHER BOOKS BY A. M. KUSI

A Fallen Star (eBook FREE on all retailers)

(Book 1 in The Shattered Cove Series)

Glass Secrets

(Book 2 in The Shattered Cove Series)

Defying Gravity

(Book 3 in The Shattered Cove Series)

The Lighthouse Inn

(Book 4 in The Shattered Cove series)

In The Grey

(Book 6 in The Shattered Cove series)

The Orchard Inn (eBook FREE on all retailers)

(Book 1 in The Orchard Inn Romance Series)

Conflict of Interest

(Book 2 in The Orchard Inn Romance Series)

Her Perfect Storm

(Book 3 in The Orchard Inn Romance Series)

For a complete list of all our books, visit:

WWW.AMKUSI.COM/BOOKS

"Boundaries are the distance at which I can love you and me simultaneously."

— Prentis Hemphill

"No one changes unless they want to. Not if you beg them. Not if you shame them. Not if you use reason, emotion, or tough love. There's only one thing that makes someone change: their own realization that they need to do it. And there's only one time it will happen: when they decide they're ready."

— Unknown

This book is dedicated to our daughters, Ellyson and Emelynn, may you forever chase your dreams despite what others tell you.

GET A FREE SHORT NOVEL

Join our newsletter to get a FREE short novel that's not available on any retailer. Plus updates about new releases, giveaways, pre-orders, sneak peeks, and more.

Visit the website below to join now.

WWW.AMKUSI.COM/NEWSLETTER

TABLE OF CONTENTS

1

CHARLI

He's alive. Finn's alive.

Charli repeated it in her mind—a desperate attempt at self-soothing. She wiped the tears that hadn't seemed to stop since she got the news five days and almost three thousand miles ago.

The sterile scent of the hospital stung her nose. She placed her hand on her growing belly.

"Your papa is going to be okay." She hoped it wasn't a lie.

She rested her palm on Finn's limp and clammy hand. His silver wedding ring was safely tucked away with his personal effects. This was the first time she'd seen him without it since the twenty-year-old version of himself vowed to love her and cherish her until death did they part. Thick white gauze had been wrapped around his head. Superficial wounds peppered the side of his rich-brown handsome face.

Could he hear her through the fog of the coma? *Wait and see.* That was what the doctor had said.

"Come back to me," she choked out.

"He will. My Finn is a fighter," Claire, Finn's mother, said, wrapping her arm around Charli.

When did she walk in? Charli tore her eyes away from the only man she'd ever loved.

Claire's warm brown gaze met hers with sympathy and shared pain. The woman's midnight complexion was a complete contrast to her own fair skin. But Claire was the closest thing Charli had ever had to a mother.

"I can't lose him, Mom."

Claire pulled her closer. Charli rested her head against Claire's heart, the side of the uncomfortable hospital chair cutting into her ribs.

"Finn has a lot to live for. He's got to meet his child. Not to mention, my son would never let anything get in the way of finding his way back to you, Charli." Claire's voice shook, as if speaking the words would will it into being.

"I don't think I can do this without him," Charli confessed as she sat up.

"No matter what happens, you're still our daughter. We'll be here for you," Zeke, Finn's father, said as he came into the room.

He opened his arms to her, a rare display of vulnerability and affection. She got to her feet and walked into his embrace on shaky legs. He patted her back with his big palm as she released a sob.

"There. There," he said awkwardly. Zeke was a man of few words and even fewer emotions. Much like his son.

"Why don't you go get some coffee and a hot meal? A walk will do you some good," Claire suggested.

When was the last time I ate? Charli turned towards Finn's unconscious body. Her stomach churned with anxiety. "I don't want to leave him."

Claire stood, taking her hand and ushering her to the

door. "You have to take care of yourself too, Charli, or you'll be no good to him when he does wake up. Besides, it isn't just you you have to think about. You're carrying my grandbaby." Claire pressed her hand gently to Charli's small, fifteen-week baby bump.

Charli nodded. "Yeah, okay. Call me if anything changes. I'll have my phone."

"Of course." Claire's eyes flashed with sympathy.

Charli put one leaden foot in front of the other. The tug to her heart to go back to the room was strong. But her mother-in-law was right. She needed to stay strong for her baby, and for Finn.

Walking through the large hallways in a daze, Charli found her way easily enough to the cafeteria. The smell of grilled meat permeated the dining area. Her stomach grumbled in response. After grabbing a simple sandwich and a juice, she paid before numbly walking towards the seating area. Charli made herself sit at an empty table and dig in. She didn't taste her food, rather devoured it quickly in hopes of nourishing her body and getting back to Finn. The phone rang in her pocket, and she jumped. Heart racing, she pulled out her cell.

Mason.

Oh.

Her heart sank. Not Claire with news on Finn.

She clicked accept and answered. "Hello?"

"Hey, Charli. I just wanted to let you know we've got everything covered as long as you need. Turns out that temp help Bently, Andre, and Mikel offered? It's not so temporary at all. It's here for as long as you need it. Jasmine even said she'd wait tables. I guess what I mean to say is, you guys focus on everything going on with Finn and take care of yourselves. We got your back here at The Shipwreck," Mason said, his voice full of sympathy.

"Thank you, Mason." Tears welled in her eyes again. Stupid pregnancy hormones turned her into a water fountain. "I can't tell you how much that means to us."

"How is he?"

She swallowed. "Still waiting for him to wake up. But the swelling on his brain has gone down and the surgery was successful. The doctors are hopeful."

Mason was silent a moment, as if struggling for the right words to make her feel just a little better. But there was no such magic. "You guys are in our thoughts. The whole town is putting together a fundraiser so that the Reeds will have a cushion when you get home."

"Mason—" Her phone beeped with an incoming call. She pulled her cell away from her ear. Claire's name flashed on the screen. *Oh god!* "I have to go."

She didn't bother waiting for his response. She switched the call over and got to her feet, stumbling out of the cafeteria and towards her husband's room.

"Is he . . ." She couldn't finish the sentence. Hope and dread sparred for dominance in her chest, halting her voice.

"He's awake!" Claire said.

Awake. A surge of emotion flit in her belly. Charli ran like her life depended on it. Nerves swirled and knotted, twisting her up. Her pulse raced, ringing in her ears. For the first time since receiving the fateful news that her husband had been in an accident, hope bloomed within her.

Tears blurred her eyes once again as she burst into the room. A doctor and a nurse blocked her view. Zeke held Claire off to her right, love and gratitude pouring out of them as they stared towards the hospital bed.

"How did I get here?" Finn's deep voice rumbled through

her, making her knees wobble. She covered her mouth and moved closer, needing to see his face.

Finn's dark eyes searched the room, unfocused.

"Baby?" She stepped forward, unable to wait any longer to touch him. She reached out her hand, her fingers grazing his warm cheek. "You're okay." Her voice cracked.

She leaned in to kiss him, but he turned his head away.

"What the hell?" Finn asked. His eyes roamed over her, his confusion edging on panicked.

"Major Reed, do you know who this is?" the doctor asked.

"Of course, he knows me," Charli snapped. The notion that her husband of thirteen years could forget her was absurd.

His beard had grown in over the past several days of being unconscious, hiding his sharp jaw. Stitches marred his warm, brown skin. She searched Finn's dark eyes, her usual source of peace, and the floor fell out from under her. "Finn?"

His brows knit together in concentration before relaxing. "Oh, yeah. You're Bently's friend, Charlotte, right?"

"What?" The room started to spin. Blood rushed to her ears. *No. No. No. This isn't real. Finn's still in a coma, and I've drifted off into this nightmare. Wake up!*

"How old are you, Finn?" the doctor asked.

Finn turned to him. "I'm seventeen, obviously."

Claire gasped. Finn focused on his parents. "Mom, Dad, what happened? Why am I here?"

"You don't remember Charli? Your wife?" Zeke asked.

Finn's gaze snapped to hers. "Is this a joke?"

The doctor stepped forward. "Major Reed, you've been in an accident. The truck you were riding in was hit and you've sustained a few injuries which include—"

Finn shook his head. "What? Why do you keep calling me Major? You've got the wrong guy. I'm a senior at Shattered

Cove High School. I haven't enlisted yet. I'm still in the JROTC."

A senior in high school? Panic clawed her chest as her body trembled in shock. Charli sucked in air through her chattering teeth.

Claire stepped forward and placed her hand on his. "Sweetheart, we're in Washington State."

Finn's gaze darted from face to face. His brows drew together, panic flashing in his eyes. "How old do you think I am?" His voice trembled.

"Thirty-three."

He swallowed.

The doctor shone his flashlight over his pupils. "Amnesia can be common with head injuries like this. Your memories may come back to you in time." He continued explaining tests they would run and listing Finn's other less serious injuries. But all Charli could do was stare back at the man she'd given her heart to when she was sixteen. Her husband, who looked at her as if she were a complete stranger.

She placed her hand over her belly growing a child they'd made in love. His panicked gaze followed her movement. His eyes widened.

His body trembled and he shook his head. "No. This isn't real!"

"I need you to try to calm down, Major Reed," the nurse said.

Finn struggled to sit up, pulling at wires. "No, this isn't—I'm not—"

"Pull yourself together, soldier!" the doctor ordered.

"Finn, sweetheart, just breathe." Claire came to his side.

"Maybe it's best if you wait outside."

Charli had no idea the nurse was talking to her until she tapped her shoulder. "But he's my husband."

The red-haired nurse looked at her with sympathy. "This is a lot for him to take in at the moment. Just give him some time," she said, leading Charli out of the room.

Charli leaned against the wall in the hallway, refusing to go farther. She collapsed to the cold, hard ground, pulling her knees as close to her chest as she could get them. Fat tears rolled down her cheeks, soaking into the grey leggings she wore.

Finn had forgotten *sixteen years* of his life. He'd forgotten *her*. He'd promised she'd never have to be alone. He'd sworn after his last deployment his service obligation would be up, and they'd raise a family. He'd made so many vows, and now he'd forgotten every single one.

Pain sliced through her heart as overwhelming grief shook her body in a violent sob. Flashes of moments shared, the life they'd built, gone in an instant.

All that was left was the unknown. For the first time since she'd married Finn, she felt alone. Stranded. Lost in a sea of shattered promises.

Will he remember me?

Would he come back to her?

Or was this the end of their fairy tale?

2

FINN

Thirty-three years old. Sixteen years gone in an instant. *No. It can't be. This is a dream. Or a sick joke.*

Charli placed a hand over her belly. He gulped down the fire and panic, his eyes widening at the small bulge. There was no mistaking it. Charli was pregnant. A hurricane of emotion rippled through him, cast in a haze of confusion. The room shuddered and wavered. This was a nightmare. He shook his head. "No. This isn't real!"

His eyes flicked to his hands. It wasn't the room that trembled; it was *him.*

"I need you to try to calm down, Major Reed," the nurse said.

Finn struggled to sit up, pulling at wires. "No, this isn't—I'm not—"

"Pull yourself together, soldier," the doctor ordered.

I'm not a soldier!

"Finn, sweetheart, just breathe." His mother's voice cut through the fog as she stepped to his side. But he couldn't tear his wide eyes away from his *wife.*

"Maybe it's best if you wait outside," the nurse said to Charli.

"But he's my husband."

Husband. Finn's chest squeezed tight, his lungs constricting. Chaos creaked and splintered inside his chest. Adrenaline coursed through his veins. Horror clawed at his throat. *Husband. Baby. I'm seventeen. There's no way I can . . .*

"This is a lot for him to take in at the moment. Just give him some time," the nurse said, leading Charli out of the room. Her watery eyes were as dark as the river Styx. And just as hopeless too.

His heart lurched. Why did it feel like this was wrong? He didn't really know her, but there was something there. Something about the way those pain-filled brown spheres called to him deep inside his soul. He slammed his eyes shut, severing the portal before she exited the room.

He fisted the sheets, every muscle tense. Monitors beeped; alarms blared. The doctor's voice curtly demanded he calm down.

Finn gasped as two sets of arms grabbed his. His eyes shot back open.

"Son!" His father's voice boomed, thrusting him out of the violent twist of panicked emotions he'd been caught in.

"Finn!" his mother cried out, rubbing up and down his arm.

"I don't want to have to give you a sedative," the doctor warned.

Finn forced himself to take slow breaths. This wasn't a dream. This was real.

"Get me a mirror," Finn rasped.

His mother frowned. "What?"

"I want a mirror."

The doctor nodded and disappeared for a moment before

coming back with the nurse and a handheld mirror. Finn took it, heaving in a deep inhale before flipping it over. He swallowed hard. His skin burned like it had been set on fire. It was him, but it wasn't. They were telling the truth. Finn was all grown up now. Gone were the patches of facial hair he thought passed as a goatee. He ran a hand over the thick scruff, the beginning of a beard. His eyes and forehead had lines that weren't there before. His face was all hard edges, even with the stitches on his chestnut skin.

"What happened?" Finn ran his finger over the white gauze on his forehead and winced.

"You and your friend, Eric, were fishing. On the highway home, a drunk driver swerved into your lane. There was an explosion. We removed a piece of shrapnel from your skull, but we believe you hit your head on impact. We replaced a piece of your frontal and parietal bone with a metal plate."

Finn squinted his eyes and handed the item back to the nurse. He turned to his mother. "It's true?"

She covered her mouth and nodded. "It's gonna be okay, sweetie. The important thing is you're alive."

His gaze flicked to his father. "I'm married?"

His father tipped his head. "Yes. And they need you."

There was no mistaking his meaning. The message his father had repeated to him all his life echoed in his head. *A man takes care of his responsibilities, son. You gotta man up; no one said it was gonna be easy. Sometimes you gotta do what's best for everyone but you.*

Finn swallowed and nodded, trying to wrap his mind around it all. His head pounded, his body aching. Exhaustion clung to every cell as he settled back on the bed, spent. His eyes fluttered closed. A warm, soft hand caressed his arm. "Rest, sweetheart. We'll be here when you wake up."

But would he ever truly wake up and remember? Or was

he supposed to live a life he didn't recall choosing? This had to be a nightmare. Maybe if he just closed his eyes, the next time he opened them he'd be in study hall and this would all be a very bad memory.

* * *

A full week later, Finn was able to stay awake for more than a few hours and he was itching to get out of the hospital. His father had to fly back to New Hampshire to take care of their bar, The Shipwreck, but his mother stayed. And Charli.

When his eyes were closed, he'd sense her in the room, her hand slipping into his. He'd almost grown accustomed to the steady thrum of electricity that radiated from the connection. When he was awake, she stayed farther away, her sad eyes flickering with hope before each new test the doctor ran, only to be dimmed a little more when the results came back. They had no idea why he couldn't remember almost half his life.

A near constant headache throbbed in his skull—another wonderful side effect. It got worse the more he tried to focus on something and strained to remember. The doctor said this would happen. Along with a laundry list of symptoms like blurred vision, pain, and emotional storms.

"If you find yourself having a memory and experiencing any of these symptoms, you need to take a break. It can do more harm than good and cause you physical pain if you stress yourself out with too much information at once. You don't want to overload your system as you heal," one of his many doctors had explained.

Charli swiped a hand over her belly as she asked, "How will I know if something is too much for him?"

It was weird to have this stranger talking about him.

"Finn will need to communicate that to you, but I'd say to go slow. Trust your instincts."

"Do you want some lasagna for dinner? I know it won't be as good as Charli usually makes, but their stuffed manicotti was pretty good the other day," his mother said, pulling him out of the memory.

He wouldn't know what Charli's food tasted like, but his mother had decided acting like nothing was different was the way to go, apparently. "Sounds good, Ma."

After another beat of silence, she nudged Charli. "Don't you want to tell him about what he's missed since the accident?"

Charli's eyes found his. "Bently and the boys all send their hellos. They said you'd better get better soon so they can kick your ass at basketball again."

His lips curved of their own accord for the first time since he'd woken in this strange place in a foreign land. She'd given him the first taste of familiar, people he knew. And from the sounds of it, they hadn't changed that much. "Good to know."

She crossed her arms and leaned back in the chair, scanning the room, looking anywhere but at him.

"It will be so good to have you back home again, Finn. Won't it, Charli?" His mother tried again.

"Yes," Charli answered, her voice half relieved, half pained.

"And I bet you can't wait to return to your own bed. Get back into the routine at The Shipwreck, Finn? And to your tinkering in the garage?" His mother pushed.

My own bed. He doubted it was the one he remembered at his parents' house.

"Yeah," he answered, mostly to appease his mother's attempts at filling the silence.

"What about—"

Charli stood. "I'm going to take a walk and get some fresh air."

"Okay, dear." His mother's tone was as soft as the expression on her face as she looked at Charli.

Finn risked a peek at the woman he had supposedly vowed to love and care for, in sickness and health, for the remainder of his life. Her dark hair was pulled into a messy bun on her head, her face clean and devoid of all makeup, highlighting the smattering of rust-colored freckles above her button nose. Her pink, pouty lips seemed soft, much like the woman they belonged to. Her cable-knit sweater hanging off one shoulder was wrinkled, most likely from spending her days in the chair in his hospital room. He couldn't bear looking any lower. Her round belly reminded him that he had a lot more responsibility than just a wife coming soon. She was gorgeous, even with the bags of exhaustion under her eyes. But not familiar in any way.

What am I going to do?

Charli's tired gaze flicked to him before she exited.

"You can go too, Ma. You don't need to stay in this room just because I'm stuck here. My therapist should be in soon anyway to do some exercises with me before they do another evaluation."

"I know. I just—I keep thinking about how we almost lost you. My only child."

He reached out to take her small hand in his. "I'm fine, Ma. Promise. It's all over. You don't have to worry anymore."

She snorted. "I've worried about you ever since you've been born. Afraid this world would take you from me. That they would see aggression where I saw energy. A threat, where I saw a strong, growing boy. You can't tell me to stop doing something that comes with breathing as a Black mother."

He squeezed her hand. There were no words to comfort

her as she'd so readily offered him. "I'm healing. My motor skills are much better, and soon we'll be back in Shattered Cove and you can make me your macaroni and cheese."

She smiled. "Sounds like a plan. You and Charli can come over once you're settled."

Right. Charli. His *wife*. His *pregnant* wife. He closed his eyes and rested against the pillow, fighting the fear that battered his rib cage. He'd made it through the worst. Hadn't he?

Now all he had to do was survive this next part.

3

FINN

Green trees whipped by outside the car window. Finn kept his focus trained anywhere but on the unfamiliar woman sitting next to him. His parents' presence was the only thing tethering him to this new reality. He still couldn't believe this was real. But every morning for the past two weeks he'd woken up to this nightmare.

It was still hard to believe the face staring back at him in the reflection of the window was him. Finn rubbed his jaw, the coarse hair scraping against his palm. His beard grew twice as fast now. His finger trailed to one of his healing cuts, sore from having the stitches removed.

The radio played low—some R & B channel his parents had on. His mother had given up on trying to spark conversation between him and Charli thirty miles ago. He preferred the silence right now. He wanted some space and something familiar.

His father turned the corner, pulling into the driveway of a small, white house with dark eggplant shutters and a front door to match.

"This is it," Zeke said, turning to him. His father's expectation was clear. *Be a man, son. A man owns up to his responsibility.*

There would be no going home with his parents, back to his room with basketball trophies and posters of his favorite bands. *Is that stuff even there anymore?* No, there would be no coddling from his father. There never was.

"Do you need help carrying in anything?" his mother asked, opening her door.

His father's hand shot out to hers, halting her. She turned to him, a silent message passing between them.

"Let the boy go, Claire. He and Charli need to get settled."

His mother nodded before facing him. Her gaze volleyed from him to Charli. "Call me if you two need anything. We're right down the road. Belle said she delivered some groceries, so you shouldn't have to run right out."

Who's Belle?

"Okay. Thank you both for everything." Charli opened the door and climbed down, her hand going to her lower back.

His panic rose. He was supposed to follow her, a complete stranger, who was carrying his baby. Only, Finn was a virgin, wasn't he?

"Take care, son," Zeke said.

That was his cue. Finn took a deep breath, opened the door, and climbed out. The sun was setting, making the sky glow orange as the cool and crisp September air sent a chill through him. Charli had the trunk open, pulling the handle of her suitcase.

"I can get that," he offered out of habit. His mama had raised a gentleman. Weren't pregnant women supposed to avoid carrying things?

She shook her head. "I can manage. It has wheels. Plus, your bag is really heavy." She nodded towards the long military duffle. He picked it up and swung it around his shoulder before closing the trunk to his parents' CRV. He followed Charli up the stone path to the house, noting the handprints in one paver. *C+F = Forever.*

The jangling of keys pulled his attention back to the house. The quiet hum of his parents' car faded as they drove away. Charli opened the door for him. He held it as she walked in, the thud and roll of her suitcase trailing after her.

Finn entered, searching for anything to spark a memory. A few pairs of men's boots and shoes lined the edge of the wall mixed with tiny heels and sandals he assumed were Charli's under the built-in coatrack. Charli slipped out of her shoes and hung up the jean jacket she'd been wearing. He did the same, following her lead.

She turned her face, peeking a glance at him before shyly tucking a strand of raven hair behind her ear. "I guess I'll, uh, give you a tour of the house?"

"Sure." He nodded.

Swiveling around, she led him along the hallway. His gaze dropped to her round ass swaying, swirling up emotions he was familiar with but on a whole other level. Sex was something he'd thought a lot about but hadn't actually gone that far with yet. Only, his pregnant wife would probably beg to differ. Would Charli expect him to have sex with her? Panic seized his chest as he stumbled before righting himself.

Pictures on the wall caught his eye. There was one of him in his heavily decorated Army Service Uniform, one arm around a dressed-up Charli. They were smiling and laughing together. He was in a graduation gown in the next frame, hoisting her into his arms with his cap on her head. She beamed at him, pride pouring from the picture. Apparently after four years of **JROTC** in high school, he'd attended junior college until he was married at twenty. After being commissioned, he'd gone on his first tour before enrolling in a bachelor's program. At least, that's what his mother had told him. He had a degree in business and couldn't even remember applying to college.

His gaze moved along to another picture of Charli in a white gown. He'd lifted her up, lips locked to hers as his hand grasped her ass. They looked happy.

"That was our wedding day," she whispered as if she were afraid the wrong movement would provoke another freak-out from him.

She'd been tentative around him since he'd woken in the hospital in Washington three weeks ago. He didn't like it. But he also didn't know what to do about it. Maybe she'd always been this way.

"This is the living room." She pointed to his right. A long grey couch decorated with white and purple pillows took up most of the space. A rectangular coffee table sat before it strewn with motorcycle and embroidery magazines.

"Nice." He wasn't sure what else to say.

"And through here is the dining room slash kitchen."

He turned, taking in the off-white cabinets and grey backsplash. The square table was built into the large kitchen island with booth-like seats around three sides.

"Are you hungry?" she asked.

"Not really."

"I'll show you where you can put that." She motioned to his bag. Pulling her suitcase behind her, she led him past a door, explaining it was the bathroom, and over to a set of stairs.

He gripped the handle of her suitcase, his hand grazing hers. A bolt of energy zinged up his arm. He swallowed as his body heated.

Her gaze met his as she tugged her pink bottom lip into her mouth. "Thanks."

She continued upwards, her round ass right in his line of view. His cock hardened at the sight of her curves leading him to what he guessed was their bedroom. That ass was going to be the death of him. Did she have to wear these leggings that left nothing to his imagination? They were so tight, highlighting the fact that there was no way she could possibly be wearing any underwear.

Finn pressed his hand against the growing erection in his pants, hoping to god she didn't turn around and see.

Our bedroom. As in, the bed he shared with *this* woman. Nerves twisted in his gut. Arousal heated his body. He may not have remembered her, but his body seemed to. If his dick had his way, he'd be inside the woman right now. But that felt wrong. She was pregnant, after all. *Can pregnant women even have sex?* He shook his head, trying to rid the thoughts from his mind. His shoulders bunched as he lifted the weight of their luggage up the steps behind her. She passed the first closed door and pointed to the second. "This is the other bathroom."

"What's in there?" He motioned to the first one they'd skipped.

She looked away and then back to him. "It's the baby's room—or it will be."

He rested his hand on the knob and turned. Taking a fortifying breath, he pushed it open. A box with a picture of a crib on it lay stacked against the wall with a window. A rocking chair sat in the corner, as well as a few other pieces of furniture and boxes. His head swam. This was all too much. A baby? He was going to have a baby?

"The bedroom is this way." Charli must have sensed his panic, because she shut the door and turned away from him.

She walked through the entrance to the master bedroom.

The room was neat and tidy. Two big, matching dressers sat against the walls. One large window opened to the backyard. A queen-sized bed with a reclaimed pallet headboard sat front and center. The white comforter looked soft. The whole house carried notes of Charli's scent, but it was strongest in here: honey and amber. Sweet and rich. It was intoxicating and comforting. That must mean something.

"You can just leave the suitcase there against the wall. I'll unpack tomorrow," she said.

He did as she said and lowered his bag next to hers. His gaze swept over the room once more, seeking anything that might jar his memory. His eyes landed on hers. Dark pools of uncertainty stared back at him.

He stepped forward, out of instinct maybe? He wanted to be closer to her, even if he didn't know her.

"Finn?" Her voice came out breathy. His hardness poked against the zipper of his pants. Charli's eyes darkened as her tongue swept over her bottom lip. His stomach muscles tensed to keep him from bending down to kiss her—which was crazy, because he barely knew her. And last he remembered, he had a girlfriend. *Laura.* What had happened to her anyway?

"I'll sleep on the couch." His voice came out gruffer than he'd intended.

She winced. Hurt flashed in her eyes.

Shit. He was an asshole. "I'm just . . ." *Scared. I've never slept next to a woman.* "Tired."

Her mouth opened and closed as she blinked rapidly, her eyes growing glassy.

Great job, idiot. You made her cry.

"O-oh. Okay. Of course. I . . . I'll get you some blankets and pillows set up." She stepped past him, her scent winding around him, lighting him up.

His hand shot out to her arm. Her face tilted to his.

Energy crackled between them. Fire licked his body from their connection. "Th—thank you." He cleared his throat and let her go.

"You're welcome." She offered him a small, watery smile. She opened a closet door and pulled out a sheet and comforter. "The dresser on the left is yours."

He opened the first drawer, finding boxers and socks. The second was full of T-shirts. "Where are my pajamas?"

She lifted the blankets and pillows in her arms, her gaze raking up his body. A slight pink colored her cheeks. "You don't usually wear anything to bed."

So some things hadn't changed. "Oh."

"But you have a couple pairs of sleep pants in the closet for when we have company. Top shelf." She nodded to the door behind her before leaving the room.

Finn found a set of black-and-red plaid fleece pajama bottoms and slipped into the bathroom to change. He'd always been hot-blooded; there was no need for a T-shirt.

After grabbing his toiletries bag, he brushed his teeth before going back down to the living room. Charli's head was buried in her hands as she sat on the blanket spread out on the sofa. Her shoulders slumped. He wished he had the right words to say to comfort her. He may not remember much of her, but he didn't like to see her unhappy.

"Thanks for getting this ready," he said, breaking the silence.

Her head snapped up. Her gaze licked every inch of his naked torso. These sleep pants were not doing much to hide his erection that seemed ever-present around her.

Charli stood. "Of course. It's not a problem."

She walked over to him, squeezing her hands at her sides as if she wasn't sure what to do about this situation either.

"Finn?"

"Yeah?"

"I'm really glad you're home." Charli offered him a small smile, her eyes glassy.

He wasn't sure what to say, not wanting to lie. This didn't feel like home to him. She didn't feel like his wife. His body might be the man she knew, but in his mind, he was a seventeen-year-old high schooler who was still dating Laura Bridges. "Thank you." His voice came out gravelly.

Charli blinked twice and nodded. Disappointment flashed in her beautiful brown eyes. Her mouth flattened. "See you in the morning."

He lay on the couch, turning his back to her as her feet padded up the stairs. Closing his eyes, he willed sleep to take him and offer some relief.

The tick of the clock on the wall was the only sound in the room. Hours passed as he tossed and turned. His stomach knotted with unease. Eventually, sleep came, but rest did not.

Finn pointed out the windshield, speaking to the soldier driving the Humvee. "Six more klicks east, and then we'll be at the meet point."

"First thing I'm gonna do when I get back to the States is ask my boyfriend to marry me," Smithson said from the driver's seat. His white smile contrasted against the tan camouflage uniform he wore. His helmet was clipped snuggly under his chin.

"Hopefully Zack comes to his senses and turns you down." Finn laughed.

Smithson gave him a goofy smile back. "I'm gonna be one lucky son of a bitch."

Finn kept his gaze trained out the window, searching for insurgents or anything that seemed out of the ordinary. The dust from the caravan in front of them made it hard to see out there in the desert.

"What about you? This is your last deployment. What are you gonna do when you get back home?" Smithson asked.

"I'm gonna kiss my girl and never come back up for air," Finn said with a wide smile.

"Sounds like a good way to go," Smithson agreed.

A loud noise blasted through Finn's ear as his world turned upside down. Glass shattered. Metal screeched as it bent and twisted. Pain radiated through his body. Blackness swallowed him.

There were screams, muted by white noise, then piercing his ears in sharp contrast. Smithson's face was frozen in fear. Gone were the military fatigues, replaced with a sweatshirt and jeans. His mouth opened and closed like a fish. Blood poured from the wound in his neck. And then his movement stopped all together. His cold dead eyes stared back at Finn, pleading for the impossible.

Finn reached out to his friend, his head spinning. A red haze covered his vision. He swiped his hand over his face. Blood. More blood. Gunfire blasted all around him. His chest squeezed tight. Ropes of fear strangled him as he clawed at his neck for air. A crushing weight settled over his chest, cracking his ribs as he tried to scream, but no sound came out. The vehicle shook as another loud blast sent him back into darkness. Death swallowed him whole.

4

CHARLI

Charli jolted awake. Scanning the dark room, she sat up. The clock on the bedside table was the only source of light in the room. *Four A.M.*

A moan filtered in through the darkness. *Finn?* She slipped her feet out of the blankets onto the rug, leaving the comfort of her warm bed. Charli headed towards the stairs, listening intently.

"Nooooo!" Finn screamed.

Charli's heart raced, panic flooding her veins. She hurried down the stairs.

Finn was tangled in the sheets on the couch, eyes closed, his skin shiny with perspiration in the moonlight.

"Finn?" she whispered, reaching out her hand to his bare shoulder. His chest heaved up and down, his body thrashing side to side as his screams grew louder.

"Finn!" Charli said more forcefully, shaking his arm with one hand and turning on the lamp next to them with the other. "Baby, wake up. It's just a dream."

Yellow light flooded the living room. Finn's eyes snapped

open, as black as the night, terror etched across the lines of his face. Fear permeated the room. His forehead was dewy with sweat.

"Are you okay?" Charli brought her palms up to his rough cheeks, forcing him to look at her.

His gaze focused on her, but the familiarity she longed for was not there. Her husband looked at her as if she was a stranger. Like he hadn't mapped her body with his tongue just a month ago before leaving for his pre-baby fishing expedition with his Army buddy. Like he never vowed to love her forever.

She dropped her hands to her sides, fisting them. Would he ever regain the memories?

"I . . ." He raked a hand through his hair, searching the room for some unknown threat. "I'm sorry I woke you."

She sat on the coffee table opposite him, his old T-shirt that she wore riding up her legs. His eyes drifted down with the movement, hesitating a moment before lazily making the ascent back up.

"Was it a memory?" Hope flitted in her chest. Were they coming back?

His eyes snagged on her chest. Her gaze dropped to the loose-fitting top that did very little to hide her body. Her nipples were clearly visible through the well-worn fabric. His stare heated her skin, the familiar hungry look on his face causing her body to respond.

Her attention focused on the dip in his neck, between his collarbone, shining with sweat. His naked, muscular chest was still heaving from the nightmare or the arousal sparked between them—she wasn't sure which.

Was it coming back to him? Was he remembering her? Charli reached out her hand to his knee. His muscles tensed and bunched underneath her touch.

His gaze dropped to her hand. "Just a nightmare."

"Do you want to talk about it?" The urge to comfort him tugged her closer. She pushed her hand up another inch on his thigh, rubbing circles with her thumb, intending to soothe him.

Finn stared at the connection. "No."

"Maybe I can help? Do you want a drink of water? Or maybe—"

"No!" He shoved her hand off his leg.

Charli winced. His rejection stung like a slap in the face. He wasn't remembering her. He'd forgotten her and every special sacred moment they'd spent together. She nodded, willing the tears to be kept at bay. She wrapped her arms around herself.

"I—I'm sorry. I just—I need some air." Finn got up and headed over to the door. The clunk of shoes being slipped on and the rustling of fabric sounded in the quiet room before the door opened and shut. She glanced out the window as Finn passed before he took off jogging down the street.

"Come back to me," she pleaded aloud to the empty room.

She got to her feet and headed upstairs. Turning on the lights as she went, she made it into the bathroom. She was too wired to find sleep—of that she was sure. Charli switched on the shower and slipped off her panties before throwing them in the washing machine on the other side of the bathroom. She pulled the shirt over her head and brought it to her nose, breathing his woodsy scent in. Swallowing the lump of emotion that clogged her throat, she tossed the shirt in before stepping into the shower. The hot water sluiced against her sensitive flesh, melding with her tears.

Is our time up? Does our happily ever after end here?

She placed her palm over her belly. "For your sake, I hope this isn't the end of our story."

No, she'd fight for Finn, and what they had. Their relationship had never been perfect, but Finn was her soulmate. He was her everything. And right now, he just needed her patience and support. She needed a plan.

* * *

An hour later, she stood in the kitchen, brewing a fresh pot of coffee. Finn opened the door, the grey ARMY hoodie he wore soaked through with sweat.

She pulled a Gatorade from the refrigerator and held it out to him as he approached.

"Thank you." He twisted off the cap and chugged it down before wiping his mouth with his arm.

"You're welcome."

His eyes met hers—so many emotions flashed in his. "I . . . do you mind if I shower?" He searched the kitchen, holding up the empty bottle.

She pointed to the recycling bin in the corner. "This is your house too, Finn. You don't have to ask. Towels are under the sink."

"Right." He tossed the plastic into the bin.

His gaze moved behind her, snagging on something before his brows furrowed and his expression turned to stone. "I'll . . . uh . . . go do that, then." He jogged up the stairs.

She turned around, searching for whatever had given him that reaction. The black and white ultrasound photograph on the fridge drew her attention. Their little bean. She traced the shape with her finger. She was eighteen weeks now. At her next appointment they'd find out if she was going to have a daughter or a son.

Was this what freaked him out? Did he feel trapped? Scared? She tried to place herself in his shoes. Finn just needed her to be strong for him right now. She'd have to forget any hope she'd had of him being there for her for the time being. Charli would start with making him his favorite breakfast.

* * *

Finn descended the stairs and met her in the kitchen. He had on a fresh pair of jeans and blue T-shirt that hugged his body just right. "Smells good in here."

She closed her eyes and turned her back to him. How many times had he said the same thing before wrapping his arms around her and kissing her neck?

"Have a seat." She motioned to the table on the other side of the island. "I'll bring it over."

She poured him a cup of black coffee and balanced his plate in the other hand. Charli set it in front of him before grabbing her tea and toast. Sitting across from him, she studied him.

Finn motioned to her simple breakfast. "Not hungry?"

She shook her head. "I'm not really a breakfast person usually, but if I don't eat something little, I still get nauseous."

"Oh. Right. Well, thank you." He nodded before tucking into his food. He slipped a slice of pancake into his mouth and closed his eyes. A drip of maple syrup escaped, and he licked it off his lips. "Mmmm."

Heat blossomed in her belly, like a flower expanding and spreading out to her limbs. She swallowed hard, clenching her thighs together. "Good?"

"I love blueberry pancakes. They're my favorite."

"I know." She smiled.

His gaze met hers, the side of his mouth quirking up sheepishly. "I'm sorry about before."

"It's okay. I know this is a lot for you. I-I just want to help you any way I can. We'll get through this together." She moved to put her hand over his and halted mid-air, not wanting a replay of earlier.

"I appreciate that." He reached out, eclipsing her hand in his warm palm.

Sparklers of hope burst in her chest. She smiled.

He drew back, taking another bite of his food before he asked, "Did that happen before? The nightmares?"

She nodded. "Occasionally. But you've never been in an accident before. You told me they were about being under attack, losing men."

He finished his breakfast in silence, as she sipped her tea and nibbled on her toast. It seemed like he needed space, so she didn't press.

"I like your ink." He motioned to her arms.

Her gaze darted instinctively to the black and white lace-work decorating her forearm. "Thanks. You actually helped me design one."

"Which one?" he asked.

"The matching ones we got." She left him the bread-crumbs, hoping to spark some memory.

His hand rested on his chest. "The compass?"

"Yes." She stood, moved next to him, and lifted her white shirt over her grey lace bra, exposing the black compass tattooed on her rib cage. "We got them before your first deployment. I was so worried about you leaving. You surprised me with the appointment." She took a shaky breath, preparing herself for the next part of the story. "You said I was your true north, and if you ever got lost, this would help you find your way back to me."

Finn's brows pulled together as he stared at her ink,

looking thoughtful. He reached out his hand, halting partway in hesitation. "May I?"

She nodded and held her breath in anticipation of his touch.

His calloused finger traced the outline of the tattoo, blistering her skin, teasing her with his tentative touch. She pressed his hand onto her needy flesh, yearning for more. His heated brown eyes locked on hers, arousal reflecting back.

He wanted her, didn't he? Finn's eyes dropped to her growing belly, and he winced before he dropped his hand, severing the connection.

"I don't remember it," he confessed.

She pushed away the disappointment, not willing to give up so quickly. "I have an idea. Why don't we start from the beginning?"

He took a sip of the coffee and nodded. "Alright."

Charli smiled. Sharing memories with Finn might help him remember. Maybe she could still get her old Finn back. Perhaps their fairy tale had a few chapters left before they got to the happily-ever-after part.

5

____

FINN

Finn followed Charli to the couch with his cup of coffee. Her amber scent danced on muted tones in the air around him. The sway of her hips drew his attention to her voluptuous backside. He swallowed, his eyes dropping to her bare legs, accentuated by the linen shorts that hugged her ass to perfection. She might have been small, but her legs seemed to go on for days in those tiny bottoms. *What color panties is she wearing today? Gah!* He hadn't been able to get her out of his head since catching a flash of pink lace under the T-shirt earlier.

Charli sat, placing her cup of tea on the rectangular table. The bedding he'd used last night was nowhere to be seen. He took the empty place beside her, taking one last sip of his coffee before setting it down. He shifted back to get comfortable. A strand of raven hair fell in front of her face, contrasted by her porcelain skin like his very own modern-day Snow White.

Charli tucked one bare foot under her and angled her body towards him. He jerked his head in the other direction, afraid to get caught staring like a pervert. But if she was his wife, wasn't he allowed to ogle her?

Finn turned back to her. Charli's light brown eyes studied him—the same color of the smattering of freckles across her cheeks and nose. It was cute. Everything about her seemed soft.

"Why don't you start by telling me what you do remember of me?" Charli suggested.

He nodded and cleared his throat. "There was a bonfire at the beach with the boys. Bently showed up with you, and we all thought you were his date. But then he, uh, pulled me aside and told me to help look out for you."

Her brows creased. "Bently said that?"

"Yeah. He just explained you needed a few friends to have your back. But I don't remember why?"

Charli tucked a piece of wavy black hair behind her ear. "You'd think this would be easy to talk about, having already had this conversation with you, years ago." She cleared her throat, her eyes searching the room as if she'd find the right words somewhere around them.

"I was in a pretty bad place when we moved to Shattered Cove. My mother was neglectful and pretty extreme in her religious beliefs. We didn't have money for basic necessities, so I didn't have much for clothing, food, you name it. Bently noticed me slipping into the nurse's room window at school one evening." She took a calming breath and smiled. "He followed me in and scared the shit out of me." Charli laughed before her face grew serious. "He caught me trying to steal pads and tampons. It was mortifying as a fifteen-year-old girl. But he warned me away from doing that again. If I got caught, I'd get into so much trouble. Instead he promised I wouldn't have to worry about it. The next day, I found a whole box in my locker."

She paused, settling her hand on her chest. "He invited me to hang out at the bonfire with you guys. At first I was terrified. Here was this popular guy asking me to chill with his friends and buying me tampons. I didn't know what to make of him. I was a far cry from the girls he usually had on his arm."

"You're beautiful," Finn said.

Charli's gaze snagged on his. Her pink lips parted and closed before she smiled, lighting up her whole face. Happiness glowed from her expression as gratitude flashed in her gaze. "Well, back then I was gangly and way too skinny with all these freckles. I felt like the ugly duckling."

"Didn't I have Laura with me at the bonfire?"

Charli's face fell. "Yeah. She was there. But you broke up soon after."

"Why?" He leaned closer.

"I walked into the library and found her and another guy huddled together in a corner, kissing. I knew you and she were together, so I asked Bently about it. He brought me to you and we let you know."

Her words were a fresh punch to his gut. "What did I do?"

"You asked me for details, and then you got mad and went after Ricky."

"Ricky Emerson?"

She nodded.

Finn shook his head. "Captain of the football team and girlfriend stealer."

Charli took a sip of her tea and returned it to the table.

"How did you and I get together?"

She took a deep breath, like she was preparing herself. "A few months later, I came to school with a black eye. You wouldn't let me leave the parking lot until I told you how I got it—the truth. You hugged me close and said I was going home with you."

"How did it happen?" His hands clenched into fists. The thought of anyone hurting this woman made his stomach turn to stone.

Her eyes grew dark as her expression dropped. "I'd rather not relive that."

He let out a long exhale he hadn't known he was holding and nodded. "What happened next?" Finn's shoulders bunched and his abs clenched as anger welled within him. He may not know Charli well, but what he did know is no woman deserved that.

"Your parents tried to get me help, but . . . my mom fought for me and lied to the police about how I got the bruise. I had to go back."

He shook his head in disbelief.

"I'd sneak out some nights when it got to be too much. You got me a phone after the first time I walked to your house. After that you would pick me up to sneak me into your bedroom. I felt safe with you. Then you'd sneak me out in the morning before your parents or my mom ever found out. This went on until I turned eighteen and left for good."

"When did we start dating?" Had he taken advantage of her in such a vulnerable state? They were only two years apart, but in high school that made a huge difference. Panic lanced across his chest. Maybe he didn't want to know the old Finn.

"It was gradual. You never really asked me out. But one night I woke up from a nightmare, and you climbed into bed with me and just held me." Her eyes grew watery as she turned to him with affection shining in them. "You usually slept in a sleeping bag on the floor when I came over."

"Did I try anything with you?" He held his breath.

She shook her head. "No. You were the perfect gentleman. No matter how hard I tried to persuade you." She smirked.

He released the tension in his body with the deep exhale.

"You waited until the dawn of my eighteenth birthday, and we shared our first kiss." Her lips turned up dreamily.

A bubble of pride welled up inside him at his young self. Charli was gorgeous. Sleeping next to her with his raging hormones and not trying anything must have been torture. He picked up his coffee and took a swig of the cold liquid.

"Then you asked me to marry you."

He coughed. "Wow. I didn't waste any time, did I?"

Light laughter spilled out of her like glowing sunshine. The beautiful sound gave him a sense of familiarity. Like he'd heard this laugh a million times before. Warmth filled his chest.

"That wasn't even the craziest part. Your parents knocked on the door and told you to come down to breakfast and bring me. Apparently, they knew you'd been sneaking me in for some time. They had a big breakfast ready. You drove me to my house to get my things . . ." Her smiling face fell, focused on the edge of her shorts as she ran her fingers across it.

What is she holding back?

"Within the month, we were married. Six months later, you joined the Army."

"Damn, I moved quick."

Charli giggled. "You've always been a man who knows what he wants and goes after it. Looking back, I can't imagine how I'd react if my daughter told me she was getting married the day she turned eighteen."

His gaze was drawn to her belly and the dainty hand resting over the small bump. "It's a girl?"

"Oh, no. I mean, I don't know yet. The appointment is in a couple weeks to find out the gender."

He nodded, taking in everything she'd just told him. He searched his mind for anything, but no memories had been triggered.

Charli pulled out her phone and tapped the screen a few times before she handed it over to him. "This is our wedding day."

He held the smartphone as his smiling and seemingly nervous face took up the screen. Finn wore a simple suit with a black bow tie. Bently, Mikel, and Andre stood by him in dress shirts and pants, laughing and teasing him from the looks of it. The camera panned around the room. All his friends and family were there.

"Did anyone from your family show up?"

"No."

Did she have anyone else?

Jasmine, Bently's younger sister, walked down the aisle first, followed by Remy, and then Emma. Finally, the music changed and Charli seemed to float over the path in a simple, white lace dress.

"Your mother bought me that dress," she pointed out.

Charli's hair had been left down, with large curls added to her already wavy hair. Her eyes were done up in smoky eyeshadow and her lips shiny. "You looked amazing."

The camera panned back to him, showing a stunned reaction on his younger face. It was like watching a twin he hadn't known existed. In the video, his grin widened. The look on young Finn's face was pure adoration and awe.

I must have really loved you.

Her body stiffened beside him. Shit. Had he said that aloud?

"Maybe you can again someday?" Charli reached out her hand to his. The touch sent a zing of electricity humming through his body. He turned toward her, her face only inches from his. Her scent and presence took up all the oxygen in the room. His fingers itched to touch her. But he barely knew her. His gaze dropped to her swollen belly. This was too much. He shot to his feet and set the phone on the table. "I—I'm gonna go find Bently."

Her shoulders drooped, disappointment flitting across her expression. "Okay. He's probably home today with his wife and kids."

What? "Bently's married? And has kids—as in, plural?"

Charli smiled. "Yeah. Took those two long enough, but they were made for each other. They foster teenagers. I'll give you the address." She grabbed her phone and tapped the screen before his phone buzzed in his pocket. "Keys to the car are hanging by the door. Unless you want to take your bike?"

"Umm, how do I . . .?" He held up the phone, not sure what he was supposed to do.

"Right. I forgot you aren't used to this technology yet." She grabbed the phone, angling it towards him to show him how to use the map setting and built-in GPS in the iPhone. "Take a right onto Starfish Avenue, then continue straight for one quarter of a mile," the robotic voice of his phone directed.

"What was that?" Finn asked, confused.

"That's Siri. If you aren't sure how to pull it up to get home, just say 'Siri, give me directions home' and she should help you."

He blinked a few times, still digesting that this was his life now—talking phones. What was next? A car that ran on only electricity?

"Just call me if you have any questions. I'm in your favorites under the phone icon."

"Thanks." He turned and walked out the door, not

looking back. Bently was familiar. His friend could help him make sense of this.

* * *

Finn checked the address on his phone one more time to make sure he was at the right house. Red flowers of all different kinds surrounded the front path. A few hung from baskets on the porch. This place was a far cry from the trailer where Bently and his siblings had grown up. Finn knocked and waited.

The door opened and a woman in scrubs smiled at him. "Finn, you look good. How are you feeling?"

She spoke as if she knew him. "Good. Uh, I'm sorry, I don't remember meeting you?"

"Oh, of course. I'm Belle." She opened the door wider to welcome him in.

"Who's here?" a deep but somehow familiar voice asked as he walked into the foyer. "Finn." The man held out his hand and pulled Finn into a hug, slapping him on the back before releasing him. "How are you, bro?"

His friend's face had aged, but he had the same jet-black hair and piercing blue eyes. His lean teenage body had grown into a man's muscular frame. The other huge difference was a light in his eyes that hadn't been there before.

Finn tucked his hands into his pockets and shuffled side to side. "Fine."

Bently nodded. "Not sure how much you remember, but this is my wife, Belle. And the one over by the TV is Anthony, Gage has a book in his face, and Amara is upstairs some-where." From the way his friend looked at his wife, there was no question where Bently's newfound spark came from.

"Wow. Things really have changed."

Belle reached up and kissed her husband on the cheek. "I'll leave you guys to it. I'm gonna go to work." She grabbed a purse hanging on a hook by the door and waved. "Bye, guys. See you tonight."

"Bye, Belle," the two boys in the living room echoed back.

"Why don't we head out back? Want a beer?"

Beer? Right. He was thirty-three years old. He could buy beer now. "Yeah, sure."

Bently grabbed two cold beers from the fridge and popped the tabs before handing one to Finn and leading him out through a rear door. Bently pulled out a chair at the patio set before motioning to Finn to do the same. Finn took in the surroundings and claimed the spot next to his friend. A volley-ball net was set up in the green grass. A single young tree stood in the corner of the yard, surrounded by stones with colorful wind chimes hanging from its branches. Music tinkled from the chimes every time the wind blew, like little bells melding together to form a melody.

"That's cool." He motioned to the tree of music and took a sip of the cool beer.

The corner of Bently's eyes crinkled as his face grew somber. "It's TJ's tree."

Finn nodded. He had no idea who TJ was, but the pain in Bently's eyes said enough; he was greatly missed.

"So, a wife? I never thought you'd settle down. Last I remember you had two dates to the dance lined up."

Bently chuckled. "Yeah. Well, I met Belle and finally had to stop running away from my problems. She made me want more and believe it was possible."

"Sounds like quite the woman."

"You have no idea." Bently took a drink.

"Charli was telling me a little about how we got together."

Bently tipped his head to the side. "That's another good woman right there."

Finn nodded. "I don't really know much about her yet."

Bently leaned forward, resting his elbows on the wooden circular table. "Charli has been through her share of hell. But she's always stuck by your side. I know you got a lot of shit going on in that brain of yours, but she needs you just as much as you need her."

What did Bently know about Charli's life that he didn't? If he was her husband, why wouldn't she share it with him? Why did she hold back earlier? Jealousy simmered in his gut, mixed with frustration at this whole situation. Pain lanced through his forehead, a dull throb pounding in his skull. He just wanted to escape this pressure that built within him. Expectations from strangers and friends he barely recognized. Living with a woman who he was legally married to and carrying a child he never remembered making. Finn was spinning into an abyss, everything rushing by him in a dark cyclone. Overstimulated and unraveling, he was being pulled in different directions.

He just needed a fucking minute to breathe.

6

CHARLI

Charli checked her phone for the hundredth time. Still no answer from Finn. She opened Bently's last text message and read it again.

Bently: *Nope. He left two hours ago. Thought he was headed home.*

That message had been sent six hours prior; it was now ten at night. She paced the living room, anxiety churning in her gut. Was it too much too fast? Did he get lost? No, he'd know how to get home to his parents. And she'd already checked with them. Claire or Zeke would call her if Finn showed up. So, where was he?

Her phone beeped in her hand. Charli jumped. She'd set it as loud as it could go so she wouldn't miss his call. Tapping the screen, her stomach sunk. Not Finn.

Zeke: *If he doesn't show by 11, we'll send out the search party.*

Charli: *Okay. Thank you.*

She tucked the phone into her pocket and bit her nail. What if he'd gotten into an accident? Or he was in trouble? She couldn't wait anymore. Charli slipped on a pair of sneakers and a jacket before she grabbed the keys by the door. He'd taken the car, so that only left her one option: his bike.

Her hand trembled on the doorknob. She didn't go out at night alone anymore. Not since—not since she'd been attacked. *But what if he's hurt?* She sucked in a ragged breath and twisted. Cold night air sent a shiver through her as she walked to the garage and slipped inside. She flicked on the light, illuminating his workspace. Scanning the area for an intruder, she grabbed a pink helmet covered in dust and slipped it on her head. Driving on a motorcycle at night was risky, but she didn't have a choice. She'd go slow and be careful.

Charli pulled the tarp off his bike and opened the garage bay. Swinging her leg over the center took a little more effort. She started the engine and it purred to life. Going through the safety check, she wanted to make sure she remembered everything Finn had taught her. He was the one who usually drove. Nerves twisted up her spine. She took a deep breath and shifted into gear.

The motorcycle jerked forward and stalled. The second try was successful. Slowly, she eased the bike down the driveway, cautiously gaining speed as she turned down the street. The crisp fall night air whipped against her face the farther down the road she got. She'd check his old haunts first.

She turned to the left, heading towards the beach. The roads were empty on these back streets, and most porch lights had been extinguished. Two high beams popped up behind her, the headlights reflecting into her eyes from the mirror. She winced and adjusted her head. Charli sped up, but so did the vehicle on her six.

"Asshole." She searched for a pull-off, but the next one wasn't for half a mile. She'd stay on the side of the road and wave him past. As she slowed and veered to the right, whoever was in the vehicle only increased their speed.

She gasped, fear blanketing her. Another inch and he might clip her bumper. "Fuck! Go around!" She increased her speed and searched the space ahead of her illuminated by the headlight for an escape route. The gravel pull-off was just ahead. She steered towards it as the horn blared behind her, never slowing down as the car passed. Charli jerked the bike to a stop and sucked in panicked breaths. Her hand rested over her heart in an effort to calm the rapid beat. "It was just some drunk asshole. You're safe." She sucked in delicious oxygen as her chest heaved.

It was too risky for her to be doing this at night. She had her baby to think of too. She shifted into gear and headed home. Maybe Finn was back.

* * *

Charli slowed as her house came into view. Her Toyota Corolla was nowhere to be seen. Her heart sank. *Where are you, Finn?*

She pulled the bike into the garage and shut the door and lights off before stepping towards the house.

"I didn't know you meant that kind of bike," Finn said.

Charli jumped back and screamed as the silhouette of a man took shape on the dark porch.

"Jeeeesus, you got some lungs on you." Finn got to his feet.

"Finnegan Jacob Reed, you scared the shit out of me!" Charli whisper-yelled.

"I couldn't find my keysss." He slurred and swayed to the side.

Is he drunk? The relief she'd felt at his return was now tainted in anger.

"Where is the car?" she asked, pushing past him to unlock the door.

"At the Pink Flamingo. They wouldn't let me drive it home. So, I got a cab."

She pushed open the door and walked in, holding it for him. "How did you remember the address?"

He stumbled in, reaching out for the wall as to steady himself. "It's on my ID."

"Right." She slipped her hand around his waist to guide him towards the kitchen table. He reeked of booze. She could yell at him and tell him how worried she'd been, but nothing would get through to him tonight. He'd have to sleep this off. "Why did you go that far? And why did you get so drunk?"

"Perks of being over twenty-one. Figured I'd see what it was like."

She only partly believed him. "Here, sit down. I'll make you something to eat."

He did as she said, his head bobbing up and down lazily. She pulled out her phone and texted Claire and Zeke to let them know Finn was home safe and then grabbed the eggs from the fridge. She slipped two pieces of toast into the toaster and got to work making scrambled eggs.

She set a glass of water in front of him. "Drink this." Returning to the stove, she piled the eggs on the plate and buttered the toast before bringing it over to him.

His large hand reached out for a piece of toast, missing it the first time. "Thank you."

"You're welcome."

She sat in silence as he gobbled up the food, refilling his water once it was empty. Charli moved to take the plate away, but his palm shot to her wrist, his fingers squeezing her firmly.

"Laura cheated on me with dicky Ricky," he growled.

"I know." She'd been the one to tell him. Had his short-term memory been affected too?

He released his grip on her, his expression softening. So, this was all because he was upset about his ex. Of course, this was still fresh for him. He didn't remember her, but he remembered Laura. She tried to ignore the sting that realization brought.

"You're so sexy."

She turned her gaze to him. *Is he still attracted to me?* In his mind, he was seventeen, after all. She was thirty-one and pregnant. His delivery could use some work though. She smiled. "Thanks."

"No, I mean it. You're, like, extra hot. It's hard for me to be around you."

"Because I'm hot?" She held back her laugh. Drunk Finn was adorable and open. The walls he'd had up were gone.

"Nahhh, because my body seems to remember you, but up here—" He tapped his head. "Up here you scare me."

"Why do I scare you, Finn?"

"I don't know."

She stared at his glazed eyes a moment longer and then grabbed his hand. "Let's get you to bed."

He leaned on her but managed to walk up the stairs. "I don't feel so good." He groaned.

Shit. Charli opened the door to the bathroom and led him over to the toilet just in time as he threw up the food she'd just made him. "Feel better?"

"A little."

She flushed and wiped his mouth with a towel. "Come on."

He got to his feet and she handed him a cup full of mouthwash. He swished and spat as she tossed the dirty towel into the washer. Taking his hand, she led him into the bedroom and pulled back the sheets on his side.

She lifted the hem of his shirt, and he helped her the rest of the way, leaving it in a pile on the floor. The moon reflected off the dark toned muscles of his body. She swallowed. Being so close to him, touching him like this and knowing she couldn't have him was pure torture.

She reached for the button on his jeans.

"Whoa, now. This is moving a little fast. Don't you think?" He chuckled. And he sounded just like old Finn, except that tinge of apprehension in his voice.

"I'm just putting you to bed." She pulled them down his muscular thighs, over his legs, and then he stepped out of the pants, leaving him in his black boxer briefs.

She guided him to the bed.

He lay down with a sigh. "It smells like you in here."

"Is that a good thing . . .? Finn?"

Light snores were her only answer.

Okay, then. She slipped out of her clothes and into an old T-shirt of his with a pair of panties. Charli climbed into bed, wanting some semblance of normalcy. She craved to be held in his arms. Pulling his hand up towards the pillows, she snuggled against his bare chest. Closing her eyes, she breathed him in. Even with the booze and mint from the mouthwash, traces of his scent were there bringing her warmth and comfort. She held on to him in the darkness, because when the dawn came, her Finn would be gone once again. At least in the night she could pretend everything was back to the way it used to be.

* * *

Early morning light filtered through the windowpane. Stifling, Charli kicked off the covers on her feet. The hot, hard body behind her was like a furnace. Finn's arms were wrapped tightly around her, one hand on her breast and his hardness poking her backside. A smile curled the edges of her mouth. She'd love nothing better than to stay like this until he woke up, but unfortunately nature called. Holding on for another minute longer, she savored the moment before she slipped out of his hold and tiptoed to the bathroom. He would wake up with one hell of a hangover.

She relieved herself and stripped naked before walking into the shower. The hot water rained over her body, relaxing her muscles. She and Finn needed to talk once he had some coffee and food in his belly. He couldn't just disappear like that again and stay out at all hours without calling her to let her know. She was his wife.

After shutting off the water, she reached for her towel, but the hook was empty. She opened the cupboard and it too was void of anything she could dry off with. "Damn it."

The fresh basket of clothes was in the bedroom, waiting to be folded. She scurried out of the bathroom and opened the bedroom door, finding exactly what she was looking for. Picking up the blue towel, she dried off her hair first before wiping the droplets from her skin. After wrapping it around herself, she looked up. Finn's heated gaze locked on to hers. She knew that look. He wanted her.

She padded over to the bed and sat on the edge by his chest. "You okay?"

"Why am I here in the bed? Did we . . .?" Finn stared at her hand holding the towel together.

"No, we didn't have sex. You were drunk. You threw up in the bathroom, and then I brought you in here to sleep it off. You don't remember?"

His brow furrowed. "Bits and pieces."

"Do you have a headache?"

"Yeah." His voice was still gravelly with sleep.

She pulled open the drawer of the bedside table and

collected two aspirin before handing it to him with the bottle of water she kept on the nightstand.

He sat up and took them. "Thanks."

"We need to talk about last night at some point."

"What about it?" he grumbled.

"You need to let me know when you're going out, where you'll be, and when you plan to come home. Preferably at a reasonable hour."

"You're not my mother. And I'm a full-grown man, apparently. I don't even know you. I shouldn't be here," he snapped.

She flinched and stumbled back a step as the blow of his words hit her with full force. Her own anger rose. "I'm your wife. And I deserve some common courtesy, so I don't spend hours worrying that you're hurt or lost or in some kind of trouble. So I don't have to call everyone we know to find out if they've seen you."

"Because my brain is fucked up and I can't remember a god damned thing?" he barked. "I can handle getting around town. I can remember a lot of things. Just. Not. You. And I sure as fuck wonder why that is. Maybe old Finn was trying to tell me something. Maybe he wasn't happy here."

With you. The words he didn't say echoed in her mind as the force of his voice shattered her hope and broke her heart. Painful chaos slammed into her chest, knocking the breath from her lungs.

She ignored the tears dripping down her cheeks as she got up and grabbed a dress and a clean pair of underwear from the pile before storming out of the room. She and Finn had had their fair share of spats in the thirteen years they'd been married. But he'd never treated her this way before. He'd always protected her, taken care of her. He'd loved her.

This Finn was not the man she married.

7

FINN

Finn wiped the bar top with the wet rag as a patron slid into the empty seat across from him. Music thumped in the background, an upbeat song that had several others grinding against one another on the dance floor. He scanned the room, noting the exits and the number of people inside. The Shipwreck hadn't changed much since he last remembered it. His parents had bought it when he was fifteen. They'd turned the former hole-in-the-wall bar into a destination for the seacoast. It wasn't every day you had a bar that looked like you were underwater.

"Finn?" the blonde across from him asked, tapping her fingers impatiently. Another person who knew his name, and another face he had no memory of.

"What can I get ya?" he asked.

"An apple martini, please."

Shit. Of course, she wanted something he had no fucking clue how to make. He turned his back, trying to look busy as he pulled out his phone and googled the recipe.

"One and a half vodka, one schnapps, and half calvados

with a peel of apple to garnish," Charli whispered only loud enough for him to hear as she passed by him.

He tucked the phone into his pocket and filled the mixer with ice. Heat flamed his cheeks. Finn didn't like being caught lacking. But she'd saved his pride by not insisting on making it for him. It was one of the few sentences they'd exchanged this week since he'd picked a fight after waking in her bed, in his underwear, with a pounding headache.

She'd walked in naked, water dripping over the most gorgeous figure he'd ever laid eyes on. He hated that his body reacted so strongly to her, like she had more power over him than he did. Couldn't he have anything he controlled anymore? When she'd tried to tell him what he could and couldn't do, that had been the last straw.

He let out a sigh as he shook the ingredients in the steel mixer. The hurt that had reflected back in her eyes had torn him apart. He'd felt her pain as if it was his own. But where did they go from here? Should he apologize? His parents usually pretended like nothing happened and eventually things were right again. But it had been a week and nothing was okay.

Finn poured the cocktail into a martini glass and added an apple peel before sliding it over to the woman.

"Thanks. Just put it on my tab." She grabbed the drink and turned away before he could ask her name.

"Shit."

"Tina Romm," an old man at the corner of the bar who looked vaguely familiar said with a heavy Ghanaian accent.

"Excuse me?"

The man nodded his bald, brown head towards the blonde, now laughing with a group of other women. "That's Tina Romm."

"Oh, th—thanks." Finn was able to find her tab easily enough and added the drink.

Finn studied the man out of the corner of his eye. His leathery hand wrapped around a local beer as he wrote in a book with a pencil.

"Mr. Owusu?"

The man looked up and smiled, his bright white teeth contrasting with his midnight skin. "I knew you'd remember me eventually. I'm unforgettable."

Finn smiled for what felt like the first time in days. Finally, a familiar face from his childhood, Solomon Owusu. "How are you?"

"Good. Good. God has blessed me. I can't complain." Solomon took a sip of his drink.

"How is the shop? You still own it or has Link taken over?"

Solomon raised his hand and swatted the air playfully. "Ah, come on. Get out of here with that. I'm not too old to work. You will have to pull the wrench from my cold, dead fingers before I give up my garage." He chuckled.

Finn laughed with him. "It's good to see some things haven't changed."

"All things work out in the end the way they are supposed to. Glory to God." Solomon raised his eyes to the shiplap ceiling.

"Repeating more lines of your infallible wisdom, Papa?" another familiar man asked, taking the empty seat next to Solomon.

He had the same rich brown shade of skin as Solomon but no Ghanaian accent. The sides of his head were shaved in a fade, with short locs on the top. "Link?"

Link's brown eyes met his as the corner of his mouth turned up. "The one and only." Link reached out his hand. Finn slapped his palm to his friend's before fist-bumping him.

"Sorry to hear about the accident, man," Link said earnestly.

"It is what it is." Finn shrugged, wishing to talk about anything but himself. "What can I get ya?"

"I'll have the same as him." He pointed to his father.

"Sand Dune Brewery's finest IPA coming right up." Finn opened the fridge and grabbed the second to last bottle before popping the top and handing it over.

Link took a long sip before setting the glass bottle on the bar. "Can't wait until they release the cranberry one for the holidays."

"How have you been?" Finn asked Link.

"Pretty busy doing all the work this old man can't." Link tipped his head to the side.

"Eh! What old man are you talking about? I know my son is not speaking about his elders this way." Solomon smacked the back of Link's head playfully as Link smirked. "You do the work I don't want to do because I'm the boss."

"Okay, Papa." Link chuckled.

"Kids these days." Solomon shook his head. "I should have sent you home to my sister to raise in Ghana after your mother died. Then maybe you'd show some respect."

"Then who would do all the work at the garage?" Link ducked in time to miss Solomon's paw swinging over his head.

"I'm just kidding, Papa." Link laughed harder.

Solomon shook his head, muttering about spoiled children before taking another sip of his beer.

"You should stop by next Friday. We're gonna have a little get-together." Link peeled the label off his drink.

"Maybe I will."

"Hey, beautiful," Link said, his eyes darting behind Finn.

"Hey, guys. Another long week at the Shattered Cove Garage?" Charli asked, sidling next to him. Her amber scent drifted over, involuntarily sparking his arousal. The white T-shirt she wore had The Shipwreck's name and logo stretched across her breasts. Had they grown recently? The shirt was tied in a knot at her side, cinching the material across her swollen belly.

"It would be long for anyone if they had to listen to this one complain about his woman troubles all week." Solomon pointed his thumb at Link.

Charli laughed, seemingly at ease with his friends.

Link just shook his head and looked at Charli, a silent message seemingly passing between them. Charli gave him a wink. A shot of jealousy lanced through Finn, burning his stomach with bile. Just how close was she to his friend?

"I need to steal this guy away for a few minutes. You two stay out of trouble until we get back." She winked at Link.

Finn clenched his fists as she reached for his arm and then hesitated as if thinking better of it, dropping her hand.

The smile faded from her lips as she turned away. "I need your help with a delivery. I'm not supposed to lift anything heavy," Charli explained as she led him out the back.

A tall man stood in the loading dock at the back of his truck holding a piece of paper and a clipboard.

"Hey, Roman." Charli walked over to the man and opened her arms for a hug.

Roman looked up from his paperwork and smiled before wrapping Charli into his arms. Finn grit his teeth together until pain radiated in his jaw. Was she doing this on purpose?

Roman released her. "Hey, Charli, long time no see." He glanced over to Finn. "Hey, buddy. I'm sorry about the accident. Glad you're home safe."

Finn nodded, unsure of how to proceed.

Charli motioned to the boxes in his truck. "Your delivery is right on time. We were almost out."

"Can't have that." Roman shook his head smiling.

"How's Ariel?" Charli asked.

Roman's eyes lit up. "She's getting so big. Wants to go out and work in the fields like her daddy."

"That girl is fearless. I wouldn't want to be surrounded by bees. No, thank you. I'll leave the dangerous work to you." She laughed.

"It's not dangerous unless you're allergic to them," Roman added.

Finn's body was on fire. Forget bees. He felt like a million fire ants were crawling all over his skin. Was Roman flirting with Charli? What kind of asshole did that to a pregnant woman in front of her husband? It sure fucking seemed as if she was flirting back.

"Let's get you some of my raw honey. Promised Ariel I'd be back in time to tuck her into bed." Roman handed Charli the clipboard.

"I'll get you a check, and Finn will help you unload. Just put the honey in the usual spot." Charli walked away, disappearing inside.

"Can you get the other two boxes?" Roman nodded in the truck, his arms already full.

"Sure." Finn grabbed the remaining goods and followed Roman inside, stacking his on top of the boxes Roman had left on a pallet in the corner of the back room.

"Thanks again." Charli handed Roman a check with the clipboard, keeping a copy of the invoice for herself.

"No problem. Let me know when you need more." Roman waved to both of them before he shut the back of his truck and climbed into the driver's side.

Charli closed the loading dock door and turned to him and opened her mouth and then closed it. She hesitated one more moment. "Thanks."

"You're welcome."

"There's a bachelorette group at the bar. I'll help you get caught up." Charli walked past him.

He turned and followed her, his stomach twisting into knots. Jealousy twisted with his anger. His shoulders tensed, drawing up to his ears, the music growing louder the closer they got to the bar. His fists clenched at his sides as his head spun. What the hell was going on with him? Why was he so angry? Was this all because of Charli? Damn it. If he could remember, everything would make sense again and he wouldn't feel so lost and out of control.

Charli grabbed a glass bottle from the fridge. The bar had become even more packed since he'd left. People pushed towards the front, waving, trying to get his attention. His sight to the exit blocked, his chest tightened, squeezing his lungs.

Pop!

Finn dove to the ground. The rubber slip guard mats pressed into his face as he covered his head. Blasts and the sound of an explosion ripped through his eardrums. He sucked in a panicked breath and prepared for the strike. Bullets rang out. The sound of metal bending and screeching assaulted the air. The acrid smell of smoke made his lungs burn. His mouth filled with the tang of blood as screams erupted. *Charli. I have to get Charli out of here!*

8

FINN

Finn opened his eyes, searching for Charli.

"Finn?" Charli kneeled beside him, her face contorted with concern. "Finn? Are you okay?"

He sat up, searching around him for any sign of danger. Nothing but the thrum of music and boisterous laughter and conversation filled the air. *It was all in my head.* Fuck. He scrambled to his feet, embarrassment heating his whole body.

"Are you okay?" Charli repeated, reaching her slender fingers around his bicep, but he ripped his arm away.

"I slipped," he barked. She flinched and backed up.

Fuck! Why couldn't he do anything right? Why did his head have to be so messed up!

"You can take a break if you need to. Mason can fill in at the bar. Jarod just got here to work out front," Charli offered.

All around the bar people were staring, their unwanted gazes burning a hole in him. Could they see how broken he was?

"I'm fine," Finn grumbled and shot past her, needing to get busy and prove he wasn't a complete invalid.

He ignored her and focused on the line of people in front of him.

"Anyone order a beer and you get it half off," he yelled. Beer was the easiest thing for him to get them and the quickest way to get the line down.

He spent the next forty minutes filling orders before the crowd thinned and he could take a breath. A hand slipped over his shoulder. He tensed and spun around, ready for a fight. His mother's face greeted him instead.

Her eyebrows drew up. "Finn? What's wrong?"

I wish everyone would stop asking me that fucking question!

"Nothing. I'm just peachy."

Charli wiped the bar behind his mother, keeping her gaze on her work.

"Come to the office for a minute. Your dad wants to talk to you," his mother said, leading him towards the back once again.

He entered the small room, and his mother shut the door. His father sat at the rectangular desk with his reading glasses on, clicking away at the computer as he checked the pile of invoices in front of him. "Hey, son." His father looked up.

"Hey, Dad. Mom said you wanted to talk about something?"

His mother took a seat on the small, floral love seat at the side of the room. "Come here." She patted the cushion next to her.

Finn obeyed.

"How were your appointments with the doctors this week?" his mother started.

Invasive as fuck. "Fine." It seemed like every other day he had one appointment or another. Each doctor had new pills, exercises, or tests they wanted to poke and prod him with. He was just a guinea pig to them. *I wish everyone would leave me alone!*

"Charli was really worried about you last week," his mother pressed.

Finn rolled his eyes and sighed. "I already got a lecture from her. I don't need one from you too."

"You'd better watch the way you speak to your mother, son." His father's tone shifted, letting him know he was on thin ice. Grown man or not, his parents wouldn't tolerate disrespect.

"Sorry, Ma."

She placed her hand on his. "I know this whole situation is really hard on you. But you're not alone. You have Charli, and us, and your friends. We all just want the best for you."

He sighed, releasing some of his pent-up frustration. "I wish I could remember more."

"It will come back. What did the doctor at the Veterans Affairs say?" his father asked.

"I have an appointment tomorrow."

"Don't be so hard on yourself, and give Charli a chance, okay? That woman has been through hell. She's given up so much for you." His mother gave his hand a squeeze.

What does she mean?

"You owe her your respect," his father interjected.

"A marriage is a partnership. Everything you do affects her and vice versa. And she's carrying my grandchild. The last thing she needs is more stress in her life," his mother finished.

Finn nodded. "Alright. I get it."

"Be the man I taught you to be, Finnegan. Take care of your responsibilities," his father added and nodded towards the door.

"I will." Finn gave his mother a hug and went back out towards the bar. But voices halted his steps from the storage room.

"Finn . . . doesn't need to know."

He could only hear pieces of what Charli was saying. His heart raced in his chest as every muscle tensed, his body on alert as he rounded the corner. The air sucked from his lungs as if he'd been punched in the gut at the sight of one of his best friends whispering in a dark corner with his wife. "What the fuck is going on?" Finn roared.

Charli jumped, and Bently spun around, arms wide as if to protect Charli. A line appeared between Bently's forehead as he studied Finn. "What the hell, man?"

"Wanna tell me why you two are over here huddled in the corner, talking about what I don't need to know?"

Bently sighed, his shoulders dropping. "I came to give Charli an update."

"On what?"

Bently looked over his shoulder at Charli, as if asking permission. Finn clenched his fists until the nails bit into the skin.

Charli looked at him with wide eyes as if she didn't recognize him. As if she was afraid of him. The thought made him sick to his stomach. She turned to Bently and nodded. "Fine."

Bently stepped towards Finn. "I got news that the same man who attacked Charli on your last deployment just assaulted another woman in Massachusetts last week. Still haven't got the fucker."

What?

Bently's gaze grew dark. "He killed this other woman. He's escalating."

"What do you mean Charli was attacked?"

Bently glanced behind him to Charli.

"I hadn't told him yet because I didn't want to burden him with anything more than what he is already going through." Charli spoke to Bently but kept her gaze on him.

She tried to protect me even though she's the one in danger?

"Do you think he's gonna come back after Charli?" Finn asked, worry cinching his gut.

"Anything is possible. She's the one who got away. He might return to finish what he started. He might not. Best to keep an eye out. Don't go anywhere alone, Charli." Bently leveled his gaze on her.

"I'll be careful," she promised.

Bently nodded. "I'll be sure to send my squad to drive by your house a few times a night."

"Thank you," she said. "I'm gonna get back to work." Charli gave Bently a quick hug and walked by him, not sparing a glance in his direction.

His heart squeezed. He wanted to fix whatever this was between them, but he had no idea where to start. "What happened to her?" Finn asked.

Bently swiped a hand over his face and blew out a breath. "She closed the bar. Mason had to go home because his daughter was sick. She was jumped trying to get into her car. He beat the shit out of her."

Finn's stomach turned to stone. Only the most depraved and insecure men laid a hand on a woman. *Coward.*

"A car pulled in and it must have scared him off before he could go any further. We had six other hits in the system with his DNA. Six other women he attacked and raped."

A chill ran down Finn's spine. Bile rose in his throat. "Was Charli . . ." He couldn't finish the sentence.

"No. She put up a hell of a fight, got the asshole's DNA under her fingernails. He was interrupted before that happened. But his newest victim wasn't so lucky."

Fantastic. A psycho was probably gunning for his wife, and instead of the thirty-three-year-old military man he should be, he was a seventeen-year-old boy stuck in a body he didn't recognize. How was he going to protect her? Finn blew out a breath and put his hand on his hip to steady himself. "You think he will come back?"

"I don't know. But since there is a chance, I wanted to warn her." Bently slapped his hand over Finn's shoulder and looked him in the eye. "Keep an eye on her. Stick close. She needs you."

Finn nodded. Bently left the room. So much stress was piling on Finn's shoulders. He needed some space. He opened the back door, sucking in the cold night air. Stars glittered above as the moon shone bright. He pounded his fist on his chest, his eyes burning and his throat constricting. Charli was hurt. She could be in danger again. Why didn't she want him to know? He'd been too busy pushing her away this week to give her any reason to trust him, that's why. Fuck! How was he supposed to protect her if she didn't let him in?

"It gets easier," a voice said from his side.

Finn spun around, fists clenched, ready for a fight. "Who the fuck are you?"

A tall man walked out from the shadows. Even in the moonlight, the scars on the side of his face were visible, twisting up the side of his mouth at an unnatural angle. "Mason. I work security."

Right. The one who was supposed to take Charli to her car to keep her safe.

"What gets easier?" Finn asked.

"The triggers. The hyper reflexes. The PTSD."

Finn didn't have PTSD. How could he? He didn't even remember his time in the service. Just that one nightmare he wasn't even sure was a memory or not. "You get injured in the line of duty?" Finn asked. If this guy wanted to butt into his business, he'd make him equally uncomfortable.

"Yup. Navy SEAL. Can't tell you where or how though," Mason said, stepping closer, his feet scraping the gravel.

"I don't have PTSD," Finn said, standing taller.

"It's not easy readjusting to civilian life. Not all of us do." Mason's gaze dropped for a moment before he continued. "But you've got a wife who loves you and a baby on the way who needs you. You gotta figure out how to navigate this, soldier. For them."

"I—I don't even remember what happened."

Mason shrugged. "The body remembers, even if the mind hid the trauma away to protect you."

"You're about as good as a shrink as you are security," Finn snapped.

Mason eyed him, guilt flashing in his gaze. A direct hit. "Pushing people away who wanna help you is only going to make this worse on you and everyone who loves you." Mason walked past him, not waiting for a reply, disappearing beyond the corner of the building.

Finn let out another sigh. Why couldn't he get a hold of himself? Was he truly losing his mind? He'd lashed out at Mason for not protecting Charli, but Finn hadn't been there either. The key to remembering things was unlocking his brain. But the question was, what was his mind trying to protect him from? The accident? Unless that nightmare was actually a memory. Or was it something else? Something more dangerous and sinister with the power to rip apart his life? Had he killed someone? *No. There's no way I could do that.*

"What are you hiding up there, Finn?" he said aloud to himself, a puff of his breath turning to smoke in the crisp air and floating up to the moon.

Maybe Mason had a point. Finn may not be sure who he was anymore, but one thing he did know is that he had two responsibilities: Charli and the baby. He needed to man up and take care of them, do better. But since when was half a man enough for anyone?

9

CHARLI

Charli slipped the keys into her pocket and shut the door to her car. She turned around, scanning the street. The hair on the back of her neck stood to attention as a shiver made its way up her spine. A mother with her baby in a stroller pushed on the sidewalk on the opposite side of the street. A few others she recognized as locals went into shops along Main Street. Nothing seemed out of the ordinary. *Maybe I'm just being paranoid.*

She checked her watch. Charli only had an hour before she needed to pick Finn up from his appointments at the Veterans Affairs. She walked towards the High Tide Diner, that prickly feeling of being watched clinging to her skin. Sweat beaded on her temple as she peeked over her shoulder. A man in a brown jacket and baseball cap followed far enough behind her that she couldn't make out his face. Her pulse spiked as she increased her speed. She took out her keys and slipped them between each finger—the only weapon she had. Almost there. Just a few more feet. Her hand slipped over the metal door handle of the diner and she pulled with all her force, whipping the door open. She scanned the street where the man had been, but it was empty. He was gone.

"Are you okay?"

Charli turned her attention back to the diner. One of their newer residents, Brynn, eyed her worriedly.

"I—I just thought . . . I thought someone was following me," Charli admitted.

Brynn's worry flashed with panic as her eyes darted to the window overlooking the street. "What did he look like?"

"Brown coat and a blue baseball cap." Charli shut the door and focused past the glass to the street bustling with other townsfolk and tourists. The tension between the women was palpable. Guilt pressed over her shoulders. Brynn had enough fear to deal with without Charli adding to it. "Maybe I was wrong. It was probably nothing."

Brynn turned to her. "Are you sure?"

"Yeah. Probably just paranoid. Bently stopped in to see me yesterday with an update on my case." Charli walked towards the counter as Brynn followed. A few other patrons looked up as she passed, one older lady smiled at her. She nodded back before taking a barstool.

Brynn slipped around the other side. "Did they catch him?" She whispered only loud enough for Charli to hear.

Brynn knew the whole story, because Charli had shared it last year at the meeting they both attended for survivors of sexual assault. Charli hadn't been raped, but he'd threatened, and he would have if he hadn't been interrupted. His slimy hands had touched her—assaulted her. No matter how hard she fought, she'd still lost in the end. She'd passed out believing she was going to die, alone in the dark. All she had been able to think about was Finn.

Brynn's warm hand landed on hers, tentatively offering her comfort. Charli met her sympathetic gaze. Though Brynn had only shared bits and pieces of her story, it was enough to know the woman had been through more pain than any human should know.

"I'm okay. I think I just need some food." Charli forced a smile.

Brynn nodded and pulled her hand away to grab a pen and notepad from her apron. "What'll it be?"

"I've been craving a mint-chocolate milkshake and a cheeseburger with bacon and extra pickles. And maybe a couple slices of pie to go."

A small smile turned up the corner of Brynn's mouth. Everything about the woman was small and muted, like she didn't want to be noticed. "I remember the cravings I had when I was pregnant with David. I wanted the weirdest things. Onion rings dipped in tartar sauce." Brynn's nose wrinkled.

"Can't say that sounds very appetizing." Charli laughed.

"Pretzels dipped in peanut butter."

"That's a little less weird."

Brynn chuckled quietly. "Pickled eggs."

Charli's mouth watered at the thought of a tangy egg. "No, thanks. Just the burger and pickles for me."

"Coming right up."

After a few minutes, Brynn came back with her milkshake. "Extra thick, so here's a spoon."

"Thank you." Charli took the first mouthful and groaned as minty, chocolaty goodness erupted on her taste buds.

A man a few seats over turned to look at her, his face glowing red before he refocused on his plate. A puff of air came from Brynn as if she'd started to laugh and stopped. "That good, huh?"

"You have no idea." It was better than sex—almost. Not really, but she hadn't had any since before Finn left for his fishing trip. Now she had to live with the man without touching him, and it was pure unadulterated torture. Though he'd been avoiding her this past week, which made it a tad bit easier. She'd had to take care of business herself, which barely took the edge off. Stupid pregnancy hormones. Today was actually the first time he'd strung more than a few words together to her. Maybe he just needed more time and space. She wanted to be there for him, but he wouldn't let her in. Something old Finn and the new one had in common.

"Your lunch, mama." Brynn slid the plate in front of her.

She inhaled, smelling the meaty cheesy masterpiece before her. "How's David doing?" Charli asked as Brynn reset the coffee pot.

A ghost of a smile danced across Brynn's lips as her blue eyes lit up. "He's doing great."

"Are you still homeschooling him?"

Brynn nodded, a shadow crossing her features. "Mm-hmm."

Charli bit into her burger before washing it down with another sip of the shake.

"I just wish there was a way for him to make some friends . . . like him. You know?" Brynn said.

"I know a guy who runs a center called Hope Facility for teens. They accept all teenagers, but he started it for LGBT plus kids who needed a safe place."

Brynn's eyes brightened. "Really?"

Charli nodded. "I'll get you the info."

"Thank you so much!" Brynn pressed her hand to her heart.

"My pleasure." Charli took another bite of her burger while Brynn refilled coffees and helped a few new customers with their orders.

"Do you need more pickles?" Brynn asked.

"No, this was perfect."

Brynn nodded. "Is it just what happened earlier, or is something else on your mind?"

"Can I tell you a secret?" Charli asked.

"Of course." Brynn leaned in.

"I'm terrified of being a mother—of being like mine. The only reason I agreed to have a baby was because Finn promised to be by my side. He believed in me . . . and now . . . it's like he's here, but he's not himself. He's not the man who left on that guys' trip. He's not even the man I married. He's short-tempered and moody. I am terrified I'm going to have to do this alone, and I'm worried I won't be enough." *And he doesn't love me anymore.* Charli placed her hand over her belly.

Brynn walked around the counter and sat in the empty chair next to her, sliding her arm around Charli's shoulders as she spoke into her ear. "Motherhood isn't about perfection. God knows, if it was, we'd all be doomed. I made a lot of mistakes as a mother—things I can never take back and will always regret. But the important thing is we love them with our whole heart, and each time we make a mistake, we apologize to them and promise to do better. Then we do just that. Motherhood is about sacrifice, and growth, and love. You don't just wake up the perfect parent. Motherhood is an evolution. The fact that you're so worried about making the mistakes your mother did tells me you won't."

Charli's throat tightened as she choked down the emotion welling in her chest.

"We only do the best we can do and hope it's enough. Keep learning. Keep growing. And follow your gut. Woman's intuition is a gift. The more you listen to it, the louder it becomes." Brynn pulled away enough to look Charli in the eyes as her voice grew serious. "Don't ever doubt yours. Even when it's uncomfortable, even when it hurts to follow that little voice. You do what your gut tells you."

Charli nodded. "Okay. I will. Thank you."

Brynn patted her back. "Anytime."

"Was David's father a part of his life at all?"

Brynn flinched away, her blue eyes growing stormy. "Sometimes it's better to do things on your own."

Her eyes flicked to the sailboat clock on the wall. "I'd better get going. Finn is getting out of his appointment soon."

"Don't forget your pie." Brynn pushed a paper bag towards her.

"Thank you for feeding me and for letting me pour my heart out. I hope I didn't upset you."

Brynn waved her off. "I'm glad I could be a listening ear."

Charli paid before heading back out to her car. She got in and locked the door before starting the ignition—a habit she'd formed as a young teen girl. Maybe if she'd gotten into her car that night, he never would have been able to touch her. She shook off the thought. *What's done is done.* Charli pulled out onto the street and drove to pick up Finn.

10

CHARLI

Charli pulled up her phone, making sure her text sent letting Finn know that she was in the parking lot. It was marked as read but Finn never bothered to respond. Maybe he had been kept longer. Or perhaps he'd had a breakthrough with his therapy?

Knock. Knock.

Charli jumped in the car seat, her pulse rocketing as her gaze darted to the window. Finn's brows drew in as he studied her overreaction.

She unlocked the car and rolled down her window.

"Sorry I scared you." He wiped a hand over the back of his head.

"All done?"

"Yeah. Do you mind if I drive back?" Finn asked.

"Sure."

He backed up, and she hopped out of the car, slipping around to the passenger side. Her hand reached out to grab the handle, but he beat her to it. Yanking her palm away before she touched him, she eyed him warily as he opened the door for her.

She hesitated a moment and then climbed inside. Apparently, he was opening doors for her now? Finn climbed into the driver's side and buckled up before shifting the car into gear and driving out of the parking lot towards home.

"I brought you some pie from the diner." Charli broke the silence.

"You did?"

"Yeah, apple or pecan pie."

"Thank you . . . Which one is your favorite?"

Charli tried not to let her jaw drop to the floor. Was Finn actually having a conversation with her now? "Apple."

"Pecan is mine." He turned at the light, getting on the highway.

"I know."

He nodded, glancing over to her before focusing back on the road.

She drew in a breath. Might as well take advantage of this moment. "How was your appointment?"

"They gave me a couple of new prescriptions. I got them filled around the corner. That's why I was a little late."

"Oh, I could have driven over there and picked you up."

"It's okay. I needed the fresh air."

She nodded, unsure of what to say. She flicked the radio on, letting the music fill the silence until they pulled into their driveway.

An idea flitted through Charli's mind. Finn seemed to be having a better day. Maybe a night out would help him not feel so stuck. "Do you think you'd want to go out to dinner tonight?" Holding her breath, she unbuckled herself. When he didn't answer, she glanced over at him.

His gaze met hers and held for what seemed like the first time since his accident. "Yeah, that sounds good. Where do you have in mind?"

"We could go into the city? To Alfonso's?"

He hesitated.

"Too bad Atlas's restaurant isn't open for business yet, then we wouldn't have to go too far."

"Atlas?"

Right. Of course, he doesn't remember. "He's dating Jasmine, and he bought the old fish market down by the bay."

"Wow. But she's so young. I mean, the way I remember her." Finn leaned his head on the back of the seat.

"She's a mom too."

He shook his head and smiled. "Damn."

"What time do you want to go? I'll call and make us a reservation." She tapped the app open on her phone.

"Uh, six?"

"Okay." Charli entered the information and secured their reservation before she opened her door and climbed out. They walked into the house, her trailing behind Finn. Butterflies of hope fluttered in her belly. The first flame of joy she'd felt in so long sparked to life. She'd shower and take her time getting ready. Charli would enjoy this peace between them for as long as it lasted. She'd dress up and put her all into this. She'd promised to love him in sickness and health. And if Finn needed her to go slow and give him space and patience, well, she'd do that. She'd do anything to find him again.

* * *

At five thirty, Charli gave herself a spritz of her favorite perfume and spun around in the mirror. Her dark, wavy hair flowed to her waist. She'd added a few curls. Her brown eyes stood out with the black eyeliner and smoky eye shadow she'd applied. Her lips were naked except for the sheen of lip balm. She slipped her hands over the black lace top that cinched under her breasts and flowed out, hiding her baby bump. She was glad she didn't have to choose between beauty or comfort. These pregnancy jeans were the best invention, and she was probably never going back to regular pants after experiencing the stretchy comfort of her new wardrobe.

She took a deep breath. "You look good. Now go make your husband fall in love with you again." Charli swallowed the nerves down and straightened her shoulders.

She exited the bathroom and walked to the living room. Finn was sitting on the couch, flipping through a motorcycle magazine. His gaze flicked to her as she descended the stairs and the paper slipped through his hands, fluttering to the ground. Finn stood, slack-jawed, eyes wide and dark. He opened his mouth and closed it, throat bobbing as he swallowed. His heated gaze raked over the black boots laced over her calves—a pair he'd bought for her last fall—trailing her body until he landed on her face. "Wow."

Heat stirred in her belly. "You don't look so bad yourself." He'd gone with a simple pair of jeans and a white-and-grey-striped, long-sleeve Henley that clung to his muscles to perfection.

"We match." She nodded to his black motorcycle boots.

"Uh-yeah. I guess we do."

"We should get going if we don't want to miss our reservation."

"Right." He shook his head as if in a stupor.

Charli slipped on her leather jacket and followed him to the car, where he opened the door for her. He drove them to Alfonso's, following her directions.

"Have I been here before?" Finn asked, opening the front door.

A flutter of hope tipped in her belly. Did he remember?

"Yeah. You took me for my eighteenth birthday. We celebrated our engagement here," Charli answered, stepping inside and waving to the large dining room. The room hadn't changed much in the last thirteen years. That was partly why she'd chosen this place. Maybe it would jar his memory. White tablecloths covered each square table with a small vase in the center with a fresh rose and baby's breath. Giant sepia photos of the Bianchi family who owned the restaurant and their nonna making large batches of sauce or pasta by hand adorned the walls.

"Do you have a reservation?" a young woman asked them.

"Yes, under Reed," Charli answered her.

"For two?" The girl tapped the tablet in her hand.

"Yes."

"Right this way." She grabbed the menus and led them past the tables full of couples and families and out a door in the back.

Crisp sea air whispered around her as she followed the woman to a table overlooking the ocean, right by an outside heater. "This is lovely. I didn't think we'd get one out here tonight," Charli said, slipping into the seat.

"Mr. Bianchi has you on his VIP list." The maître d' smiled.

"Well, I feel special." Charli grinned as Finn took a seat across from her.

"Here are your menus. Your server will be along shortly to take your order. Can I get you a drink to start?" She handed them the black parchment; the menu items were printed in silver ink.

"I'll take a warm apple cider, please," Charli answered.

"I'll have a beer. Do you have Sand Dune's pumpkin ale?"

"Yes, sir, we do."

"Sounds good."

"It will be right out," she promised and disappeared.

Charli turned to look over the water as the waves lapped the rocky shore. The sky was orange and purple as the sun set, casting them in a burnt glow.

"You really look amazing tonight," Finn said.

Charli turned her attention back to him and smiled. "Thank you."

"There's something familiar about this place." Finn scanned the room, eyes squinted in focus.

Her stomach flipped. "You remember it?"

His forehead scrunched in concentration before he shook his head. "You know how you run into someone and you swear you know them from somewhere, but you aren't sure where?"

"Yeah."

"That's what this feels like."

"We came here a lot. It was a tradition for us. We celebrated our engagement here and then every anniversary after that."

"Every one? Doesn't seem so creative."

She smiled. "You used to say if it isn't broke—"

"Don't fix it," he finished as their eyes met.

Was it coming back to him?

"My dad used to say that all the time. Guess I got that from him."

She swallowed her disappointment.

"Why are you on the VIP list here?" he asked.

She glanced at the menu as she answered. "Frank Bianchi's daughter got into a situation one time at The Shipwreck. I noticed she needed an out. That's actually why we created the Angel shot."

His eyebrows rose in question.

"It's plastered all over the women's bathroom at the bar. If they feel they are in an uncomfortable situation and need help getting out of it, they order the Angel shot. You give them water and order them a cab, while getting security to intervene if necessary—to get her away from the guy usually."

"Oh, that's cool."

"You also served with Frank's son, Frank Junior. You guys are—or were—friends."

Finn nodded. He opened his mouth as if to say something and then closed it before looking out the window.

"Andre and Mikel told me to let you know that when you feel up to it, they'd love another set of hands working on Atlas's renovation. After that they are moving to work on Jasmine's place."

"Mikel and Andre started that business after all?" He chuckled.

"Yes. And Jasmine opened The Lighthouse Inn down the road."

"Damn. It's really cool to see how much everyone's accomplished." He knocked his knuckles on the wooden surface of the table.

"They are happy."

"Are you?" His voice wavered.

"Am I . . . happy?"

"Were you . . . before . . . before my accident?"

She focused on the setting sun as she answered. Memories of their laughter spilled into her mind, bleeding from her heart. "Yes. I mean, our life wasn't perfect. We had struggles like any other couple. But . . . I was excited for you to get out of the Army. I felt like we were ready to start the next phase of our life." She placed her hand over her belly. "I was very happy."

Charli turned back to him, his brown eyes full of emotions that he'd never reveal. Sadness, grief, guilt, and others she had no name for.

"Here's your drinks." A man interrupted the moment, setting her cider in front of her and his beer before Finn. "I'm Daniel, and I'll be your server tonight. Do you know what you'd like to order? Or would you like to hear the specials?"

Finn picked up the menu. Charli scanned the items one more time, the local fare all sounding so delicious. "The specials, please."

"Our chef prepared fresh pasta with Alfredo sauce, broccoli, and organic sausage from the Ever farm in Durham. Or we have Nonna's lasagna."

"I'd like the lasagna, please." Charli handed over her menu.

"Of course."

"Me too," Finn said.

"It will be out shortly," Daniel promised before he left them alone.

Charli sipped her cider, soaking in the cinnamon and warmth.

Finn mirrored her with his beer. "It's so weird being able to order a beer and not be carded." Finn shook his head.

"You didn't exactly avoid alcohol in high school." She laughed.

He pulled his bottom lip between his teeth as he shook his head. The action sent a pulse of need throbbing through her. Heat blanketed her skin. She slipped off her jacket, trying to cool down. Good god this man was going to be the death of her. His dark eyes never left her, only making the stirring within her worse.

"We had some good times at the beach." He smirked.

"Do you remember the time you and the guys went skinny-dipping?"

His eyebrows drew together in concentration and he nodded, his eyes lighting up. "Yeah. Vargas was there. That water was so fucking cold." He chuckled. "Wait, were you there?"

"No, but Vargas told me all about it the next time you guys had a bonfire."

"We were crazy little shits." He smiled. "How is Vargas?"

"She's a deputy working with Bently at the Shattered Cove PD. She and her wife have a little boy."

"Good for her. Did I do anything to top public nudity?" Finn asked.

Charli couldn't hold back the smile as memory after memory flicked through her mind.

"What did I do?" He leaned forward, excitement sparking in his gaze.

"Well, let's just say you kinda had a thing for public spaces and partial nudity."

His eyes widened as a worried expression painted his face. "Oh, shit. You gotta tell me now."

She giggled at his expression. "Nothing like that." She placed her hand over his to assure him. Sparks of attraction burst within her, warmth blossoming inside her at the connection.

As she licked her lips, his attention darted to them. "You, uh, liked to take me to places where we could get caught at any moment."

"Doing what?" He breathed out, his voice heady. The

energy between them was charged with longing and anticipation.

"You'd put your hands on me usually, slowly moving from
my breasts to between my thighs." She swallowed as his eyes
darkened to almost black.

"What did you do?"

Charli twisted her head to look over her shoulder, making
sure no one was close enough to hear. She leaned towards him
in a whisper. "I pretended like I wanted you to stop."

"But you didn't?" His eyes locked on to hers, his head
tipping closer so that the wisps of his breath teased her lips.

"Never. And you knew that. We'd talked about it the first
time."

"Where?" He took a sip of his drink, his hand shaking
ever so slightly.

"Lots of places. The office at the bar. The storage room.
The walk-in fridge. The beach. A changing room once." She
smiled.

"Was that it? I just touched you?"

She shook her head. "No, you fucked me." Sometimes
with his mouth, other times with his hands, or that perfect
thick cock.

His grip squeezed the glass bottle so tight she thought it
might crack.

"Other times, I'd touch you."

"Here you are," Daniel said, setting their plates in front of
them.

Finn jumped at the intrusion and then turned to look at
the sun as it slipped behind the line of the ocean. His chest
rose and fell rapidly as he drained what was left of his beer.

Heat blanketed her skin, rising up her neck and burning
her cheeks at the sight of her husband coming so undone by
her explicit confessions. She wanted more than anything to

run her foot up his leg, past his thigh, and press against what she was sure was a hard dick and tease him.

"Thank you," Charli said to the server instead, sounding a lot calmer than she felt.

"Can I get you another beer, sir?" Daniel asked.

"I'll have some hot cider now."

They tucked into their food as the stars sparkled above them, the moon shining over the dark water. The salty breeze swept over them from time to time. The conversation switched to lighter topics, catching up on people from their past. She told him stories of fun times they'd shared. By the time dessert was brought out, her face hurt from smiling so much.

"Ready to go?" Finn asked as the server cleared their plates and returned Finn's credit card.

"Yeah." She slipped her coat over her shoulders and took the hand Finn offered to help her from her seat. He didn't let her go after that, and her belly flipped. Hope squeezed her chest tight. Happiness bubbled up. After his aloofness and cold demeanor this past week, this moment seemed like she'd hit the jackpot. Maybe her Finn was coming back to her after all.

She walked by his side to the car as he opened her door. She turned around to face him, his chiseled jaw more prominent in the moon and shadows now that he'd shaved. "Finn?"

"Yeah?" His breath tickled against her lips, smelling of sweet apple and cinnamon.

"Thank you for tonight. I had a really good time." She stood up on her tiptoes and melded her mouth to his. Finn's soft lips tensed. She moved away, but then his palm gripped the back of her head, pulling her towards him. He kissed her back, much like the first kiss they'd shared—it was sweet and innocent. Still, it turned the flame inside her to an all-out blaze. She ached for him. And if the pressure against her belly was any indication, he wanted her too. But she wouldn't push him. Not tonight. Not after he'd given her this amazing gift. It had been months since he'd had his hands or mouth on her like this. She'd savor it.

Finn backed away, his expression full of manly desire and boyish surprise.

She smiled. Maybe things were going to work out for them sooner than she'd thought.

11

FINN

Finn took another sip of his beer as he clicked play on a video on the laptop. Charli's whole face lit up as she smiled and laughed. Finn's chuckle overlapped hers in the recording.

"What are you doing?" Charli asked him.

He zoomed in on her freckles and then back out. "Just looking at the most beautiful woman I've ever laid eyes on," Finn answered her.

Her eyes glittered with happiness, joy overflowing. She was breathtaking. There was not a trace of the pain and hesitation he'd become accustomed to in her eyes.

"Boy, is that a line if I ever heard one." She snorted.

"Not a line. Just the truth."

"You trying to get laid, soldier?" she teased, her eyes darkening.

He growled. The camera turned to the blue sky with bits of green grass poking up at the edges.

She squealed as if he'd grabbed her. "Finn!"

The screen rolled again, this time capturing the two of them lying in the grass. His eyes focused on her like she was his whole world and then some.

"I can take you whenever I want. I don't need a line for that."

"Oh, really? What makes you so sure?" Charli's eyebrows rose.

His finger slid over her neck, trailing down the middle of her breasts. She shuddered. "The way your body trembles under my touch." He dipped his nose to her neck and inhaled. "You smell so fucking good. Rich as sin and sweet as heaven."

"Finn." Charli's voice was breathy.

Finn's cock grew hard. He shifted in his seat, eyes locked on the screen.

Finn leaned in and kissed her nose and then the smattering of freckles on either side of her face before he landed his lips on hers. She moaned, her hands wrapping around his shoulders.

He pulled back and smiled lovingly at her before tracing his thumb over her cheek and down her jaw. "Because you want me too. And I'm all yours, baby. Now and forever."

She moved his mouth back to hers.

Fire and so much emotion radiated in his chest. His eyes remained glued to Charli and himself on the screen.

A rustling noise filtered through the speakers and then Finn's finger hovered over the screen before it ended.

Wow. He shut the laptop and ran a hand over his face. He could feel the warm sunshine on his skin as if he were there, in that moment, who knew how long ago. He slammed his eyes closed. The prickly sensation of grass danced across his skin. His finger pressed against his lips. He could taste her kiss on his mouth. But was that because she'd kissed him last night? Or was it the memory from that day in the recording? He reached out into the deep, dark fog of his mind, grasping for anything tangible.

Sparks and glimmers. Flashes, long enough to know something was there but not what memory it was. The vision slipped through his fingers like sand.

Click.

He opened his eyes as the sound of keys jangling drew him back to the present. "Charli?"

"Yeah, I'm home. Just getting my shoes off." Charli appeared around the corner a moment later. Finn checked his watch; it was seven thirty at night.

She walked in holding her lower back before falling into the cushions next to him.

"How was your meeting?" he asked.

She shifted, placing a pillow behind her, and pulled her foot over her knee, rubbing it with her hand. "It was okay."

"What was it for?" He grabbed her tiny foot and settled it into his lap.

She stiffened, her eyes darting to him. As he pressed his thumb into the arch, she tipped her head back and moaned before relaxing into the sofa. The sound shot straight to his dick. Just like it had when he'd watched the video.

"It's, uh, kinda private. But it's a meeting for survivors of sexual assault and trauma."

His hand paused. Bently said she hadn't been . . . but maybe someone else had? "Your—" He cleared his throat. "Your attacker . . .?" He couldn't even say the words out loud.

She shook her head. His shoulders relaxed away from his ears as he returned to massaging her foot.

"He didn't rape me, but he did sexually assault me in . . . other ways. It helps me to go to the meetings."

He nodded and switched to her other foot. If he ever got his hands on the fucker who thought it was okay to put a hand on a woman—*his* woman. Shit. *His* woman? Well, Charli was his wife. Couldn't get more *his* than that.

She moaned again as he squeezed the edge of her foot, working his way up to her tiny toes. He shifted her foot away from the steel rod in his pants. There wasn't much she had to do before that traitor stood to attention. But those fucking delicious sounds coming from her and the sensation of her skin on his was enough for him to worry about coming in his pants. Jesus, fuck! What the hell?

"You used to do this for me," Charli whispered as if she wasn't sure she should speak.

He tipped his face towards her, like he had any other choice than to look upon perfection itself. "I did?"

"Mm-hmm. All the time when I got off my shifts at the bar. Although it usually led to something else." Her voice came out breathy and wanting.

He swallowed, his body burning with white-hot flames of desire for this gorgeous woman beside him. "I may not remember you in here." He tapped his temple. "But my body seems to remember you."

Every fucking molecule seemed destined to bend towards her, seeking more flame. She was pure sunshine, and Finn didn't care if she incinerated him. He just needed to capture some of her warmth, a burst of her solar flare. Burning alive had never been more enticing.

Charli leaned forward too, her hand reaching to cup his face. His jaw, peppered with rough bristles, brushed against the buttery softness of her skin. Her chest rose and fell more rapidly, sending bursts of her sweet breath against his lips. Still, she continued her caress as if his roughness was what she desired. Her brown eyes heated, locked on to his, holding him prisoner in her wanton gaze. "Finn?"

His name was soft against his lips, breaking his self-control. He crashed his mouth to hers. Red and white flashes of searing heat lashed against his skin, burrowing to his core. One hand fisted in her hair, pulling her closer, and the other cupped her neck.

He swallowed her moan with his own sound of pleasure. Leaning over her, he laid her on the couch, cursing the clothes between them. Charli's tongue dipped into his mouth, and he lost all ability to think, forced only to feel. Her hands gripped his shoulders, her nails digging into his flesh.

It was too much and not enough all at the same time. Needing more, he ran his palms down her arms until he found her hands. He lifted them above her head and held them against the armrest, his fingers interwoven with hers. She bit down and raked her teeth across his bottom lip, making him growl and press his hard cock directly against her hot center. His body burst into flames from the contact. Finn thrust again, seeking relief, the sensation from the friction incredible, wishing to dive deep inside her. Nothing else mattered.

Charli let out a whimper and wrapped her legs around his waist, urging him on. The couch creaked with every thrust. Her kiss drugged him, intoxicating him with the duality of her taste and her tongue. His palm slid down her arm to the curve of her breast and over her hard nipple. *Jesus, she's so soft, yet firm.* His cock twitched as he explored the luscious peaks. Excitement built as he satisfied his curiosity and explored her body.

She arched her back. "Finn!" His name on her lips only made the pulse inside his cock beat faster. With her hand now freed from Finn's grip, Charli's fingers reached for the button of his pants, releasing some of the pain caused by the harsh denim prison that had contained his engorged dick.

He palmed her breast, loving the way it fit perfectly in his hand. She only kissed him back harder. Her hand slid over the waistband of his boxers. He hissed as her soft touch seared his skin like a tattoo.

Sliding his hand over the swell of her belly, he froze. She was pregnant. There was a baby in there. *Shit!*

He jerked off of her, scrambling to his feet. "Fuck! I'm sorry, Charli."

She winced and sat up, running a hand over her belly.

Had he hurt her? Was the baby okay?

"I'm sorry," he repeated. "I shouldn't have—"

She held up a hand and nodded. Hurt and rejection flashed in her eyes. "It's okay. I get it."

But she didn't. Not really. Damn it! He didn't want to cause her any pain. That was why he'd backed off.

She got to her feet, straightening her clothes and brushed past him.

"Charli?"

"I'm going to bed." Her voice was strained as if she was about to fall apart. She didn't turn around to look at him as she walked up the stairs.

He sighed and sat on the couch. "What the fuck were you thinking, Finn?" He'd dry-humped her on the sofa. Had he squished her? Was she alright?

"Of course, she isn't, dickhead," he snapped at himself.

Why did this have to be so hard? He should march up there right now and tell her she was the most beautiful crea-ture he'd ever laid eyes on. That he wanted to be the Finn in the video for her. But what if he'd screwed it up by thinking with his cock? He should have been more worried about her instead of crushing her into the couch like that. He buttoned his pants.

Finn lay on the sofa, slinging his arm over his eyes. Each place she'd touched him now felt cold. What if he went up there and she told him he'd never measure up to her expecta-tions, because he was only a shadow of the man he once was? If he went upstairs, he'd only disappoint her more. He had no idea what he was doing sexually. Not to mention he'd prob-ably hurt her, and she probably wanted nothing to do with him now. No, he'd stay here and hope tomorrow would come and that the sun would rise with it.

* * *

After two hours of tossing and turning on the couch, Finn gave up. He shrugged his sweatshirt on and slipped his boots over his feet before going out to the garage. He placed his palm to the wall until he found the plastic switch and flicked the lights on. The space was organized neatly, all but for the sheen of dust over everything except the motorcycle that sat front and center in the single bay. He ran his hand over the gleaming metal and cherry red paint. It was beautiful. He turned, taking in the array of tools hanging on the wall by the workbench. A few shelves with odds and ends were stationed across the room. Several boxes had been stacked in a corner, leaning against the shelving unit with labeled bins.

He walked over to the bench, finding more magazines and a few manuals on the mechanics of engines. A smaller leather-bound book between them caught his attention. He pulled it out and turned it over in his hands before opening it. His own scrawl stared back at him. A journal. A dull thud pulsed in his head—a flicker of a memory, more like a wisp of smoke.

He flipped the page, Charli's name catching his eye.

I don't know how long I can keep doing this. Charli . . . I just can't do this anymore. She can't choose him again. We won't survive it. Maybe one day she'll forgive me. Maybe one day I'll forgive her. But Damon has to go. It would destroy her to do it, so I'll make that choice for her. I can't share her like this. She's my wife. She isn't his to love and protect. Only mine. If I have to break her heart to get him out of her life, I will. Real love doesn't hurt someone the way he hurt her. I'll show her what it is to be loved, and eventually she'll move on from him.

What the fuck? Piercing pain split his vision as he searched the page. There was no date on the entry. In the videos Charli had shared with him they'd been so happy. But here it was in black and white—his own damn words—not everything was as it seemed. What had Charli done? Who was Damon? Had Charli cheated on him? Had Finn been planning to leave her? Was this all a lie? He needed answers. Flipping the page, the words blurred as the room spun.

He clenched his fist and slammed the journal onto the counter, his chest heaving. Damn it! His own body was betraying him. He squeezed his eyes shut. He'd thought he could trust Charli. Apparently, he'd been mistaken. But she'd been kind and patient with him. She'd done so much. Would a woman like that lie? Maybe he should ask her? *But how can I know she'd tell me what really happened?*

It was here in his own damn handwriting. Wasn't it? She couldn't be trustworthy if she'd been having an affair. She'd just been taking advantage of this whole situation. Hadn't she? He'd kissed her—what was the point? She was a stranger. Would he ever find out the truth?

12

CHARLI

Charli scrubbed the dishes in the sink and checked the clock. Five p.m. Finn had been gone when she woke up like he had the last three mornings, and the only reason she knew he'd returned was the music blaring from the garage. She'd brought him out lunch but he'd refused it, saying he wasn't hungry. But she was starving—for him. Seeing him with grease on his cheek, his jeans clinging to his sculpted ass, and that white T-shirt covered with black stains. Good god, she'd nearly melted into a puddle at his feet. She was used to going months without sex because of his deployments. But he was here, sleeping in the same damn house, torturing her. Not to mention, today was her birthday. And birthday sex was always something extra special when he was home. And when he wasn't—they'd made up for that too.

He'd been quiet, withdrawing again. Hadn't they made progress? Maybe she'd pushed him too hard. Fuck! This was so frustrating. She just wanted to help, but she didn't know how. *I want my Finn back.*

The door creaked open. She turned around with a smile,

89

only to have it disappear entirely as she laid eyes on the second man through the door. She swallowed and cut her eyes to Finn. "Hey." Her voice wavered.

Finn wiped his hands on a dirty rag before slipping it into his pocket. "You know Stewart?"

Charli nodded, flicking her gaze to the pale man beside him. Stewart didn't look much different than the last time she'd seen him. He was as oily as ever. His narrowed blue eyes made her shift uncomfortably. He smiled smugly. *Why is he here?* "Yeah, it's been awhile."

Stewart rubbed a hand over his long beard before turning to Finn. "Yeah, but I understand you had other things going on. Being pussy whipped only lasts so long. I knew eventually you'd come to your senses."

Charli cut Finn a questioning look. Surely, he'd say something, stand up for her. He'd cut Stewart out of their lives years ago.

Finn just stared back at her with a blank look.

"You up for a ride? Catch up for old time's sake? I got this place we can have a few drinks you're gonna love." Stewart chuckled, insinuation in every syllable.

What was going on?

"Yeah, sounds good. I'll be ready in an hour," Finn said, brushing past her to the fridge to grab two Gatorades. He threw Stewart one.

The man caught it and waved it in the air. "Sounds good. I'll be back." He turned and left, the front door closing behind him the only sound in the room.

Finn drained the drink and tossed the bottle into the recycling bin.

"We're supposed to have dinner with your parents tonight."

"Well, I'm going out instead," he snapped, giving her his back as he headed towards the bathroom.

Charli blinked a few times. She shook her head, anger welling up. He may need her patience, but he wouldn't speak to her like that.

She followed him, opening the bathroom door. He had his clothes off down to his boxers.

"Jesus! Haven't you heard of knocking?"

"What is going on with you?"

He stood straighter and rolled his eyes. "Nothing."

"Finn, you don't—you can't talk to me like that. I want to help. I want to be here for you."

His jaw clenched as he looked away, hands balled into fists.

"*You* cut Stewart out of your life years ago. And I don't trust him—"

"And you're the expert on who's trustworthy, huh?" His brown eyes burned with warning. What was she missing?

"I just want you to be careful." Her voice trembled, her emotions much harder to control with the pregnancy hormones.

"I know Stew. I remember *him*."

But not me. She flinched, his message loud and clear. "You also remember Bently, Mikel, Andre, or Link. Why not hang out with them?"

"What do you have against Stewart?" His voice rose louder. "Were you the reason I abandoned my friendship with him?"

She shook her head, tears welling. "No. I mean, you decided it on your own. I told you he made me uncomfortable, but I never . . . You made that choice, Finn. You outgrew the friendship. He stayed partying, always trying to get you to see other women. He never grew up. He still hasn't. He's reckless. And I've always had a bad feeling about the guy."

"So, you don't trust me. That's what this is about."

"I trusted the man I married with my life. *My* Finn would never let a man speak like that to me. My Finn loved me." Her voice cracked as the tears fell. "But I don't know who you are anymore!"

"Well, that makes two of us, then."

She sucked in a breath and backed up as if his words had been a physical blow.

He stepped forward, his hand on the wall. "I'll be out late. Don't wait up."

He shut the door. The lock clicked into place in more ways than one.

Charli clapped a hand over her mouth, trying to contain the sobs. The world as she knew it crumbled around her. Her chest splintered as a thousand tiny arrows pierced the most vulnerable pieces of her. She took one shaky step after another to the entryway, slipping on a pair of shoes and grabbing her jacket before snatching up her keys. She ran to her car and started the engine. Navigating out of the driveway through blurry eyes, she just needed to get out of there. Her heart couldn't take anymore.

Somehow, she made it to her in-laws'. The only family she had left, except for her friends. Charli wiped her face with her sleeve before climbing out of the car and marching up the steps. She took a ragged breath before knocking.

Claire opened the door, her bright smile disappearing the moment their eyes connected. "What's wrong?" Claire searched over Charli's shoulder, presumably for Finn.

She stepped forward and fell into the woman who'd become her mother's arms. Claire held her and guided her inside, shutting the door behind them.

Zeke walked into the room. "There's the birthday girl— Charli? What happened? Where's Finn?"

"He—he's out with Stewart."

"Stewart?" Zeke scratched his head. "That deadbeat?"

Charli nodded. "We had a fight and he . . . he just . . . I don't know what to do."

"I'll call him," Zeke said, his tone serious as he left the room.

"This just doesn't sound like Finn," Claire said, pulling herself away to fill up a glass with water and set it in front of Charli.

"He's not . . . he's not himself. His moods are all over the place. He goes days barely speaking to me. We had a good time a few nights ago. We went to dinner and had a great conversation. I thought we were getting somewhere. And then he just shut me out again."

"The doctor said these things are common for Finn's condition. Has he remembered anything?" Claire asked.

Charli shook her head, unable to give voice to her hopelessness.

Claire took her hand, squeezing gently. "Finn is a good boy. He won't do anything reckless."

The old Finn wouldn't. Even the seventeen-year-old Finn wouldn't. But this new angry version of him was someone else entirely. And now Charli had no idea what her husband was capable of.

13

FINN

Sexy, seductive music blared from the speakers as bodies pulsed to the beat. The air was hot and thick as Finn followed Stewart through the crowd at The Pearl Necklace. They'd ridden their bikes for a couple of hours up and down the coast, stopping for dinner along the way. Stewart had said he had just the surprise to finish their night off together. But this wasn't what he'd expected. The scents of different colognes and perfumes mingled together making it hard to breathe. Red light cast a warm hue over the dark room. Women danced on stages, topless as they gyrated behind the bars of a cube. One in the center used a pole, spinning her body and winding around like a snake as lecherous eyes full of lust watched her.

Finn's gaze widened as he took in the room. He'd never been to a place like this—at least that he could remember. His cheeks heated as he caught glimpses of the women dancing. His body was aroused and full of discomfort at the same time. His lead feet stayed behind his friend as Stewart pointed towards a table in the back corner marked reserved.

Stewart sat in one side of the booth, and Finn took the other.

"Is it okay if we sit here?" Finn yelled across the table.

A scantily clad woman appeared with a black tray, setting a napkin in front of both of them.

Stewart leaned forward. "Yeah. My boss, Angelo, keeps it open for his employees." Stewart grabbed the ass of the waitress and pulled her closer as she bent forward. He said something in her ear before she nodded and turned to leave. He smacked her behind.

"That's quite the perk," Finn said, tapping his leg.

It was loud in here. And the crowd wasn't helping. The woman returned, setting a couple of glasses in front of them. She poured them half full of amber liquid before leaving the bottle in the center of the table.

Stewart picked his up and raised it in a toast. "To new beginnings and fresh starts."

Finn lifted his, clinking the glass to his friend's. "To a fresh start."

The liquor burned his throat and he winced.

"Good stuff, huh?" Stewart smiled and waved to someone over Finn's shoulder.

"Yeah." Finn took another sip.

"You deserve to let loose once in a while." Stewart picked up the bottle and refilled Finn's glass.

"What do you do for work now?"

"I'm into a little bit of everything. Come on, man. We're here to get drunk and enjoy the ladies. No shoptalk. Tonight is about showing you everything you've been missing." Stewart lifted his drink again.

Finn took another gulp, the bite getting easier the more he drank. The alcohol flooded his veins as a warm buzz took over his body. He relaxed into the velvet seat. A soft hand wrapped around his shoulder, a strong floral scent cloying to its owner.

"Hey, baby. You two look lonely over here. Thought you could use some company," she purred, slipping onto his lap.

Finn tensed. *Charli.* He was a married man. Even if Charli had cheated on him, he wasn't that kind of guy. He moved over, setting her onto the cushion next to him.

She giggled. Two other women surrounded Stewart. His hands hung over their shoulders, fondling their breasts.

"Do you prefer blondes?" Stewart asked.

"N-no. I just—I'm married."

"What Charli doesn't know won't hurt her," Stewart said before pulling down the top of the redhead next to him. He whispered into the other blonde woman's ear. She leaned in and sucked the exposed nipple of the redhead into her mouth.

Fuck that was hot. Finn's pants grew tight, and the brunette next to him slid her hand over his thigh and kissed his neck.

His hand shot out to stop her. "Stop."

She pulled back, her eyebrows drawing together as she licked her ruby red lips. "You seem so tense. Let me help you relax."

She sucked his earlobe into her mouth and he jerked away. "What's your name?"

"Whatever you want it to be," she said saccharine sweet. When he didn't say anything, she replied, "Candy."

Doubt it. "Okay, Candy, look, you're a beautiful woman, but I'm not available. You'd be better off finding some other guy here."

"You don't want a taste? I can give you the best blow job you've ever had." Her voice was saccharine sweet in his ear.

Shit, that sounded good. But her touch made his skin

crawl. Because she wasn't Charli. *Damn it.* He was so fucked up.

"What the fuck is this?" A big man stood over their table, his shoulders broad. He was young, mid-twenties maybe. Two men flanked him either side. Stewart pushed the women apart in front of him and sat forward. "Hey, Angelo. Just showing my friend here what a nice place you have."

The big man pinned Finn with two dark eyes. He ran a hand through his long black hair and slicked it back. Gold rings glinted on his fingers.

"I know you," Angelo said, stepping forward.

"My friend, Finn Reed," Stew supplied.

Recognition flashed in those dark eyes before his gaze turned menacing. His face twisted into a snarl.

"Finn was in an accident. He's got amnesia. He forgot everything. Remember, I told you?"

Why was Stewart talking to his boss about him?

"Isn't that convenient?"

Actually, it was far from it. A sick feeling twisted in Finn's gut. The wisp of a warning flit into his consciousness and left before he could grasp it. *Damn it.*

"You having a good time?"

"He doesn't want my company." Candy pouted, thrusting her barely covered breasts out.

Angelo's eyes narrowed. "My club's pussy ain't good enough for you?"

Finn sat straighter, his body growing rigid. "No, I just—I'm married," he repeated.

Angelo's smile was predatory. "Yeah, I remember."

This guy knew Charli? A chill skated up his spine. He needed to get out of here. "Look, I better get home. Thanks for the drinks." Finn nudged Candy out of the booth so he could stand. Even at his full height of six-three, Stewart's boss towered over him by another three inches.

"You don't leave until I excuse you," Angelo growled.

"Look, buddy, I don't want any trouble." Finn risked a glance at Stewart, who nervously stared at his boss as he got to his feet.

"I'll show him out."

"No. My boys will show him the door." Angelo nodded, and the two men flanking him grabbed Finn's arms.

Their hands clamped down and Finn jerked and pulled away reflexively. His knees bent slightly, hands lifting in front of his face into fists. "I know the way."

"Don't fight them, Finn," Stewart said, sympathy written across his features as he followed them. He waved to his boss, who stood there, eyes glued to Finn as he was dragged towards the door.

"What the fuck?" Fine. If Dumb and Dumber wanted to hold his hand to the door, whatever. As long as he could get out of this place.

They pushed him out into the cold air, digging their fingers into his flesh.

"Ease up, man!" Finn yelled.

Dumb laughed before Dumber's fist came out of nowhere. Finn ducked, but the crony's knuckle grazed his cheek. Pain split his face as he dropped low and moved reflexively, taking out Dumber's legs. *Where did I learn that move?* Maybe his body remembered more than he thought from his time in the military. A small bloom of comfort flit through his chest that his old self was still in his subconscious.

Stew jumped onto the other guy's back. Finn pulled his fist and swung, meeting flesh. Dumber groaned in pain, swearing as he swiped his hand and missed.

"Stop!" Angelo's voice boomed.

Finn backed up, arms up, ready for another fight. But the glint of the metal of a gun pointed at him had him raising his hands in surrender. "They attacked me first, man."

"I got this handled, boss," Stewart said.

Angelo's thumb cocked the gun.

Finn held his breath. *I should have listened to Charli. Should have given her a chance to explain the journal entry.*

Fuck, he'd acted like an ass. And all for what? Is this how it all ended? Flashes of their last conversation slammed through his mind. He ground his molars, ashamed.

The blare of a siren split the tense night air. The sound gave him a shred of hope as they grew louder.

Angelo's gun never wavered. "Next time you think of taking a swing at one of my men or setting foot in my club, think again," Angelo said as red and blue lights reflected off the metal building. He tucked the gun into his waistband and smirked. "Over here, officer. This one got too handsy with the dancers and then attacked my security."

"That's not what happened!" Finn shouted.

"Put your hands behind your back," the cop ordered.

"He's lying. These guys attacked me," Finn argued, looking over to Stew to corroborate the truth. Stew's gaze shifted to Angelo's and then he shook his head. *Asshole.*

Angelo walked over to say something to Stewart as Finn tried to reason with the cop. But it was no use. The cold metal bite of the cuffs pinched his skin as he was shoved into the back of a police cruiser.

He stared down at his knees. Shame and regret swirled inside him for how he'd acted towards Charli and blown off a family dinner. Anger burned his chest, frustration tightening his airways. It was like he had been thrust into a game where everyone knew the rules but him. He didn't know who to trust. But one thing was clear. He'd fucked up big-time tonight.

* * *

Five hours later, Finn had his personal effects in a bag in his hand and his angry father in the driver's seat next to him. Zeke was silent. He hadn't said a word to Finn after the phone call. His parents' was the only number he'd had memorized, and thankfully, they'd never gotten rid of their landline.

The tension was so thick in the car—Finn could have probably cut it with a knife. He'd sobered up long ago and had hours in that cell to feel the full impact of the weight of his choices bearing down on him. He'd been terrified to call his parents from jail. Disappointing them was still his biggest fear. Of course, it didn't help that Charli had been right. He owed her more than an apology. *Damn it! How could I be so stupid?* Finn cleared his throat as the sign for Shattered Cove whizzed past them. His ears heated and his chest squeezed tight as anxiety rattled through his bones.

"I'm sorry." His voice cracked. "I'm sorry for . . ." *Getting into trouble. Calling you in the middle of the night and scaring Mom half to death. For hurting Charli.* "Everything."

His father's solemn expression didn't change. Had he even heard Finn?

"It won't happen again—"

"Damn right it won't happen again, Finnegan Jacob Reed," his father snapped gruffly, making Finn jump.

Zeke shook his head and sighed, his voice coming out more evenly. "I've never, not once in your life, been disappointed in you, son. Not until tonight."

Finn lowered his head, his shoulders dropping with the heavy shame.

"You're not behaving like the man I raised. I taught you better than this. And on all the nights to be an asshole, you chose her birthday."

"I know, Dad—" *Wait, what?* It was Charli's birthday? *Fuck.*

"You could have been killed tonight! Where would that leave us? Or Charli? Your child? You owe that woman respect." Zeke slammed his hand on the steering wheel before he turned down Finn's street. "You went and shirked your responsibilities, and all for what? Some naked, nameless women?"

Finn cringed at the disgust on his father's face. *I did more than that. I yelled at her and said horrible things I can't take back.* It seems Charli hadn't told his parents about that. *She protected me even though I was a total asshole to her.*

He couldn't bear the thought of his father thinking he purposely went to cheat on his wife. "It wasn't like that. I had no idea where Stew was taking me. I didn't—"

"You went in though. You drank there. You sat there. And apparently, you got handsy with the dancer."

"That was a lie. I didn't—"

His father turned his glare on him, and Finn shut his mouth. It didn't matter if he was seventeen or thirty-three. His father was right. Finn had royally messed up. Had he destroyed his life in a single night? His parents' disappointment was one thing, but now he had to face Charli and explain where he'd been all night. His *wife*. Finn scrubbed a hand over his face as his father pulled into his driveway.

"You and Charli were so happy before the accident. You two are a match made in heaven. That woman has stood by you through deployments, family emergencies, when you two had nothing but two pennies to rub together. Whatever you've got going on in that head of yours, you need to fix it for Charli's sake." His father sighed.

She's been by my side from the beginning. In the hospital, even when I freaked out on her. Since we've been home and I've been cold to her. Fuck. I need to trust her and have faith in the old me who chose her.

"Thank you, Pops."

His father's chest heaved up and down like he was containing a hurricane behind his ribs.

"I really am sorry." Finn lifted the handle and stepped out of the car before shutting it.

His father rolled down the window, turning to face him once more. "You'd better make this right, Finn. For Charli and that baby. Or at least be man enough to set her free."

Ringing filled his ears as his father slipped the car in reverse and left. Panic scorched his chest at the thought of leaving Charli. She was still someone he didn't know well, but what he had seen of her was enough to know she was someone special. He'd hoped they could begin a relationship, but then he'd found his journal and the doubts had crept in. *How could I have thought anything different? Why did I jump to conclusions about her lying and cheating on me to manipulate me?* Probably because his head was so fucked up. He clenched his fists and ground his teeth together in frustration. Looking back, his erratic moods and behavior were a bit more evident. *I can't even trust myself.*

Finn turned his face up to the cold, night sky. Not a star was in sight, and the moon was nowhere to be found. The street was covered in darkness except for a stray streetlamp or two dotting down the road.

Finn shook his head and faced the house as the motion light switched on. He drew in a breath and steeled himself as he walked up the steps.

After pulling his keys from the bag, he twisted them in the lock and opened the door, slipping inside. The small light over the stove was on. He shucked off his boots and hung his coat. He needed a long shower to wipe the grime of that club and the jail cell off his body. He reeked of the place. And was that glitter on his hands? That shit got everywhere. He crept through the living room to grab his bag from behind the couch when his eyes landed on the small figure curled on her side around his pillow. Finn stepped closer, the low light bright enough to see the tracks of old tears across Charli's cheeks. Guilt sunk in his gut like a stone. Her small hand rested against her belly, and all Finn wanted to do was pick her up and hold her in an attempt to ease some of her worry.

He'd been a selfish bastard tonight. And it was time he started thinking about Charli and their baby's well-being too. His father was right—as usual. Finn needed to man up and take care of his responsibilities. Charli didn't deserve this from him. He'd loved her enough once to tattoo his body for her—and marry her. He'd have to trust that the old Finn knew what he was doing.

Reaching out his hand, he brushed the strand of hair from her face. Her skin was buttery soft, eliciting a familiar buzz that happened whenever he touched her. Her eyes fluttered open, as he held his breath. It was time to face the consequences.

14

CHARLI

armth spread over Charli as she opened her eyes. The blurry room in front of her came into focus. A dark figure bent over her. She jolted up and screamed.

The man jumped back and stumbled. "Shit."

Finn?

The light switched on. The burst of brightness made her wince. Her head was pounding as it usually did after hours of sobbing. She must have drifted off at some point. Charli glanced at the clock. Three in the morning?

"I'm sorry. I didn't mean to scare you," Finn said.

"Did you just get home?" she asked, standing. She sucked in a sharp breath. Every muscle ached. Sleeping on the couch had not been a good choice. Especially after overdoing it cleaning the house from top to bottom. But she'd wanted to talk to Finn when he got back. And his pillow smelled like him. She'd scavenged for any shred of comfort, no matter how small. *Where has he been all night?*

His eyebrows drew together and his lips flattened. "Yeah. Sorry."

Anger roiled in her belly. *If he thinks he can just come and go as he pleases, treating me like a doormat, he's got another thing coming.* She let her gaze wander over his features, searching for something, anything at this point that gave her hope that this wasn't over. His lip was swollen and cut. His eye darker around the rim.

"What happened to your face?" she gasped, stepping closer to get a better look. A whiff of cheap perfume hit her sensitive nose and she froze. Her heart raced and her mind sought an explanation that wouldn't leave her heart shattered as a result. She sucked in a breath and stepped away from him.

His gaze met hers before regret flashed in them and they dropped. Her stomach twisted into a thousand intricate knots as she shook her head. Tears burned her already irritated eyes.

He'd not only dismissed her feelings earlier, blew her off, brought that dirtbag into their home and let him disrespect her, but now he'd . . . cheated on her?

"I got into a fight."

Obviously. "I didn't hear your bike."

He shifted on his feet, hands digging into his pockets—a nervous gesture. "I got a ride home."

From the owner of the horrid perfume? *Did he sleep with her?* She swallowed and turned towards the stairs, her pulse pounding in her head. Pain lanced up her side as she hissed and grabbed her belly.

Finn's arms wrapped around her, holding her steady. "Are you okay?"

She was anything but okay. Her husband had been out all night and come home smelling like another woman, booze, and piss. And he'd gotten into a fight. This wasn't Finn.

"Just leave me alone, Finn." Her voice trembled as she

pushed him away and started up the steps. Her knees wobbled and her body trembled. Maybe in the morning they could make better sense of this. Right now, it hurt too much.

"Charli, please?" Finn's voice tugged at her heart, making her halt her steps. She flicked the hall light on and turned to him.

His gaze landed on her face, and he cringed. She must look a mess right now with bloodshot, swollen eyes from crying. Something sparkly glinted off his cheek. Glitter?

"I messed up by choosing to go with Stewart. He was familiar to me. I just . . . I wanted to feel like myself for one night. I didn't want the pressure or to feel like I was letting anyone down. I was pissed at you." The words stumbled out of his mouth, and then he took a fortifying breath. "I should have listened to you." Finn's thumb rubbed the tears from her cheek as he took her face in his calloused palms.

She closed her eyes, relishing his gentle touch.

"I may still feel like I don't know much about you, Charli. But I do know I don't like to see you hurtin'. I've done a piss-poor job at keeping that from happening."

She opened her eyes, needing to witness the sincerity in his.

Pain was etched across the lines in his face and determination in the creases of the corner of his eyes. "That stops now. I want to be a better man. For you. And for our child."

Charli couldn't stop the bubble that expanded and filled her insides with bright rays of faith. Was this real? Could they really begin anew? She'd been here the whole time, just waiting on him. If Finn was all in, it meant she could have her life back.

A small smile tugged at the corner of her lips. Finn's expression immediately relaxed, hope shining back in his brown eyes. Charli swept her gaze over him. The bubble deflated at the imprint of red lipstick on his white collar. Bile rose in her throat as the floor dropped out from below her. Her knees gave way and she collapsed to the stairs.

Finn's arms immediately wrapped around her. "Charli? What's wrong? Is it the baby?" His worry seemed so sincere. But so had his eyes only a moment ago.

She pushed him away with all her might, and he stumbled back, catching himself on the railing. "What the hell?"

Charli got to her feet, one hand on her belly as she moved through the pain tearing her up inside. But she needed a straight answer. "Did you fuck someone else?"

He blinked and took a step back, presumably from her harsh words. "No!" He shook his head vehemently. "Charli, I'd never—"

She pointed to the lipstick stain. "Then what the fuck is that? And why do you smell like perfume? You're covered in glitter."

He pulled his collar and looked down, understanding or maybe recognition flitting across his face. Holding his hands up, he said, "It's not what you think."

"Stop! Just stop. I don't want to hear another word from your mouth."

"But I can explain—"

"Finn, if you have even an ounce of care for me in your heart, you won't say another goddamned word."

His mouth snapped shut.

Charli turned and went up to her bedroom, locking the door and climbing into her bed as the pain of heartbreak doused the little bit of faith she'd had left. Her tears stopped as she lay there alone in the dark, lost in her grief. A cold numbness settled into her bones at the realization that her marriage was really over.

15

CHARLI

eep! Beep! Beeeeep! Fire! Fire! Fire! Charli jolted upright as the alarm shrieked. The smell of smoke had her jumping out of bed and rushing down the stairs as she ignored the soreness in her muscles.

Curses came from the kitchen as Charli searched for the source of the emergency. Finn waved a dish towel over a smoking pan by the window he must have opened.

Charli released a breath. She walked over to the sink and turned the water on. She grabbed Finn's arm, tugging him over. "Put it under there."

He listened. The hot pan sizzled and popped as steam rose.

"Wave the towel under the alarm," she directed.

He obeyed, and a moment later the alarm stopped screeching. She surveyed the kitchen. Lumpy pancake batter dripped down the edge of the bowl by the stove. The room reeked of burned food. A colorful assortment of roses from the counter had her stomach hardening and her body heating with anger.

"What the hell is this?" she snapped.

"I, uh, got you flowers, and I was going to make you breakfast in bed," Finn said, tucking his hands in his pockets.

"You think a bouquet and some burned pancakes are going to make up for you cheating on me?"

His mouth dropped open as he shook his head. "N-no. Never. But that isn't what happened last night."

She shook her head as he looked helplessly around the room.

He picked up a mug and handed it to her. "I made you tea. I read that too much caffeine isn't good for the baby, so it's decaf."

She stared at the cup. He was trying. She should take it. Though if he had cheated, she'd more likely want to throw it at him. But if there was any thread of truth that he hadn't . . . She owed it to the Finn she'd made vows to, to listen. Finn had never been a liar.

Charli reached out and accepted the olive branch in the form of tea.

The relief on Finn's face was fleeting as he shuffled his feet. "Can we talk?" Three words Finn rarely, if ever, used.

She nodded and walked over to the couch in the living room, needing to get away from the lingering smell of smoke.

"I wish I had known it was your birthday yesterday," he started.

"Oh, yeah? When was I supposed to tell you? Sometime over the last few days when you were ignoring me? Or maybe when you cut me off about going out with Stew?" His name tasted bitter on her tongue.

Finn sat on the cushion next to her. "You're right. I've been a complete, selfish asshole."

She sucked in a breath. Even the old Finn didn't really admit when he was wrong. He usually just acknowledged her hurt, gave her some mind-blowing orgasms, and then they moved on.

"What did I usually do for you on your birthday?" he asked.

She sipped the tea. It was a little sweet, but not bad. "We'd spend the day together—usually most of it in bed. And then you'd give me a gift, and we'd have dinner with your parents before we got home and spent more time tangled together. Sometimes you'd surprise me with short trips to a cabin or a beach house. I never knew what to expect. But it was always the most special day, ever since you proposed on my eighteenth."

He nodded and looked down. "I'm really sorry I screwed up. Looks like I have a lot to learn from the old Finn."

"Thank you for apologizing. But that doesn't erase what happened last night." Charli set the cup on the coffee table.

Finn ran a hand over his head. He'd showered at some point, but his bruises were darker and angrier today. "I'd like to explain what happened after I left."

She sat back, grabbing a pillow to hold in front of her as if it might protect her somehow from the blow his words were sure to deliver.

"I followed Stew to a club in the city. It was . . . it was a strip club." His eyes didn't waver from hers.

Her stomach pitched and her muscles grew rigid. The steel wall she'd let down around him so long ago snapped upright as if the last decade had never happened. As if they'd never tumbled together sharing their bodies and baring their souls with whispered promises of everlasting love.

"I didn't know that's where we were going, but I still chose to stay. And I'm really sorry for that . . . We had a couple drinks and then some women came over."

Charli studied his face for any sign that he was being

untruthful or omitting pieces. But his gaze never strayed and nothing but regret and sincerity were reflected back.

"One got close to me and sat on my lap—I pushed her off and told her I wasn't interested, that I was married. But she was persistent. She kissed my neck, leaving that smear on my shirt. *Nothing* else happened with her. I swear."

"Okay." What else could she say? Did she believe him? Yes. But it still hurt.

"Then Stewart's boss showed up with a couple of security guys and started some shit. I said I'd leave, but he had his muscle drag me out and then they started hitting me, so I fought back. The cops were called—"

Charli's hand flew to her mouth.

"His boss told them I'd gotten handsy with the dancers, and he arrested me. I called Pop to bail me out, and he brought me home."

Not another woman, then. The revelation should make her feel better, but there was still the fact that Finn had been arrested, dismissed her warnings about the man, and let him disrespect her in their home. "How could you be so reckless?"

Finn shook his head, his shoulders dropping. "I know. I should have never gone."

"It isn't even just that. You treated me horribly. When I told you about my feelings towards Stewart, you ignored them. He disrespected me, and you just stood there, letting it happen."

Finn looked down. "I was an idiot. I know I can't go back and redo things, but I swear I won't make the same mistake again."

"You could have been killed, Finn. After what happened with . . . Jesus, Finn. You know better than to go to those places and be around people like that. Even at seventeen your mother would have brought out the slipper if you so much as thought about going to a strip club. I could have lost you. And then your child would have grown up without a father. Is that what you want?"

"No." He shook his head and reached out his hand to her bare knee. She was still in his old T-shirt, her usual sleeping attire. "Damn it. I fucked up. But I swear to you, it won't ever happen again. I realized last night that I—I care for you, Charli. And I just . . . I'm committed to trying to be a better man. I want to make this work. If . . . if you're still willing to try with me?" Vulnerability shone from his eyes. "Do you believe me?"

She took a deep breath, mustering the courage to reply. "I do. But you hurt me, Finn. I can't . . . If we do this, I need you to talk to me. I can't handle it when you get angry and walk out like that, leaving me wondering if you're going to come back or what you're doing. It reminds me of . . . a past I'd like to forget."

His brows drew together, unspoken questions reflecting in his eyes. "I promise. I'll do better."

She picked up the mug and took another sip of the cold tea.

"Did we fight a lot . . . before? Did we ever hurt each other?" His question seemed weighted. Did he remember something?

"We argued just like any other couple. But it was never like this."

"Oh," he said, sounding discouraged.

"But you were never one for apologizing either. I like that about the new Finn."

A small smile tipped the edge of his full lips. "What was the old Finn like?"

"He—*you* were a hard worker. You cared about your friends and family. You spent a lot of time tinkering in your garage. You'd work at The Shipwreck with me. We were perfectly in sync behind the bar together. We worked hard and had lots of fun in between. You always brought that to my life —a lightening of sorts. When everything got too heavy, you'd be there to carry some of the weight." Her heart twisted. Could they have that again?

"Sounds like I was a good guy."

"You were. And I know that you're still in there. You've been through something traumatic, and it's just gonna take some time." She slipped her hand over his.

His attention moved to the connection. Flipping his palm over, he weaved his fingers in between hers. "How about we do something special today, just the two of us?"

Her belly flipped. Swallowing down the tiny flicker of hope that bubbled up, she asked, "Like what?"

His thumb traced over the soft flesh of her hand. "I scheduled a couple's massage for us—a prenatal one for you. I figured since you've been under so much stress, and I noticed you've been in pain . . . I just . . . You work so hard, maybe too hard. I figured you could use something relaxing."

Emotion welled in her chest. Gratitude and faith wound around her heart. Maybe, just maybe, Finn was finding his way back to her.

16

CHARLI

Two hours later, Charli lay on her side, naked under a sheet on a table next to Finn. Notes of lavender danced through her senses as soft, instrumental music and the sound of rushing water filled her ears. Strong, warm hands pressed into her skin, working out the kinks and buildup of stress she'd carried for the last few months.

"Mmm," she moaned. God, that felt good. She was putty in the masseuse's hands. Her limbs had been turned to jelly. It felt so good. She didn't even mind the bits of oil now coating her hair as his nimble fingers pressed into her scalp. "Ohhhh, that feels so good."

"Happy to help." Tom, her masseuse, chuckled.

Charli glanced over to Finn's table. The sheet was tucked into his boxer briefs, showing the two dimples on his lower waist. Dimples she'd run her tongue over countless times. His muscular back and arms were being kneaded by another masseuse, Julie. The yearning to replace the woman's hands with her own hit her hard. The result of a decade of condi-tioning—every time she and Finn had had arguments in the past, they'd have make-up sex. Maybe that was why it felt as if they hadn't resolved everything. She closed her eyes. She wanted to connect with him for more than just physical pleasure—though that would be welcomed too. No, she needed to be intimate with him to feel fully connected.

Tom pulled the sheet higher and pressed the warm material against her oil-slicked skin as Julie did the same to Finn.

"Alright. Take your time getting up. There is a water bottle for both of you on the table; be sure to hydrate really well today. Come on out when you're ready, but no rush," Tom said as he and Julie left the room.

Finn sat, his hands resting over his lap. His eyes were half-closed and groggy. "How was that?"

She smiled dreamily. As she tipped her head, stretching her neck, the sheet dropped. A rush of cool air blew across her bare breasts.

Finn's eyes widened and darkened. There was no hiding the erection that rose under his blanket.

"I'd better get dressed," she said, wanting him to stop her, wishing he'd make a move. Her nipples pebbled under his stare as he licked his lips. Gooseflesh sprinkled her body in awareness. She stood, letting the sheet slip away, leaving her in nothing but her underwear—a light pink silk thong. Bending to give him a good view of her ass, she plucked her leggings off the chair in the corner and slipped them on. His gaze burned her naked flesh.

She sucked in a breath as his body pressed against hers. Rough, calloused hands rested on her shoulders. A tiny moan slipped from her. *Is this really happening?* His hot exhale tickled the fine hairs on her neck, sending a bolt of lust rocketing through her. The flames of arousal licked her skin as his deep voice rumbled in her ear. "Do you have any idea how fucking beautiful you are?" Finn asked.

She closed her eyes, savoring the moment.

"This is what you do to me." His cock pressed to her lower back, inciting swirls of desire spinning through her.

Charli spun around, her nipples grazing his chest. His lust-laden eyes were glued to hers. He trembled as she spread her hand over his stomach. The urge to reclaim some of what she'd lost nearly bowed her over. She stroked her hand over his cock. He hissed through his teeth. His hands gripped her shoulders hard enough to leave a bruise. It only fueled the fire blazing inside her.

"I could take care of that for you?" Charli rubbed her thumb over the head of his cock. It jerked.

"Today is about you," he said through gritted teeth like he was barely in control.

"What if this is what I want? What if I told you this would make me feel good?"

Finn's eyes darkened before he turned to the door. "Is it locked?"

She shook her head. "That's part of the fun."

He looked at the closed door once more, nervously.

"They said to take our time." She winked, hoping to set him at ease.

He nodded his consent. She slipped her hand under his briefs as she lowered to her knees.

"Fuck." His hand gripped the back of her hair. Wetness seeped into her panties at the show of control. It seemed his body did remember what she liked.

"Maybe we should wait—" His mouth said one thing, but his body said another.

She wrapped her hand around his thigh. "I want to touch you, Finn. I want to taste you." She licked her lips and then flicked her tongue over the engorged head of his cock, lapping up his salty precum.

"Oh, fuck. Charli. I'm not going to last."

She sucked him into her mouth as he groaned in pleasure, the sound ricocheting through her, stirring her arousal into white-hot flames. She cupped his balls and took him all the way to the back of her throat just the way he liked it.

He pulsed and throbbed in her mouth. "Fuck, Charli."

She pulled him out, licked around the head of his cock, and said, "Fuck my mouth." Pulling him back into her parted lips, she sucked him down once more.

"Fucking fantasy come to life," he groaned as his hips thrust, pushing him in and out of her.

Her nails dug into his ass, urging him faster, taking him deeper.

Finn must have gotten the message because the tip of his cock reached the back of her throat with every surge. She swallowed around him, fending off the urge to gag.

His thighs clenched and his balls drew up in her hands. "I'm gonna—" He came with a strangled groan, his thigh muscles bunching under her touch as she swallowed him down. He leaned over, pulling her mouth from him as he lifted her into his arms. He slammed his mouth to hers. His tongue delved between her lips and he squeezed her ass. Finn set her onto the table she'd just had her massage on and stepped between her legs. One hand grabbed her breast while the other gripped the back of her neck, locking her into place. Her belly pressed against his body.

"Is this okay? For the baby, I mean?" he asked, concerned.

"Yes. Don't stop."

He bent over, taking a nipple into his mouth and swirling his tongue over it. Her inner muscles clenched together in rapture. "Oh, god. Yes, Finn." Pleasure and something more burst through her.

"Charli, baby. You're so perfect," Finn growled.

He'd called her Charli-baby, like he used to.

"What did you say?" She wanted to hear it again and again—a sign that her Finn was returning. That maybe they could find their way back to how things used to be.

"You're perfect."

She shook her head. "No, you called me Charli-baby."

He straightened, his gaze meeting hers. "Is that okay?"

She blinked back the tears. For once, she was crying out of happiness. "You used to call me that all the time."

"I did?" His gaze wandered to the side of the room before coming back to her.

"Yeah."

"Charli-baby?" He licked her nipple, scissoring his teeth over the light brown bud.

"Mm-hmm." She tipped her head to the side.

"That was the best experience of my life." He grinned.

The corners of her mouth turned up in a bittersweet smile as her chest squeezed. Memories of the day he'd asked her to marry him, their wedding day, and the moment she'd told him they were pregnant were all lost to him. *At least we're making new ones.*

"But now, I want to make you come all over my mouth."

Her smile fell as she swallowed at his husky promise. "What are you waiting for?"

Finn crashed his mouth back to hers. *Finally. Finally. Finally. Knock. knock.*

He pulled his face from hers and shifted as if to block her body from the door. Tom's voice came through the closed exit. "Just wanted to make sure you two were all right."

"Yes, we'll be right out," Finn said.

"We're *coming,*" Charli added giving him a smirk, making her innuendo clear.

Finn gave her a goofy smile. "Come on. Let's finish this at

home." He tossed her the pink bra and her white-and-black-striped T-shirt.

She bit her lip. He rushed to get his clothes on. Finn was back—at least, glimpses of him. This could work. They would get through this. Together.

17

——————

CHARLI

Charli laughed as Finn scrambled to open the passenger door for her before the rain soaked them. He ran to the driver's side of the car and dove in, shutting them out of the steady drizzle. He wrapped his hand around her wrist and brought her in for a kiss before the most satisfied smile crossed his lips. Warm light spread from her chest to the tips of her fingers and toes. She couldn't contain her glee. Her belly fluttered and flipped with excitement. It was like a piece of her life had finally been put back together after the hell of Finn's accident. There was no way she was letting this moment go without taking full advantage of it.

He started the engine, then pulled out of the parking lot. His hand darted out to capture hers as he steered them to their destination. The windshield wipers were the only sound besides their rapid breaths.

"I can't believe we just did that . . . in there." He shook his head. Droplets of water cascaded down his temple, weaving around his angled jaw.

"Just like old times," she mused.

He met her gaze and smiled before focusing on the road. "When we get home, it's your turn." His thumb rubbed a circle over her hand, a gesture he'd made countless times before the accident.

He turned onto their road. The last time she'd pushed him, he'd taken off and avoided her for three days. She didn't want that to happen again.

"You don't have to, Finn. It's okay. I don't want you to feel pressured."

He pulled into the driveway and shut off the engine before turning to her, his eyebrows drawn together. "I want to taste you. I want to know what that beautiful face looks like when you come apart. But if you want to wait, I can be patient."

She licked her lips and clenched her thighs together. A mix of old love spun into new appreciation and affection. Her belly fluttered. "I . . . I can't handle if you pull away from me again after this and repeat what happened last time."

He placed her hand against his mouth and brushed his lips over her knuckles. "I won't run this time. Promise."

She nodded. "I want you."

He tore out of the car and ran around to her side before she'd even opened the door. She took his hand and they dashed towards the house. The cold rain drizzled over them and pelted the tin roof. He pulled out his keys, body trembling. Her heart squeezed tight. The door opened and then his hands were on her, slipping her coat off her shoulders, letting it drop in a pile on the floor. She kicked her boots off frantically next to his. His hungry eyes were glued to her as he struggled to remove his wet jacket. Heat unfurled in her belly, spreading to her extremities as a wolfish smile broke out on his handsome face. It was a familiar expression; one she hadn't realized she'd missed as much as she did until this moment.

Shoving their shoes out of the way with his foot, he picked her up in his arms.

She let out a squeal. "Finn!" Her arms instinctively curled around his neck.

"You won't fall. I've got you."

His words spun up and twisted inside her with a blend of longing and adoration. She clung to his promises as he set her onto the countertop in the kitchen and stepped back. He bit his lip, his gaze roaming over her with lust-filled appreciation. She shivered, not from the cold, but anticipation. There was a glimpse of the old Finn in the way that he looked at her as if she were the most beautiful creature in the world.

Stop staring at me and touch me. "Finn?"

"I just . . . don't know how I got so lucky. I don't know why I didn't see it before."

A tinge of pain tweaked through her heart at the reminder of where they'd been just a mere twelve hours ago. She shook her head, ridding the thoughts. She wanted to be here, in this moment, savoring the way his eyes feasted on her. The place where she was wanted, with the potential for love . . . someday.

"Touch me. Please," she begged, needing him.

He stepped closer, cupping her face before his hot lips melded to hers. He tasted like the musk of man, fresh rain, and the sweetness of hope. He tasted like *her* Finn.

His tongue traced the seam of her mouth as she sighed, opening to give him access. Fingers twined through her hair, tugging out her hair tie. Her hands wrapped around his waist, pulling him so that he was flush against her core. Slipping her feet over his powerful thighs, she squeezed, needing the friction.

He sucked on her tongue and dropped his hands to her waist, pulling up the wet shirt that clung to her body. Cool air rushed over her skin at the loss. Goose bumps skated over her exposed flesh and her nipples hardened to the point of pain. His exhale was her inhale as he gazed in her eyes, dark and heady.

"Is this okay?" he asked.

"Yes. I'm all yours, Finn." Her voice was breathy. Could he hear the plea in her words? *Love me. Come back to me.*

Finn slipped his shirt over his head, his mouth glistening from her kisses and those dark brown spheres hungry. She traced the ridges and valleys of his muscles over his shoulders, down his pecs before swirling her finger around his nipple. He groaned and pressed her hands to the counter.

"Take your bra off."

She slipped her hands behind her, unclasping the fabric and letting it fall to the ground. Their gazes locked.

Finn hissed before his mouth clamped over her nipple. Wanton desire turned his eyes coal black. His brows drew together as if it was taking all his control not to rush this. She sucked in a breath, closing her eyes—the sensation was so powerful. His hot tongue, sucked and teased her hard bud as his free hand kneaded the other breast. The rough callouses of his palms added another layer of sensations coursing through her. Heat pooled in her core, soaking her panties.

"Yes! Finn. Oh, god." Her nipples had always been sensitive, but the pregnancy hormones brought another level of intensity to the action. Pressure built. A hollow ache stretched from her clit to her womb.

He pulled her nipple and tweaked it with his fingers before rolling her breast in his hand. His mouth flicked and sucked, scissoring his teeth over the sensitive flesh.

Stars burst from behind her eyelids as she squeezed her thighs around him, clinging on to his head, digging her fingernails into his scalp. "Ahhh!"

Finn lapped at her flesh as she came down. He sat up, and she nuzzled into his neck.

"Did you just?"

She nodded.

"You can do that? From just . . ."

"Sometimes."

"Fuck, that's sexy. Lie down."

She looked up at him, dazed and relaxed. "Why?"

"Because I'm gonna find out all the other ways I can make you come."

Swallowing, she obeyed, lying on the cold granite countertop as he peeled off her leggings and panties.

"God damn, you're soaked." He pressed his finger between her folds, lightly tracing over her clit. She arched her back and sat up. "Ohhh. Finn." He slammed his mouth onto hers, stealing her words as his finger rubbed her throbbing sensitive nub. Her legs dropped open as pressure built in her center. Prickles of desire burst from every nerve ending, a million sensations exploding through her at his touch. He slipped a finger inside her and swallowed her moan. He was so close to *that* spot.

"Curve your finger," she directed.

"Like this?"

"Fuuuuuck." She threw her head back in ecstasy as pleasure coursed through her. "I need more," she begged.

He added another finger and sucked on her neck. The bite of pain and tension of building pleasure erupted like hot lava, burning her up from the inside out. She screamed and raked her fingernails over his back. "Finn!"

"You're so beautiful, so sexy when you come." He added a third finger and blackness filled her vision.

"I can't . . ." She shook her head. She couldn't take anymore.

"You can," he promised huskily.

Strong hands gripped her naked thighs, pulling her ass to the edge of the counter.

"Watch me. Watch me make you come," he ordered, sounding so much like the old Finn, *her Finn.* Dropping to his knees, his hot tongue licked her clit like a frenzied flame of ecstasy.

She propped herself up on her elbows and held her breath, incapable of words.

"You taste so fucking good." His head bobbed between her thighs as he lapped the arousal dripping from her slit. His tongue flicked between her slick folds, torturously gentle.

"Finn," she begged.

"Just one more time, Charli-baby. Come for me and let me see that gorgeous body blush." His dark eyes locked on to hers as he sucked her clit into his mouth and slipped two fingers back inside her.

She screamed. Rapture encompassed her like a tidal wave, rendering her incapable of thought and action, leaving her helpless to anything but feeling. She surrendered, riding the wave to completion as her orgasm rocketed through her. Her body turned boneless and limp.

The room came back into focus. Finn licked his lips before reaching out to cradle her in his arms, her ear against his chest, the tattoo of his heart pulsing in sync with hers. Emotion welled in her eyes. For the first time in months, she felt truly connected to her husband.

Her legs were still trembling as Finn stood. His strong arms lifted her, carrying her up the stairs to their bedroom. Finn laid her on the bed and kissed her softly on the mouth. She dropped her hand to his hard cock, pressing against the denim.

Finn's grasp snaked over her wrist, halting her.

"I want you inside me," she said.

He looked down, over her naked body, his eyes snagging on her belly. "I don't think . . . I mean . . . I—"

"Because of the baby?" she asked, holding her breath, steeling herself for the rejection.

He shook his head and lay next to her, holding out his arm for her to lie on. "No. I mean, you said it's safe. But it's more than that. I just . . . I've never . . . I don't remember ever having sex before."

"Oh." *Right.* This Finn, who'd expertly commanded her body just a few minutes ago, was a born-again virgin. "That's okay. We can go slow." She could wait to have sex. It might kill her, but she could.

He released a lungful of air as his muscles relaxed. After a moment, he asked, "How was I?"

She smiled and turned her face to look up at him as she snuggled closer. "Perfect."

He grinned, pride gleaming in his eyes. His finger traced over the tattoo on her rib cage, sending a shiver through her.

"Is it always as amazing as that?" Finn asked.

"Only ever with you."

His thumb pressed against the jagged scar on the side of her belly. "What's this from?"

She cringed. *I wish I could forget.*

"Is it from the attack at the bar?"

She closed her eyes, Damon's face flashing in her mind as her heart lurched. Regret and grief tainted her joy. The scar tissue was a permanent reminder of when her love hadn't been enough. Her history with Damon might be too much for him. The doctor said to avoid overly stressful topics, and she didn't want to ruin this perfect moment with things she couldn't go back and change. She'd tell him . . . eventually. But she wouldn't risk his healing—not when they were making progress. "No. But I'd rather not talk about it now. Let's just enjoy this." She turned so her back was against his front. His arms encircled her, holding her close.

Finn rubbed the scruff of his five o'clock shadow in the dip of her neck before he kissed her shoulder. "Thank you, Charli."

"For what?"

"For believing in me." Finn squeezed her before nuzzling his cheek against hers. Charli relaxed, cocooned in his warmth and the brightness that the bloom of hope offered.

18

CHARLI

Charli leaned back as far as possible in the leather seat of the Seaside Cinemas movie theater, trying to relieve some of the pressure of the growing baby on her bladder. Soft music played in the speakers as the couple on the screen kissed for the first time.

Finn turned towards her, the light coming from the large screen projecting color onto one side of his face. The other was hidden in the shadows of the otherwise dark room. "You okay?" He squeezed her hand gently.

Her chest squeezed at the action. After the massage earlier, he'd surprised her by continuing the birthday celebration with a movie. It wasn't the most romantic idea, but she had to remember that Finn was still a teenager in his mind.

"Yeah. Just brings back memories, being here," she whispered.

He leaned in, his clean scent washing over her, melding with the smell of buttery popcorn between them. "Did we come here a lot?"

"When we were teenagers, before they redid the whole thing. Back then it wasn't quite as fancy."

His expression dimmed just a little. "I'm sorry. Maybe we should go somewhere else. I should have thought of that . . ."

"Hey." She moved her hand to the side of his face, pulling him closer before kissing him. "This is perfect. I needed a low-key event after the afternoon we had."

His hand eclipsed hers, holding it against his cheek. "You sure?"

"Absolutely. Reminds me of some other fun we got into here." She wiggled her eyebrows up and down suggestively.

"Oh really?" His deep voice rumbled in his chest.

"Shhhhh!" someone a few rows ahead chastised them.

She giggled, leaning into his ear. "Let me go to the bathroom, and when I come back, I'll see if I can suck those memories out of you—one way or another." She winked before standing.

"You need me to go with you?" he asked.

"No. Be right back," she whispered before walking down the aisle to the stairs leading to the exit.

She pulled open the door to the theater and squinted at the bright lights as she made her way to the restrooms.

A man exited the men's room ahead. Something about his familiar frame caused her breathing to halt. He looked up, recognition flashing in his dark eyes.

Charli's blood turned to ice. A thousand tiny pinpricks of fear leeched into her veins. It was *him*. Her attacker! She made a split-second decision and ran for the women's restroom, not looking back to see if he was following her. She slammed the door shut, leaning all her weight against it as she clicked the bolt into place, locking her inside.

Her chest heaved as blind terror leapt into her throat.

Drawing out her phone with trembling hands, it took her two tries to unlock it.

The door behind her squeaked as someone tried to open it.

Bang! Bang! Bang!

Charli pulled up Finn's contact and pressed send. He was the closest to her. He would save her.

Bang! The door thudded against her again.

It rang and rang several times before Finn's hushed voice answered. "Charli?"

"H-he's here! Help me!"

"Where are you? Who's here?" Finn's voice was louder this time, the movie in the background getting quieter.

"The man who attacked me. Outside the women's bathroom. Go right out of the theater."

"I'm coming, baby. Hold on." Finn's firm promise brought her comfort. She wasn't alone this time.

Every muscle tight, she pressed her ear against the door, straining to listen.

"Charli?" Finn's voice through the phone made her jump.

"Yes?"

"I'm outside the door, Charli-baby. No one's here."

She unlatched the lock, peeking out the crack before opening it fully. She fell into his waiting arms, relief crashing into her from his touch.

"H-h-he was here. Is he following me?"

Finn squeezed her tight against his chest, his head swiveling left and right. The muscles under her hands bunched tight, as though his body was on alert. "No one was out here when I got out of the theater. We should call Bently."

She nodded stiffly, her entire body shaking uncontrollably.

Finn rubbed her back, pulling her closer into his body and wielding it like a protective shield. "Bently . . .? We have a problem . . . Charli and I are at Seaside Cinemas, and she said the man who attacked her was here . . . She's safe. I've got her . . . Okay . . . will do."

With her face still pressed close to his chest, the sound of fabric rustling suggested he'd put the phone away in his pocket.

"Bently's on his way. He said to go out to the front and wait for him." Finn kissed her forehead.

Charli tried to walk, but her legs locked up and wouldn't budge. Her chest constricted, making it hard to breathe.

"Hey. Hey. Shhhh. You're safe now. I've got you. No one is going to hurt you, honey." Finn wiped her cheeks, his hands coming away wet from her tears.

"I was alone, and I thought . . . I was so scared." The confession burst out in a sob.

Finn picked her up, cradling her like a child as he carried her to the main lobby and out the double set of glass doors leading to Main Street. "If that prick thinks he can come for you, he's got another thing coming. I won't let him hurt you again, Charli. The old me might not have been able to protect you, but I will. I'm here. You're safe."

Sirens in the distance got louder as Bently's familiar patrol truck skidded to a stop, another patrol car pulling up next to him.

Bently jogged over to them, with Deputy Vargas and Officer Rafe Owens following swiftly behind him.

"Did he hurt you?" Bently asked Charli.

She shook her head. "I saw him and ran."

Bently nodded and pointed to the other two police officers. "You two take the east side. I'll go west. We've got unit three guarding the exits."

Vargas and Owens didn't waste time, darting inside the movie theater.

Bently brushed his thumb along her cheek. "We'll get him." Hope burst in her belly, fluttering up her chest.

I hope so. She wanted to put this nightmare to rest.

His gaze turned to Finn. "Get her home and lock the doors. I'll stop by after for a statement."

Finn nodded and carried her to their car. He opened her door and set her inside before getting in the driver's seat. His hand immediately found hers, holding tight as if he knew he was her only lifeline right now.

Their day had come full circle. And here she was, back to feeling like her world had just been turned upside down again.

* * *

As they arrived home, Bently's name flashed on her phone. She answered, pushing the speaker button.

"Did you get him?" she asked, not bothering with greetings.

Bently's sigh on the other end told her all she needed to know. "He got away. We searched the whole place. I'll review the footage from the concession stands and exits. Maybe we can get a lead. We'll get him, Charli. I promise."

She nodded, even though he couldn't see her. Here she was, back to square one. He'd been close enough for her to smell his cologne. Was he taunting her? Playing with her like a cat with its prey?

"What do I need to do?" Finn asked, his voice rough with frustration.

"Keep the doors locked. Stay vigilant. Don't let her out of your sight. I'll have you on our patrol route. If you see or hear anything, call me right away." Bently's tone was far from his usual jovial self. That alone told her how serious it was.

"Done," Finn agreed.

"Try to get some rest," Bently added.

"Thanks. Good night," Finn said before he tapped the screen, ending the call.

"Come on. I'll run you a bath and tuck you into bed." Finn grasped her hand, leading her up the stairs. She followed numbly.

Trying to remember that stress wasn't good for the baby, she made her best effort to relax in the hot water as Finn stood watch. And when he helped dry her off and put the large T-shirt over her head before pulling back the covers, she repeated the mantra in her head: *I'm safe. I'm safe. I'm safe.*

Finn slid the blankets over her, sliding into the spot next to her and holding her in his arms against the beating heart in his chest.

"Sleep, Charli-baby. I'll keep watch over you. I've got you."

She closed her eyes, burning from exhaustion like she'd never known. Drained from the emotional roller coaster of a day, she gave in to sleep. His warm body chased the chill from her bones that even the hot bath hadn't gotten rid of. His heartbeat lulled her into slumber. Here, in his protective embrace, she could almost believe that she was safe—at least for now. But the sun would rise, tomorrow would come, and with it the reality that someone wanted her dead.

19

CHARLI

"Finn?" Charli called from the hallway the next day.

"In here."

She walked into the bedroom and froze at the metal glint in Finn's hands. Her pulse jumped.

He turned the gun over before bringing his attention to her face. "Why is this in the drawer?"

Charli sat beside him. "You gave it to me after your last deployment—taught me how to use it too. After the attack, you wanted me to have something since I was home alone all the time."

"Can you . . . do you mind telling me what happened?"

Charli blew out a breath. "I worked closing. You already know why Mason wasn't there. There had been a guy who wouldn't take no for an answer at the bar earlier that night. Young college-aged kid. I had to have Mason kick him out. I went out to the car, and before I could put the keys into the door . . . he came up from behind me."

The memory flashed through her mind as fresh as the moment it happened.

"Stupid bitch. Thought you could embarrass me like that. Do you know who the fuck I am? Nobody treats me like that and gets away with it." He wrapped his arm around her neck and shoved her against the car, stealing her oxygen.

She moved out of reflex—so many hours of training in self-defense with Bently and Finn. Jabbing her fingers into his side, she pinched his flesh as hard as she could while she stomped on his foot.

He swore, loosening his grip around her neck enough for her to run, but he grabbed her hair and pulled her back before shoving her to the ground. "I'm gonna make you pay for that." He reached for the button on her jeans.

She screamed and swung her arms. Pain split her head as he punched her and swore at her. His spittle flew onto her face as she clawed at him, struggling with all her might. But he was bigger and heavier. Feeding off her pain, his hands were on her body, groping her breasts roughly. Vomit rose in her throat in revulsion. "No! Please no. Stop!"

Then his hands were on her throat as his weight settled over her chest, squeezing the air from her lungs. Leaning down, he bit down hard on her lip. Her lungs burned as he choked her. Realization that she was going to die was blaring in her mind until everything went black.

"Charli?" Finn's thumb brushed away a tear on her cheek. She hadn't even realized she'd started crying. "You don't have to if it hurts too much."

"He just . . . he hurt me. He hit me and choked me until I blacked out. I woke up cold in the empty parking lot and crawled to my phone. I managed to call emergency services through the shattered screen and they came. From our security footage, we know he ran off after a car pulled in. Scared him enough so that he didn't finish what he'd started."

Finn's hands clenched into fists. "I'm sorry I wasn't here for you."

She laid her hand over his, pulling it into her lap. "It's not your fault. And it's all in the past. I'm just hoping they catch him before he hurts anyone else."

"If I ever get my hands on that fucker," Finn threatened.

"As much as I love this protective side of you, promise me you won't do anything to jeopardize our life?"

He shook his head. "Never. I'm not going anywhere this time." He kissed her temple. "I'll be here to protect you . . . and the baby."

She met his gaze. He hadn't really brought up the child growing in her womb, choosing more to act like it wasn't happening. "Do you want to come to my next appointment and find out what we're having?"

His eyes lit up. "Yeah—I mean, if you're okay with that."

She smiled. "I'd love for you to be there." She placed his hand on her belly, studying his reaction.

Finn's eyes focused on her bump with part apprehension and part curiosity. "It feels like I woke up in someone else's life, and it's a good life—don't get me wrong—but it doesn't feel like *my* life. Do you know what I mean?"

Charli nodded and dropped her attention to the scuff on the wooden floor, trying not to let him see the disappointment in her expression.

Finn's finger lifted her chin so she had no other choice but to face him. "But I want this life. I want . . . you. I want to be the Finn you married. The one you made this baby with. It's just gonna take me some time to get there."

Her chest squeezed tight. "That makes me happier than you know."

He leaned his forehead against hers, his arms wrapping around her.

"We're in this together," she promised.

"Together," he repeated before his lips slid over hers, sucking her bottom lip into his mouth.

She coasted her palm up his thigh, his hand wrapping over hers and placing it where he needed her touch most. His cock pressed against the zipper of his pants. He groaned when she slid her fingers over him and deepened the kiss.

She giggled and pulled back. "We have to be at the bar in thirty minutes, and I still have to shower."

"We can shower together and save water?" He moved his eyebrows up and down suggestively.

"Something tells me that won't make it any faster." She laughed.

He traced the edge of her smile. "I love when you laugh. Your whole face lights up, and everything seems right in that moment."

She sucked in a breath, his sweet words hitting her like a punch to the chest. "Well, I do know the bosses pretty well. I think they'd understand if we were a teeny bit late." She bit her lip.

He smirked. "Then I'd better get to it." Finn pressed his mouth to hers as happiness swirled and dipped in her belly like millions of lightning bugs buzzing with hope and anticipation. Emotion welled in her heart. It was some of the old, and a lot of new. But one thing was for certain—she was falling in love with this man all over again.

✳ ✳ ✳

An hour later, Charli sliced the limes as Mason came up behind her with fresh ice.

"How's everything going?" he asked before dumping it into the ice box.

"Good." She scanned the room. Finn was helping the band for the night set up on the stage.

Mason tipped his head. He was a man of few words—and

they were usually gruff. He looked more like a lumberjack—tall and broad with a big beard and half of his face badly scarred. But when you got to know him, he was just a big teddy bear underneath.

"It's actually going really well. Finn always has an adjustment period when he comes back from deployment where he's off for a while before he levels out. That's sort of what this feels like. But this time has been so different."

"I'm happy to hear it's going better. I'm here if you guys need anything."

"Thanks, Mason."

"No problem."

The doors opened and customers filed in. By ten that night the place was at full capacity. The band was doing a cover of "Dangerous Game" by Klergy. The drumbeats blasted as she weaved through the crowd to deliver another round of drinks. Setting the cocktails around the table, she yelled to the girl who had ordered them, "Enjoy!"

The girl smiled and shouted, but her words were lost in the noise of the bar and the crash of the symbols and electric guitar. Charli slipped the tray under her arm and turned back to the bar, pushing past a couple basically sucking each other's faces off. She dipped her head and pressed on.

The fine hairs on the back of her neck stood on end. It was the same feeling she'd gotten in the street when she'd thought someone was following her. She peered over her shoulder, searching the sea of faces. She froze. Her heart stuttered and her stomach dropped. Fear splintered through her, rendering her immobile. She became caged in past terror, locked in present panic. It had only been a moment. A flash of that familiar face she'd stared at until her world went black, believing it was truly the end. *He* was here. Her attacker.

She sucked in a strangled breath, her skin itchy and hot as she backed up. Two hands wrapped around her shoulders. She spun round, adrenaline and the primal need for survival spurring her actions. Lifting the tray, she readied herself to swing, to fight, but halted at the last second as Finn's face came into focus behind her.

"Finn!"

His eyebrows formed a triangle, worry cinching them together. "What's wrong?" His eyes darted behind her, searching for the source of her terror.

"He's here," she choked through the tremors that racked her body.

"Who's . . .? Motherfucker!" Finn's confusion warped into anger. He stepped in front of her to block her from the crowd. "Where?" he asked.

"C-call Bently." She slipped her phone from her pocket.

"Where is he, Charli?" He pulled out his phone and texted. Mason's name flashed on his phone.

"What are you doing?"

"Making sure he can't leave. Come on." Finn took her hand and walked her to the bar, waving over the other mixologist, Ken. "Take over."

Ken nodded as Finn led her to the back room. "What does he look like, Charli?"

"He—he's white with black hair and brown eyes. He's tall, taller than you." He looked different than before—a little older. His hair was longer than last time.

"Okay, you wait here in the office."

She clung to his arm, panic snaking around her spine. "Don't leave me, Finn."

He pulled her into his chest, his hand holding her head as he kissed her temple. "I'm not leaving you. I got you. No one is going to hurt you again." He pulled out his phone once more. "I just need to tell Mason what to look for. Bently is on his way. We'll get him this time, sweetheart."

She closed her eyes and relaxed into his arms. *I'll be okay. Finn is here.*

Fifteen minutes later, there was a knock on the door to the office. Charli jumped. Finn stepped in front of her. "It's just Bently." He twisted the knob and let the sheriff in.

"I did a sweep with Vargas, and a couple guys are watching the exits from the outside. There isn't anyone who looks like the sketch. Do you think you can come out and take another look? We'll be right by your side."

Her body trembled. "I was just saying to Finn, his hair has gotten longer."

Bently nodded. "I know this is hard, but we won't let anything happen to you."

She sucked in a breath. This man had killed other women, and he was never going to stop. If she could do something to help catch him, she had to try. "Okay."

Finn and Bently flanked her sides as they walked back to the bar. Charli's eyes scanned the place where she'd seen him last. Several people turned and looked, most likely wondering about the police presence. The lights had been turned on, even the music was subdued. Charli searched the faces, but none of them were *him*. Had it been her imagination? Had she seen someone similar and panicked for no reason? Doubt crept into her mind. Anxiety twisted her belly into knots as she took one more hard look around the room. One man sat in the dark corner, his back to them, next to a blonde woman.

Charli's pulse quickened. She pointed towards him. "Is that—"

Finn took off towards the man before she could finish her sentence, anger radiating from him. Silence descended upon the room as the music stopped and everyone turned to gawk.

"Finn!" Bently yelled. "Fuck! Vargas!"

"I got Charli." Vargas, the beautiful deputy, sidled up to her protectively as Bently went after Finn.

Finn's hand landed on the guy's shoulder, whipping him around.

It was *him*—the man she had kicked out of the bar, the one who attacked her. Finn pulled him out of the chair by his collar, winding his fist back. But before he could release it, Bently tackled him to the ground. All three men ended up on the floor.

Curses and a muffled groan rang out. Gasps echoed each other as Bently growled, "Stop before I have to arrest you too." Bently locked his arms around Finn placing him in a choke hold. "Calm down. We need this to be clean."

Vargas ran over towards the perpetrator, who was trying to scramble to his feet. She drew her gun, ordering him to stay down with his hands on his head.

"What the hell is going on? I didn't do anything!" he yelled.

"Fine!" Finn yelled. Bently got off him, keeping a wary eye on her husband. Finn's gaze was hard and dangerous as he got up, his chest heaving. He faced Charli. "He won't hurt you again."

She nodded. Air rushed from her chest as weight she hadn't known she'd been carrying slipped from her shoulders. Her body sagged in relief, and her knees went weak. Finn was beside her in an instant. His arms wrapped protectively around her. Tucking her head to his chest, he led her back to the office. Her chest tightened, her lungs squeezing tight.

I'm okay. I'm safe. The baby's safe. They got him!

"I'll need to call you after we get things straightened up at the station," Bently said from the doorway.

"Thank you, Bently," Charli said.

"Of course. I promised we'd get him."

She closed her eyes and leaned against Finn. "I want to go home."

Finn brushed a lock of hair away from her face and kissed her. A sense of calm washed over her with his touch. "I got you, Charli-baby. No one is gonna hurt you on my watch."

His promise brought her comfort. She stood on shaky legs, his arm supporting her. They'd actually caught the bastard. Her mind was still reeling. Now she only had one man to worry about.

She'd have to trust Finn and believe the promises he'd made and hope he could be the man they both needed.

20

FINN

Finn's eyes fluttered open. Bright rays of sunshine shone over Charli's body pressed against his so perfectly—like she was made for him. A few grey steaks glittered from the reflection in her otherwise coal-black hair. He took his time, his gaze roaming over her features. Dark eyelashes and a button nose. The urge to kiss every single light freckle smattered over her cheeks rose within him like a tidal wave. Her mouth parted, those honey-tinged lips calling to him. A small scar tucked underneath her chin on her otherwise pure complexion. How did she get that? There was so much about Charli that was new to him, and still he wanted to know everything there was to know about her. She swallowed, her long slender neck bobbing, drawing his attention down farther still to the rise and fall of her breasts. The sheet covered the rest of her, but the image of her naked was burned into his brain.

He'd actually slept pretty well last night for the first time since he'd been back. After the adrenaline had worn off, they'd both crashed in each other's arms. He leaned in and kissed her temple. She wrinkled her nose before she smiled. Her eyes fluttered open, her whiskey gaze focusing on him.

"Good morning, beautiful."

"It sure is. I thought last night . . . you . . . everything was a dream." A frown creased her brow.

He pressed his lips to her nose and then her mouth. "I promise, it's all real. I'm right here." *And I'm not going anywhere.*

She relaxed and snuggled into him, kissing his naked chest. "I like waking up with you."

"Me too."

"Oh, I can tell." She giggled, pressing against his morning wood.

He groaned. "I have some errands to run this morning." He nipped her shoulder. "But before our shift, I'd like to take you out to lunch." Finn nuzzled his nose against her neck before kissing under her chin. He couldn't get enough of her, wanted to leave his mark all over her. Christ, when had he become so territorial?

"I'd like that," she answered.

He pulled back enough to look at her. She gave him a dreamy smile.

"Stay here. I'll be back to pick you up. We can run by the station to give Bently what he needs, and then I'm gonna feed you." He gave her another kiss on her mouth before rolling out of bed.

Finn got dressed and took one more parting look over his shoulder. Charli's eyes locked on to him with a mixture of desire and joy. He'd do whatever he could to keep that expression on her beautiful face. He gave her a wink and left the room.

* * *

Twenty minutes later, Finn sipped his coffee he'd picked up from the Stardust Café. Running into Remy had been a surprise. She'd grown up and married Mikel of all people. He shook his head in disbelief and stepped into the line at the pharmacy.

"Finn?"

He turned around, his jaw dropping. Laura, his ex, stood with a hesitant smile on her face. Her dirty blonde hair was swept up into a bun. Pink colored her cheeks. Her blue eyes sparkled, matching the scarf with some fancy designer logo printed on it. She was older, but somehow more beautiful than he remembered her. His heart squeezed. The feelings he'd had for her were still fresh. Something unfinished lingered between them, but he had a feeling it was due to the fact that to him no time had passed. "Laura?"

Her smile widened. "I'd heard you were in an accident and forgot everything."

He swallowed. "Just everything since I was seventeen. I remember you. How have you been?"

She bit her lip and batted her eyelashes at him. "Pretty good. How about you?"

"It's been . . . challenging. But better now."

Laura looked over her shoulder before she leaned in and said, "I'd love to catch up sometime for old times' sake. There're some things . . . I'd really like to talk to you about."

Finn nodded. *Like about what happened between us?* "Okay."

She grinned and pulled out her phone. "What's your number?"

He rattled off the numbers and then his phone dinged.

"There. Now you have my number and my address too. In case you have some free time. I work from home, so I'm usually around." She tucked her phone back into the large purse hanging from her arm.

"Maybe I'll stop by."

"I hope you do." She licked her lips. "Well, I'd better go. Have a good day."

"You too." He waited until she'd disappeared down the aisle before he turned away.

"Can I help you, sir?" the pharmacy tech asked.

"Picking up prescriptions for Finn Reed. There should be three."

He pulled out his phone, clicking on Laura's message before adding her to his contacts. Nerves skated across his chest, his belly twisting. Maybe talking to Laura could help him piece together more of his past. Maybe it would help him be more at peace with his present.

"This new one has some additional side effects to be aware of, so make sure to read the inserts."

"Mm-hmm." Finn nodded, half paying attention.

He paid for his meds and jogged back to his car. After popping the lid on the one his doctor said would help level out his moods, he washed the pill down with his warm coffee.

Shifting the car into gear, he headed home. The thought of telling Charli about his run-in with Laura was fleeting. What did it matter? He hadn't done anything wrong. And Charli was just beginning to trust him. There was no need to rock the boat.

* * *

They'd been forced to see that fucker, Phillip Feller, through the glass today when Charli picked him out of the lineup. After they'd squared things away at Bently's office, Finn drove them to get lunch, the events of last night still very fresh in his mind.

He opened the door to the diner for Charli and entered

behind her. The blue and white tables were another familiar sight. He'd spent countless days here eating and joking around with his friends. His first date with Laura had been here. *Damn.* He needed to focus on the woman he was with, his wife.

"Do you want to sit in a booth?" Charli asked.

"Sure." He placed his hand on the small of her back and led her to an empty one in the corner.

She angled in, her belly close to the tabletop.

"Are you okay here?" He pulled out a menu from the basket behind the condiments.

"Yes. Still have room." She smiled.

A woman came over, setting two bundles of silverware in front of them before pulling out her notepad. "Good afternoon."

"Hey, Brynn. You remember Finn?"

Brynn smiled hesitantly at him. "Yes. Good to see you again."

Finn nodded. "Nice to meet you."

"Do you know what you want? Same cravings as before? Burger with extra pickles and a shake?" Brynn turned her attention to Charli.

Charli smiled. "You know me too well."

A pang of hurt bounced through him. He should know these things. He'd been home for weeks, and he still didn't know what his wife was craving.

"And for you?" Brynn's eyes only met his for a moment before she stared at the menu in his hands.

His gaze searched the list of items. "I'll just have the same as Charli but with no pickles. You can give them to her."

"Got it. I'll bring your shakes in a few minutes." Brynn tapped the pen to the paper before she turned and left.

"She seemed nice," Finn said, unwrapping his set of silverware.

Charli placed a hand on her belly. "She is."

"How did you meet her?"

Her gaze dropped. "At the meeting I attend, actually. But don't say anything about that to her."

"I won't," he promised. Brynn also attended the meeting for survivors of sexual assault? Maybe that's why she'd shied away from him. His grip tightened on the spoon he unwrapped. He'd just about had his fill of men who thought they could lay a hand on a woman. Damn if Charli wasn't the bravest woman he knew. She brought out the protective instincts in him like no one else.

"So, pickles, huh?" He smirked, changing the subject.

The corner of Charli's mouth turned up. "Don't judge."

He lifted his hands, palms facing her. "Me? Never."

She laughed. His heart skipped at the sound.

Warmth and light radiated from her. This woman affected him. And just maybe, he was falling for her, one tinkling laugh at a time. But something was still holding him back. A part of him remained tethered to the past. Questions left unanswered, festering in the back of his mind. Maybe he did need to meet up with his ex for some closure. And perhaps she could help him trigger valuable memories. Then he could put whatever they'd had behind him and move on to a future with Charli.

21

FINN

The paper on the examination table crinkled as Finn helped Charli climb on top of it. The hospital gown she wore flapped open, giving him a tantalizing peek of her backside.

"Where should I, uh, stand?" he asked, searching the tiny room that was no bigger than a decent closet.

"Over here, by my head." Charli patted her left side with a tiny space between her and the wall.

Finn walked around, taking in the large machine that looked more like an outdated computer from a bygone era.

Charli reached out and grabbed his hand, giving it a squeeze. "Are you nervous?"

"Never," he answered far too quickly.

She shot him a look of disbelief.

"Okay, maybe a little." The truth was his body was buzzing like a hive of honeybees.

She gave him an easy smile. "I promise the ultrasound is actually pretty cool."

He swallowed the bundle of nerves that stuck in his throat.

He was about to get a sneak peek at his child.

Knock. Knock.

The door to the tiny room opened and in came a young woman in a white lab coat and purple scrubs. She gave them a warm smile before sitting. "Hello, I'm Karli, and I'll be your ultrasound tech today. How are you feeling, mom?"

Charli grinned. "Excited."

"Are we finding out the gender?" Karli asked, slipping on a pair of gloves.

"Yes—" Charli turned to Finn, uncertainty in her expression. "I mean, do you still want to know?"

Did he want to know if he was going to have a son or daughter? It made it that much more real. "Yeah. Whatever you want."

"You must be dad?" Karli lifted the sheet from Charli's belly, tucking the blanket over her legs into the top of her underwear.

"Yeah."

"Well, let's take a look at baby, then. We'll check out the organs today and make sure everything is growing as it should, listen to the heartbeat, get a few pics for your scrapbook, and then find out the assumed gender." Karli squirted some sort of gel onto Charli's belly. She winced.

"Are you okay?" Finn asked worriedly.

Charli gave him an assuring squeeze on his hand. "Yes. It's just cold."

Karli picked up a fat wand-looking instrument and pressed it over the jelly on Charli's bump. The black screen lit up with lines and swirls of white. A suction type of sound filled the room, a mixture of white noise and rushing water at a steady and fast rhythm.

"Heartbeat sounds great." Karli clicked a few keys on the keyboard in front of her.

"That's the baby's heartbeat?" Finn asked in awe. His eyes were glued to the tiny screen. The profile of a baby—*his baby*—became clear.

"Sure is. Strong, just how we like them." Karli moved the wand around, skipping to various places she named—kidney, heart—her voice blending into the background as his heart raced. The steady rhythm of his child's heartbeat captured his full attention. It was both the oddest and yet most beautiful sound he'd ever heard, with the exception of Charli's laugh. A warm, comforting emotion welled in his chest. How could he fall in love with someone he'd never met?

He tore his eyes from the screen to glance at his wife. She was already looking at him, her bottom lip tugged into her mouth. "Are you okay? Is this too much?" she asked quietly.

He brought her hand to his mouth and kissed it. "It's pretty amazing."

Her smile seemed more out of relief.

"Okay, let's see if this little one will cooperate and show us the goods." Karli drew his attention to the screen. "Baby sure is wiggly today. I bet you can feel that, mom."

"That's the baby? I thought it was gas," Charli asked, her voice awed.

"Sure is. The movements will get stronger the bigger baby gets." Karli tapped a big button on the keyboard.

"It's like a little flutter. I've been feeling them for a few weeks." Charli's grin was unmatched, and her brown eyes sparkled with joy. He sucked in a breath. She was gorgeous, glowing like she'd swallowed the sun. He found himself sucked in, like a riptide. There was nothing he could do to stop it. He would have to hold on for dear life, because he was once again powerless to his wife's beauty. Life shone from her—the very definition of goddess. He was just the lucky bastard who got to experience this with her.

"Looks like baby has a . . ." Karli squinted at the screen.

Finn shifted on his feet in anticipation.

"Penis."

"A boy?" *I'm gonna have a son?*

"Yes." Karli wiped off Charli's stomach. "Go ahead and get dressed. I'll come back and let you know when the doctor is ready to speak with you in her office."

She handed Finn a printout of the pictures. He grasped the images, tracing his finger over the profile of his son. Finn's heart squeezed. His knees weakened.

Charli sat, wiping her belly a little better before climbing off the table. "You don't look so well. Sit." She pushed the stool the tech had been using over to him.

Finn sat, unable to argue. The room was spinning. He hung his head, staring at the pictures in his hands as Charli got dressed.

She kneeled before him, hands resting on his thighs, and tipped his chin up to meet her gaze. "How are you really feeling about all of this?" Worry creased her brow.

"It's a lot . . ."

She sucked that bottom lip into her mouth again, biting down.

He pressed his thumb against her lip, pulling it away from her teeth. "We're gonna have a son."

Nodding, her eyes searched his. Tension grew thick in the room. A heavy cloud of expectation and uncertainty gathered between them.

"It's so much more real now." He cleared his throat, emotion clogging.

"I know you don't remember, and it's more difficult for you . . ."

He pressed his hand over her belly, reaching out for some sort of connection with the tiny human growing inside his wife. His son. "I'm amazed. But I'm also excited, and if I'm being honest, terrified."

"Me too." She sighed into his arms. "I'm scared I'm gonna mess this all up."

He rubbed the back of her head as she snuggled against his chest. "We've got this. Together."

If only Finn could remember, then everything would be easier.

* * *

Later that evening, Charli wiped down the bar. Music from the sound system played, allowing the small crowd still going strong a rhythm to dance to. She reached below to pick up a case of beer.

Finn's hand shot out to stop her. "Hey, I'll do it. You shouldn't be lifting these anyways." He brought the case to the fridge and restocked the bottles.

"I'm not made of glass. I can still lift things, just not more than fifty pounds." She huffed.

"Don't want to take any chances. Besides, I'm here. Might as well let me do it." He broke down the box as she pressed a hand to her lower back.

She shifted her weight from foot to foot. Stubborn woman was clearly uncomfortable and in pain, and yet she kept pushing. He set the box in the back room as she filled a drink order for Link and his dad.

When he returned, he wrapped his arms around her from behind, tucking his chin to her neck, inhaling her scent.

"Finn." She giggled, swatting his arm.

"Why don't you go home early, draw a bath, and relax. I'll close up with Mason."

She turned to face him. "Are you sure?"

"Yeah. I can handle this. I'll walk you to the car and see if Mason can drop me off after."

Her gaze roamed over him, studying him in part surprise, part happiness. "Okay."

He kissed her lips, pulling her tighter in his arms, but being careful of her belly. When he released her, Charli's cheeks were flushed and her eyes glazed and watery.

Worry cinched his gut. "Are you alright?"

She nodded, swallowing. "It's just . . . I feel like you're coming back to me."

He smiled. If only he felt it too. *If only I remembered.* All he was doing was trying to keep his head above water. But if she was feeling better, he was doing something right.

"Come on. Let's get you home."

* * *

When Finn returned, Mr. Owusu gave him a knowing look. "I can remember when my wife was pregnant with Link. I was so protective of her."

Finn nodded. "Any advice?"

"Looks to me like you're doing a fine job. One thing I wish I had at the time was access to more knowledge about the whole process. Back then, and in my country, we men didn't really learn much about the process a woman's body goes through." Solomon took another sip of his beer. "Enjoy this part, because when they come out, that's when the real worry starts." Solomon chuckled.

"You're scaring him, Papa." Link nudged his father.

"Well, maybe he will get lucky and his baby will be an angel. You were a troublemaker. Still are," Solomon teased.

"It's a boy," Finn admitted.

"It's good to ease into the parenting thing with a boy.

Count your blessings, son. Having a girl, now *that's* terrifying," Solomon said, staring past Finn.

"Emma was just as troublesome as me, if not more," Link argued.

"Ahhh, my Emma can do no wrong. Her heart is always in the right place," Solomon added.

Link huffed. "Yeah, she's had you wrapped around her little finger since her mother brought her to us."

"She needed someone to look out for her, god knows that woman wasn't." Solomon tipped back his bottle and drained the last of his drink.

"I think she's your favorite." Link peeled the label from his bottle.

"She is." Solomon smiled.

"Papa! Seriously?"

Finn chuckled at the astonished expression on Link's face.

"She's my favorite daughter, and you're my favorite son." Mr. Owusu got to his feet.

Link just shook his head and took another sip. "I run your shop for you, and this is the thanks I get."

"Ahhh, don't throw a tantrum, Link." Solomon looked to Finn and winked. "See, he's still trouble."

Finn smiled. Watching these two go back and forth was one of his favorite things to do when they came in during his shifts.

Solomon patted his hand, meeting Finn's eyes. "You keep doing what you're doing. Just be there for her and listen. Women love a listening ear. Take care of her, and she'll take care of you. Charli is one of the good ones."

Yes, she was. He was beginning to realize that, bit by bit, day by day. Charli wasn't one to run away when things got hard, or she'd be gone by now. So, what was still holding him back from going all in?

22

CHARLI

Charli stepped into the bath, sighing as the hot water enveloped her in a steamy, lavender-scented hug. Little bits of the Epsom salts bit into her flesh, but it didn't matter. For the first time in hours, she was off her swollen feet and able to enjoy the silence.

Finn had been right. She needed this. Her belly poked out from the water, the line of suds forming a rim around her pink flesh. She pressed her hand on her baby bump as her son moved inside her in tiny, clustered flutters.

"Your daddy is acting more and more like his old self every day."

She closed her eyes and relaxed her head on the edge of the tub, taking a deep breath of the steam-filled air. "We have to find a name for you." What would Finn choose? She'd have to ask him. She picked up her phone to text him when an unopened message caught her eye.

Sender unknown: *I've waited long enough. I'm coming back for you.*

Chills skated across her skin. This couldn't be her attacker;

he was in jail. So, who would send her this? Was it a wrong number? Or maybe . . . was it Damon? She hadn't changed her number, so that if he ever needed to, he could reach out to her.

Charli: *Who is this?*

When an answer didn't come after a few minutes, she dialed Bently. Her nerves were a stone ball in her belly.

"Charli? What's wrong?" Bently's voice was groggy and panicked like he'd just woken.

Shit. She pulled the phone away from her ear to check the time. It was after midnight. Sometimes it was hard to remember not everyone kept the same late-night hours as she did. "Nothing. So sorry. I didn't look at the clock before I called."

"It's fine. Are you okay?" he asked.

"Yeah. I just . . . I wanted to check and make sure Phillip Feller was still in jail?" Her voice trembled as fear cinched her chest, making it hard to take a full breath.

"Yeah, Feller's still in custody. Waiting on DNA results, and then we can go through the next steps . . . You're safe, Charli. We got him," Bently assured her.

She let out a sigh of relief, her shoulders falling. "Thank you. I'm sorry I woke you."

"No problem. Call me anytime, night or day. You know I'm here if you need me."

"Good night," she said.

"Night."

She switched off the call and set her phone on the counter by the bath. Maybe it had been a wrong number after all . . . Or maybe it was secrets from the past catching up to her.

23

FINN

Finn pulled out the worn, brown leather journal from between the stack of engine manuals. His thumb pressed over the soft material. *Are my answers in here?* Only one way to find out. He sat on the metal stool and flipped open to where he'd left off last time.

He's gone. I drove Damon myself. He won't be coming back anytime soon. I made the decision for Charli, because she needed me to. But if I tell her, she'll be swallowed by the guilt of her broken promises. So, I'm confessing my secret the only place I can, here in these pages. I hope she'll forgive me if she ever finds out. But even if she doesn't, I'd do it again. I'd do anything for her to not to have to feel like she's being torn in two different ways. She shouldn't have to choose between him and me. I understand we are two parts of her heart, and to ask her to make that decision would be asking her which limb to remove. I did this for us. So we could have the life she always dreamed of. I can give it to her. And I will.

Finn turned the page, his eyes unfocused. The back of his neck pinched and tingled. *Who is Damon? Did Charli love him? How could the old Finn just overlook that?* On his quest for answers, he only seemed to have more questions. He took a deep breath, ignoring the growing headache, and continued on the next page.

I surprised Charli by taking her to a bed-and-breakfast in the mountains for the weekend. It was just what we needed. We spent most of the time christening every sturdy surface, both indoors and out. I asked her what she thought of starting a family. She was terrified. I hate that her mother did this to her. That Charli questions herself because of that bitch. I promised her we could wait until she was ready, and once I got out of the Army, I'd be with her every step of the way. Someday, Charli will see what she's truly capable of. And I'm gonna be right by her side to tell her how proud I am of her.

Finn's brows drew together as he closed the book. The pieces to this puzzle didn't make sense. He should ask Charli about it, but if she didn't know the secret Finn had kept from her, it might do more harm than good to their already fragile relationship. He'd just begun mending things from the last time he assumed things. He had two choices: trust that the old Finn knew what he was doing and follow his lead, or ask Charli and risk this blowing up in his face. He had responsibilities to Charli and his son. *If only I could remember.*

A memory unfurled in his mind's eye, like a wisp of smoke. He closed his eyes, reaching for the clue to his past. Pain pulsed in his skull as drops of sweat beaded on his brow. It was right there, just a puff of a recall. His head spun, dizziness melding with the violent alarm blaring in his head.

Finn sucked in a breath, his hand darting out to steady himself on the worktable. *No.* It might be better if he just let it go and trust these memories would come back to him eventually. He couldn't afford to have an emotional storm like last time and end up hurting Charli again. The doctor said to take his time and process each new piece of information. So that's what he'd do. For now.

"Finn?"

He jumped to his feet, hiding the journal in a drawer with tools and shutting it just before Charli entered the garage. He spun around, hands slipping into his pockets.

Charli eyed him suspiciously, one eyebrow cocked upwards. "Hey."

"What's up?" His voice rose an octave and he cringed.

She surveyed the area around him. "What are you doing out here?"

"Just going through some things."

She nodded. Her hand splayed over her belly while she bit her lip—an action he'd come to know as her nervous tic. "I wondered if you wanted to go into the city with me? I need to get some things for the baby."

"Yeah. Maybe we can stop for a late lunch?" He stepped closer, tucking a stray lock of hair behind her ear, letting his hand linger on her soft cheek.

She closed her eyes and shivered before she smiled, meeting his gaze. "That sounds perfect."

* * *

An hour later, Finn pushed a cart filled with contraptions he'd never heard of, and more diapers than he'd ever thought they'd need.

"Isn't this cute?" Charli held up a knitted grey sweater with a baby bear on the front that looked like it was made for a doll. It seemed way too tiny for a human.

"Is it for an old man or a baby?"

She chuckled. "Babies do kind of look like old men with their bald heads and wrinkles."

He picked up a white, long shirt-type thing with buttons on the bottom. The writing on the shirt said *My dad is the best!* "How about this one?"

She studied the shirt and shook her head. "I think we can do better. How about this onesie?" This time she held up a camouflage one that said *Soldier in training.*

Finn squinted. He might be retired from the Army, but he didn't think of himself as a soldier. He had no memories of any time spent serving. Just scars and a metal plate on his skull. And the nightmare.

She must have sensed his turmoil because she hung it back up and picked another. "Maybe this one would be better." The onesie was navy blue with a wrench and hammer. It said *Daddy's sidekick.*

He smiled. "Yeah, I like that one."

She picked out a few more outfits and slipped them into the cart.

"Is he really gonna be that small?" he asked.

A hesitant smile tipped the corner of her mouth. "Yes. He will be little and vulnerable, relying on us for his every need." The clothing trembled in her hand.

He reached out, grasping his fingers around hers. The journal entry had at least given him insight into why she was scared, even though it was vague. "You're going to be a great mother."

Her eyes widened. "How do you know?"

He traced his thumb over her wrist, gently rubbing it in circles. "Because you're so patient. And kind. I can tell by the way you hold your belly, like you're trying to soothe him and let him know you're there even when he's safe inside you."

Her lashes fluttered closed.

He pressed his hand to the side of her cheek, tipping her face up to look at him. "I know because everything I learn about you tells me one thing. You are the most capable and brave woman I've ever known."

She blinked her glassy eyes, gratitude glowing back at him.

She leaned in, pressing her soft lips to his. This kiss was dipped in affection and rimmed in hope. And when she pulled away, something that looked a lot like his future stared back at him.

"Have we ever done it in a department store?" Finn asked.

Charli snorted before she laughed. She was fucking adorable.

Her eyes lit up mischievously as she sucked in her bottom lip. "The changing room in the men's section is usually less busy."

His stomach flipped and tipped as if he were at sea. Finn's cock pulsed at the idea. "Are you serious?"

She leaned in and whispered, "Only if you promise to do very bad things to me."

He'd have thrown her over his shoulder if he wasn't afraid of hurting the baby. Instead, he grabbed her hand, abandoning their cart. He pulled her towards the sign for the men's section as she giggled behind him.

"What about our stuff?"

"It will be there when we get back." Or they could go grab it all again. He didn't care about anything but the fact that he was going to explode if he didn't get this woman alone in the next few seconds.

Finn looked over his shoulder. In between the rows of clothing, a few people milled about, their attention everywhere but them. He led Charli into the room, pushing her through the first open door to the changing stall. Flicking the lock, he spun around. Charli's chest was rising and falling almost as rapidly as his. The lights and the three-sided mirrors showed him so many delicious angles of her at once. He traced his hand over her collarbone. She was wearing some sort of loose-fitting sweater over leggings. His lips replaced his fingers.

Charli gripped his head. "Finn?"

He hooked his thumbs into the elastic waistline of her pants and pulled them down her legs. "Step out of these so I can fulfill your conditions."

She followed his request, and her obedience sent a thrilling bolt of lust through him.

"You're not wearing any panties?" he asked hoarsely.

"Didn't want any underwear lines." She shrugged innocently, a gleam in her eye.

He growled before pressing his nose to her pussy, breathing her in.

"Please? Finn. Touch me." Her begging only added fuel to the fire raging in his body.

Something inside him snapped. "Turn around. Take your clothes off. Put your hands on the mirror."

She did as he said, stripping down until she was completely naked with her back to him as she leaned against the glass.

He pressed himself against her backside, his hands digging into her hips. Brushing his rough stubble against her soft neck, he spoke in her ear. "Do you see the way your cheeks flush pink with every order I give you?"

She nodded.

"Answer me."

"Yes." Her cheeks bloomed even darker.

"I think you like when I tell you what to do. Don't you?" He didn't know how he knew this, but he did. Maybe it was the hours they'd spent bringing each other to heaven with their hands and mouths. Or maybe it was this gut instinct that grew more powerful each time they were together. It just felt right.

"Yes." She swallowed.

He pressed his hand to her neck, applying pressure on both sides as her eyes darkened with her own lust.

"You like that?"

"God yes."

"Do you know how fucking perfect these tits are?" He palmed both of them in his hands, her back flush against his chest. Her fingers whitened against the glass. He flicked her nipples and pinched. Her thighs squeezed together.

"Keep them open for me." His boot pressed her foot, widening her stance.

"Now look at yourself. Look how these perfect breasts fit in my hands." The contrast of his brown skin against her paleness only added to the starkness of the erotic image reflecting back at them.

One hand trailed down her stomach, cupping her sex possessively.

She gasped. "Finn?"

A door opened and closed next to them. The sound of hangers clanking and metal scraping filled the room.

"Don't make a sound," he whispered in her ear.

She nodded.

The swoop of clothing dropping to the floor as someone else changed right next to them and the reality that they could be caught only added gasoline onto the all-out aching blaze of lust scorching through his body. Goose bumps covered her flesh. Her skin was hot to the touch. He slipped a finger over her clit and she bucked and hissed. Clamping a hand over her mouth, he reminded her quietly, "Not a sound or I'll stop."

She nodded, her eyes pleading with him to continue. He pressed her clit again. Charli squeezed her eyes shut, her body trembling.

A rush of adrenaline sluiced through his veins at her submission. Arousal burned him from the inside out. His muscles tensed, stretched taut with the rush of power at knowing she yearned for his dominance. Fuck, he liked being in control for once. "That's it. Take it like a good girl. Open your eyes. Watch what I do to you," he continued his whispered commands almost on instinct. Like he knew exactly what to say to turn both of them on.

Her gaze was glassy and drunken, lids half-closed as he pressed his finger inside her. He moved his digit up and down a few times before adding another. Her lips widened beneath his hand, but she remained silent.

"You're so wet. Is this for me?"

She nodded. The blush on her skin spread across her chest.

He added a third finger. Dropping to his knees, he used his other hand to press her clit.

Her hips rocked as she fucked his hands. Her mouth opened in a silent scream as her inner muscles clenched around him. Her hazy gaze met his in the mirror as she came undone. She dropped her hands, leaving sweaty palm prints on the glass. Her body relaxed as she turned to face him. He stood, pressing his lips to hers. She melted against him, pliant with euphoria and drunk on pleasure.

Footsteps padded outside their stall before another door opened and closed, a lock clicking into place. More company.

She reached for the button on his jeans. But his hand halted her. "Get dressed."

"But what about you?" Disappointment flit across her expression, and damn if it didn't make him harder. The woman had shown him more than once how magical that mouth was. But this was about her. He wanted to prove to her that he could take care of her, be there for her. That they were in this together.

"That *was* for me, beautiful." He kissed her again. "I wanted to show you how grateful I am for all you've done."

She smiled, and god damn if it didn't make his heartbeat

falter. "Hearing you say that means a lot to me. I think . . . I think we'd been together so long we started taking each other for granted somewhere along the way."

"Maybe we can do it right this time."

Her eyes glistened with hope as she nodded.

"Now get dressed so we can go pay for the stuff and get lunch."

"Yes, sir." She saluted him.

"Smartass," he said under his breath.

"I thought you liked my ass." She wiggled her hips in front of him.

He leaned against her ear. "I'd like to smack that ass until it turns pink, but that would get us caught in here."

Her mouth dropped open. Maybe he'd taken it too far?

She licked her lips and whispered back, "Promise?"

Fuck me. The old Finn knew what he was doing when he picked Charlotte. She was a goddess among women. It was time they took this to the next level.

24

FINN

Finn pushed the mop across the bare, wood floor. Alternative music quietly bled through the near-empty bar. Charli was busy behind the counter, wiping everything down while she chatted with the last two stragglers.

"Your ride is here." Mason held the door open for the couple.

They got up, leaning against each other and giving a wave.

Mason locked the door behind them. "Do you guys need anything before I go?"

Charli swiped some of the hair that had come loose from her braid out of her face. "No, we got this. Go home and get some sleep before you gotta get that little girl of yours up for school."

"Aspen isn't quite so little anymore." He chuckled. "She likes to remind me of that every day."

"I bet. She's twelve now, isn't she?" Charli asked.

"Twelve going on sixteen." Mason rubbed a hand over his scarred face.

Finn put the mop back in the bucket and wheeled it towards them.

Mason turned to Finn. "Be thankful you're having a boy. They may be trouble of a different kind, but damn if I know what to do with a teenage girl."

Finn nodded. Being responsible for a young woman was a terrifying thought. It seemed there was so much more to be worried about.

"Alright, I'll see you guys tomorrow. Lock up behind me, Finn," Mason reminded him as he turned and headed out the front door with Finn on his heels.

Finn clicked the lock closed and walked towards Charli. She bent over, restocking the bottom fridge. Her firm ass was so round and tempting. His cock twitched in his pants.

Approaching the bar, he flipped the first stool upside down on it. The song switched to Andy Grammar, singing about not giving up on each other. His hands wrapped around the metal of the second one as an idea popped into his mind. He moved around the bar as Charli stood, wiping her brow.

"Dance with me?"

Her eyes sparkled as she smiled. "Let me turn it up." She untied her apron, placing it on the counter before adjusting the volume.

He reached out his hand and she took it. Finn led her to the dance floor, spinning her in his arms. She giggled. Holding her closer, he pressed his cheek to hers. Hands intertwined, bodies molded against one another, they danced. The lyrics, though sung by another, were ripped straight from his heart. Charli was a good woman. She'd stuck by him when he'd lost everything. She was understanding and patient. Charli was perfect. He might have gotten hit on the head, but he wasn't stupid. They had something between them—something most people searched their whole lives for. He could love this woman. He wanted to. He was already more than halfway there. It was time he showed her he was ready for more.

"You're so beautiful." He backed away to look into the windows of her soul, studying her face. The corners of her eyes creased when she smiled. And damn if the curve of her lips didn't do something to him. The hand on her waist tightened; his other went to her neck. Leaning in, he pressed his lips against hers. Sparks and shimmers buzzed through his body. A firestorm burst to life inside him from just the feel of this woman in his arms. Liquid heat poured over him. She moaned, her mouth opening to him. She sucked on his tongue. A bolt of lust shot straight to his dick. He ground against her so she could feel what she did to him.

"I want you, Charli-baby."

Her eyes met his, the question shining back.

The song switched to something else. The heavy bass line throbbed a pulsing, rhythmic beat. Slow, sensual lyrics wrapped around them, tangling them up in a web of desire.

"I need to make love to you," he confirmed.

"I want that too." She smiled.

"Let's go home, then." He grabbed her hand.

"No. I can't wait any longer. I need you inside me." She grabbed his T-shirt, pulling it over his head.

Finn looked towards the cameras.

Charli's hand slipped into his, tugging him towards the back room. "Office."

He followed, shutting the door behind them with a click. His heart raced, while his body throbbed with fierce yearning. *We're really about to do this.* "This is what you want?"

She nodded, reaching for the buttons of his pants, eyes on his. "Tell me what to do."

"You like when I boss you around?" He smirked.

"Only when we're doing this." She smiled.

"Take me in your hand."

She obeyed, unzipping his pants, pulling down his boxers, and allowing him to spring free. The gust of cool air was a stark contrast to his hot flesh.

"Now get on your knees."

He held her hand to help her down.

Her pink tongue darted out, licking her lips as she eyed his erection, salacious hunger smoldering in her wanton gaze.

"Suck my cock."

Hot lips enveloped him a moment later. He hissed. Fuck, she was good at this. Her tongue swirled over the head before she ran it along the underside. His hands threaded through her hair as he slowly fucked her mouth. His dick grew harder.

Her fingernails raked down the inside of his thighs. A prickling sensation wound up his spine. He pulled out of her mouth, helping her to her feet and tearing down her leggings. She stepped out of them.

Charli pointed to the couch. "Take your pants off and sit there."

"Now who's giving orders?"

She smirked. "It's my turn to be in control."

Fuck, that was hot. He quickly stripped and sat on the sofa. Charli took off her remaining clothes and climbed onto his lap.

"Don't I need to get you ready?" he asked.

"Sucking you off is one of my favorite things to do. Feel for yourself." She grabbed his hand and placed it against her sex. Finn slipped a finger inside her slick folds. Her eyes closed as her breath hitched. "See what you do to me?"

"How can you be real?"

Her eyebrows scrunched up in question.

"If this is all a concussion dream, I don't want to wake

up." The confession slipped from his lips—a truth he hadn't been able to admit to himself until this moment.

Charli's expression softened. "I love you, Finn."

Restraint frayed, and he thrust two fingers inside her.

Her head rolled back as she moaned. "Yes, Finn. I need you. Please. I've waited long enough."

She lifted her hips and he lined up the tip of his dick with her pussy. Her hot wetness teased the head of his cock. The urge to be buried in her became overwhelming.

He pushed her hips down, sliding the first few inches inside her, her hot pussy choking his cock. Christ, she was perfect. Overwhelming pleasure magnified and compounded with each pulse of his cock inside her. He clenched his ab muscles, trying to hold back the animalistic urge to plow into her. His dick tingled with a mixture of fire and icy spears of desire.

"More," Charli pleaded.

Don't come. Don't come. He grit his teeth, fighting the desire to explode inside of her. He flicked her clit, buying himself time to get back in control of his body.

"Mmmm, stop teasing me. I need to fuck you."

He wanted to dive so deep in this woman he might never find the way out. Getting lost in Charli seemed like the best idea he'd had yet. He gripped her hips and slammed her over him.

She gasped.

"Is this okay? Did I hurt you?"

"It's perfect. You feel so good." She rose on her knees before sliding back down his shaft.

His forehead pulled together in focused ecstasy. Nothing was better than this. Holy fuck, did she feel like heaven riding him. Her tits bounced with each grind of her hips. A pink blush painted across her ivory skin and up her neck. Her lips were swollen from his mouth and his cock. And those whiskey eyes locked on him, sucking his soul into their depths.

"Finn?"

"Yes?"

"Touch me."

He leaned forward, sucking one of her hard nipples into his mouth. She grasped the back of his head, pulling him closer.

"Yes! Harder," she pleaded as she rocked faster in his lap.

The slickness of her tight heat drove him closer and closer to the point of no return. She guided his hand to her sex and pressed his finger against her clit.

"Mmm. Make me come."

He raked his teeth over her nipple and swirled his thumb around her clit. Her inner muscles clenched impossibly tight around him. Her limbs clamped around his body, her thrusts becoming more urgent.

Charli's mouth dropped open in a litany of curses before she screamed, "Finn!"

Pressure gathered in his spine as euphoria washed over her expression. He thrust his hips, driving into her as she clung on to him, riding her own waves of ecstasy.

"Come with me," she choked out.

"You want me to fill you up?"

"Yes. Fuck, yes. Finn!"

His stomach muscles clenched. His face contorted in uncontrolled rapture. As Charli spasmed around his cock with her orgasm, Finn came with an unstoppable force, emptying himself inside her.

"Charli!" Her name fell from his lips before he locked them on to her mouth, kissing her as they both came down from the high. He pressed his forehead to hers. Only the sound of their heaving breaths fell between them. His cock was still pulsing inside her. He didn't want to leave her warm embrace.

"I was wrong."

She pulled away far enough to search his eyes, her forehead scrunched in question.

"This was the best experience of my life."

A smile broke free on her face, but it didn't reach her eyes.

He'd forgotten too much. Would it ever come back? Or would Charli have to live with his impairments for the rest of their lives together? He brushed his thumb over her lips. "I can't wait to make a million more memories with you."

Finn kissed her long and slow before tucking her into his arms as he slipped out of her. The loss was instant. Finn wanted to bury himself back inside her, and he would the first chance he got. But for now, he'd hold her. He'd meld his lips to her temple, press her naked skin against his, and live in this moment for as long as she'd let him.

25

FINN

Finn tossed and turned in bed, unable to fall asleep. Slipping his arm out from under his sleeping wife, he gave her a kiss on the cheek before quietly sneaking out of the room. He grabbed his computer and headphones, setting them on the kitchen bar. After taking a seat, he pulled up the photos and videos.

Picture after picture of himself and other guys in uniform with a desert background loaded on the screen. One man snagged his attention in particular. He zoomed in on his face. *Smithson.* The guy from his dream. So, it *was* a memory. Was this the man who'd died in the accident that had stolen all of Finn's memories? They'd been friends.

Finn plugged in the headphones and clicked play on the video with the two of them. He closed his eyes and rubbed them, searching the fog of memories. His mind exposed flickers and flashes of Smithson laughing, joking, and then being serious with gunshots firing in the background. Smithson's voice triggered a flashback.

"We could extend your trip another week and go see a buddy of mine in Oregon to catch some Dungeness crab," Smithson said, turning to look at Finn from the driver's side.

"Tempting offer. But I need to get back to Charli."

"You know if I called her, she'd tell you to stay and enjoy yourself." Smithson chuckled.

Finn laughed. "Yeah, that woman would do anything for me, even to her own detriment. Nah, working on her feet at the bar is getting harder for her the more pregnant she is. I need to go home to help her relax a little. Plus, I'm missing her something fierce."

Smithson shook his head. "Damn, if I had found a woman like that, maybe I could have considered swinging both ways."

Finn punched his shoulder playfully. "Hands off. She's mine."

"Yeah, yeah. Don't get your panties in a wad. I'm perfectly happy with my husband." Smithson's eyes got that dreamy look.

"We are some lucky bastards, aren't we?"

"Fuck yeah we are," Smithson agreed.

"Hey, have you heard from—" Smithson's question was cut off by the screech of tires and the crash of metal.

Flashes of the dream mingled with the new memories as he was thrust into another.

Gunshots rang in the distance, getting closer. Bullets whizzed by them. Smithson and another soldier flanked him on either side as they moved through the compound.

"Fuck! Incoming!" Smithson threw his weight over him as an explosion rocketed behind them.

Ringing whined in his ears and the tangy taste of iron filled his mouth. Smithson rolled off his back. Finn sucked in a dust-coated breath and coughed. Squinting through the rubble, he checked his brothers-in-arms. "You okay?" He couldn't even hear his own voice.

Four dust-caked figures gave him a thumbs-up.

Movement caught his attention in the corner of the building just a moment before the enemy was on top of him, stabbing a knife into his shoulder. Pain split through his arm. Adrenaline coursed inside him.

Finn screamed and fought him off. He pulled the 9mm from his waist and shot his attacker in the side of the head. Blood and god knew what else splattered across Finn's face, soaking into his uniform. Panic ripped through his body.

A hand clamped on both sides of his neck. Finn spun around reflexively, the headphones tearing from the laptop before it crashed to the ground. His chest heaved as he pinned the enemy's throat to the wall. *Protect. Serve.* The enemy choked, the only noise in the otherwise quiet room.

Nails scraped his arms.

No. Not the enemy.

Charli!

"Fuck!" He tore his arms away from her as she slumped to the ground in the dark. He flicked the light on, terrified to see the damage he'd done. Charli's knees tucked into her chest as she stared at him with wide eyes filled with fear.

"I-I'm so sorry, baby. I thought—I thought . . ." He reached towards her, and she flinched, sending a wave of shame and anger roiling through him. His chest cinched tight, his lungs unable to draw a full breath. Finn grabbed his hair at the top of his head, pulling in frustration as he dropped to his knees in defeat. *What have I done?* He brought his hands in front of him, staring. *What kind of a monster am I?*

"I'm so sorry." His voice came out in a whisper.

Charli coughed and grabbed his hand and pulled herself up. "No. I'm sorry. I shouldn't have snuck up on you like that."

"This isn't your fault." He lifted her chin to inspect her throat.

"I'm okay, Finn. Really. It was just an accident." She placed her hand over his, her eyes still wary.

"I could have killed you." His voice sounded like he'd swallowed shards of glass.

Worry marred her features. "Finn, this isn't your fault. It's not a big deal. I promise. Let's just take a hot shower and go to bed."

Her words said one thing, but the slight tremor in her hands and the wide-eyed look on her face gave away how shaken she truly was.

He backed up, dropping her hand. He couldn't go near her. What if it happened again? What if he hurt her worse next time?

"You go. I just need some time alone."

Hurt flashed in her gaze. "Okay, if that's what you need. But know I'm here for you." She bent over and picked up the fallen laptop, checking it over quickly before turning her concerned gaze towards him.

Emotion clogged his throat, so he nodded before he left to the garage.

Opting to use his bike, instead of smashing his fist through the drywall, he grabbed a helmet and zipped his coat. He needed the cold wind to tamp down some of this anger that still burned inside him.

He started the motorcycle and drove towards the coast.

Fifteen minutes later, under a canopy of stars and beside the crashing ocean, Finn perched his helmet on the seat. Icy sea breeze whipped against his frozen cheeks. He welcomed the pain, the numbness. Everything was so fucked up in his life. Just when he and Charli had taken a huge step in their relationship, his body had betrayed him—again. It was bad enough he couldn't remember shit about her. Instead he'd discovered he was, in fact, a killer. Unless it wasn't a real memory.

He slipped his hand over his shoulder where the knife had

pierced his skin. The rough stubble of a scar gave him his answer. An injury from a fight he didn't remember joining. He was capable of taking a human life. And sometimes his fucked-up head couldn't determine what was real and what was a flashback. What kind of man put his hands on a woman like that? *I'm a monster.* He wasn't good enough for her.

"Half a fucking man," he growled and kicked the sand.

Charli's terrified expression flashed in his mind. "She deserves someone better than me. More than I can give her."

But she and that baby are my responsibility.

"Maybe they'd be better off without me. Charli needs a man who can give her everything. Who can keep her safe." His hands clenched into iron fists at the thought of another man touching his wife. "Damn it!" he yelled.

How can I fix this? He never wanted Charli to be hurt by him again. He'd figure this out himself. Charli didn't need one more thing to worry about. This was his problem to solve.

"Ahhhhhhhhhh!" he screamed out, the crashing waves swallowing up his cries.

Finn dropped to his knees. The cold sand bit through his jeans. He was drowning, lost in the darkness, searching for any sign of help. Where to go from here? How could he find his way back—back to the Finn he'd been in that journal? The man who'd spent weekends away in the mountains fucking his wife? The one who was capable of saving her? The man who would do anything for Charli?

Finn sucked in a sharp breath of salty frigid air, shoulders slumped as he looked towards the heavens. Dark grey clouds had moved in, the North Star nowhere to be seen. He was alone on a deserted, frozen beach, with no guiding light.

You said I was your true north, and if you ever got lost, this would help you find your way back to me. Charli's words echoed in his mind.

If only it was true. If only the ink in their skin had some magical ability to bring his memories back.

If only he'd never woken at all.

179

26

FINN

The next morning, Finn lifted the phone, checking the address once more. *49 Seal Cove Lane.* Laura's house. He hung his helmet on the motorcycle and slipped the keys into his leather jacket. Taking a lungful of cold air, he walked across the crunchy leaves that had fallen towards her door. Nerves wound around him, twisting inside him.

He lifted his hand at the door and hesitated. Charli's hurt expression flashed in his mind. *I need to do this for us.* Watching those videos had brought back memories. Maybe if he started from where he remembered with Laura, he'd recover the moments lost with Charli.

He rapped three times on the door and waited. His stomach flipped as he shifted from side to side on his feet. He hadn't been this nervous since he'd asked Laura on a date.

The door opened, and Laura's blue eyes met his, her lips twisting in a pleased smile. "Hey, stranger."

"Howdy." He cringed. *Am I a fucking cowboy now?* "I was in

the neighborhood and thought I'd take you up on your offer to talk."

Her eyes lit up. "Come on in." She moved to the side to allow him to pass.

He squeezed by her in the small space.

"Can I take your jacket?"

"Sure." He shrugged the coat off and handed it to her. She hung it on the coatrack behind the door.

"Let's go sit in the living room. Would you like anything to drink?" Laura asked, leading the way. She wore a simple pair of dark-wash skinny jeans and an oversized sweater that hung off one shoulder. Her golden hair fell to her shoulders with curls that were not natural to her normally straight hair.

"Nah, I'm good."

She motioned to the couch, and he took a seat. She joined him, her thigh touching his. He moved a little farther away.

"How have you been?" she asked.

"Good. Fine."

One of her eyebrows rose as she tilted her head disbelieving.

"It's been difficult getting . . . into the swing of things," he confessed.

She reached her hand out, resting it on his knee. "I'm so sorry you had to go through that. I can't imagine waking up having forgotten so much of my life. You're a really strong man to conquered that and still try to make things work between you and Charli."

He sighed. Maybe Laura understood him better than he realized.

"I was wondering if you could help me." Finn turned his head to face her.

She squeezed the hand on his knee. "I'd do *anything* for you, Finny." Her eyes shone with genuine care.

Did she still have feelings for him? Did she feel bad about cheating on him?

"I wondered if you could give me some closure."

"How so?"

"Just, can you tell me what happened between us?" *Maybe it will spur the memories I need back with Charli.*

She stiffened, pulling her manicured hand to her lap. Her shoulders drooped. "Where do you want me to start?"

"The last thing I remember is us going on that date to the fair."

She smiled. "Oh, that was the best date ever. Do you remember the bear you won me?"

He smiled. How could he forget? He'd used every last dollar in his wallet to get it for her. She'd pouted because Julie Kent's boyfriend had already gotten her one. Laura had always been in some silent competition with the other girls. But that was understandable when you came from two parents who only cared about winners. He'd been able to look past her rough edges and see the girl beneath who needed him to show her she was good enough.

"Yeah. That was fun."

"You told me you loved me that night." Her gaze bore into him. "Do you remember what else you told me?"

He swallowed and nodded. "I told you I'd never leave you. That you and I were forever."

She nodded jerkily, turning away slightly. She was silent a moment before she wiped a tear from her cheek.

"I'm sorry. If this is too much, I can go," Finn said, moving towards the edge of the couch.

Her hand shot out and grabbed his thigh. "Why did you do it, Finn? Why did you leave me for her? What did she have that I didn't?"

His brows furrowed, pain reflecting in her turquoise eyes.

"You cheated on me with Ricky."

She shook her head. "She told you that. Because she wanted you for herself."

"What?" *No. That can't be true.*

"She lied to you, and you believed her after you told me you loved me. After you promised me forever. I guess I never was enough." She pulled her arms into her lap.

Finn was torn, his mind running a million miles a minute. One part wanted to comfort Laura. The other wanted to run out of there and track down his wife and ask her what the hell was going on. Would Charli lie to him? No, she didn't seem like a liar.

Stewart warned me she changed me.

Laura let out a humorless laugh. "After all that, she still cheated on you when you were deployed. Are you even sure that baby is yours?"

The air was ripped from his lungs. His chest threatened to snap under the weight of the blow Laura had just delivered. Confirmation of what he'd suspected. He turned towards her, his body rigid. "What are you talking about?"

"I'm sorry. I know you don't remember, but I can't stand by and watch you destroy your life anymore. I still love you, Finn. I never stopped. Even though you hurt me more than anyone ever has. I still want you to be happy." She placed her hand on his cheek.

He shook his head. "Damon." The pieces of the puzzle clicked into place.

"Finn?"

Shooting to his feet, Finn needed to get out of there. "I-I'm sorry. I've gotta go."

He grabbed his jacket off the rung and opened the door, running out.

Mind spinning, his heart racing in his chest. He slid on his jacket before grabbing his helmet. Finn got on his bike and flipped his black visor down. Revving the engine, he took off down the otherwise quiet street.

Everything inside him was at war. Spiderwebs of connections lit up. Synapses fired. Panic built. Anger roiled. Houses whipped by. Every muscle was tense as the world as he knew it came crumbling beneath him.

Charli isn't like that. Is she?

Was he that blinded by the lust between them? Was she that good at playing him? No. The last time he'd gotten a conflicting story off Stewart, Finn had made some big mistakes. It had all turned out to be a misunderstanding. He needed answers.

By the time he turned into the familiar neighborhood, he'd made the decision to keep his meeting with Laura to himself.

He parked his bike and walked up to his parents' house. Opening the door, he called out, "Mom? Dad?"

"In the kitchen." His mother's voice called from deeper within the house.

He took off his shoes, leaving them by the door, and hung his coat before finding his way to his parents. The scent of cinnamon and apple clung to the air.

His mother stirred a pan of cooking apples. Her smile faded the closer he got. "Finn?"

His father looked up from the e-reader in his hand, slipping the reading glasses off his nose.

"Hey, guys."

"Is something the matter?" His mother wiped her hands on the apron at her waist.

Should he tell them what Laura said? They were clearly on Charli's side from the beginning. Maybe it was better to avoid mention of what he'd just learned.

"No. I'm just tired. I . . . uh . . . remembered some stuff last night."

Claire's eyes glittered, the hopeful smile returning to her face. "You did?"

"About Charli?" Zeke asked.

Finn shook his head. "No. About my time in the Army. But it got me thinking. Maybe if I heard more about Charli, I could remember things about us too."

"Did you ask her?" His father picked up his cup of coffee and sipped it, his gaze studying Finn.

"Yeah. I mean, we've talked a lot about the past. I thought maybe hearing your version of how we got together might help."

"You two thought you were so slick, sneaking in the window. You forgot about the fact that your bedroom was right by ours, and we slept with the window open most nights." His father chuckled.

"Why didn't you say something?"

"We trusted you. We asked you about her, and you explained her situation at home. We knew you were taking care of her, because that's who you are, Finn. I raised a man who did right by the women in his life." His father shrugged.

You were the perfect gentleman. No matter how hard I tried to persuade you. Charli's words repeated in his head.

"Although somewhere along the line, your friendship turned into something more," his mother added.

"What was Charli's home life like?"

His parents looked at each other before returning their gaze to him. "Haven't you asked her that?" Claire shut off the stove.

"It came up a couple times. She said she would rather not talk about it."

"It's hard for her. Her mother was a basket case. She

belonged to some sort of fundamentalist cult. That poor girl took the brunt of it."

This didn't make any sense. Who was he to believe? He couldn't make the same mistakes he did last time. He'd watch and wait. There had to be some answers in his journal. From his own words, he was the one who'd kept secrets from her. But if she had cheated with this Damon guy, could he forgive her like the old Finn apparently had?

"Why are you asking us all these questions instead of her?" His mother's head tipped to the side in question as she studied him.

He swallowed. "I just wanted to see her through your eyes, I guess." It wasn't a total lie.

"What I see is a remarkable young woman who has become a daughter to me. But what is important is what you see," she pressed.

Finn scratched his beard, leaning back in the chair. "She's brave. And she's loyal—I mean, Charli's been there for me since the hospital. She's protected me in so many ways already."

"That's our girl." His father smiled.

"But, sometimes . . . I feel like she holds some stuff back."

His mother's brows drew together. "Didn't the doctor tell her to be careful with how much she brings up so that you aren't overloaded with too much?"

"Yeah." He conceded.

His mother patted his hand. "If anyone could overcome the obstacles you two have been given, it's you guys. You couldn't have asked for a better partner."

Finn took a deep breath before letting it out. He wanted to believe Charli was what they said and he'd seen. But Laura's words had burrowed into his mind leaving holes of doubt.

"You'd better get going if you plan on helping Charli with the deliveries today," Zeke said, checking his watch.

"Right." Fin nodded. He gave his mother a hug and kiss on her cheek and waved to his dad on his way out.

* * *

Finn wiped his brow, needing a drink of water and a break from stacking boxes in the back room. He stepped into the main area behind the bar to find Charli leaning over the timber slab, laughing with a couple of guys who were looking at her as if she were their next meal.

His fists clenched at his sides as he stepped closer.

"How about we take you out fishing sometime?" the first guy asked.

Who the hell hit on a pregnant woman?

Charli wiped down the counter. "Fishing is more my husband's thing than mine."

He stopped, relief washing over him as she clearly let these guys know she was taken.

She looked up, meeting his eyes, and offered him a smile. "Speak of the devil."

He studied her intently. The curve of her lips seemed genuine. Her golden-brown eyes shone with honesty.

What the hell was he doing? Who could he trust? What could he believe? *If only I could remember for myself.* He'd hurt her. She'd stayed by his side. She was carrying his child—as far as he knew. He owed her the benefit of the doubt. So, he'd wait. And watch. And hope to hell he was doing the right thing. The last thing he wanted to do was create friction in their already fragile relationship. Things were good right now. He wouldn't do anything to disrupt that.

27

CHARLI

Sunlight glittered through the frosted windows. Charli walked over to her dresser, searching for her favorite earrings. It took a minute but she found them. Slipping them into her ears, she studied the rest of her items. Normally she was very particular about how she organized things. Something was off. Where was the picture of her and Finn? She searched the room, her eyes landing on the side table. A shiver ran through her. Charli opened the side drawer, relief flooding her at the sight of her gun. After the baby was born, they'd have to lock it away with Finn's hunting rifles.

Maybe Finn moved the photo? She'd ask him once he got back. He was staying out more and more the past few days. Ever since he'd pinned her against that wall, he'd withdrawn again. *How can I get through to him?* How could you get someone to stop beating themselves up for something they couldn't control? Unfortunately, she had a lifetime of experience in that department. It was impossible.

Her phone dinged.

She pulled it from her pocket and her stomach turned to stone.

Unknown: *It's been too long. You haven't changed, but I have.*

Charli: *Who is this?*

Unknown: *You'll see soon enough.*

Charli's heart thundered in her chest. Was this Damon? Was he okay? She dialed Brynn.

"Hello?"

"H-hey."

"How are you?" Brynn asked.

"I-I don't know. I'm getting some strange texts."

"From Phillip? Your attacker?" Brynn's voice was panicked.

"That's just it. He's in jail."

"Who else could it be?" Brynn asked.

"It might be . . ." *Someone from my past. Someone I never thought I'd see again.* "I don't know."

"Are they threatening?"

"Not really. I'm probably just being paranoid." Charli dismissed the idea.

"I know you're working closely with the sheriff. Maybe it's worth mentioning to him," Brynn suggested.

"Yeah. I'll do that. Thanks for . . . listening."

"Anytime."

"Have a good day off."

"You too." Brynn hung up.

The creak of the floorboard made Charli jump. She slammed a hand to her chest. "Finn?"

Her husband walked into the room, studying her with dark clouds in his eyes. "Who was that?"

She should tell him about the texts. But what if she worried him for no reason? He'd had an enormous amount of stress thrust on him already because of her situation. If Finn wanted any hope of recovering his memories, the less stress the better for his healing. No. She'd protect him from this. It wasn't her attacker—he was in jail. And if it was Damon . . . well, that definitely would be too much for him to handle right now. Charli eyed the phone in her hand before returning her gaze to his face. "Brynn."

"Mm-hmm."

"Hey, did you move the picture of us from my dresser?" She stood.

He shook his head.

"Are you sure?" She leaned over to check if it had fallen behind the dresser. *Nope.*

"I didn't touch your stuff," he said coldly.

"Okay. Never mind. I'm sure it will turn up at some point. You ready to go to Link's bonfire?"

"Sure."

She reached out and placed her hand on his chest—the first contact she'd had in days. He tensed under her fingertips. Lately she'd been going to bed without him, and he'd resumed sleeping on the couch. *Because he's afraid of hurting me again.*

"I miss you, baby." She leaned her cheek against his pec.

"I'm right here. I didn't go anywhere."

She turned her face to his. "You're here. But you're not *here*." She tapped his temple.

His hand wound over hers, lowering it back to his chest.

"It was an accident. And no harm was done. Stop blaming yourself." She leaned on tiptoes. Her hands wove behind his neck, pulling him down for a kiss.

Conflict flashed in his gaze. His lips flattened in a thin line.

"Please, Finn?"

At her plea, his gaze turned soft, dropping to her mouth. His lips crashed to hers, possessive and unrelenting. A surge of lust shot through her as his hands wrapped around her body, picking her up off the floor. She locked her legs around his waist, raking her teeth across his bottom lip, giving it right back to him. He groaned, squeezing her ass hard before he lowered her to the bed, settling his weight over her. His tongue dove into her mouth, taking, blurring, stirring her arousal to a peak. Finn's intensity seemed desperate, like he needed to prove something. To her or himself, she wasn't sure. Heat blanketed her every cell. He palmed one of her breasts, squeezing to the point of pain. Sweet agony. It only fed the fire wreaking havoc in her core. Molten lava spilled from her most secret places. He lowered his head to her chest, biting her nipple through the thin fabric of her blouse.

She moaned.

"Say my name," Finn ordered.

"Finn."

"Louder!" he growled.

"Finn!"

His eyes stared intently at her, his gaze animalistic and feral. She'd never seen him like this before. A thrill of excitement made her clench her thighs around him. He slipped his hand over her stockings, over her thighs. He cupped her sex, pressing her clit through the thin barrier. After gripping the stocking fabric in his hands, he ripped it apart.

"Finn!" Her eyes widened as she gasped.

Pushing her silk panties aside, he shoved two fingers inside her. She closed her eyes and bucked her hips.

"Open your eyes. I want you to see who's fucking you. Want you to know who's bringing you this pleasure."

She obeyed, eyes locked on his every movement as his fingers fucked her relentlessly. She fisted her hands into the sheets as he hit that sensitive spot inside. Pressure built. She held her breath, thrashing her body. Reaching out her hands to his shoulders, she raked her nails over him.

"Tell me who you belong to," he commanded.

"You. You, Finn."

"Tell me this pussy is mine," he growled.

"It's yours."

"Just mine," he insisted.

"Only ever yours," she said, breathless.

His eyes bore into hers.

"Please, Finn."

"What do you want, Charli-baby?"

"Make me come," she pleaded.

Pressing his thumb to her clit, his fingers continued to thrust in and out of her. Stars burst in her vision as her muscles clamped together. Finn's mouth possessed hers as every nerve ending exploded with an avalanche of sensations.

"Turn over." His hands helped her get onto all fours in her orgasmic haze.

Cool air flushed over her as he pushed her skirt over her waist. The sound of tearing echoed in the room as he destroyed what was left of her stockings. The crackle of a zipper lowering warned her of what was coming next. His hard cock plowed into her in one thrust, burying himself to the hilt.

She gasped. His hand pressed her back down. She arched her back for deeper penetration, squinting her eyes closed at the intensity of pleasure ripping through her body with every thrust.

"You're mine, Charli. Every fucking inch." His hips pistoned in and out of her, flesh slapping against hot flesh.

Her body grew limp, unable to do anything else but experience every peak, every plunge, every nerve ending glowing with the all-encompassing intoxication of pleasure. It was complete rapture. His grunts and her moans melded into a muted symphony of the soundtrack of ecstasy.

"Yes! Fuck! Finn!" The only three words left in her vocabulary.

Wave after wave crashed over her until it blurred into one giant tsunami of pleasure.

He sucked the sensitive skin at the crux of her neck, the bite of pain sending her rocketing towards a new plane of euphoria. She opened her mouth to scream but nothing came out. Her eyes rolled back as she gripped the sheets. Charli's inner muscles locked up, squeezing Finn like a vise.

"Mine!" Finn roared as he came and pulsed inside her. His hands dug into her hips hard enough to leave bruises.

Holy shit. That was the hottest sex they'd ever had. Maybe the old Finn could have learned a thing or two from this new guy.

"Wow." She was still trying to catch her breath.

Finn pulled out of her, and she rolled over. Conflict warred in those dark pools. His chest heaved with each intake of oxygen. He blinked as if even he was surprised at the ferocity of what they'd just shared.

"That was pretty fucking hot."

He stared at her silently.

"Was it good for you?" she asked, doubt creeping in.

"Yes." He turned away, mumbling something that sounded a lot like, "That's what scares me."

"I really liked these stockings," she called after him.

He stopped in the doorway, turning back to her with a smirk. "Sorry."

"No, you're not." She giggled.

"You're right . . . I'm not." He walked out of the room, the bathroom door shutting a moment later.

Charli smiled, her body still humming with satisfaction. She couldn't move until the bones returned to her legs. Then she'd take a quick shower and they could go to Link's party.

Remy and Mikel would be there along with their other friends. It would be good for Finn to see people from high school.

The sound of water running filtered through the room. Maybe this was a turning point for her and Finn. The sex was explosive—it always had been, though not at *this* level. Damn, her husband had wrecked her in the best of ways. Was this his way of making up for the last few days of distance? Perhaps now they could move on. Her smile grew as the baby in her womb fluttered and kicked. She placed her hand over the swollen bump. Happiness descended over her like a warm, weighted blanket. Everything was right again in her world.

But every mountain had a descent. The higher the peak, the farther the fall. Hopefully this one wouldn't destroy her.

28

CHARLI

Charli threaded the needle through the white material, creating small Xs in a pattern. Cross-stitching brought her a sense of calm. Every stitch was organized and tidy. Each small, seemingly insignificant pass of thread added to the overall picture. The words "I don't spew profanities. I enunciate them like a fucking lady" was complete in the center. All she had left to do was finish the pine trees underneath in soft purple and grey. Charli smiled to herself. Emma would get a kick out of this one.

Finn walked in and set a steaming cup of tea on the table in front of her. "Here you go."

"Thank you." She tipped her head up, hoping he'd offer her a kiss. No such luck. He hadn't touched her since they'd had sex a week ago. *At least he's sleeping in the bed with me now.* It was hard to keep up with his hot and cold moods.

"You're welcome." He nodded.

"Do you want to watch something?" she asked, motioning to the TV.

"Actually, can I use your phone? Mine's charging." His

eyes darted to the ground and then back to the small circular tapestry in progress in her hands.

"Sure." She slid it out of her pocket and handed it over.

He accepted it and moved towards the chair opposite her, his back turned. She reached for the tea and took a sip. Warming notes of ginger and the tang of lemon burst on her taste buds. *Perfect.*

Charli's focus returned to the needle as Finn's heavy steps padded closer. She looked up. His jaw clenched, and his brown eyes narrowed with rage directed at her. His shoulders bunched near his ears with tension that radiated from him.

"Finn? What—"

"What. The. Fuck. Is. this?" He pointed with a shaky finger towards the last message she'd received from the unknown number.

Unknown: *I can't wait to have my arms wrapped around you again.*

Her eyes flicked back to his as she set down her needle work.

"It's not a big deal. It's probably a wrong number." *Or Damon.* But she wasn't ready to get into that with Finn. Maybe it was selfish of her, but she needed to leave the past in the past. Because the pain of losing the only other man she loved was too much. And if Finn found out now, it would do more harm than good for his recovery.

"Wrong number?" He scoffed and shook his head.

"Look at me, Finn." She stood up, facing him.

His eyes blazed, brutally puncturing her with the chaos raging within them. "This isn't the first time, is it?" he grit out.

"No."

His chest heaved as his hands fisted at his sides. "How many times?"

"Um . . . like, two or three maybe."

"You don't even know?" he snapped.

Why did this feel like they were talking about two different things? She reached for the phone. "It's all still there. I even asked who it was. Look for yourself. Scroll up."

He lifted the cell and clicked the button, scrolling. His hand clamped so tightly around the device she was surprised it didn't crack.

Finn let out a shaky breath. His shoulders drooped. He wiped a hand over his face.

She reached her hand out to his shoulder. "Baby—"

He threw her phone across the room, shattering it to pieces. She jumped. Her hand went to her mouth, eyes wide. "What the hell?"

Pure rage glimmered in his eyes marred by confusion. Regret flashed as he flicked his gaze to her. He reached out, and she stepped back, her hands drawing out in front of her instinctively. She'd never seen this side of Finn before in all the years they'd been married.

His hand paused before he pulled it back. "I'm sorry."

"You just destroyed my phone. That is not okay." Her body trembled with her own anger.

"I thought . . . fuck!" he yelled, pacing back and forth.

"What's going on, Finn? Talk to me."

He shook his head and turned around.

Charli reached for his arm, tugging him towards her. "Please, talk to me, Finn. Tell me why you're so upset."

He shook his head, not meeting her eyes, and pulled away before disappearing out the front door. The rumble of his motorcycle faded into the distance a minute later.

She turned towards the remnants of her phone, tucking her trembling hands into her pockets. Tears bled to the surface. She couldn't help Finn if he didn't let her in. And now she questioned whether it was safe for her to even be with him. He hadn't laid a hand on her, but if her past taught her anything, abuse came in many forms. Her heart lurched. Her Finn would never hurt her. But the last few weeks reminded her too much of her life growing up—walking on eggshells, never knowing when her mother would explode. No. She wouldn't put up with this from Finn. This wasn't healthy.

* * *

Charli raked the leaves into a pile. She'd had enough sitting for the day. Anxiety spun her up, doubt curling her stomach into nervous knots. Her heart was in confused torment, her love at war with her mind, tangled in a past she remembered and he didn't. It was as if she were drifting at sea, unsure which way the current was taking her, lost in the darkness of chaos.

A flutter vibrated in her belly and then another. Charli pressed her hand to her abdomen. "Hey, little man." She sighed. He could probably sense all her unease. Guilt crashed over her. She was already screwing this motherhood thing up. "I'm sorry, sweetheart. I'm just worried about your daddy . . . But I'll find a way to get through to him."

This would only work if Finn wanted it to as well. She couldn't fight for a marriage if her husband was running the other way. She inhaled a determined breath and resumed her raking.

"Twinkle, twinkle, little star," she began singing softly. The fine hairs on the back of her neck stood on end. Prickles skated across her skin. The weight of being watched tore into her. She searched around the yard. A dog barked in the distance. Leaves rustled in the breeze. A chill crawled through her. Heart racing, she dropped the rake and went in the back door, locking it behind her with a trembling hand.

She turned and gasped at the man standing in her kitchen. Terror and memories from the past splintered and cracked the fragile ground she'd carefully constructed since she'd last laid eyes on his face.

He stepped closer. "I told you I'd be coming back for you."

29

FINN

Finn pulled out the box with a new phone for Charli and gripped the flowers in his other hand. He'd really made a mess of things. *Again.* The moment he'd seen that text, he'd lost it. Laura had said she cheated on him. His journal mentioned another man named Damon. But Charli had never given him a reason to doubt her. That anger though, it was like someone flicked a switch and all he saw was red. He hadn't even been in control of his body anymore; the rage had taken over. Finn had to apologize and lay everything on the table.

He opened the door and stopped short. A tall man with a grey sweatshirt stood with his back to Finn.

"Damon?" Charli asked, her voice filled with disbelief. "You . . . you're here?"

"I couldn't stay away any longer. I had to see you. Had to make this right," Damon said.

Finn's stomach roiled. The items in his hands dropped to the floor, along with any hope he had of making things right with Charli. She'd lied to him. Laura had been right all along.

Her eyes met his—fear reflected back with her soft gasp.

Yeah. You've been caught.

He turned away without hesitation, slamming the door behind him as he jumped on his motorcycle. Knocking the helmet to the ground, he didn't waste time picking it up. Instead he revved the engine and tore out of their driveway.

He pressed harder on the gas once he was on the long stretch of road, until houses whizzed by in a blur. Freezing wind lashed at his skin. Finn welcomed the numbing pain to quench some of the boiling rage tearing apart his chest. His shredded heart sent a bolt of searing pain through him with each haggard beat. Why did it hurt so much? *Because I love her.* Hot tears burned his eyes, blurring his vision. He shook his head and grit his teeth.

A truck passed on the other side of the road. A cop. *Shit.*

Red and blue lights lit up behind him as a siren wailed. *Just what I fucking need.* He slowed down and pulled to the side of the road, glancing back.

Bently opened the door to his truck and climbed out. *Thank fuck.*

"What the hell, man? Why are you going so fast?" Bently took off his aviators and stuck them in his pocket, his expression hard.

"Charli's cheating on me."

Bently's eyebrows drew together. "What are you talking about?"

"Did you know? All this time?"

Bently held out his hands. "Whoa, whoa. Slow down. What happened?"

"I came home and there was a guy in my kitchen. She called him Damon."

The blood drained from Bently's face. "Damon is back?"

Finn nodded.

"And you left her alone with him!" Bently rushed to his truck. "Get in! Now!" His friend's tone left no room for argument.

Finn parked his bike and ran to the passenger's side before scrambling in and barely shutting the door as Bently whipped the car around.

"Did he have a gun or another weapon?" Bently asked, pressing the gas pedal to the floor.

"No, I don't think so. Bently, what's going on?"

"The last time she and her brother were in a room alone together he stuck a knife in her gut trying to get to you."

Chills washed over Finn. *Her brother?* Panic gripped him like a vise. *I left her with him.* His wife and child were in danger because of his jealousy. *Her brother.* "Fuck!" He slammed his fist against the dashboard.

Bently shut off the sirens before they turned onto Finn's street. He parked around the corner and slipped out of the car, drawing his gun. "Stay here."

"Not a fucking chance."

His friend ground his teeth. "Then stay the fuck behind me, and don't do anything stupid." He crouched low as he approached the house, saying something into his radio to dispatch about backup.

"I'm gonna peek in the window. See if I can locate them." Bently continued towards the back. Finn pressed his back to the siding of his home and waited. Each second was an eternity crawling by.

"They're in the kitchen at the table. I don't see a weapon. I texted Charli. We'll see if she can answer."

Finn grimaced, guilt sitting in his stomach like a stone. "Her phone is broken. She won't get the message."

Bently let out a frustrated sigh. "I'm gonna knock and see

what situation we have. He might talk to me. But you'd better stay here, out of sight."

"I can go in the back," Finn offered.

His friend seemed to think it over. "I have backup three minutes out."

"Don't wait. *Please.* That's my family in there."

Bently nodded. "Stay out of sight." He walked up to the door and knocked. The shuffling of feet came closer, and Charli opened the door.

"I was in the neighborhood and thought I'd stop by. See how you were doing," Bently said as if this was any other day.

"It's okay. Damon's okay," Charli said, opening the door wider.

Finn stepped forward. Charli's eyes flicked to his, eyebrows drawn together. Bently went inside, saying something on his radio, as she stepped down and approached Finn. "My brother is here. I haven't seen him in . . . years."

"I'm sorry. I assumed the worst, and then I just left you."

"Did you think I was cheating on you?" Her wide, brown eyes searched his.

He nodded. "I found a journal in the garage. It mentioned Damon, but it never said who he was to you. I filled in the blanks myself. And then . . . I went to see Laura—"

Charli's mouth dropped open as she reared back. "Wh-why?" Her tone incredulous and laced with pain.

"I thought maybe talking things over with her could trigger a memory . . . and give me some closure."

She wiped her glassy eyes. "You went to talk to your ex— the one you remember—when you won't even have a conversation with me?"

"That isn't—I wasn't trying to hurt you."

She blew out a puff of air and shook her head. "Well, you did. Deeply. I've tried everything I can think of to help you.

To get through to you. It seems like we are making progress and then you freeze me out. I can't do this, Finn. These secrets are eating me alive."

He reached out and cupped her face in his hands. Her eyes closed like she couldn't bear to look at him.

"Charli-baby, I don't know what to say, except I'm so fucking sorry. Laura told me you lied about her cheating on me, that you were the one who had other men while I'd been deployed."

"And you believed her?" His wife's eyes narrowed on him, pain and disbelief shimmering in her tears.

Regret clawed at him. Shame weighed his shoulders down and held his voice hostage. He nodded.

"Wow. I don't know what else to say to that. I understand you see me as a stranger, but to think that low of me." She turned away, backing out of his arms. Charli slipped through his fingers along with the last remnants of hope.

"I swear to you, I won't keep anything else from you. I will try to talk to you. Open up about . . . all of it. I'll do whatever it takes to show you I'm in this. I want this life with you, Charli. I want to be a better man. Help me find my way." He held out his hand to her, waiting for her to give him a shred of faith he didn't deserve.

She hesitated, looking between him and his hand. "I vowed to be your wife. In sickness and heath. In the good times and the bad times. But I will not put up with you icing me out, smashing things, and scaring me again. You need time to cool off—that's fine. But *tell* me. Don't just storm off making me wonder if you'll ever come back. I'm on your team. Everything I do is for *our* life, together."

He dropped to his knees, leaning against her belly as he wrapped his hands around her thighs. "I swear it."

She threaded her fingers through his hair. "I want to believe you, Finn."

"I'll show you," he promised, kissing her belly and standing up.

Damon appeared in the doorway, looking sheepishly at Finn. "I'm sorry I didn't call ahead. I figured you wouldn't let me come."

Finn's brows drew together as he stood. "I'm sorry." Sorry for not remembering. Sorry for not being enough. Sorry for keeping secrets.

"I was telling Charli and Bently, I got help in that place you sent me to. I'm on the right medication. It helps with the hallucinations. I mean, I still hear them, but I know they aren't real."

Hallucinations?

"I got a job. I have my own place now in Colorado. I'm doing good. So, thank you." Damon stretched out his hand to Finn.

Finn shook it.

"Damon was telling me all about how you and Bently found him the treatment center in Colorado," Charli supplied, a flash of hurt crossing her features as she looked to Bently. "Seems the old Finn and the new one both knew how to keep secrets," she added.

"You promised me you'd never send me back to a hospital after what happened the last time." Damon reached out to grab his sister's hand. "Finn knew you would blame yourself. So, he and Bently convinced me to go get help in order to protect you. That's all I ever wanted."

Charli pulled him into a hug. "I know, big brother. I know. It wasn't your fault. I know you'd never hurt me willingly."

"But I did. And I needed help. I got it. And I'm doing

good. I just . . . wanted you to know that. I didn't want you to worry. And I really needed to see you."

"I'm glad you came."

A car pulled up in the driveway, and a tall, blond man stepped out, giving a wave as he approached slowly. Damon waved back. "I'd like to introduce you to my husband."

Charli covered her mouth, tears welling in her eyes. But this time they seemed like tears of joy. "Who's the lucky guy?"

Damon chuckled. "I am . . . Steven, this is my sister, Charlotte, and her husband, Finn. And that's our friend Bently," Damon introduced them.

Steven reached out his hand to shake theirs. "So glad to finally meet you. Damon's told me so much about you."

Damon wrapped his arm around his husband's waist and kissed his cheek. His eyes shone with affection. Steven smiled, a slight blush creeping up his neck.

"We're just visiting for the weekend. But maybe we can come back after my nephew is born?" Damon asked, his gaze flicking uncertainly between Charli and Finn.

"I'd love that." Charli grinned, her eyes shimmering with hope.

* * *

After a little conversation, Steven and Damon excused themselves for dinner reservations in the city.

"Come by tomorrow. Stay for dinner," Finn offered.

Damon smiled, the light shining in his eyes matching his sister's. "We'd like that."

Finn wrapped his hand around Charli's waist. Charli moved away, breaking the connection as they waved goodbye. Regret clamored inside his rib cage, slicing through flesh and leaving lasting reminders of just how bad he'd fucked this up.

Bently cleared his throat, standing in front of them. "Listen, I was on my way here to deliver some news when I passed by Finn."

Charli's body stiffened. "What is it?"

"The man you identified, Phillip Feller, he admits to being at the bar that night and getting too rowdy. Said he never came back—didn't attack you."

"It was him." Charli was adamant.

"The DNA results—took so long with the backlog . . . Phillip wasn't a match."

"No—there's no way." Charli shook her head. "I saw him. It was dark . . . but he . . . it had to be him. Who else would have done it?"

Bently reached out, pulling Charli into a hug. "Sometimes when something traumatic happens, your memory isn't the most reliable. It could be someone who looked like him. We'll find him, Charli. But until then, stay safe. Don't go out alone." Bently's gaze bore into Finn's. "Keep her close."

"I will," Finn promised.

"I'll have one of my guys go get your bike and return it if you want?" Bently offered as Charli slipped from his arms.

Finn handed over the keys from his pocket. "Thanks, man."

Bently nodded before reaching out to Charli's shoulder. "Charli, I made you a promise when all this happened. I intend to follow through. I'll get him." Bently headed to his truck.

Once he was out of sight, she gave a long exhale and turned towards the house. He followed her.

She sat on the couch, rubbing her arms.

"Are you cold?" He grabbed a blanket and laid it over her lap before settling in next to her.

"Thanks." After a beat of silence, she said, "My mother

belonged to a very religious fundamentalist cult. She took a vow of poverty, which meant we lived in squalor. I didn't even have a mattress. Our clothes were hand-me-downs, at best. It was just her, my brother, and me for the longest time. She had a few boyfriends. But when I got older, their gazes lingered. My mother blamed me. Said I was wicked. An adulterer. Temptress, she called me. Said I needed to be saved. That's when the beatings happened."

Finn clenched his fists, tension twisting up his spine.

"Damon is my half brother. He started hearing voices when he was eighteen. My mother was convinced they were from God. That my brother was a holy prophet. You have to understand, when you're raised like we were, you don't question your parent. We were taught that children should obey their parents no matter what, or it was a sin. That being hit was discipline. And it was our mother's duty to beat the devil out of us."

He reached out his hand to her knee in comfort.

"When I got older and learned about mental health in high school, I realized my brother had schizophrenia. I convinced him to go to the hospital and talk to someone." She closed her eyes as tears ran down her face. "They shocked him. They . . . they were supposed to help, but they just made everything worse. He didn't trust me after that. My mother got him back, took him off the meds, and by that time I had started seeing you. She convinced him that you were the devil trying to take me away. That you would hurt me."

He shook his head, wrapping his arm around her, drawing her closer.

"He showed up to our house, and you got between us. He had a knife, thinking you truly were the devil, that you were holding me against my will. I moved between you, hoping to plead with him. But . . . he came at us with the knife." She looked down and lifted her shirt, showing off the jagged scar. "That's what this is from."

"The journal said that I made the choice so you didn't have to. I was trying to protect you," he offered.

She dropped her top and nodded. "I know that now. And while that was truly what I needed at the time, I wish you would have told me. Before the accident or even after you found the journal. He called me once months later to let me know he was okay. That he was going to stay away so I could live my life and be safe and happy. He wouldn't tell me anymore. I went five years without knowing if he was dead or alive. Wondering if he was safe or on the streets somewhere."

"I wish I had too."

She turned to face him. "I have never cheated on you, Finn. I've never even thought about it. You're it for me. You were my first . . . and I want you to be my last."

He rubbed his thumb gently over the corner of her mouth. "I want that."

"You can ask Ricardo if you want confirmation that Laura did cheat. He runs the apiary with his brother, Roman."

He shook his head. "I trust you."

Her eyes bore into his, searching. "Do you?"

"I think maybe we've spent too much time looking behind us and not enough looking forward. It makes me feel stuck. I just want to take the next steps to move on with you, if you'll have me."

She leaned in, her forehead resting against his. Charli's breath whispered across his lips. "I'd like that too. But I'm still hurting from what you did. You not only hid your interaction with her from me, but you sought her out and went to her house. Do you know how betrayed that makes me feel? When you won't even communicate with me?"

He gripped the back of her neck, holding her in place as

his thumb rubbed back and forth on the sensitive spot behind her ear. "I will regret that for the rest of my life. It felt like you were keeping things from me, and I . . . It was cowardly of me to go to her rather than come to you."

"Everything I've kept from you was because I didn't want to stress you out. I thought it would be too much. We were building something great here. I just felt like I wasn't sure what was too much."

"No more." He ran his nose over hers. "I swear to you, Charli-baby, I'm in this. No more secrets. And I need the same from you. If it's too overwhelming, I'll tell you."

"And no more Laura?"

"No more of my ex. Promise." He pulled her into his lap, holding her to his chest. One hand on her hip, and one hand over the ink compass tattoo covered by her shirt. Closing his eyes, he vowed to follow her through the darkness like a guiding light. He may not remember their past, and he might have made a mess of their present. But starting now, he'd carve out a future with his wife. The woman he loved. The woman who was quickly becoming his everything. If only he could become the man she needed.

30

CHARLI

The next night, Charli pressed a hand to her lower back in an attempt to calm the dull ache. She winced as she kicked off her shoes, her swollen feet screaming to be freed from the confines of her Converse. Being on her feet for so long at the bar was getting harder the farther along in her pregnancy she got.

Finn shut the door behind them and bent to organize her shoes.

"Thank you."

He stood, wrapping his arm around her waist and ushering her towards the stairs. "Let me run you a bath."

"God that sounds heavenly."

"I picked up some more of the Epsom salts earlier. Do you want some of that too?" he asked, his hands dropping to her hips as she climbed the stairs.

"Yes." She reached for the bathroom doorknob.

His hand covered hers. "Let me get it ready. You go lie down on the bed."

"But I'm yucky from work," she whined.

"I'll change the sheets after."

"Okay. If you insist." She gave in.

He chuckled and disappeared into the bathroom as she made her way to the bed, climbing under the sheets. Every joint ached. She sighed, slinging her arm over her eyes.

A few minutes later, Finn's hands pressed under her.

"What are you doing?"

He smiled, lifting her in his arms. "Bringing you to your bath."

She clung to his neck. "I can walk."

"You're in pain," he said as if that answered everything. Her heart fluttered. *He's taking care of me like he used to.*

He carried her into the bathroom. The flicker of candlelight reflected off the steamy water. Notes of lavender permeated the small room.

Finn set her on her feet before dragging the shirt over her head. She lifted her arms to help. He tossed her top into the washer before unsnapping her bra.

She moaned in relief. There was nothing like freeing her breasts at the end of the day, especially now that they were the size of melons.

He kissed her shoulder and turned her around. His eyes remained glued to hers in rapt attention as he slipped her leggings down, bringing her thong with it. She couldn't help the blush that crept across her skin. Every single day she was growing bigger. Did Finn still find her attractive? Sex with the lights off or in the heat of the moment was different. The last time he'd taken her was from behind. What if he got grossed out by the changes her body was going through?

Finn balled up her clothing and threw it into the open washing machine. "Your bath awaits." He motioned to the large tub.

She took the hand he offered to steady herself as she stepped into the hot water. Groaning, she settled herself onto her back. "Oh my god. This is just what I needed."

He smiled down at her. "I'll go take care of the bed. There's a bottle of water by the edge."

"Thank you."

He left her alone to soak. The tension and pain left her body with each passing minute in the large tub. She closed her eyes, relaxing.

Sometime later, he returned, tossing the sheets into the washer.

"Do you mind if I start this? Or would you rather wait until you're out?"

"Can you wait?"

"Yeah." He crouched by the edge of the bath, dipping his finger in the water and swirling it around.

"Do you want to join me?" She held her breath.

"Definitely." He smirked.

He shed his clothing. She sat forward, making space behind her before he climbed in. He pulled her shoulders towards him, until she relaxed against his chest. Cupping water in his hands, he splashed it over her breasts and shoulders. His warm fingers massaged her neck.

"What do you want for our future?" Finn asked.

She took a deep breath before answering. "I'd like for us to connect more. To have better communication. To have fun together and build a family. I don't want to be anything like my mother. I want our son to have so much love he never has to doubt if he belongs." She pressed a hand to her belly.

Finn's palm eclipsed hers. The contrast of his brown skin against her belly striking and beautiful. *Will our son have his father's skin tone? Or maybe a mix of both of ours?*

"That sounds good to me."

"What do you want?"

"To see you and our son happy. To be enough." His voice cracked.

"You've always been enough, honey. Every time I needed you, you were there. Even when I didn't know it." *Like with Damon.*

His only response was to kiss the top of her head.

"What do you want for yourself? Are you happy at the bar?"

"I like it. I mean, the noise gets old, but I like the backend side of things. It's amazing to see what that place has turned into since my parents first bought it when I was younger. I'd like to continue that legacy. Maybe expand someday to offer some appetizers."

"That's a great idea. Have you talked to your dad about it?" She smiled.

"Not yet."

"I'm sure if you go in with a plan and all the details, there's no way he'd turn you down."

"Maybe." He scooped up more water with his other hand, splashing it over her chest. "Do you think we could have that future you dream of? With me . . . without me remembering before?"

Maybe it was easier for him to talk when they weren't face to face, but this seemed like Finn was opening up, letting her in like she'd hoped. "I'm not going to lie and say I'm not frustrated or tired of how things have been going. I was feeling like I was in this marriage alone. And I understand this is a special circumstance. But we're at a crossroads. We have to choose each other or this will tear us apart."

His chin rested on her shoulder as he spoke into her ear. "I don't want to lose you. I don't want the past to pull me down.

I want to move forward with you like we said. I choose you, Charli-baby." Finn tipped her chin to look at him. "I love you."

She blinked. A thousand tiny explosions erupted in her chest, bursting with pure joy. Her belly flipped and tumbled. Tears of happiness welled in her eyes. *He loves me.*

"When I saw you with Damon and thought he was . . . it ripped my heart out. I realized it hurt so much because I love you more than I've loved anyone before." His thumb wiped away the tear that dripped down her face. "Don't cry, beautiful."

"I'm just . . . you don't know how long I've waited to hear you say that." She sucked in a sharp breath, sitting up.

He turned her around to face him, pulling her body flush with his. Her slick skin slid against his. Charli's nipples tightened and peaked over his hard chest.

Finn's cock nudged her abdomen, quickly hardening. Warmth enveloped her, glowing from within. Strong hands wrapped around her face, guiding her lips against his. Tendrils of want uncurled from her center, winding their way through every cell. The heaviness of yearning urged her on. A fog of desire settled between them in a haze. His tongue dipped into her mouth. Tasting. Seeking. Reclaiming.

She raked her teeth over his bottom lip. Groaning, his hands slid over her bare thighs, over her ass. He squeezed. A possessive bolt of lust shot through her.

"I love you," he said, his voice gravelly.

She kissed him again. Sliding her legs either side of him, she lifted herself up to straddle his erection. Tilting her hips, she guided the tip of his cock into her slick pussy lips. He glided inside her soaked flesh as a feeling of *home* rushed over her.

"Fuuuuuck!" He jerked as she slowly lowered herself over him.

His eyes snapped to hers, lips parted. Everything else disappeared into those brown pools locked on her.

Raking her nails over his chest, she slowly began to move. She rode him up and down as he hissed in pleasure. He leaned forward and took her nipple into his mouth as she continued to fuck him. Water spilled out of the tub with each rise and fall of her hips. Nothing mattered but the man under her. The overwhelming raw need to see him come undone rushed over her like a woman possessed. Each bated breath was a prayer—every clench of her inner walls a plea that he'd understand just how much she loved him. Their lovemaking was a wordless symphony, their erotic movements an incantation, a conjuring of souls.

"You're so goddamned perfect. So sexy." The words dripped from his lips like golden honey.

Fingers dug into her hips as he thrust harder against her. Lips locked, tangled in a dance of fevered promises. Skin blistered in brutal demand with each wet, torturous glide of his saturated body against hers. Water splashed. Steam rose. Her body was about to combust. His palm cupped her breast, flicking her nipple before pinching it. Her toes curled.

"You like it when I ride you like this?" Her voice no more than a breath.

"Fuck yes, Charli-baby. You. Only you," he repeated as if he wanted her to know she owned him as much as she belonged to him.

Pressure gathered in her center. He grabbed her hips, guiding her faster up and down over his shaft. He leaned forward, his pubic bone hitting her just where she needed it as he tugged her lip into his mouth.

"Yes. Yes. Yes," she repeated.

He dipped a hand between them, pressing on her clit. Her eyes burst wide open. A flash of light exploded in her vision as she orgasmed. Finn continued to drive into her, flicking her clit as her climax continued.

"Finn!" Every muscle clenched around him as a look of awe and love shone in his gaze.

"That's it, baby. Come for me." His words only added an extra push into the oblivion of the longest orgasm she'd ever had. Wave after wave crashed and ricocheted inside her. She soared, ecstasy rippling through her, penetrating every molecule until nothing existed but her soul drowning in bliss.

The only thing that would make this moment any better is to have her husband come with her. She gripped his shoulders, increasing her pace as she fucked him. Using all her strength to lift her hips, she rode blessed gravity as she came down over him, squeezing him again and again with her pussy.

"Fuck! Yes, baby. I'm close," Finn ground out, both hands dropping to squeeze her ass.

"Come with me. Fill me up. Give me everything," she chanted, her movements frantic, needy, and desperate.

Wild unbridled pleasure erupted through her as his arms tensed around her.

"I love you too, Finn. I love you," she cried as another wave of bliss pushed her over the edge and soaring into the abyss of euphoria.

His face contorted in controlled chaos. "Charli!" He came roaring her name. Finn's abs flexed under her hands as he pulsed inside of her, warm spurts of him filling her up. Her thighs locked around him as aftershocks pounded through her.

His mouth melded to Charli's, soft and sweet. Resting his

forehead against hers, he said, "I love you, Charli. You're it for me too."

If she'd been holding back any piece of her heart from this man, it was gone now. He'd stolen every part of her for the second time in her life. And it was the best feeling in the world.

31

FINN

Finn wrapped the fluffy towel around Charli before drying himself off. "I'll be right in after I clean up this water." He dropped another towel onto the ground to mop up some of the mess they'd made.

"Don't be too long." She smiled sleepily at him.

He bit his lip as she walked away. Finn turned to look at himself in the mirror. Droplets of moisture glistened from his hair. His eyes had that faraway quality to them. *I'm in love with my wife.* He grinned. Something else the old Finn and new version had in common. *She loves me too.* A burst of something warm and hopeful tumbled in his chest.

He finished cleaning and started the washer before rejoining his gorgeous, naked wife in bed. She was on her side with a pillow between her knees. Finn dropped his towel and slipped under the covers, molding his body to hers like two puzzle pieces designed to fit perfectly.

She lifted her head and laid it on his arm. "Finn?" she asked before she yawned and turned over, facing him. She lay at an angle, her belly resting against his side.

"Yeah?" He leaned his cheek to her head, inhaling her sweet, rich natural scent.

She traced circles with her finger over his bare chest. "Would you be open to seeing a therapist? I think maybe it could help you work through some stuff instead of holding it all in. You'd have someone neutral to talk to about everything."

A jolt of panic zipped through him, quickly replaced with embarrassment. Therapy was for chicks and white people. Why would he want to go talk about his feelings with a stranger? He had a hard enough time verbalizing them with his wife. No. He didn't need that. "Nah. That's not for me. I have you. You're all I'll ever need. We can do this together— just the two of us. We're a team, remember?"

"I know, but sometimes it can help having someone from the outside looking in." She dropped her palm to his pec.

"How about we shelve that idea for now?" He kissed her head and rested his head against the pillow.

"You'll talk to me?"

"Promise."

She seemed to accept his words. Her breathing evened out a few minutes later as she drifted off to sleep in his arms. The curtains were closed, save for a sliver of moonlight that passed through illuminating a portion of her face. He took the time to study her profile. From this angle, he could make out the slope of her forehead, the dip to her nose, and a few of her darker freckles. Her long eyelashes dusted over her fair cheeks. She was gorgeous. *And all mine.*

He stayed like that for an hour, relishing the feel of her in his arms. But just like most other nights, sleep evaded him. Slipping his arm out from under her, he was careful not to wake her as he quietly grabbed a pair of grey sweatpants and a matching hoodie from the chair in the corner and left the room. He slid on a pair of shoes, picked a set of keys, and locked the house behind him as he headed towards the dark garage.

The sun wouldn't be up for a few hours. Stars were scattered across the sky. The distant sound of an owl hooted in the otherwise silent night. He entered and flicked the light on, going straight for the leather journal. He sighed, the fog of his breath creating a small cloud in the freezing space. He carried it back to the house and flipped through the pages.

Finn was a man of few words, and that was no different when writing, it seemed. This journal appeared to be an outlet for him. *Or a place I kept my secrets.* That thought had him hesitating. Did he want to read on? What if he found something else that would disrupt the fragile peace he and Charli had made? They were in a good place right now. She wouldn't blame him for his past choices when he couldn't remember them, would she? *No.*

But damn, this was his only direct access to the memories of his past locked somewhere inside his head. He turned the page and read on.

I fucked up. I fucked up and I don't know how to fix this.

Shit. Maybe he should just close the book now. If he didn't know, he couldn't be responsible for it, right? Damn it! There was no way his curiosity would let this rest. Finn took a deep breath, steeling himself as he continued.

I'm almost seven thousand miles away from Charli and I still managed to fuck up her life. She was attacked the other night. I wasn't there. I wasn't there to protect her . . . And worst of all, it's all my fault she was targeted.

What. The. Fuck? Finn slammed the book shut and tossed it onto the coffee table like it was on fire. His chest heaved as he bolted to his feet. Pacing back and forth, he pulled the ends of his hair.

"What the fuck did you do, Finn?" He cursed.

Maybe I didn't mean it like that. Perhaps I just blamed myself for not being here when she needed me. His stomach dipped, bile rising in his throat at the words repeated in his head. *It was my fault she was targeted. Targeted.*

He sunk to the ground defeated, his head in his hands. "What did I do?" He slammed his fist against his head again and again. "Why can't I remember?"

The pain did nothing to jolt his memory. He sat there alone with the weight of his past choices bearing down on him, snuffing out his hope that there would be smooth sailing from here on out. His heart squeezed tight in a fist of regret and guilt. Staring at his open palms, he said, "What have I done?"

How could he have done something to put Charli in a position to be harmed in the worst way? What kind of man was he? Maybe Charli would be better off without him. He shook his head. No. He'd spend the rest of his life making this up to her. He'd protect her with his life. But there was no way he could tell her about this.

He picked up the worn journal, searching for any more details to help him, but the remaining pages were blank. He ran back out to the garage and dropped the book in a metal garbage can. Flicking the cap off a container of lighter fluid, he poured some over the journal before dropping a match. Flames burst over the pages, eating them up, distorting them until nothing was left but ash. This was one secret he'd take to the grave so that he and Charli could have a fighting chance. That old Finn was gone. It was time he accepted that. He'd make up for his past sins, both known and unknown. They would move forward. As long as the past didn't come back to haunt him.

32
──────

CHARLI

After another week, Charli and Finn had found a rhythm to their daily schedules. Finn's lips pressed against her cheek, waking her up. He smelled like he was fresh out of the shower, clean with an amber musk. She smiled and opened her eyes.

He handed her a cup of ginger tea. She sat, gratefully accepting the gift. "Made you some toast too, if you want?" He set the plate on the bedside table.

"I like this breakfast-in-bed thing. What time is it?"

He lifted his watch. "Noon."

"I overslept. You should have woken me." She sipped her tea. It was the perfect temperature.

"You need your rest. You're growing my baby boy. Besides, it was my fault you were up so late." He winked.

"Several orgasms before bed is my favorite way to be put to sleep." She grinned at what had become their nightly routine after work. He'd run her a bath, massage her body, and then when she couldn't take it anymore, he'd give it to her until she was boneless and limp, falling asleep in his arms.

Though he'd only take her in two positions with her growing belly: from behind or with her riding on top, because he'd read on some website those were the only comfortable ones for pregnant women.

"I'll keep that in mind." He smirked. "You sure it's still safe? With the baby and all?"

"Yes." She nodded. "You know there is something we haven't discussed?"

His eyes flicked to hers, brows drawn together worriedly. "What's that?"

"We haven't picked out a name for him."

Finn blew out a breath, his shoulders relaxing as he came to sit on the edge of the bed, facing her. "What about Ford?"

"Like the car?" She scrunched her nose skeptically.

"It's a cool name for a kid."

"How about Noah?"

"Like the ark? No." He shook his head.

She laughed. "What else you got?"

He thought for a moment, looking around the room before he turned back to her. "How about Jamison?"

"Hmmm. I kinda like that. We could call him James or Jamie for short."

"Or J," he offered.

"We'll keep it as our top choice for now, but let's stay open to new ideas."

He leaned in, lifting her T-shirt up to expose her belly. He pressed his hands to either side of her stomach and spoke against her skin. "What do you think about that, little man? Are you a Jamison?" He chuckled.

Flutters filled her belly as a few rapid kicks pulsed in her abdomen.

Finn's laughter stopped abruptly as his eyes widened. "Was that . . .?"

She smiled and nodded. "You felt him?"

Finn kissed her belly. When he pulled away, his wide grin nearly blinded her. Excitement danced in his eyes, wonder and awe tangling in his expression. "I guess he likes the name we picked out."

"Or he likes his daddy's voice."

Finn's eyes grew glassy as he turned his attention to her. Her heart squeezed at the raw emotion pouring from her husband. He climbed over her and kissed her mouth.

"Thank you for this. For being my wife. For growing our son inside you. For being the most amazing woman I've ever known."

Tears were welling in her own eyes now. She threaded her fingers through his. "Thank you for doing all this with me. For giving me a chance. For loving me."

"I'll always love you. You're my true north, remember? I'll always find my way back to you."

She leaned forward, capturing his lips with her own. Demanding and needy. Wrapping her arms round his neck, she pulled him closer. He slipped in next to her, always so careful of her growing belly. His mouth remained locked with hers. Their tongues tangled and teeth nipped.

Finn pulled away, lowering the sheets to expose her legs. He lifted her shirt over her belly as he settled between her thighs. A wave of self-consciousness barreled through her. She grasped his shoulders, halting his descent.

"What is it?" He furrowed his brow.

"I just . . . I don't want you to do that."

He quirked his brow. "You don't want me to go down on you? Did I do a bad job before?"

"No! No. Nothing like that. You were wonderful. Amazing."

"Then why haven't you let me do it all week?"

She shifted her shirt down and covered her face with her hands, heat rising to her cheeks.

"Hey, what is it? You can tell me anything."

"It's stupid."

"Sweetheart, tell me." He pulled her hands away from her face.

"I can't reach down there anymore. I can barely see to shave my legs." She flicked her gaze to his, and the bastard was smiling. "You think this is funny?"

He chuckled. "You think I'll care that you have some body hair?"

"Well . . . yeah. And the giant basketball above my va-jay-jay."

His smile disappeared as he lifted her shirt once again. "This is the body of a goddess. This gorgeous, swollen belly . . ." He kissed her stomach. ". . . is growing a human life. And these"—he pointed to the stretch marks that had begun appearing on her skin despite her faithful use of lotion—"these are Jamison marks. It's his tattoo. The mark of a warrior." He kissed each one gently.

Tears welled in her eyes for the second time, his words and actions squelching any embarrassment she'd had.

"And this pussy." He dipped his fingers inside her slick folds. She gasped, her hips jolting upwards.

He bent his head to her sex, inhaling. "This is the door to heaven. The portal of life. And no real man cares if it has some bushes or a whole damn forest outside."

His tongue laved between her folds. She moaned, fisting the sheets on the bed. He fucked her with his fingers while swirling her clit with his tongue.

She'd never felt more worshiped, more beautiful than in this moment. "Finn," she begged.

"You're so fucking delicious." He sucked her clit into his

mouth and hummed at the same time he added another finger. His digits hit the magic spot inside her. Charli's orgasm detonated like a bomb exploding inside her, destroying everything else in its path except the pure bliss that rocketed through her.

"Fuck! Finn!"

"That's it, baby." He crawled alongside her, pulling her against his chest. He kissed her, her essence still on his lips.

Her breathing slowed, and her eyes drooped. Riding a cloud of sunshine, she snuggled into him.

"If it bothers you, I can help. But don't shave for me. I like you just the way you are, whatever that way may be." Finn traced his fingers over her back.

"You'd help me?" She tipped her head to look at him.

"Of course. Is that what you want?"

She nodded.

Finn got up and took her hand. "Come on, sweet thing. Let me take care of you."

She followed him into the bathroom. He turned on the bath as she stripped. Once it was full enough, he motioned her inside. He sat on the edge, picking up the bottle of soap. She lifted the first leg out of the water. Finn gripped it with his hand, eyes locked on his task. He squirted some soap into his palm before rubbing it over her tender folds and the outside of her pussy. She shivered with his gentle touch. He grabbed the shaver, dunking it into the water before gliding it over her flesh. Taking care with the razor, his hands swept along her legs making sure he didn't miss a spot. It shouldn't have been erotic, but it was. The way he took tender care of her. How he'd accepted her in all forms. *I truly have the best husband in the world.*

He finished the first leg, glancing up to her as he switched to the second. "What?"

She smiled. "I'm just thinking about what I did to deserve such an amazing man."

The light in his eyes dimmed before he looked away, bringing the shaver up her other leg. "I'm just doing what any decent man would. I'm the lucky one here." He finished the last part of her thigh. "Spread your legs apart. Let me see that pretty pussy you want shaved."

She obeyed. But damn if she didn't feel exposed. The blush returned to her cheeks.

"Are we doing all the way or do you want a landing strip?" He squirted some of the soap in his hand before he massaged it over her sex.

Desire pooled in her core. She'd just had an orgasm, but her body was ready to go again. "You pick."

He smirked and dipped the razor in the tub before bringing it to her skin. He carefully swiped it around her sex. He was thorough, pulling her lower lips apart.

He cleaned the shaver and set it on the edge of the tub. Then he splashed some water over her. Two fingers slipped inside her. His gaze captured hers in their dark pull. Goose bumps rose on her flesh as he worked in and out of her. Her pussy was still swollen and sensitive from earlier. She bucked her hips.

"Finn?" She closed her eyes, as he flicked his thumb over her clit. Nearing the edge of the cliff, she begged, "Make me come."

Cold air tickled her hard nipples, a contrast to the hot water of the bath and the liquid fire spreading through her limbs.

He added another finger, stretching her in delicious pleasure.

"Whatever my goddess wants, she gets." He pressed his thumb to her clit as he fucked her unapologetically with his curled fingers. He used his free hand to pinch her nipple, sending a shockwave of ecstasy tearing through her.

He pulled his hands from inside her just before she came. "All done."

She closed her legs and groaned in protest. "I want you."

Finn removed the plug from the bath. It began to drain. "Rinse off and then we'll continue what we started in the bedroom." He winked before getting up and walking out.

God damn, this man. This truly was their second chance. Her belly flipped as the baby inside kicked repeatedly.

She placed her hand over her swollen abdomen and smiled as joy burst in her chest, blanketing her in the warmth of contentment. She had a man who worshipped her, and a healthy growing baby in her womb. *My life couldn't possibly get better than this.* A shiver wound through her. She'd thought the same once before. *But this time is different.* She just knew it.

33

CHARLI

Charli stirred awake, the dull ache in her back alerting her that it was time to switch positions. She rolled to the other side, adjusting the pillow between her thighs for extra support. Reaching out her hand, it met nothing but cool sheets where her husband was supposed to be. She blinked her eyes open, searching the dark room.

Where is Finn?

She slipped out of bed, grabbing a silk bathrobe from the catch-all chair in the corner and tied it around herself.

Did he leave me alone?

Opening the door, she walked down the hall towards the sliver of light that escaped the baby's room. The door was cracked open. She peeked inside, pressing on the knob to open the door farther. The breath stalled in her lungs and her heartbeat faltered. Knees weak, she took in the sight before her.

Finn had his back to her, bent over the mostly finished crib. Screwdriver in his hand, he twisted his veined arm. His grey sweatpants hung low on his waist, and his shirt was nowhere to be found. Her eyes wandered over the space for the first time in days. He'd put everything else together. The small dresser by the window with the changing table on top. The rocking chair sat in the corner next to a smaller side table. A bouncy contraption for the baby that Jasmine insisted she buy stood in the other corner.

She pressed her fingers to her open mouth. Her chest squeezed tight, love bursting like a bubble of sunshine in her rib cage. Tears welled in her eyes.

Damn these hormones. She sniffed.

Finn jumped and spun around, the screwdriver wielded in his hand like a weapon. Relief blanketed his expression as his shoulders lowered. "Hey." He ran a hand over the back of his neck, something he did when he was embarrassed or self-conscious.

"You did all this?" She motioned to the organized baby furniture.

"Yeah. I just figured I should get it all ready so you can put things where you want them. Get everything prepared . . . Wanted it to be perfect for you." He looked at his hands.

"Finn, this is . . . Thank you." She stepped forward and wrapped her arms around him, squeezing tightly, infusing him with her gratitude. "It looks so good."

He hugged her back and kissed the top of her head before she pulled away enough to look at him.

"I have a lot of catching up to do. You're almost into your last trimester, and I feel like I missed so much." His brown eyes clouded with regret.

"The important thing is you're here now. We have plenty of time. Come to bed with me?"

He glanced to the crib. "I should finish this."

"It's the middle of the night, honey. Come on. Let's get

some sleep and you can finish tomorrow." Charli tugged his hand towards the door.

Finn hesitated.

Charli gave him what she hoped was a seductive smile as she raked her eyes down his delicious body. "Let's go. I need a midnight snack, and you're on the menu."

He smirked and dropped the tool onto the dresser. "Well, if you put it that way." He slapped her ass before following her to the bedroom, where she did exactly as she'd promised.

* * *

The next night, Charli pushed her way into the back room, the noise from the music dying down just enough to hear herself think. Finding the clean towels she was after, she took a moment to stretch. Bending at her waist as far as she could —which wasn't much—she twisted, trying to stave off the back pain. Being pregnant was beginning to suck. Yes, she couldn't wait until her little boy was in her arms, but damn if it wasn't getting harder to do basic tasks.

It will all be worth it.

She stood, rolling her head from side to side. A hand clamped over her shoulders. She jumped and gasped.

"Just me, Charli-baby," Finn said, massaging her sore muscles gently as he handed her a glass of water with the other.

She took it from him and gulped down the cold liquid. "Thank you."

"You okay?"

"Yeah, just came for some clean rags." She waved them in her hand.

He wrapped his arm around her waist and guided her

back to the bar, giving her a kiss on the cheek as he went to fulfill more drink orders.

Charli did a sweep of the room. The waitress Sandy was busy delivering a tray of drinks to a large table. A small group had gathered around the bar. That was where she was needed. She'd been working here since she was twenty-one and was fast and efficient after all these years. She and Finn had been in sync, even managing to learn a few party tricks with slinging bottles. But Finn had forgotten all of that. He was still a newbie at making drinks, which meant he was slower. Charli started on one end. She'd work her way down the line.

"What can I get ya?" she asked a man with a plaid shirt.

"Two Coors Light."

She winced. Might as well have ordered water. She grabbed the bottles from the fridge and took his payment before moving on.

A few customers later, Finn's angry voice rose above the music. "That is a manhattan. If I make it again, it's gonna taste the same! Don't like it, order something different."

Charli handed a woman her cosmo and turned to figure out what was going on.

A big guy towered over the woman by his side, arms crossed as he leaned in towards Finn, pointing at the drink in question on the timber counter. "This tastes like shit."

Finn stepped forward. She placed a hand on his arm. His muscles tensed, but he turned towards her.

"What's the problem here?" she asked Finn.

"This guy ordered a manhattan and says it doesn't taste right." Finn crossed his arms, mirroring the big man in front of him.

"Okay, let's see what we can do." She took the drink off the counter and dumped it down the sink. She grabbed Finn's arm and led him a little farther away, grabbing a mixing glass. "Make another."

"It's gonna taste the fucking same," he argued.

"Humor me? It's bad for business if you argue with the customers without at least trying to appease them once."

He grumbled and shook his head, picking up the bottle of vermouth.

Charli pressed her hand to the top of the glass. Speaking loud enough for only him to hear, she said, "Okay, that's your first mistake. You have to add three or four drops of the bitters first."

He took one slow, deep breath and nodded.

She handed him the small glass bottle of dark liquid. "That's bound to happen when you're learning. If you ever feel unsure, just ask. I'm here to help and happy to do so."

After dripping the bitters in, he measured out one ounce of rouge vermouth and dumped it into the mixing glass. Next, he picked up a bottle of whiskey.

"This is the one you used before?"

"Yeah." He held out the bottle to her.

"It's the wrong one. For manhattans we use rye whiskey." She grabbed the Wild Turkey 101 Rye and handed it to him.

"Oh." He took it and measured out two ounces before adding it to the mixture. He grabbed a spoon and then topped it off with ice. Stirring it, he flicked a glance to her. "I'm sorry."

A loud burst of laughter rang out, and Finn's body jolted. His eyes scanned the room as his shoulders bunched to his ears.

She placed her hand on his lower back, leaning in. "There's nothing to be sorry about. You got this. It's a lot of different recipes to memorize. You'll get there." She offered him a smile.

He nodded and grabbed a stemmed glass.

She picked up the handle of the spoon and continued to stir. "Because the cocktail doesn't usually come with ice, we stir it until we get the dilution we want. You'll learn to feel it out, but to start, I'd stir about thirty to forty seconds." She passed him the glass after adding a strainer. "All set to taste."

He grabbed a straw, dipped it into the drink, and pressed his thumb to the top to lock some liquid in before bringing it to his mouth. He nodded. "Tastes almost the same to me."

"Almost." She winked.

He strained the amber liquid into the glass before sliding it across the bar to their waiting customers.

The woman sipped it and nodded towards the big guy at her side. She smiled. "It's perfect. Thank you."

Finn nodded and grumbled, "You're welcome."

Sandy came back to the bar with an empty tray.

"Can you manage the bar for a few minutes?" Charli asked her.

"Sure, no problem," Sandy agreed.

Charli grabbed Finn's hand. "Come here for a sec."

He followed her to the back room. She opened the large walk-in refrigerator door and pushed him ahead of her. The blast of cool air was like a breath of fresh air. The bar could get stifling, depending on how many people were inside, and lately she'd been getting even hotter because of the pregnancy hormones.

"What are we doing in here?" Finn gave her a sly grin.

She smacked his chest playfully. "Not that, so get your mind out of the gutter, dirty boy."

His laugh seemed to ease some of the tension from his body.

She walked into his arms, pressing her cheek against his chest. A staccato beat pulsed against her ear. She pulled away and pressed her hand against his pec. "Your heart is racing."

He shrugged. "What can I say? You have that effect on me."

She'd love to believe that was the case, but he'd been jumpy all night and getting short with customers. This was something else. "Are you feeling a little overstimulated by the noise and the crowd?"

His gaze wavered before he shifted on his feet.

"Since your first deployment, crowds were difficult for you." She pressed, hoping he realized some of this wasn't completely new.

"They were?"

She nodded. "Why don't you take the rest of the night off? You can come pick me up at midnight." They only stayed open until two on Friday and Saturday nights.

He pinched the bridge of his nose, the florescent lights highlighting the dark circles under his eyes.

"You need rest."

He sighed.

"Are you having trouble sleeping?" Finding him working on the crib in the middle of the night surrounded by other pieces of completed furniture told her he hadn't been getting as much sleep as she'd thought.

He nodded again, turning to look towards a shelf of beer.

"Is it because of the baby? Or are you having more nightmares?" Charli ran her hand over his rough stubble.

He returned his attention to her, his shoulders drooping. "Both. Neither. I don't know. It's just hard for me to fall asleep."

"Well, why don't you go home and try to take a nap until I get off?"

"I don't want to leave you. You're the one who should be home relaxing." He placed his hand on her belly.

"I'm fine. Let me do this for you, while I still can. Lean on me and I lean on you, remember? This is your turn to do the leaning." She reached up on tiptoes to kiss him.

He groaned and squeezed her tighter against him. "Fine. I'll be back to get you at eleven thirty. I'll help close and you can sit down and relax. I'll run you another bubble bath and give you a massage. How does that sound?"

She smiled. "That sounds like perfect teamwork, Mister Reed."

His eyes glittered with affection and desire. "I love you so fucking much."

"Right back at ya." She winked playfully.

He gave her one more searing kiss before taking her hand and walking out to the bar with her. "See you at eleven thirty."

"Only four more hours." She kissed his cheek.

"Go easy on your mama." He bent to kiss her belly.

The gesture melted her insides to goo.

He waved to Sandy before heading out the door. Charli slipped right into the groove next to Sandy. The crowd was dying down and mellowing out.

"Charli!" a familiar voice squealed from behind her.

Charli turned around in time for Emma to wrap her arms around her.

"What are you doing here? I thought you were in Japan."

"I was. Me and the guys had a show in Boston yesterday, and I have a whole twenty-four hours before I have to be on a bus to New York City. I thought I'd stop and see Papa." Emma motioned over her shoulder to Solomon Owusu.

The Ghanaian man waved to Charli, his warm, white smile contrasting with his dark brown skin.

Charli waved back before returning her attention to Emma. A loose strand of her friend's blonde hair fell across her fair skin. Charli reached out and pinched the blue-and-purple-tipped ends between her fingers. "I like the new colors."

Emma beamed. "Aren't they fun? My manager thought they'd add to the whole rocker-chick credibility."

"Is this the same manager who's been after you for a date?" Charli asked.

Emma looked at the ceiling and shrugged. "She is a gorgeous and persistent woman, but I don't mix business and pleasure anymore."

"Uh-huh." Charli winked.

Emma shook her head. "Seriously!"

"Okay." Charli lifted her hands up, palms forward. "Where is Link?"

Emma stiffened and crossed her arms over her chest, the gleam in her eye distinguishing at the mere mention of her stepbrother's name. "He found out I was home, so he took the opportunity to disappear again. I don't think I've seen him since last Christmas when we were forced to be in the same room for Papa." Pain flashed in her eyes.

Charli laid her hand on her friend's shoulder gently.

Emma shook her head, as if she could rid the unrequited feelings she had for her stepbrother that way. It was no secret to Charli that Emma had a huge crush on the man. On the rare occasion she did see them in the same room, Emma couldn't keep the truth hidden. It was written across her face. *Maybe that's why he stays away.*

"Anyways. Tell me about you. How are you and Finn doing?"

Charli grabbed Solomon's usual drink and didn't even try to hide her smile. "It's going really good."

Emma snickered. "You mean you've been getting some good dick."

Charli smacked her friend in the arm. "You have no filter."

Emma shrugged. "That's what you love about me. Now give me all the dirty details."

Charli handed Solomon his drink before walking back to Emma. "It was rough there for a while. But I think things are finally starting to settle down, and I'm hopeful for our future."

Finn had communicated with her tonight. He'd done as she suggested without a fight. This teamwork thing was working out. He really was trying. He'd fallen in love with her all over again. And maybe this time, they could do it right—mixing the old with the new to create an even better relationship than they'd had before. Finn was more open, their communication was getting better, and the sex was as hot as ever. This was the second chance they never knew they needed.

34

FINN

Finn kissed Charli's shoulder before he rolled over in bed, checking the time. Three in the morning. Sleep was yet again evading him. He turned back to his sleeping wife. She was curled on her side, hugging a monster of a pillow. She'd fallen asleep while he massaged her tonight, snoring lightly before he'd even finished. Guilt sunk in his stomach like a stone. She trusted him, and he was keeping a secret from her after he'd promised not to. But things were just starting to get good between them. He couldn't remember what had actually happened. And for all he knew, he'd just blamed himself for not being there. *Then why did I burn the journal?*

He sat up, rubbing a hand over his face with a yawn. Exhaustion weighed heavily on his shoulders. *Why can't I sleep?*

Finn tiptoed out of the room quietly. After slipping into the bathroom, he flicked the light on. He relieved himself and then opened the cabinet and removed the bottle of pills his doctor had prescribed that were supposed to help stabilize his moods. He shook his head. The only thing they did was make him numb. Maybe that's why he couldn't sleep. He tossed the bottle into the garbage bin and made his way down to the living room.

Stretching out on the couch, he picked up the book he'd been reading, *What to Expect When You're Expecting*. After flipping the light on, he opened to where he'd left off.

Finished reading the chapter, he laid the book on his chest. It was amazing to understand the process of pregnancy and what changes were happening week by week. But to have his own wife going through it was extraordinary. Would his son have her eyes or his? Would Jamison have darker skin like his daddy? Or a mix of the two of them?

Daddy. I'm gonna be a father. The realization never got less exciting—tinged with terror. He closed his eyes, trying to imagine his son's face.

"We could extend your trip another week and go see a buddy of mine in Oregon to catch some Dungeness crab," Smithson said, turning to look at Finn from the driver's side.

"Tempting offer. But I need to get back to Charli."

"You know if I called her, she'd tell you to stay and enjoy yourself." Smithson chuckled.

Finn laughed. "Yeah, that woman would do anything for me, even to her own detriment. Nah, working on her feet at the bar is getting harder for her the more pregnant she is. I need to go home to help her relax a little. Plus, I'm missing her something fierce."

The words came out with a resounding warning blaring in his mind. He'd been here before. No—he was dreaming again. He turned to look at his friend, but instead of Smithson sitting in the driver's seat, it was Charli. She had tears streaming down her face as she held a bundle in her arms. My son.

"Please, Finn. Help us!" she cried.

"Stop the truck, baby," he pleaded, reaching out to her. But she was too far away.

She shook her head, eyes pleading. "I can't. You're the one driving."

He turned, and sure enough the wheel was on his side of the car now. He pressed the brake as hard as he could, but nothing happened. His muscles were too weak, his body sluggish.

"Stop! Finn, Please!" Charli begged.

The baby in her arms wailed. Frantically, he stomped his foot on the brake. He knew what was coming next. He had to stop the car before—

Tires screeched. Glass crashed and shattered. The truck groaned on impact in an eerie metallic scream. They flipped.

"Charli!" He reached out for her, but his vision was darkening. His hand touched something wet and sticky. Drawing it back, he realized it was blood. The car was saturated in it.

"Charli!" he screamed.

Her head lay against the broken window, shards of glass embedded in the side of her face, terrified brown eyes locked on his. "You did this. It's all your fault."

"Charli! Baby! Nooooo!"

Finn bolted upright, sweat pouring over his body. His chest heaved as he sucked in oxygen. Violent panic took hold as his heart raced.

Soft, warm arms wrapped around him. "Finn?"

He pulled Charli close, inhaling her amber scent, needing her to ground him.

It was just a dream. Charli's safe. The baby is safe.

"Shhhh," she soothed. "It's just a nightmare."

He threaded his fingers through her hair and tucked her head to his chest. He should be the one protecting her. Instead, here she was holding him once again as he broke down, his mind betraying him.

She deserves so much more.

Anger rose, sloshing out and spilling over him. He clamped his eyes closed. Maybe his subconscious was trying to tell him something. Maybe his wife and child would only be hurt by him. *Or maybe I'm the one who put Charli in danger to begin with.*

35

CHARLI

Charli walked into The Oyster. The scent of old and new books wrapped around her, pulling her farther into the shop. The large sculpture in the middle was what had caught her attention first. A woman reading a novel, her expression one of fascination and pure joy as her hand reached out as if to turn the page. The entire sculpture was made from pages of books.

Charli scanned the rows of novels. Smaller sculptures were scattered around the store, some more realistic like beehives. Others were more fantastical like a mermaid perched in the folds of an open book with one page textured to look like waves.

"Good afternoon. Can I help you?" a soft voice asked from the left. A woman stood behind an L-shaped desk cluttered with several books stacked with no rhyme or reason.

Charli approached the woman with a smile. "Hello. I'm looking for some books on breastfeeding. Would you have something like that here?"

The woman tapped her bottom lip with a neon-yellow

nail. "Yes. I think we do in the parenting section. I'll show you." She slipped off the stool and walked ahead of Charli. The clicking noise drew Charli's attention down to the golden yellow retriever by her side with a vest marking him as a service dog.

"I'm Pippa, by the way." She flicked her twisted hair over her shoulder.

"I'm Charli."

Pippa led her down the narrow aisle, turning sideways seemingly to avoid knocking the books with her curvy hips. "Yes, right here. There's a few to choose from. Is there something else you are looking for?"

"No, this is perfect. Thanks."

"No problem. Let me know if you need anything." Pippa continued through the row with her dog following right behind and turned left out of sight.

Charli ran her finger over the titles and picked up two out of the three. She checked her watch. She still had some time to kill before collecting Finn from one of his many appointments at the VA. She moved through the aisles, grabbing a romance novel that seemed interesting, before making her way through what she assumed was the self-help section. Each row had a quote to hint at the theme rather than actual titles. This one was, "In life, nobody will help you until you're willing to help yourself." Charli shifted the books in her arms, continuing until her eyes caught on one in particular. She picked it up, scanning the back. *This would be perfect for Finn.*

She added it to her pile and went to the register.

Pippa put on a pair of blue glasses and smiled. "Find everything you need?"

"And then some." Charli laughed.

"That's usually how it works." Pippa giggled as she

scanned the books before slipping them into a paper bag one at a time.

"Are you the owner?" Charli asked.

Pippa nodded. "For a few years now."

"I can't believe I haven't been in here. The artwork is pretty unique."

Pippa bit her bottom lip. "Thanks."

"Did you do them?"

A tentative smile curved the corner of Pippa's mouth up. "Yeah. It's just a hobby."

"Wow. Well, they are pretty amazing. Do you sell them?"

"When someone's interested." She handed over the bag with Charli's purchases. "Fifty thirty-two."

Charli passed over her credit card. "Thank you. I'll definitely be back again sometime soon."

"I appreciate your business." Pippa returned the card with a receipt. "Have a good day."

"You too." Charli waddled out the front door—because that's what it had come to. Walking normally was no longer possible with how big her belly had gotten. The crisp November air sent a chill through her. She pulled her coat closer together. Charli looked both ways and crossed the street. She needed something warm to drink from the Stardust Café.

The door opened and a woman rushed out, bumping into Charli.

"Sorry," Charli apologized.

"Excuse you," the other woman said, looking up from her phone.

Charli's breath caught, her belly churning with a mixture of jealousy and anger. *Laura.*

"Oh hi, Charlotte. Hard to avoid crashing into you these

days. My god you are huge." Laura's eyes darted to Charli's stomach as her eyes widened.

Bitch. "Yeah, well, that's what happens when Finn puts his baby inside me."

Laura's cheeks tinted with pink. "Yeah. I saw him the other day. He stopped by my house and we had a great chat. We got real cozy. Gee, I hope everything is okay at home these days. Tell him I said hi. Or maybe I'll just text him and see what he's up to later." Laura smiled with an evil gleam in her eye.

"What the fuck is wrong with you? Why have you always been such a bitch? Are you mad at yourself for losing your chance with him? Sorry, but that ship has sailed," Charli snapped, anger roiling inside her.

Laura seemed momentarily stunned, her mouth opening and then closing like a fish before she huffed. "I could never be jealous of you. Despite what you have him believing, you're still the same trailer-trash girl with a crazy brother who I went to high school with. Finn deserves better."

A mixture of shame and rage overflowed, sloshing inside Charli. She closed her fist. God, she wanted to hit this skank so bad. "Go fuck yourself." Charli turned and rushed into the café, the bells juggling above the door joining the condescending laughter from Laura outside.

Remy was behind the counter. She looked up, her smile fading as Charli got closer. "Hey, mama, you okay?"

Charli took a deep breath, fighting the tears burning the back of her eyes. "These damn hormones have turned me into a water fountain."

"I don't miss those days. Let me get you a drink and a cookie. That will help you feel better," Remy offered.

Charli nodded. "Can I have a decaf pumpkin spice latte and two double chocolate chip, peanut butter cookies?"

"Coming right up. Why don't you have a seat? I'll bring it to you."

Charli pulled a twenty out of her pocket and slid it over the counter to Remy as she nodded. She found a seat and took off the scarf from around her neck before setting her bag of books on the ground next to her.

A few minutes later, Remy dropped off her goodies and sat across from her with a sigh.

"Long day?" Charli asked, taking a bite of her cookie.

"Began at four. Phoenix has decided that he doesn't like to sleep anymore."

Charli cringed. "Sorry."

"Eh, I had to be up at five anyways to start the bread. We've had more orders for loaves, so I added that to the menu for special order." Remy picked a loose thread from her pants.

"I would rather do the late nights than the early morning." Charli took a sip of her coffee. She'd just pretend it had caffeine.

"That's why you run the bar." Remy chuckled. "Mikel was going to invite Finn and you over for dinner some night, but we wanted to make sure he was settled enough."

Charli nodded. Warmth flooded her chest and tears pricked the back of her eyes. She wasn't alone in this small town, and she and Finn had people beyond his family who cared for them. "That sounds great. Text me and we can plan it."

Finn was leaning on the side of the building with his arms crossed when Charli pulled outside the VA. The baseball cap he had on was turned to the back. He looked up when she parked next to him.

"Let me drive." He opened her door.

"I'm capable."

He eyed her belly. A wave of insecurity rippled through her—Laura's words coming back to sting her. Was she a whale after all?

"It's not safe. Your belly nearly touches the wheel. If we got in an accident, you'd be safer in the passenger seat."

Oh. Of course, he's worried about the baby and my safety. She nodded and unbuckled before she climbed out and walked around the other side. His hand rested on her lower back as he opened the passenger side door and helped her in.

"Thank you."

He lifted her hand to his lips and kissed it before shutting her in. After he climbed in the driver's side, he drove them towards home.

"How did your appointment go?" she asked.

"Fine."

"Did you discuss your flashbacks?"

Finn sighed. "Did you end up getting the book you wanted?" He motioned to the bag at her feet, completely ignoring her question.

She tucked her hair behind her ear. Reaching down to grab the bag took more effort than it should have. "Yes. And I picked up one I thought might be helpful for you." She pulled out the PTSD workbook.

His eyes flicked to her purchase before focusing back on the road. His jaw clenched as his hands squeezed tight on the steering wheel. "I don't have PTSD."

"You exhibit a lot of the symptoms," she said carefully.

"How can I when I don't remember any of what happened?"

"What about your nightmares?"

He shook his head. "They're just dreams. Probably not real."

"Did you tell your doctor about them?"

"No."

"Finn—"

"I don't have PTSD," he repeated.

"You have panic attacks."

"So do a lot of people," he argued.

"What about trying some alternative ways to get the memories back? Like, maybe hypnotherapy?"

"I'm already going to the doctor every other day. I don't need any more fucking appointments!"

Charli sighed, frustrated. "You don't want to see a therapist, and you obviously don't want any more doctor visits. So I thought maybe trying something different or even just taking a look at this book could help."

"Charlotte—" He slammed his hand on the wheel.

He *never* called her by her full first name. Not unless he was angry or something was really bothering him. Well, tough luck. He couldn't fault her for trying to help. She wasn't going to walk on eggshells again. He promised he'd work through this with her. And she was going to hold him to his word. "You promised me we'd figure this out together. I'm simply offering you a way to do that."

He remained silent.

"I ran into Laura today." *Literally. Too bad I didn't knock her over or spill something hot on her.*

Finn growled. "I thought we agreed to leave the past where it belongs?"

"She had some interesting things to say to me."

Finn shook his head and turned down their street.

"Is her number still in your phone?"

He swallowed, a flash of guilt crossing his expression. "I guess. I never deleted it."

Her nails bit into the flesh of her hands. Her body heated with a flash fire of green-tinted anger. "Is she texting you?"

"I haven't texted back." He sighed and parked in their driveway. Pulling his phone out from his pocket, he tapped on the screen. He turned the phone towards her, so she could see what he was doing before he pressed Laura's contact information. "See? No responses to her since the time I told you about. I wouldn't lie to you." Finn locked his gaze onto hers. "Show me how to delete the contact and I will."

She let out a deep breath, some of her anger dissipating. *The bitch was just trying to start trouble.* Why now after all these years? "Okay." Charli tapped the phone, effectively blocking Laura rather than just deleting the contact. She picked up the book she got for him and held it out. "Please just take a look at this before you dismiss it. I did some reading, and I think you'd be surprised to find out you have a lot of the symptoms. Hypervigilance, trouble sleeping—"

"Damn it, Charli. Can't you just leave it alone?" Finn snapped before bolting out the door. He opened hers and held out a hand to help her down. His jaw clenched again, and his muscles tensed and bunched by his ears. Anger radiated off him in waves. But his touch was gentle as he guided her to the front door, one hand on the small of her back like always. He stepped in front of her to unlock the door before ushering her inside.

Finn bent at her feet, helping her untie her shoelaces and stack her shoes neatly before standing. "I'm going for a walk to clear my head. I'll be back."

She nodded before he left out the door.

He turned. "Lock up behind me."

Charli did as he said, clicking the dead bolt into place as he left.

Sighing, she shook her head. *At least he told me this time and didn't run off without an explanation.* "He's trying." *Maybe I let my anger with Laura get the best of me and took it out on him.* "Ugh!" she screamed in frustration.

We can't do this alone. But Finn wasn't willing to read a book, never mind seek outside help. Maybe when he calmed down they could have another conversation about it. Or perhaps this whole thing was pointless. Was this the best it got for them? Riding the highs and lows of Finn's moods and whims? Could she live with that? Or would they grow resentful of each other eventually? Only time would tell.

36

FINN

Finn walked behind Charli, entering his parents' house with his hands full of desserts she'd made.

His father greeted them first, pulling Charli into a short side hug. The sight of his usually stoic father softening in his wife's presence brought a twinge to his chest.

"Happy Thanksgiving." Zeke motioned towards the kitchen. "Claire is in the kitchen. She can tell you where to put the dessert."

Charli moved down the hall, her shoulders relaxing. She seemed more at ease at his parents' than she did in their house. Ever since she'd come home with that book a few days ago, there'd been a thick layer of tension between them. *I know she's only trying to help.* But it was embarrassing. He'd had enough issues with his accident and then his choices after. He just wanted to move on and forget the bad. Talking about the past never helped anyone, never mind the fact that he couldn't even remember most of it himself. *And what I do find, I don't want to remember.*

Zeke's hand clapped over his back, shaking him from his thoughts. "How are you doing, son?"

"Good." *As I can be, considering.*

"How's everything with Charli?"

"Better."

Zeke nodded. "I'll put the game on. Bring me a beer and come join me and Mason."

And that was the end of their uncomfortable discussion.

Mason's here?

Finn headed down the hall. Feminine laughter filtered out of the bright room. The savory scent of roasting turkey and herbed vegetables grew stronger with each step he took towards the kitchen. His mother stirred a pot over the stove, looking up as he entered.

A feeling of déjà vu washed over him, halting his steps. How many times had he walked into this same scene?

Charli sat at the breakfast bar, decorating what looked to be cookies alongside a young girl.

"How about we use some orange sprinkles on this one?" Charli asked.

The little girl smiled and nodded, brushing her reddish-blonde hair from her face. "And rainbow sprinkles for the turkey cookie?"

Charli chuckled. "Sounds festive."

"Hey, sweetheart," his mother said, greeting him. A smile split her face. "You can set those on the small table by the window." She pointed to a card table covered by a brown tablecloth.

He did as she said and opened his arms for his mother's embrace. She squeezed him tight before backing up.

"Dinner won't be ready for another forty minutes."

"Okay. I'll bring Dad a drink."

"You sure you don't want to help decorate cookies?" Charli asked, offering him a tilted smile.

He hadn't decorated cookies since he was about the girl's age, maybe twelve? "No, thanks. I'm gonna watch the game with Dad."

"Boys." The little girl rolled her eyes.

Charli and Claire laughed.

"Keep thinking that way. I'm sure your daddy will be able to rest easy," Claire joked.

Charli must have read the question in his expression. "Oh, Finn, this is Aspen, Mason's daughter."

"Hi." He waved.

"Do you like chocolate chip or sugar cookies better?" Aspen asked, her eyes studying him closely.

"Uh, chocolate chip?" His answer came out more like a question.

"Did he pass inspection?" Charli teased.

"Yes. You'd have to be crazy to pass up chocolate." Aspen giggled.

"Well, I'd better leave you ladies to it." He headed to the fridge to pull out two beers, and then grabbed a third for Mason. He turned around and stopped.

Aspen stared up at him. "You don't remember me, do you?"

"No, sorry, I don't."

She searched his face for another minute. "That must be scary."

He nodded. It was fucking terrifying. Having half your life stolen from you and waking up without even knowing what you missed. One day you're just a teenager rushing into the lake naked with your friends, and the next you're a grown man with a wife and a baby on the way. *Scary* was an understatement.

"My daddy said that you might be different."

Finn's brows knit together. "Did we hang out before?"

She nodded. "You helped my dad build my tree house."

"Oh." He didn't know what else to say.

She looked towards Finn expectantly.

"Is it a cool tree house?"

She smiled, her whole face lighting up. "Yeah, there's a window seat where I sit and read my books."

"That sounds awesome."

"It is. Well, I'm gonna go finish decorating the cookies." Aspen waved and skipped away.

Charli's eyes met his. She smiled, and he gave her a wink, hopefully setting her at ease.

Finn made his way into the living room as the doorbell rang.

"Can you get that?" Zeke asked.

Finn handed the men their beers, nodding to Mason before he went to the entryway. Opening the door, two familiar faces came into view.

"Damon, Steven, glad you guys could make it." Finn stepped aside so they could enter.

Steven's hands held out a pie. "Thanks for having us. Where should we put this?"

"Kitchen, down the hall."

Steven walked ahead. Damon turned to face Finn. "Thanks for this. For giving me another chance."

Finn nodded, shifting his weight to the other foot. "Charli's in the kitchen, but us guys are watching the game. Can I get you a beer?"

"No, thanks, messes with my meds, but I'd love some coffee." Damon nodded towards the kitchen.

"I'm sure my mom's got some ready." Finn returned to the

living room as laughter rang out from the kitchen where their two new guests had disappeared.

Finn took a seat on the couch, tipping the beer to his lips, watching blankly as the football moved across the screen. He tried to focus, but he couldn't enjoy this moment. It was like he wasn't fully there. His body was going through the motions, laughing at the right time, responding with short sentences.

The buzzing sound in his head grew louder as he sat down for dinner with the family. Everyone else seemed to be enjoying their time. Mason was more reserved than the other guests, but he still had everyone breaking out into fits of giggles. Aspen seemed a lot like her father, but more inquisitive. She seemed to hang on every word Charli or Claire said, a bit of wonderment in her eyes. Damon and Steven went on and on about how delicious dinner was. It looked good, but for some reason Finn found himself forcing the food down. Everyone seemed happy to be together, sharing stories. But Finn was like an outsider looking in. He was numb. *Why am I like this?*

He drank his fourth beer, getting up to grab another.

Charli's eyes snagged on his as he stood, her brows drawn together in concern. "You okay?" she asked quietly. Still, a few sets of eyes tracked his movements.

He leaned and kissed her cheek. "Just need some air."

Dropping the glass into the recycling bin before he grabbed another beer from the fridge, he then headed out the back door. The cold November air slithered through his Henley, biting his skin. The crisp temperature was a nice break from the overly warm home. All the trees had shed their leaves, save for a few evergreens in his parents' backyard. A few big bags full of leaves sat off to the right. His mother's garden had already been ripped up, void of the vegetables she'd long ago harvested.

The door behind him opened and shut with a creak. Heavy footsteps padded closer, Mason appearing at his side.

Mason offered him a cigar.

"No, thanks." Finn pressed the glass bottle to his lips, taking another long pull of the alcohol zipping through his system, loosening him up. "Didn't know you smoked."

"Only occasionally." Mason flicked the lighter open, puffing on one end of the large cigar. "How are you doing?"

"Fantastic," Finn answered sarcastically, focusing on the worn garden gnome at the edge of his parents' privacy fence.

Mason pulled out his wallet, his beefy fingers digging out a black business card before handing it to him. "This lady is the best. Lots of experience and credibility."

Finn accepted the paper as he took another swig of his drink. His muscles grew rigid as he scanned the name. *Rebecca Cole. Veritas Counseling Services specializing in EMDR for PTSD.*

"Did Charli put you up to this?" Finn snapped, the beer in his mouth turning bitter. *Was she telling his business to anyone who would listen?*

Mason just shook his head, blowing out a cloud of smoke. "Charli didn't tell me jack shit. But from one vet to another, I can recognize the signs."

Finn pressed his beer to his temple, a migraine taking hold. "I don't fucking have a problem."

"That's what my wife said too. Two months later . . ." Mason shook his head before taking another puff of his cigar and blowing it out. Mason turned to face him, locking Finn in his steady gaze. "I was once where you were at. I know you don't think you need help. You probably think you can handle this all on your own. And maybe you're right, but maybe . . . you're wrong." He pressed the butt of the cigar out on the dirt before tucking it into his fist as if waiting to dispose of it inside.

"What do you care?"

Mason sighed and looked out at the dreary sky. "That woman on the card saved my life, saved my relationship with my daughter. You and I were friends once upon a time. Even though you don't remember me, it doesn't erase the fact that I want the best for you. It can't hurt to try it out. Man up and do it for your girl, and that little boy in her womb, until you can do it for yourself." With that, Mason turned and went back into the house.

Finn stared at the paper in his hands and shook his head. How could he talk to a stranger when he couldn't even be completely honest with his wife? "Fuck," he grumbled, squeezing the bridge of his nose. His head was pounding. He crumpled the paper and tossed it in the firepit off to the side. *The only woman I need to talk to is my wife.* Hopefully she'd understand.

The door creaked open again before warm arms slipped over his waist from behind. Notes of honey and amber wrapped around him almost as tightly as Charli's hug. "You doing okay?"

"Just have a headache."

She threaded her hand through his and led him over to the lawn furniture. Settling onto the couch, she wrapped her sweater tighter around her and motioned to her lap. "Lie down and put your head here."

He set his drink on the glass table to the side and lay on his back, his legs hanging over the arm of the other end. Her belly pressed into the side of his face as Charli's fingers massaged his temples.

He groaned. Her touch was like magic, easing the tension and dulling the pain. She worked her fingers all over his scalp, down to the base of his neck and upper shoulders before returning to his temples.

"I love you," he said.

"I love you too, always."

He hoped she remembered that promise, because his confession would surely put it to the test.

37

CHARLI

Charli rolled over in bed and groaned. The blankets were the perfect temperature and the mattress and pillow so cozy. However, the baby jumping on her bladder was not ideal. She pushed the covers off her and waddled to the bathroom. After relieving herself, she washed her hands. The reflection in the mirror stared back at her, rosy cheeked, hair mussed. Her belly stretched against the fabric of Finn's old T-shirt. She lifted the material and turned sideways. *Twenty-six weeks today.* She smoothed a hand over the taut skin. *We're more than halfway there, buddy.* She craned her head to the side. "Not sure how much room I have left for you to grow." She chuckled.

Charli brushed her teeth and then went back to the bedroom to change. No sense in returning to bed now.

She headed down to the kitchen. The smell of breakfast wafted up to greet her. Finn had thankfully perfected the art of pancake making. Although, he'd steered away from making eggs after she'd puked from the smell alone and had to leave the house for an entire day until the scent was gone.

"Hey, you." She grinned.

He smiled back, but it didn't reach his eyes. After flipping the last pancake in the pan, he plated it and set it on the breakfast bar in front of her.

She climbed onto the stool as he placed a cup of tea and the bottle of maple syrup to the side. "This looks delicious. Thank you."

"Anything for you." His gaze locked on to hers, holding her captive.

A sliver of unease rippled through her. "Everything okay?"

Instead of answering, he walked around and took a seat next to her. "Eat up. Gotta keep you nourished." His hand spread out over the side of her belly.

That was a non-answer if she'd ever heard one. But she was starving. In her second trimester, she'd become a breakfast person after all. She slathered the hotcakes in syrup and cut into them before taking a big bite.

Sweetness exploded on her taste buds. "Mmm, these are so good. Did you already eat?"

"I had my coffee already."

She frowned and cut another piece, gobbling it up before pushing the plate away. "You going to tell me what's wrong or are we going to act like you're giving me straight answers?"

He sighed, rubbing his thumb over a drop of syrup on her chin before sucking it into his mouth. "I need to tell you something, but I wanted you to eat first."

She straightened. "Just tell me."

He looked down at his hands, shoulders slumped. "I found another journal entry about your attack."

"Okay." She breathed a sigh of relief. He just wanted to talk about that night. She could handle this.

He licked his lips and met her gaze. "The entry made it

seem like I knew why it happened. Like it was my fault you were *targeted*."

Her brows knit together. "You . . . you were deployed, honey. I'm sure you just felt guilty for not being here to protect me."

He shook his head. "I don't think that's the case. I got a bad feeling it was my fault."

"Let me see the journal. Maybe I can help make sense of it."

He cringed, his eyes darting away, suddenly taking more interest in the engine grease under his fingernails. "You can't because . . . I burned it."

"The journal?"

He nodded.

"Why?" She shook her head. It didn't make sense . . . unless—*No.* "You tried to hide it from me?"

He didn't answer.

"Was this before or after you promised no more secrets between us?" Her voice trembled as she squeezed her hands together in front of her. Anger overflowed and her skin prickled with heat.

"After." His brown eyes clouded over with regret.

"I see." Her body stiffened as if turning to stone.

Finn's hand wrapped around hers, but she pulled away. Once again, he'd broken a promise. *I thought we were getting somewhere.*

"Charli-baby, we'd just made up after everything, and I stumbled on that. I thought it would tear us apart if you knew I was responsible for that happening to you. I just wanted to leave the past where it belonged." His voice was pleading.

"I don't get why you would keep this from me. There was no way you could be responsible for that. We could have talked through it. You promised me, and then you not only kept it from me but burned all the evidence. That was a pretty clear choice." Her voice was short and clipped.

"I know, baby. I've regretted it every day since."

"Why are you telling me this now?"

He placed a hand on her knee. "Because it was wrong. I fucked up. And I want to make it right, starting with honesty."

She shook her head. "You've had chance after chance."

"I know, sweetheart." His voice cracked, regret seeping from the edges.

"I told you that I needed honesty."

"I swear I'll do better." He squeezed her knee.

"We need help. We've tried this on our own, Finn. Talking about it between us obviously isn't working."

"No, don't say that. A month ago, we wouldn't be here. We've come a long way. I'm sorry it's been so rocky, but we can get past this." He leaned closer, determination in his eyes.

"Why do you want to?" Her voice was almost as empty as she felt.

He frowned. "What do you mean?"

"I mean, you woke up in a hospital and had no idea who I was. No memory of making your son. Is it just because I'm pregnant? Is that why you're staying?"

He wiped his hand over the tears she hadn't realized were streaming down her face. "I love you, Charli, more than I've ever loved anyone. Maybe it started out of a sense of obligation, but what I feel for you now is real."

She nodded. "But maybe love isn't enough to make this marriage work."

"What?" he gasped. "No, no. Don't say that. I made a mistake, and I take full responsibility for it."

"I can't trust you, Finn!"

He flinched, eyes growing glassy. His hands dropped to his sides in defeat. "That's why I told you. So you'd see I was telling you the truth, that I was trying to be honest." His voice was quiet.

Why keep the damn secret in the first place? "What you hid wasn't even a big deal. The fact that you intentionally kept it from me was."

"Can't you see I'm trying?" His tone sounded broken, much like the look that flashed in his eyes.

Her heart lurched. She loved him. She hated to see him in such despair and pain. But at some point, she had to put her needs first. "Can't *you* see I'm at the end of my rope? I've given you everything, Finn. I asked for one thing in return —honesty."

"But that's why I told you this. To prove to you I was done keeping secrets." He stood with a growl of frustration.

"You don't get to be mad at me for this, Finn. You broke my trust. You can't demand it back. You promised me honesty one moment and then lied to me the next. You went to see your fucking ex without even so much as a heads-up. I know you think you're still seventeen, but god damn it, even as a kid you know how small-town people talk. You had to know I'd find out." Her chest heaved up and down.

He let out an exasperated sound. "That was before."

"How about the fact that you still won't see a therapist? Or that you never tell me anything about your VA appointments or ask me to go? Your feelings are a no-fly zone just as much as your nightmares and flashbacks. So you see one little omission, and I see the last fucking straw." She got to her feet and headed for the stairs.

"Where are you going?" he asked.

"We are not going to get anywhere like this. We're talking in circles. I need some space."

"Space." He spat the word.

She didn't bother responding, instead opting to go back

upstairs. Seemed getting out of bed hadn't been that great of an idea today after all.

Charli climbed under the covers, letting the tears fall. Reaching across the nightstand for a tissue, she bumped something.

Crash!

She stared through blurry eyes at the upside-down picture frame. Gingerly, she picked it up. Spiderwebs of cracks spread out over the picture of Finn and her on their wedding day. Was this a sign? Was their marriage as broken as her heart?

38

———

FINN

Finn slammed the drink on the bar top a little harder than he should have. Some of the liquid spilled over the edge. "Here ya go." He added it to the customer's tab and headed down the line for the next order. He nodded to the guy waiting. His voice would surely get swallowed up in the loud music.

"Hard cider."

Finn grabbed a glass and brought it under the tap, filling it to the rim before sliding it to the patron. He peeked over his shoulder as the guy dug cash out of his pocket. Charli was at the other end, smiling and laughing with a few men as she passed them their drinks. Finn's guts twisted and his stomach soured. She wouldn't even look at him since he'd opened up to her earlier today. Even after he'd forced her to come downstairs and eat before their shift. *I really fucked it up this time.*

"Hey, buddy." His customer held out the cash.

Finn grabbed it.

"Keep the change."

"Thanks." Finn plugged it into the register before putting the whole extra two dollars in the tip jar.

Charli's throaty laugh pulled his attention back to her end once more. Fire lit in his veins. He was the one who was supposed to make that melodious sound come from her. Instead, he brought her nothing but grief it seemed. *How can I fix this?*

Every other time he'd screwed up she'd been quick to set him straight and then move on. This time *she* was shutting *him* out.

As the night wore on, Finn kept a close eye on her. She winced every time she bent over to grab something from the coolers. And from the way she shifted on her feet, he could tell they were bothering her. Her hand took up almost a permanent residence on her lower back. Maybe it was time she stopped working. Did she want to? They hadn't even talked about what would happen after the baby was born. Did she want to stay home with the baby? Or did she want to go back to work?

At eleven, the crowd had begun to thin out. Closing time was only an hour away seeing as it was a weekday. Finn brought a group of girls a round of shots. When he returned, a very glassy-eyed man was leaning over the counter talking to Charli as she shook her head.

"I'm sorry, buddy. I think you've had enough. Can I call you a cab?" Charli asked, pulling out her phone.

"Awww, come on now. Just one more itty-bitty drink. It will be our ssssecret," he slurred.

Finn walked over to Charli's side. "She said you've had enough. Cab or Uber?"

Charli cut him a look. "I have this handled."

The drunk guy stood a little taller. "Who the fuck you think you are, telling me what I can or can't do?"

"Let's everybody calm down. We're getting ready to close soon. And you've reached your limit, sir. I'm gonna go ahead and call you a ride." Charli tapped her phone screen as the man's hand shot out and grabbed her arm.

"I don't—"

Finn didn't think. He reacted. Pure, rage-fueled adrenaline shot through his system as he jumped over the bar, his fist flying to meet the drunk guy's jaw.

A stool crashed and someone screamed. Finn saw red. *Protect Charli* was his only objective. He lifted his fist and brought it down again, bone crunching under his knuckles.

Someone grabbed his arm as he brought it up, he shoved them away before swinging his fist into the bastard who'd dared to lay a hand on his wife.

This time the hands that grabbed him were made of steel. A headlock stole his air.

"Stop! It's me," Mason commanded. "Someone check on Charli."

Charli? What was wrong with his wife? Finn tapped the arm that locked him in place.

Mason released him. Finn took one look at the drunk bleeding all over the ground, his hazy eyes now shining with fear.

Finn spun around, searching for Charli, wanting to make sure she was okay. Every customer surrounding them just stared openmouthed.

"What the fuck were you thinking?" Mason growled, bending over and grabbing someone's hand from the floor.

No.

Charli winced, holding her belly as she got to her feet.

"Baby—"

She held out her hand, tears glistening in her eyes as she shook her head. "Don't come near me."

Mason wrapped an arm around her, guiding her to the back room.

"Everybody out!" Finn yelled before turning to the waitress. "Get them out and lock up."

The man he'd beaten wobbled to his feet, taking off through the doors first. *What the fuck did I do?*

Finn followed his wife, opening the door to the office. Mason stepped in front of her protectively, as if Finn was a danger to Charli. *But I wasn't the one who tried to hurt her.*

"Shit, Charli, I'm so sorry. Do we need to go to the hospital? I didn't know you were behind me. I—"

"I'm fine. I just want to go home." She wiped her eyes, getting to her feet.

"Do you want me to drive you?" Mason asked.

Finn's fists clenched.

Charli glanced at Finn, her eyes full of pain. "No. Finn can take me. Could you close up for me?"

"Of course," Mason said.

"Thank you." Charli walked towards the door. Finn stepped aside so she could pass.

Mason's hand clamped on his shoulder before he could follow. "Do you realize what happened tonight?"

Finn shrugged away. "Yeah, I fucked up. Again."

Mason ground his teeth and shook his head. "You need help, Finn. Things are getting worse. Don't choose your pride over your family."

"That's not what I'm doing."

"Isn't it though?" Mason looked him dead in the eyes.

Finn stepped forward until they were chest to chest. "Listen here, motherfucker. I don't know why you think you have me figured out or have the right to comment."

Mason took a step forward, pushing Finn back a few inches as he stared down at him. "I know because I've been you, asshole. I was arrogant enough to think I didn't need anybody's help. Pushed my wife away and was so caught up in trying to be a man and hold it together. Fake it till you make it, right? I was so blind as to what I thought being a man, a husband, and a father meant, I didn't see that my wife was drowning." Mason's usually stoic expression cracked open just a little. Tortured pain bled out, saturating the room with it. "Don't make the same fucking mistakes I did. Get help . . . before it's too late."

Mason took off, leaving him alone with that revelation. Was that what he was doing? Charli said she was at the end of her rope. *I could have seriously hurt her and the baby.*

Finn rushed out, the urgent need to fix things hastening his steps. His chest creaked and wavered with the fear that he'd screwed things up beyond repair. He'd do it. He'd go to counseling, get better. Fear slicked through his veins like ice at the broken image of his wife's stony expression. He'd do whatever it took to see the light shining in her eyes once again. Or he'd die trying.

39

CHARLI

The ache in Charli's back was nothing compared to the vicious tearing and shredding of her heart. Finn had gone too far this time.

"Are you sure we shouldn't go to the hospital and have you checked out?" Finn's worried voice cut through her as he pulled into their driveway.

She clamped her eyes shut, holding the tears at bay. She needed to be strong for this next part. Rather than answering, she opened the door and headed towards the house. The heat at her back told her Finn was not far away. He reached ahead of her and unlocked the door before opening it.

Charli walked in and hung her coat. Her husband dropped to his knees to remove her shoes as he usually did. *I'll miss that. I'll miss him.* She inhaled a shaky breath.

After he'd stacked the sneakers, she waddled to the bathroom and closed the door. She exhaled a sigh of relief at the short reprieve and relieved herself. Afterwards, she washed her hands and splashed cold water on her face, delaying the inevitable for another minute. Running her hand through her hair, several strands came out. She held them over the trash. An orange prescription bottle caught her attention. She let the hair go and picked the medicine up. *Finn's medication. Why would he—* She shook her head, heart sinking. This explained his more erratic mood swings.

She drew in one more fortifying inhale and opened the door. Finn was leaning against the wall in the hallway, his arms crossed over his broad chest. Regret-filled brown eyes met hers before darting to the bottle she held and then back again.

"What's this?" she demanded.

"I don't need it."

She nodded, a cold realization sinking into her marrow. A numbness settled over her. "Right, I forgot. You don't need anyone's help."

"That's not true—"

"Just stop." She sucked in a breath. Her lungs squeezed tight like she was drowning in the weight of the past and the dying hope for an impossible future. *I can't do this anymore.* "I asked you for honesty."

"I didn't want to be a burden. You have enough to worry about—that's why I kept it from you."

Her laugh was cold and empty, just like she felt inside. "And how is that working out for you?"

His shoulders drooped.

"It seems like all we do is fight and argue. You keep secrets, and then we make up. Round and round we go in this vicious cycle. Details change, but everything else remains the same."

"Baby, when that guy put his hands on you, I just snapped. I wanted to protect you like I've failed in the past."

"I told you I had it under control. He didn't hurt me, Finn. *You did.*" The last two words were spoken more quietly, yet they held the most power.

He winced as if they had been a physical blow.

"Part of working in a bar is knowing you're gonna get assholes who can't handle their liquor sometimes. That's why we have a system. You know I was alerting Mason."

He stared down at his feet. "I don't know what to say."

"I can't keep going on pretending everything is okay. You're not sleeping. You go from zero to one hundred when you're upset. You're not getting help. And now I find out you've stopped taking your meds. I can't be the one to help fix you . . . As much as I want to be everything for you, I'm human, and I have my limits. Only you can fix your problems." She trembled, mustering up the courage for what she had to say next.

"You're right. I'm gonna—"

"I love you, Finn, with all of my heart. But I can't do this anymore. Not if you're not going to get help and change for the better. It's not safe." She pressed a hand over her belly, hoping he would understand.

He shook his head, falling to his knees. "No, baby, please. I'll go. I'll do whatever I have to, to make this work. I don't want to lose you."

"I want to believe you. But right now, these are just pretty words that you've promised before. Your actions haven't lined up with them long-term." She closed her eyes, her own heart breaking, smashing to smithereens as she said the words she never thought would leave her mouth. "I want you to move out."

Finn stood, his hands cupping her face, panic and pain bleeding from his eyes in the first tears she'd seen him shed in their whole marriage. It felt like all the air had been sucked out of the room, replaced with chemicals that stung and burned, slowly poisoning her to death.

"You want a divorce?" He blinked, shock and disbelief marring his expression. He shook his head and begged. "No, sweetheart. *Please*. I love you."

She shook her head and leaned her cheek against his. Their hot tears melded together. "Show me. Show me you love me by loving yourself and getting help. This doesn't have to be the end. But I can't keep going on like this." She kissed him, infusing her last spark of faith in him into the joining of their mouths.

Finn held the back of her head like he wasn't ready to let go. This was goodbye. For now, at least. *Maybe forever.* She hadn't given up on him. But right now, she'd have to love him from afar.

He tipped his forehead to hers. His shoulders sank in defeat. "Stay with my parents. I don't like the idea of you staying here alone. Not when *he's* out there. I want you to be safe."

"I'll be fine."

He backed up, letting his arms drop to his sides. "Look, you can be mad at me and think I'm an asshole, but there's no way I'm leaving you vulnerable. I'm not running away this time . . . I'm sleeping on the couch tonight." He held up a hand to halt her rebuttal. "I'll leave in the morning. But not until I have a security system installed. Like it or not, baby, I love you. And I'll respect your wishes. But you are my wife first and foremost, and I *will* protect you. When I'm assured you are safe, as much as it kills me, I'll do what you need. Because I do love you. And I'm gonna prove it to you."

She blinked, staggering back a step. His words should have

felt like relief, but they were bittersweet. How could she trust they were anything but half-empty promises?

He walked away, disappearing down the stairs. Her belly flipped. She hoped he really did it this time. But sometimes butterflies and red flags felt scarily similar.

40

CHARLI

Seven days. It had been one, long week since Charli had heard Finn's footsteps in the entryway or the rumble of his motorcycle from the garage. He'd left her the car and had Bently pick him up after the security system was installed and tested. Claire and Zeke had insisted she take the week off after they'd heard about what happened. Needless to say, she'd gotten a lot of cross-stitching done.

Charli pushed her feet on the rocking foot stool that had come with the glider she'd purchased for the nursery. Everything was put together. The walls were decorated with woodland animals. A mobile with stars hung above the crib that Finn had stayed up two nights to complete. The drawers were stocked full of tiny clothes and diapers.

The baby kicked, making her suck in a breath and wrap her warm palm over her belly. "Ouch. You got your daddy's strength, that's for sure."

Her smile faded as she inhaled shakily. Her whole life, she'd never wanted to end up like her mother. Charli was terrified she'd repeat the same mistakes. Would she have those maternal instincts? Finn had thought so. Before his accident, he'd convinced her she would be amazing. She hadn't believed him one hundred percent, but with him by her side, she'd felt unstoppable.

And now it's just me. She closed her eyes, trying to keep the emotions at bay. Twenty-seven weeks into her pregnancy, it was getting harder to do. *How many times can I lose the same man?* The destruction of her heart and the constant vicious ache was almost worse than when she'd thought he wouldn't wake up from his coma. Because this time, she wasn't hoping for a medical miracle outside her control. This time, she'd given everything to save him and it hadn't been enough.

She patted her stomach where a little hand or foot thudded. "I don't know what I'm going to do, buddy. But I'll give you my best. And we'll figure out the rest together as it comes."

Knock. Knock.

Her eyebrows knit together. "Who could that be?" Charli leaned forward, struggling a little bit to get up from the moving chair. The knocks repeated as she reached the doorknob. *Is it Finn? Was she ready to see him?* Drunken moths of indecision spun her up and fluttered in her belly.

"Coming." As soon as she opened it, the unease settled. "Claire."

Her mother-in-law smiled and held out a covered dish. "Hey, sweetheart. I brought you some food." Claire kissed Charli's cheek and entered as Charli moved to the side to let her in.

Charli's phone rang from her pocket, the security company calling. "Hello?"

"Hello, ma'am. The silent alarm was tripped in your home, and we wanted to see if you were safe?"

"Oh, yes. I forgot to shut it off when I answered the door."

Charli shut and locked the front before entering the code into the gadget by the entrance.

"That's not a problem. I will cancel the emergency services as soon as you give me the passphrase."

Charli closed her eyes, a pang of tortured pain splintering through her at the one Finn had chosen. "Compass."

"Perfect. Have a great day, Mrs. Reed."

"You too." Charli hung up and walked to the kitchen where Claire was sliding the casserole into the oven.

"Everything okay?" Claire motioned to the cell as Charli slipped it into her pocket.

Charli nodded. "Yeah. Finn had a security system installed, and I'm still getting used to how it works."

"And how is my grandson?" Claire pressed a gentle hand to her belly.

"Running out of room." Charli forced a chuckle.

"Oh, I know it seems that way." Claire laughed.

"I can't believe I have at least eleven more weeks of this. I'm not even going to be able to walk." Charli waddled around to the stove and grabbed the kettle before filling it with water from the sink. "Tea?"

Claire nodded, opening the cupboard and pulling out two mugs. "It will all be worth it. There's nothing like the day your child enters the world. It's a birthday for you as well. The mother in you will be born."

"I hope so," Charli said, flicking on the gas.

Claire pulled her into a hug. Charli relaxed against her surrogate mother, inhaling Claire's mango and cocoa butter scent. "You will be an amazing mother." Claire squeezed her tighter. They stayed like that for a few more seconds before her mother-in-law released her.

"Thank you for saying that. I'm sorry I couldn't . . . that Finn and I . . ."

"Oh, hush. You forget I birthed that boy. He came into this world two weeks late—stubborn from the very beginning. I know what it is like to be married to a Reed. I have faith Finnegan will come around and pull his head out of his ass." Claire chuckled, adding a chamomile tea bag into each cup.

Charli sighed, a smile tipping the edge of her mouth. "I just wonder if there was something I could have done better."

Claire shut the stove off and poured the hot water into the two waiting mugs. Charli spooned honey into hers and stirred before carrying it over to the table.

Claire followed, blowing on the steamy cup in front of her before setting it down. "Marriage isn't easy. It's full of its ups and downs. Some more than others." Claire smiled. "What no one talks about is the forks in the road. Sometimes life happens, and for whatever reason someone's needs are not being met. You can love each other with every precious cell in your body and still it won't be enough."

Charli's chest squeezed. Tears burned the back of her eyes. Was Claire telling her this was well and truly over?

"It's like if you are injured. You're bleeding, losing blood, and getting weaker. In marriage, you're connected to the other person. When they win, you win. When you lose, they lose. If you don't speak up and let them know you need medical attention, that you need to fix this wound, you will bleed out—become dead weight—thereby losing yourself and taking your partner down with you." Claire took a sip of her tea before continuing. "You told Finn he was bleeding, and he didn't want to acknowledge it. You did all you could. It's up to him to ask for the help he needs and take action to get it. Without help, he's dragging you down. And, honey, that's not a healthy marriage."

Charli wiped the tears that had escaped off her cheeks. "Aren't you supposed to be on his side?" She chuckled.

Claire gave her a sympathetic smile. "I may be that boy's mama, but you're my daughter too. We love you as our own. We want you both to work this out. But more than anything, we want you both happy."

"Thank you so much for being there for me."

Claire pulled her in for another hug, patting her back soothingly. "Zeke and I have been where you two are."

Charli blinked, stunned. "You have?"

Claire nodded. "Finn was only two when I packed him up and went to stay with my mother. It was the longest six months of my life."

"I had no idea."

"We've never spoken about it. It's not a subject he's proud of. But I was done being ignored and having my opinions disregarded. He needed to make a choice. If he wanted me in his life, I wanted an equal partner in decision-making." Claire sipped her tea.

"That look you give him, when you guys disagree over the big things," Charli said, realization dawning.

Claire laughed. "I save it for the important stuff. Zeke feels better making most of the decisions. I learned it's his way of feeling like he's showing me love by protecting me. And after I understood that, it made me more appreciative. It doesn't work for everyone. But every marriage is different. Every partner has different needs."

"Wow. You're a pretty amazing woman, Claire."

"I know." She fluffed her small afro with a playful gleam in her eyes.

Charli drank some of her tea. "How is he?"

Claire took a deep breath. "In pain. But also, determined . . . He's been out late the last couple nights."

Charli's heart lurched. *Was he with Laura?*

"That casserole should be warm by now." Claire got to her feet.

Charli stared at the half-empty mug in front of her. If Finn wanted a life with someone else, she'd get over it . . . eventually. Because she loved him and wanted him to be happy, even if that couldn't be with her. As long as it was anyone but Laura.

Claire returned, setting a plate in front of her of steaming vegetables and meat in a savory mix.

Charli's stomach grumbled in hunger. "You didn't have to do this."

Claire tsked. "You're growing my grandson. I remember how tiring pregnancy was. Let me spoil my daughter."

"Where's yours?"

"Oh, I'm gonna get going. Told Zeke we could check out Atlas's new restaurant, Atlantis, for dinner."

"That sounds fun." Charli forced a smile even though the thought of another dinner alone made her stomach sink.

"Do we need to do anything about the alarm?" Claire asked.

"I shut it off. You're good to go."

"Okay, well, make sure to turn it back on when I leave." Claire gave her a concerned look.

"I will, right after I finish this dinner that's calling my name," Charli promised.

"Take it easy. It's supposed to snow later this week."

"I will. Have a great night." Charli waved as Claire left, the click of the door the only sound in the quiet house.

Charli tucked into the food. At least there was one ache she could quench.

. . .

Charli wrapped a coat around her, but there was no hope buttoning it over her growing bump. She held it together as she walked out to the mailbox, collecting the junk mail and bills. A black SUV was parked on the opposite side of the street, diagonal from hers, with someone visible in the driver's seat.

Was it there this morning when I brought out the garbage?

She'd never seen it before. Maybe one of her neighbors had company. But that didn't explain the sour feeling in her belly. She stared at the SUV, jumping when the engine started abruptly. Charli scurried to the house, panic rushing over her. Suddenly living here alone seemed like the worst idea. At least inside she'd be safe.

She yanked the door open as the engine revved, sounding closer. She spun around in time to see a man wearing a pair of sunglasses and hat staring in her direction as he drove by in the SUV.

Charli let out a sigh when he was out of sight and shook her head. "I'm just paranoid."

The sound of another car pulled her attention back to the driveway as an unfamiliar Jeep drove in. Finn got out of the driver's side. God, he looked good. She tucked her hair behind her ear. It was too late to run inside and make sure she didn't look as shitty as she felt. Would he see the bags under her eyes and run the other way? No, this man had seen her at her worst and only held her closer once upon a time. *Before the accident.*

Finn slipped his hands into his leather jacket pockets and approached her hesitantly. "Is it okay that I'm here?"

She nodded, afraid of her own voice. *Is he here to tell me he wants a divorce? That he's with Laura?*

"Can we talk?"

Charli pulled the sides of her coat together to ward off the chill of the winter air, though it was fruitless. His eyes dropped to her belly.

"Yeah, let's go inside."

He followed her silently as she entered the house, dropping the junk mail in the recycling as he set the alarm behind them. *Always the protector.*

She shrugged off her coat and hung it before placing the bills on the counter to deal with later. "Are you hungry? Your mom dropped off some food."

He shook his head, hanging his jacket and kicking off his boots. "I'm good."

She looked at the couch. There were too many memories there. He must have read her mind because he took a seat at the table. She sat opposite him, nervously tapping her fingers against the wood.

"How have you been feeling?" he asked.

"Health-wise I'm fine."

He nodded, licking his lips. "I . . . uh . . . I don't know where to start or how to tell you this."

Charli's stomach twisted into a thousand intricate knots, her dinner threatening to make a reappearance. She held her breath. *This is where he says he's done and walks away.*

"I've started seeing someone."

Lightning striking her soul would have been less painful than those four words. Her eyes burned, and her lungs halted abruptly. Her chest caved in, destroyed by his confession. She clasped a hand over her mouth, hoping to hide the scream that threatened to finish the job his words had started and tear her into two.

41

CHARLI

"Jesus—no—that's not what I meant. A therapist! I'm seeing a therapist. I mean, I'm going to therapy." Finn held his hands out, seemingly recognizing the assumption Charli had jumped to.

Charli choked back a sob as she breathed a little easier. Her heart rattled and scraped with each pain-filled beat.

"Fuck. This is not how I wanted this to go." Finn stood, raking a hand over his face before squeezing the back of his neck. He looked at her, brows drawn together in concern, eyes shining with too many emotions to read.

He got down on his knees, pulling her hands into his, turning her so her feet hung off the edge of the booth seat. "There has never been anyone else and there never will be." His hoarse voice dripped with conviction.

"Your mom said you'd been out late the last few nights, and I thought—"

He sighed, shaking his head. "I was with Mason, Bently, and the guys. I . . . was asking for their help."

"What?"

"Let me . . . start from the beginning." He got back up and sat across from her once more. She was thankful for the table between them. She needed the little barrier to remind her that as much as she wanted their marriage to be repaired, she needed more.

"After I left, I called a therapist Mason had recommended. I've had three appointments this week. And I plan to go biweekly for the rest of the month. After that, I'll still go, but maybe only once a week."

He'd really gone? "How was it?"

"It . . . was hard. I . . . It's hard for me to talk about my feelings, never mind to a stranger."

He'd done it after all. She nodded.

"She asked me questions I never thought to ask myself. And I realized a lot of things. I see how my actions have hurt you, and I want you to know I take full responsibility for them." He leveled his gaze on her.

"I appreciate that. And I'm sorry for any way I've hurt you."

"I went back to my doctor at the VA and got a new prescription. I told him why I stopped the meds, and he recommended a different one."

She nodded.

"I'm telling you all of this to let you know I *heard* you . . . I have been taking a good, hard look at myself and this life I've been living, and I realized I'm not happy."

She winced. Finn's truth had sharp edges.

"I think I've been trying to follow an old playbook and fit into this cookie-cutter mold of what I think my dad would want me to do, mixed with my own assumptions of what I should be for you. But I'm done with that." Finn licked his lips.

Charli held her breath.

"I want to start over with a clean slate. I want to find out what you need from a husband and tell you what I need from my wife. And I want us to find a way to make this work. I'm gonna work on my communication. I'm gonna keep my word. I won't be perfect, but I'll be consistently better." He reached out his hand, palm up on the table, his show of vulnerability silently asking if she would join him.

She hesitated. What if this was just part of the constant cycle they seemed to be lost in?

"I'm not asking you for anything you are not ready to give. I'll wait as long as it takes to earn back your trust and prove to you every day how much I love you. I'd like to start by dating my wife."

These damn tears never stopped. Fucking pregnancy. She wiped her face and reached out her hand to his. The gentle touch was a mix of pain and comfort. "It might be awhile. I don't want to repeat this cycle again."

"And I get that. I don't either. Whether it's a month or a year, however long it takes, I'm going to be better."

"I want that too."

The corner of his mouth turned up in a cautious smile as his eyes flashed with hope. "Would you be willing to go with me to my therapy appointment Monday evening? I saw neither of us are on the schedule at the bar."

She nodded. "I can do that."

"It's supposed to snow this weekend, so I'll pick you up in the Jeep."

"Whose car is that?"

He shrugged. "We needed a bigger car with the baby coming. This one has four-wheel drive for the snow. I'll be leaving it here for you and taking the Toyota back if that's okay?"

"You bought me a car?"

"It's safer for you and the baby," he said carefully, like he was afraid she would get mad—when the opposite was happening.

Some of the ice around her heart melted. "I appreciate you thinking of us."

He squeezed her hand a little more firmly. "Always."

After another beat of silence, his gaze flicked to the entryway. He got to his feet, sighing. "I really don't like you staying here alone."

"I'm fine. I'm safe. You made sure this place is Fort Knox."

"Maybe we should get you a dog?"

She laughed, and the sound felt foreign after the rough week she'd had. "I don't need a little yippy thing peeing all over the house."

He shrugged on his jacket before slipping on his shoes. "I was thinking more like a guard dog. Something big and protective."

Like you? "We'll see. I don't think I could walk it every day, especially having to balance on the slick sidewalks with this big belly. I probably won't be able to reach the water bowl in the next few weeks," she joked.

His hand tipped her chin up to look at him. "I would take care of it for you."

It would be one thing if you lived with me. But I'm not ready to let you back in just yet. "I'll think about it."

"Okay. I'll see you later."

"I'm back to work tomorrow." She nodded.

He frowned. "Don't you . . . I mean . . . we never talked about this, but do you plan on working up until the baby is born? Wouldn't you rather stay off your feet and relax the rest of this pregnancy?"

The questioned stunned her. "I—uh—well, I think I'd go

crazy staying home all day by myself. This week has been hard enough as it is. I want to keep busy."

He waited a moment and then said, "If that's what you want. Just know, you don't have to work if you don't want to. I'll take care of you, even if . . . if I don't move back in."

Damn these hormones. No, she wouldn't cry again. He was promising to love her from afar. To provide for her even if she didn't let him back into her life. *God, I love you so much.* Why did this have to be so hard? She had to stay strong, for her and the baby, but also for him. "I appreciate the offer."

He leaned in and kissed her cheek, lingering an extra moment as he spoke into her ear. "I love you." The rumble of his voice sent everything inside her tumbling and spinning.

"I love you too."

He smiled as he pulled away. "We're gonna fix this together. And we're gonna be better for it."

"I hope so."

He turned around, switching the key fob for the Jeep with hers on the wall. Finn entered the code into the alarm before he opened the door. "Stay safe."

"You too."

He shut the door with a click, the gadget on the wall beeping twice with the reengagement of the alarm system. She stared out the living-room window as he backed out of the driveway. His taillights faded, leaving behind embers of hope flaring to life in her soul.

Maybe they could do this. Maybe it wouldn't work out. At the very least, she believed they were both giving their all this time. She'd fight for her marriage, but she'd also fight for herself too.

The baby in her belly kicked three times in succession. It seemed even their unborn son was rooting for them.

42

CHARLI

Charli opened the front door for Finn. He smiled, his eyes lighting up as if he was overjoyed to see her. Flecks of snow dusted across the short, dark locks on the top of his head, down the faded sides, and on his shoulders. He was wearing the black, military-style peacoat she'd gotten him last Christmas. He stepped inside and shut the door behind him.

"Good afternoon." He held out a bag towards her.

"What's this?" She took it from him and peered inside.

"I noticed you needed a coat that fit over your baby bump."

She stared at him a moment. *He bought me a winter jacket?* Her heart stuttered as she pulled the turquoise puffy fabric from the bag.

"The receipt is in the bag in case you don't like it or it doesn't fit. But the sales lady assured me it was warm and comfortable." Finn slipped his hands into his pockets in a self-conscious gesture.

"It's perfect." She fought to hold back the emotion threatening to leak from her eyes—again. Setting the bag down, she slipped the new coat on. Finn must have noticed her struggling to locate the zipper over her bump because he clasped the sides for her and zipped it up.

"Thank you."

"No need for this?" he asked, lifting the tag from her wrist.

She shook her head.

He pulled the plastic tab off and dropped it into the bag. "Ready to go?"

As ready as I'll ever be. "Yeah."

She followed him out. He offered his hand, and she stepped down the newly shoveled and salted steps. *When did he do that?*

"Careful. It's slippery." Finn's care tugged on her heartstrings. He'd always been a good man. That was never in question.

He helped her into the car before he climbed in the driver's side. Holiday music bled from the radio, and the instant blast of heat was comforting. Finn drove them to their destination without another word. It was a comfortable silence. The closer they got to the city, the more Finn tapped on the steering wheel. She wanted to reach out and comfort him, knowing his nerves were getting the best of him. But it was too easy to slip back into the role she'd carved out for herself of giving him everything regardless of how it affected her. If they were truly going to work through things, she had to see his growth.

"This is it." Finn slid the Jeep into park, eying the brick building in front of them.

Charli studied the sign on the door, *Veritas Counseling Services.*

He released a long breath and climbed out of the vehicle before opening her door for her and helping her out. His palm stayed on her lower back, guiding her to the entrance. She walked in ahead of him to a small waiting room with several plants and a couple of beige couches.

Finn moved over and pressed what looked to be a doorbell before he gestured to one of the sofas. "We can wait here."

Charli had barely taken a seat when the door on the other side of the waiting room opened. A woman who couldn't be much older than her stepped through with a warm smile directed at Finn. "Hello. Are you ready for our session?"

"Yeah." He nodded, turning towards Charli. "This is my wife, Charli."

The woman brought her attention to Charli. "Nice to meet you. I've heard a lot about you. I'm Rebecca Cole." She reached her hand out.

Charli returned the gesture. "Nice to meet you as well."

Rebecca waved her hand towards the door. "Well, come on in. Can I get you some water, tea, or coffee?"

"I'm fine thanks." Charli followed her in, Finn's heat at her backside.

The room had a single rectangular desk organized neatly. In front of that was a chair where Rebecca sat, pulling a yellow notepad onto her lap with a pen. Finn guided Charli to the white couch across from her with only a small coffee table separating them. Several framed degrees and certificates lined the walls in between large, abstract paintings with cool, soothing colors.

She unzipped her coat and slipped her arms out of it before resting against the soft cushion of the overstuffed couch.

"Let's get down to it. Charli, do you know why Finn asked you here today?" Rebecca asked.

Charli gave Finn a brief glance before focusing back on

the therapist. "To work through our issues?" Charli gave a self-depreciating laugh.

"Finn? Why don't you tell Charli what you told me during our last session?"

Finn nodded and turned to face her. He cleared his throat. "I'm afraid I'm going to lose you for good. I'm afraid I went too far and hurt you too much for you to stay in this marriage."

She nodded, swallowing the ball of emotions that rose.

"Charli? Finn filled me in on the events leading up to the argument you two had, but I'd love to hear from your perspective where you are at with everything. If you're willing, of course." Rebecca sat back and tucked a dark strand of her hair behind her ear, her focus solely on Charli now.

"I want this marriage to work. I love Finn with everything in me. But I can't take the secrets, the lies, and omissions."

"That is quite understandable. Part of my job is helping spouses of those affected by PTSD find a way to implement boundaries with their partner and still remain supportive. One of the ways we do that is getting to the root of each of your needs and your hard limits for your relationship. This is unique to every couple. Is that something you'd be interested in doing?" Rebecca asked.

Charli inhaled. Did she want to rehash this and try this new approach? *If it can save my marriage, it's worth a try.* "Yes."

Finn let out a breath he must have been holding as relief flitted across his features.

"Okay. Why don't you tell Finn everything you need from a husband? These should be things that unless you have them, you will not be happy in the relationship. They are different from wants in that way. These are your non-negotiables."

Charli turned towards her husband. His brown eyes met hers, full of cautious hope.

"I need you to communicate with me about everything. I don't want to have to guess if you're in a bad mood or if something's wrong. I want you to tell me. I don't want you to keep things from me, even if you're afraid they will hurt me. I just need honesty."

He nodded.

"I need to be able to rely on you and trust you in order to feel safe. I need for you to hear me."

"Is there anything else?" Rebecca asked.

"I think that's the main things that are missing."

"And what are your non-negotiables?"

"Lying, omissions, vagueness, and your temper."

Finn winced.

Rebecca scribbled on her pad of paper and looked towards Finn. "Finn, do you think you can meet Charli's needs for honesty, open communication, and controlling your temper?"

"I want to." He rubbed a hand over the back of his neck.

"What would hold you back?" Rebecca asked.

"I'm afraid I'll mess up again, and then she'll leave me for good."

Charli opened her mouth to respond, but Rebecca spoke first. "So, what will you do to ensure you are trying the best you can?"

He sat forward, elbows on his thighs. "I'll have to enlist help."

Whoa. The Finn she knew hated showing weakness and had the misguided belief that seeking help was a show of fragility.

"And what does that look like, specifically?"

"I continue my therapy with you. And I will be more open with my wife and my good friends who can hold me accountable."

"If Finn does these things, how would that make you feel, Charli?" Rebecca set her pen down.

"Surprised."

"Why is that?" Rebecca prodded.

Charli turned to Finn. "Because he doesn't talk about things with anyone, much less me, unless I pull it out of him. Though, since his accident, he's been more open than in the past."

Finn's wary gaze studied her. "I started to, this week. I told the guys what's been going on. And I asked them if they'd hold me accountable. I trust them, and I know you do too. I just thought that extra guidance would be beneficial. Whether or not you choose to stay with me, I want to be a better man and a good father."

A small smile tugged at the corner of Charli's mouth, emotion overwhelming her. He was putting action to his promises after all.

"Why don't we talk about your needs now, Finn?" Rebecca interjected.

"I need support and understanding when I just need some space to work through things in my head. I also need you to make me feel like I can tell you when I mess up without being afraid you will walk away every time."

Rebecca held up her hand. "I just want to point out the language you used, Finn. You said *make you feel*. Charli is not responsible for your emotions. You are. If you need something in order to feel safe, then name it, but you can't expect another person to be responsible for your emotions. She can't be your sole source of happiness. People are imperfect, and they will let us down. How will you deal with those fears of being left? And how can she support you through that?"

Finn ran a hand over his beard. "I, uh, I guess I just want to know that she will try to understand that I make my decisions based on good intentions and to let me explain and work it out."

"Charli? Is that something you can commit to? Listening to Finn with empathy?" Rebecca asked.

"I want to say yes. But for example, you burning the journal so I wouldn't find out and then telling me about it much later . . . that felt like your word didn't matter."

"Why is that?" Rebecca asked.

"Because he had just promised me no more secrets, and then he went and hid the evidence to something that wasn't even a big deal. He lied by omission, and then told me like I was supposed to be happy he'd decided to tell me the truth. I just wanted it from the beginning. How can I believe him now? He gave his word before and then betrayed me right after."

Finn shifted in his seat and sighed. "I don't know what I can do to prove to you that I'm going to do better. Tell me what to do, and I'll do it. I want to fix this more than anything."

Rebecca cleared her throat. "Just to recap, Charli, you don't trust Finn's word right now. And, Finn, you want to earn that trust, but as a human you're bound to mess up and you're terrified of that."

They both nodded.

"The only way to rebuild trust is through complete transparency, consistency, and effective communication. Finn, you're going to have to be extra open and communicative with Charli while being patient and showing her consistently that you are working at being better." Rebecca turned to Charli. "And you will have to decide if you're willing to let him earn that trust back. That's the only way this relationship will work where you both have your needs met."

Charli tucked a strand of loose hair behind her ear.

Rebecca continued. "Transparency for you might look like checking in with each other every day, allowing Charli to ask questions, but also offering up information yourself, Finn. I recommend you pick a time that's good for the both of you without distractions and when you're both emotionally and mentally prepared for the conversation."

"I can do that." Finn turned to Charli.

"Good communication doesn't happen overnight. You will both have to work on it. Some topics might be hard to talk about at first but will get easier in time. One way you can do this is through what I call Relationship Checkups. When you're just starting out, I recommend you do this once a week. As things progress, you can push it back to monthly. I want you to sit down together and verbally rate the different areas of your marriage on a scale of one to ten. How is your sexual intimacy? How is your emotional intimacy? And what can you do this week to make it better?" Rebecca stood, walking around her desk and grabbing a paper from a file. She handed them each a copy.

"These are more questions for your checkup. These will help you dive a little deeper each week and hopefully guide your discussions to get to the root of your needs and open dialogue for coming up with a plan to improve those needs being met."

Charli accepted the paper and skimmed it over.

1. What is one thing you really enjoyed this week (your high)?

2. What was really challenging for you this week (your low)?

3. What can I do for you to make your life a little easier next week?

4. On a scale of 1-10, how would you rate our sexual intimacy this week?

    • *What can we do to make it better next week?*

5. On a scale of 1-10, how would you rate our emotional connection this week?

- *What can we do to make it better next week?*

6. *On a scale of 1-10, how would you rate our intellectual connection this week?*

- *What can we do to make it better next week?*

7. *On a scale of 1-10, how would you rate our friendship and ability to have fun and enjoy each other's company this week?*

- *What can we do to make it better next week?*

Rebecca cleared her throat. "This is where the consistency piece comes into play. After you've verbalized these needs, you both have an opportunity to follow through with improving these areas even though it may push you out of your comfort zone. By doing this consistently, even if you fall short sometimes, you'll prove to each other you are trustworthy and safe."

"What if she gets mad at something I rate lower?" Finn asked.

"The important thing is to prepare your mindset coming to the table when talking about these things. Criticism is never easy. But if you both keep in mind that this is for the good of both of you as a team, it will get easier. If someone is getting upset, take a break and come back to it. These types of hard conversations work best when you're both calm and open-minded enough to listen to each other with empathy."

"Okay." Finn turned to Charli. "Would you be willing to do this with me every week?"

The flash of vulnerability in Finn's eyes made her chest squeeze. The thought of discussing all of this with Finn every week was a little overwhelming and scary. Did she want to see how she was measuring up? Regardless, the promise of being able to measure his consistency of being honest and following through was tempting. "Of course," she agreed.

Relief painted his expression as his shoulders lowered with a sigh.

"Well, that's our time for today. I'll see you Wednesday for our next session, Finn. And, Charli, it was nice meeting you. I hope to see you again. My door is always open to you." Rebecca stood.

They exchanged goodbyes before they walked out to the car in silence. Finn shut his door and turned the ignition on. The lights reflected off the glass. The sun was already fading beyond the mountains in the west. Winter's early darkness was ready to swallow them up if the quiet tension in the car didn't first.

He turned to her, his gaze full of swirling emotions. "Can I show you something?"

"Yeah."

He slipped the car into reverse. The buildings passed as a light snow drifted from the cloudy grey sky. The closer they got to Shattered Cove, the further her thoughts drifted. *Am I making the right choice for me and the baby? What if I trust him again and he breaks my heart by lying to me? What would it take for Finn to heal and for us to be happy? What if it doesn't work and we end up resenting each other? We might make things worse. At least we can still be civil at the moment. But what if we hurt each other again and ruin everything?*

Could he really heal and get better? Or were they doomed to repeat past mistakes?

43

CHARLI

The sound of the waves crashing against the shore was otherwise in the darkness. Finn shouldered a backpack and grasped her hand in his, enveloping her in warmth and safety as he guided her towards the lone lighthouse covered in holiday lights. The salty sea air whipped, sending a gust of snow flurries into her face.

Finn slotted a key in the door before opening it for her. She followed him inside with blind faith. No matter their issues, Finn would always keep her safe. "What are we doing here?" she asked in a whisper.

He flicked on a light, illuminating a stone stairwell to their right. "I wanted to show you something."

He tugged her hand and guided her up what seemed like endless stairs. Her thighs burned by the time they reached the top. The glassed-in room was empty except for the large rotating light in the middle, shining out to sea.

Finn walked over to a door leading out to what looked like a type of circular balcony surrounding the top of the lighthouse. "The view is better out here." He squeezed her hand reassuringly.

"Alright."

He led her outside, as the icy wind whipped against her face. The coat was warm, but her leggings didn't do much to ward off the chill that swept through her body.

His arm wound around her and pulled her close. "Too cold?"

"Getting there."

"We don't have to stay long. Just wanted to show you this." He pointed out to the distance. Beyond the dark waves, lights dotted the coast. All manner of colored dots glittered and flashed along the beach for the upcoming holidays.

"Wow." Her breath created a fog in front of her, rising like smoke to the heavens above. Millions of stars littered the sky in between the few clouds left. The new moon was nowhere to be seen, making them stand out that much more. When comparing herself to the vast beauty of nature like this, everything else seemed so small, including her.

"It's beautiful," she said as another salty gust of wind lashed against them.

Finn reached out and tucked a strand of hair behind her ear. "Almost as much as you."

Her breathing hitched before she burst out with a laugh. His low chuckle followed, sending a rush of warmth from her belly to her extremities.

"Too cheesy?" He smirked, the light from the lighthouse illuminating half his face.

"A little clichéd." She shivered again.

"Let's get you inside." He guided her back to the small door and into the glass room. The crashing of waves was muted in here, and the sudden loss of wind lapping against her face was a nice reprieve.

He took off the backpack he'd been wearing. Unzipping it, he pulled out a small blanket. He laid it on the ground before gesturing to it. "Have a seat."

She crouched, carefully getting to the edge so she could lean against the wall for back support. "I don't know if I'll be able to get back up by myself," she half-joked.

"I'll carry you down if I have to." He winked before handing her a sandwich.

"What's this?" She took it and unwrapped it.

"Figured you'd be hungry after the appointment." He opened a thermos and poured a steamy cup of what looked and smelled like hot chocolate.

"Mmmm." She greedily accepted the cocoa.

He chuckled. "Damn, if I knew you liked it so much, I would have brought more."

"This is perfect." She inhaled before taking a small sip. Creamy chocolaty sweetness burst to life on her taste buds. Her stomach growled for more than just liquid nourishment. Charli took a bite of the sandwich as Finn dove into his dinner.

"Thank you for feeding me." She set what was left of her sandwich back in the wrapper and took another sip of her rapidly cooling hot cocoa.

"I like taking care of you." His eyes met hers.

"I know you do. But sometimes . . ."

"I take it a step too far?"

She nodded. So, he did get it.

"Thank you for coming with me this afternoon," he said, balling up the paper wrapper and tossing it into the backpack.

"It was enlightening."

He sighed and angled his body so he could look at her. "If you're up for it, I'd love to talk about some things with you."

She drained the rest of her hot chocolate and set it down. "Okay."

"Is your trust something I can still earn back or is it too late for us?"

She blew out a somber breath. "Honestly, Finn, I want to trust you. I don't want us to end. I still want forever with you. I'm willing to give us a chance, but I need to see progress and consistency like Dr. Cole said."

Finn's gaze swept the room before landing back on her. "I want forever with you too. And I'm willing to try to communicate better with you. I'll try not to overstep when it comes to protecting you."

She gave him a small smile. "That's all I ask."

He ran a hand over the back of his neck. "Then it's time I was honest with you about some other things."

Panic lanced across her chest as her pulse quickened. Worry cinched her guts into knots. *What now?*

"Those nightmares I woke up from a couple times? And that time in the kitchen when you surprised me?" He looked at her.

"Yeah?"

"I'm pretty sure they were memories."

She blinked, understanding wrapping around her.

"I think I remember right before the accident. And then some time when I was deployed. I think . . . I think I killed someone over there." His voice broke.

She reached out to his thigh, squeezing in comfort. "You were in a war zone. You did what you had to to survive and come back to me."

He bit his bottom lip. "I remember talking about you to my friend, the one I was in the accident with, Smithson."

Charli's mouth tipped in a sad smile. "You two were pretty

close when you were both serving; when you were in the same unit. His husband called the other day to see how you were doing."

"Really?"

"Yeah. Zack said he'd love to see you sometime but he understood if it was too much, especially since we assumed you didn't really remember Eric."

"I wish he'd made it through the accident. It feels like I should be grieving him, but I don't really know him." Finn's hand rested over hers, his thumb drawing lazy circles on the soft flesh sending a buzz of energy pulling through her. "I remember Smithson talking about proposing to Zack and how much he seemed to love him. We also spoke about how much I adored you, and how lucky we were to have found you both."

It wasn't necessarily a memory of her, but of his love for her. She was grateful for that at least. "Thank you for sharing that with me."

"At first I didn't tell you because you felt like a stranger to me. And then I was still processing the fact that I was a killer. And I had come so close to hurting you. I didn't want you to think of me as a monster."

She shook her head, tipping his chin up to look at her with her hand. His rough stubble scratched against her flesh as his gaze met hers. "I would never think of you that way. You did what you had to do. Survival isn't always pretty. It's messy and dark and even violent for some. You would never take a life unless you thought it was absolutely necessary."

"How can you be so sure?"

She placed her other hand over his heart. "I don't know the details, but I know you."

"Can I kiss you?" he asked, leaning his forehead against hers.

Part of her was terrified of the intimate act, letting him back in with so much on the line. The other part of her wanted to offer him some solace and connect with her husband.

"Yes." Her voice came out with a breath.

His lips fused to hers, hungry yet slow, almost reverent. She opened for him as he wrapped his hand around the back of her neck, his thumb tracing the edge of her jaw. Heat bloomed in her core, spreading to her limbs faster than a wildfire.

She raked her teeth over his bottom lip. He groaned before dipping his tongue inside to taste her.

Charli pulled away, staring into the glassy eyes filled with unbridled desire across from her as she caught her breath.

"I promise to be here for you in whatever capacity you need. I swear I'm gonna earn back your trust and be the man you deserve. I'll wait as long as you want. But I'm not going anywhere, Charli-baby." He ran his thumb over her bottom lip, still slick with the taste of him. "Thank you . . . for loving me enough to not give up."

"Always."

He lifted her hand to his lips and kissed it, almost as if he could sense another kiss would be too much for her. "Let's get you home." He stood, gathering what was left to put away before helping Charli to her feet. Finn tucked the blanket into his backpack and zipped it up.

Carefully, they descended the stairs with him leading the way out to the Jeep.

Once they'd started towards their destination, Finn turned down the radio and asked, "After the baby is born, do you want to stay home with him for a while? Or do you want to go back to work?"

Charli blew out a breath. "Ideally, I'd like to stay home for the first six months or so. Then maybe start back with short shifts only once or twice a week. I told your parents I'd be happy to help with payroll and ordering after the first couple months."

He nodded as if taking it in.

"What would you want?"

"Honestly, I just want you to be happy. I'd definitely prefer you to be home the first year, since I read there is a lot of development that happens during that time. But maybe we could schedule opposite shifts when you go in, so that I can be home with him."

"You read about it?"

He shrugged. "Went to that bookstore in town and Pippa helped me find some good books to start. Makes me feel better with more knowledge about the subject."

She smiled, pride welling in her chest. "You are something else, Finnegan Reed."

He gave a nervous laugh. "Is that a good or bad thing?"

"It's very good," she assured him.

"Any more ideas on a name?" he asked.

"Mmmm, I like Elijah."

"Hmm, not bad. I still like Jamison. But I might be willing to settle for Aiden."

"Oh, I like that one."

"It means born of fire or fiery," Finn said, turning into their driveway.

"Wow, you've really done your research."

Smiling, he said, "I still vote for Jamison."

He turned the engine off and walked around to her side of the car. The Jeep was much higher than their little Toyota, so she was thankful for the extra hand for balance. This growing belly threw everything out of whack. He followed her to the door before sliding in the keys to open it for her. The warmth of the house immediately warded off the chill from the short distance from the vehicle. She hung up the coat as he bent to help her with her snow boots.

The thoughtful action stirred a landslide of emotions in her chest. She needed him. Craved him. Loved him. She wanted to throw caution to the wind and take him upstairs to bed where they could make love and drift off to sleep with intertwined limbs and tangled souls. But it was too soon. She needed to see real change, or they would end up right back where they started.

As if he read her mind, Finn said, "It would make me feel better being here with you so you aren't alone. But I will also respect your wish for space while I earn your trust back. When you're ready for me to come back, I'll be here. Even if I have to stay on the couch."

"I appreciate that. But you're right—I'm not ready."

A flash of disappointment flit through his gaze as he nodded. "Set the alarm behind me." He held her face in the palm of his hands and kissed her forehead. "Love you."

"I love you too."

He turned and walked out the door with a click. She leaned her head against the wood, the silence in his wake deafening.

"Charli?" Finn's muffled voice asked through the door.

"Yeah?"

"Set the alarm."

She did as he'd instructed. "All set."

"Good night," he said before his heavy footsteps moved down the stairs and faded.

She sighed as she moved through the house. Her belly rumbled for food even though it hadn't been that long since she'd eaten. Her bones ached for a hot shower or even better, a bath. And her heart tugged with longing for the man disappearing out of her driveway and down the road. At least two of the three could be mended tonight.

44

FINN

Christmas had always been Finn's favorite holiday. And even though he couldn't remember spending any with Charli, it still felt wrong to wake up in his old room at his parents' house. *Does Charli feel this missing piece inside her too?*

He warmed his hands over the heater in the car, which had just started to get hot after the short ride to his home from his parents'. He hadn't bothered to wait. Getting to Charli was his priority. They may not be living together at the moment, but they were still married. She deserved a proper Christmas breakfast followed by the gifts he'd gotten her.

After pulling the gloves back on, he grabbed the bag of presents and food before exiting the car. His feet crunched on the bits of ice and salt scattered throughout the pathway. He'd come last night to make sure everything had been taken care of in case she needed to leave for any reason.

Nerves skittered up his spine the closer he got to the door. *Will she already be up?*

He knocked first and waited. A few moments later, the curtain on the side of the house swished, drawing his attention to the window before the lock clicked open. *Good girl for checking.*

Charli's sleepy gaze caught on him. Her dark hair was piled in a messy bun on the top of her head, her cheeks pink, eyes bright. She was stunning in her red plaid sleep pants and a T-shirt he recognized as his own, growing increasingly tighter around her midsection.

"Merry Christmas, hot mama."

The pink on her cheeks darkened to a scarlet red. "It's too early for your charms."

He chuckled, leaning in to kiss her cheek before walking past her. She shut the door, clicking the bolt into place once again as he removed his coat and boots. "I brought breakfast." He lifted the bag, heading to the kitchen.

"Smells good. Tell me those are Mama Claire's cinnamon rolls."

"One and the same." He lifted the casserole dish out of the bag and slipped them into the oven before turning it on. "They just need to warm up."

"I could kiss you." She looked longingly towards the stove.

He laughed. "I won't stop you."

Her gaze flicked to him, uncertainty tainting the desire.

Finn pulled out the can of whipped cream and thermos with fresh hot cocoa. "Why don't you get us a couple mugs?"

She went to the cupboard, while he set the bag of gifts in the living room under the small tree he'd helped her put up earlier that week.

Banging came from the kitchen, prompting Finn to investigate what had earned his wife's wrath. Charli lifted the rolling pin and brought it down on the plastic bag, eviscerating what was left of the peppermint candy.

"Not a fan of candy canes?"

She rolled her eyes playfully before opening the bag and sprinkling the crushed treat over the whipped-cream-topped mugs of hot cocoa.

"You love these. We drink them every Christmas." Charli pushed the drink towards him.

He picked it up, giving it a cursory sniff. Peppermint, chocolate, and fresh cream. He sipped, licking the remnants off his upper lip. "Mmm. That *is* good."

She laughed, reaching her finger out to swipe some of the whipped cream he'd obviously missed off his nose before sucking her finger clean.

Fuck that was hot. His cock twitched in his jeans. *Down, boy.* His wife was driving him mad simply by being her adorable self. She had no idea the effect she had on him, did she?

"What else do we do on Christmas together?"

She smiled, her skin crinkling at the edge of her eyes. "Actually, I'm the one who usually makes breakfast while you get the coffee ready. You put on holiday music and get the fire going. We eat, and then we exchange gifts before we . . ." She trailed off, clearing her throat.

"Keep going. Sounds like you were getting to the fun part." Though all of it sounded perfect.

She laughed. "Then you usually ask me to dance to 'The Christmas Song' by Nat King Cole. And . . . one thing usually leads to another."

"That sounds better than the Norman Rockwell version." He chuckled.

She sipped her cocoa, the blush spreading from her cheeks to her elegant neck.

"I happened to bring you some things."

"You did?"

He nodded, holding his hand out to her. She took it and

followed him into the living room. After setting her drink on the coffee table, she took a seat on the couch. Finn walked over to the fireplace and flicked the switch to turn the gas flames on. Pulling out his phone, he opened the music streaming app, choosing a holiday music channel. He offered her a smile and grabbed the bag beside the tree.

"There's a few with your name on them under there too." Charli pointed.

Finn grabbed the small stack in his other hand and set them all on the coffee table. "Can you believe next year we'll be doing this with baby Jamison?"

"Or baby Elijah," she teased. "You open yours first."

The anticipation of seeing her face when she opened what he'd gotten her was killing him. But if she wanted him to go first, he would. He grabbed the top gift, ripping the paper. "A beard kit."

"I noticed you were starting to grow yours out. There is a bunch of different samples so you can decide which you like best." She sipped her cocoa.

"Thank you. Do you like the beard? Or should I go back to shaving?" He ran his hand over the short growth.

She swallowed, her delicate throat bobbing with the action, drawing his attention to the place he wanted to kiss and taste for himself to see if she was as sweet as he remembered.

"I like you either way, but I think I like the beard more—at least for the winter." She offered him a mischievous smile.

"Then it stays."

Finn tore open the next gift. "A Kindle?"

She tucked a piece of hair behind her ear and nodded. "For when you can't sleep."

Emotion welled up in his chest at the thoughtful present. "Thank you."

She handed him the next one. He opened the rest of the gifts. She'd gotten him new socks, a nice dress shirt, and a six-pack of a holiday special edition IPA from Sand Dune Brewery. He returned to the kitchen to take the cinnamon rolls out, spreading out the icing his mother had sent and leaving them to cool on the counter.

When it was time for her to open presents, Finn shifted in his seat. Charli unwrapped them one by one: a Taser that hung from a key chain, scented herbal Epsom salts for her bath, and the baby carrier that Remy and Mia had sworn was an absolute necessity. All he knew was it sounded like a drink.

"Thank you so much. These are so thoughtful."

"There's one more." He motioned to the corner of the table.

She picked up the elongated, blue velvet box wrapped in a gold bow. Running her fingers over the shimmery trident logo of Poseidon's Treasure, her eyes flicked to his before focusing back onto the task at hand. She pulled one side of the ribbon, letting it fall into her lap. As she opened the lid, she gasped. One hand covered her heart while her eyes grew glassy.

"May I?" Finn asked.

She nodded, handing him the box. He slipped the silver necklace out and held it up to her. She turned, her hand going to the base of her neck to hold the few strands of hair that escaped her bun. Finn clasped it but she didn't turn around. He leaned his cheek against hers, as her fingers traced over the shining diamond-encrusted North Star.

"You're my guiding light, Charli-baby. And this is a reminder that I'll always come back to you. Because without you, I'm lost."

Her warm tears slipped down, soaking his own face. A tiny sob escaped her lips. He held on tighter, wrapping his arms around her with both love and protectiveness. She was his everything. And he'd show her every day for the rest of his life.

"Thank you." Her voice was no more than a whisper.

He kissed her cheek. "Anything for you."

* * *

Three hours later, they had eaten their fill of cinnamon rolls, and he'd cleaned the kitchen and cleared out the wrapping paper while she took a shower and got ready. He drove them to his parents' where she promptly kicked him out of the kitchen despite his protests that she should rest and not be on her feet.

Slowly, guests started to arrive. His parents' house had always been a gathering place for those without other family during the holidays, and this year was no different.

Mason arrived with Aspen and his brother, Sebastian. Damon and Steven were right behind them with a bottle of wine and whiskey from a distillery in Colorado. The shy woman from the diner, Brynn, arrived with a pie, cookies, and her teenage son, David.

The doorbell rang. Finn opened it, not bothering to hold back the smile as a cold gust of wind entered along with Link, his dad, and Emma.

"Hey, man. Merry Christmas." Link gave him a slap on the back and a quick hug.

"You too. Solomon." Finn nodded to the old man who clapped him on the shoulder before handing over his coat.

"A good day to celebrate," Solomon said, following his son inside, his voice rising as he greeted Finn's father. They'd been friends for as long as Finn could remember.

"Emma. Wow. You sure have grown up." It was the first time he'd seen her since his accident.

She smiled before giving him a hug. "If only everyone could see that." She cut a glance towards Link before plastering on a smile. "Where is the pregnant goddess?"

Finn chuckled. "In the kitchen with all the other ladies."

"Oh, they kicked you out, huh?" She smirked.

"Do me a favor and tell her to sit down and drink some water."

"Okay, daddy bear."

He laughed and shook his head as she disappeared into the kitchen.

Laughter and voices rose from the different areas in the home. Aspen and David were playing a card game with Sebastian and Steven. The ladies were all in the kitchen. Thankfully Charli was seated at the island, a cup of what seemed to be hot cocoa in front of her while she laughed with Emma and Brynn. Finn's mother chatted away with Damon while they inspected the turkey next to the ham. All manner of savory smells drifted out of the warm kitchen.

His parents' home was brimming with love, laughter, and holiday cheer. The difference between now and Thanksgiving was like night and day. Rather than the numbing hopelessness and anger he'd had a month ago, now he could feel the warmth of the season and the joy of having so much to celebrate and be thankful for.

"Retirement! Ha! Coming from you, that's rich." Solomon slapped his knee and shook his head at Zeke.

Finn leaned against the doorway to the living room, observing the men around the tree.

"I'm stepping away from the bar. I only do the books as it is now that we hired more help. Claire and I want to take a trip to the Bahamas this spring," Zeke said, taking a sip of his whiskey.

"You should listen to Mr. Reed, Papa. Maybe you should

take a trip to Ghana and see Aunty," Link suggested before lifting the beer to his lips.

"You should be the one to go to Ghana. You need to practice your Twi." Solomon waved his hand dismissively.

Link shrugged.

"How are you doing?" Mason asked, standing next to him.

The instinct to dismiss the question with a simple "fine" was on the tip of his tongue. Instead, he spoke the truth. "I'm okay. I just wish I hadn't fucked up. I don't like her staying at the house alone."

Mason nodded. "You still seeing Dr. Cole?"

"Yeah. Once a week. Thank you, by the way, for recommending her."

Mason took a long pull from the bottle in his hands. "Stick with it, and I'm sure it will all work out."

"Dinner is served." Claire's voice came from behind them.

Finn went in search of Charli as the kitchen grew even more crowded. Everyone lined up for the buffet-style dinner.

Charli was now seated in the dining room, her drink in front of her.

"Hey, honey, can I get you a plate?" Finn asked.

She looked up at him, her eyes shining with affection and gratitude and genuine happiness. "Would you? My feet are killing me."

"Be right back."

Finn grabbed a place in line and loaded up a plate with a little of everything before returning to her. Damon had taken the seat on one side of her, but the chair on the other remained empty when he returned with his own food.

Everyone gathered together, sharing food, joy, and cheer. Link was the last to join them, opting rather to sit at the kitchen bar with the teens than take the empty seat next to Emma.

"What's that about?" Finn leaned over and asked Charli.

She glanced between her friend and Link before turning to him with a shrug. "Not quite sure, but it seems to get worse every year."

After dinner, some of the guests broke off into games. The more the drinks flowed, the louder it got. His family's home wasn't small, but it wasn't huge either. His head rang from the extra noise. His chest tightened as anxiety twisted. Needing some space, he stepped out the back door, not bothering with a coat. Sucking in the crisp winter air, he tipped his head towards the pine trees at the edge of his parents' yard creating long shadows in the quickly fading sunlight. The snow sparkled, reflecting the illumination from the windows in the house. The door behind him opened and shut with a click. Finn turned.

Charli's worried gaze was directed at him. "You okay?"

He hesitated. "It's too crowded in there for me."

"We can go home. I'm pretty tired myself."

He studied her. "You sure?"

She nodded, turning to return inside. He took a step to follow her, but she stopped.

"Finn?" Charli turned back to face him.

"Yeah?"

"Can you . . . I mean . . . Would you stay tonight? I just . . . don't want to be alone on Christmas," Charli asked, biting her lip.

Finn stepped forward, tugging it free with his thumb. He smiled. "I still owe you that dance."

"I'm not . . . I mean, I just wondered if you'd hold me tonight." Her eyes looked up to him, vulnerability flashing.

"Absolutely." Holding her tonight would be the best gift he could have asked for this Christmas. And just maybe the magic of the holiday season could repair some of what was broken. Maybe Finn could be the man Charli needed.

45

FINN

It was New Year's Eve, and the bar was loud and crowded. They'd tripled up on bartenders tonight, and Mason had got together a few more guys for extra security. Finn pulled the handle of the beer tap, carefully filling the order for one of the customers. Despite his request, Charli was busy as ever taking orders at the other end of the bar. Her stride represented much more of a waddle at thirty weeks into her pregnancy. She reached for a bottle, the strain evident on her face with her belly against the shelf.

Finn handed the beer to the customer. "It's on the house." He came up behind her before picking the vodka from the shelf and handed it to her.

"Thanks." She smiled.

"Isn't there some payroll that you can work on in the back room instead?"

She huffed. Her eyes narrowing. "I am not made of glass. I can do this . . . I just might need some help reaching stuff."

He chuckled. "Alright."

She mixed the drink while he leaned against the counter. "You doing okay?"

His body hummed with the constant need to be aware, looking out for danger. This was one of the most difficult parts of his PTSD—the hypervigilance. His therapist had given him some techniques to ground himself, but he would need a break sooner than later. "I might step out back for a few minutes."

She nodded. "Now might be a good time while there's a break in the crowd."

He kissed her cheek, leaving his hand on her belly. Being close to her was like touching a live wire. Every synapse in his body fired with yearning and desire. He had relished holding her Christmas night. But he'd also returned to his parents the next day not wanting to push her. He'd be patient for as long as it took to show her he was trustworthy. "Be right back."

Finn disappeared out of the main room, firing off a text to Mason to keep an extra eye on Charli while he was gone.

He passed through the storeroom before opening the back door, which was surprisingly already unlocked. The frigid temperature blasted through his body, offering relief to the rising panic, grounding him. Exhaling, his breath became a fog carried away by the wind. He stepped out and shut the door. The motion-sensor light switched on, illuminating the delivery bay as he sat on the steps. A dumpster and recycling crate stood off to his right.

Finn ran a hand over his beard before resting it over his thigh. A flash of light drew his attention to the gravel. He inched forward, picking up the cigarillo butt from the ground. *Who was smoking out here?* Something about it was familiar. He brought it closer to the light and froze. The smoked-tobacco-melded-with-cherry filled his nostrils. The memory pummeled over him like a freight train.

Darkness. So much darkness. A puff of smoke bloomed in his vision. A man. An arrogant voice eerily familiar setting Finn on edge with his pulse racing.

Finn reached out, swatting the smoke away, but it only seemed to make it worse.

"You have a lot of people counting on you, Major Reed."

"How do you know who I am?" Finn heard himself ask.

It was like the car dream all over again—he had no control.

"I know a lot of things about you. Like you and your pretty wife run the bar. Your parents' address. And we have a mutual friend who assures me you can keep your mouth shut."

"Are you threatening me?"

The man gave an amused laugh. "I don't make threats. I make promises. Think about it. You're gonna need a side hustle if you want to buy that house."

Finn stiffened. How did he know Finn and Charli were trying to buy a home? "Look, buddy, I don't know who you are or what you want, but I'll take a wild guess and say it isn't exactly above board. I don't want any part of it. And you ever come near my family and you'll regret the day you were born."

Another puff of smoke. Finn coughed, nearly choking on it. Menacing laughter rang out, growing with each second.

"You don't know who you're dealing with. But you will. You don't turn down mi familia. Carelli doesn't ask twice." The man's brown eyes locked on to him.

His face was still shrouded by darkness, but those eyes. He knew them.

Just as soon as it had started, the flashback evaporated, leaving nothing but the subtle hints of smoky cherry in the wind.

Finn shot to his feet and bent over at the waist, sucking in icy lungfuls of air. "Fuck!" *What the hell did I get myself into?* Rage boiled in his veins as much as dread. Because he was positive Charli's attack was, in fact, because of him, and now he knew the answer of who'd done it was locked inside his memories. But why? Because Finn turned down something? Who was Carelli? This guy sounded like a mafia wannabe. He closed his eyes, willing the memory to return, reaching for the flashes of the past. They slipped through his mind's fingers, disappearing into wisps of nothingness. Finn's blood turned to ice.

"Charli," he gasped, running up the steps and pulling the door open. He halted, fear crashing over him.

If she knew without a doubt it was his fault she was attacked, she might leave him for good. Before it had just been a guess, but now . . . now Finn was sure. Charli would be scared for her safety and the baby's, and rightfully so. If he kept this to himself, maybe he could enlist Bently's help and protect her without her ever having to know.

"No." As much as it was going to kill him, he'd have to tell her so she could make the choice. He'd promised her. If it took him peeling back the layers of his flesh until he was exposed as the cause of her pain, he'd face it. Because Charli deserved better—even if that meant it wouldn't be him. He loved her enough to give her everything and let her make her own decision. It just might tear him apart in the process.

Finn walked back inside, his shaky steps purposeful and determined. Charli's spine was stiff. A scowl marred her gorgeous face as her eyes narrowed across the bar. Finn followed her line of sight. Laura leaned over the bar, shouting over the noise to Charli with an evil grin he hadn't seen before. There was nothing but malice in her eyes.

"I don't see how Finn can stand to look at you. It's no wonder he's back at his parents'. Word around town is y'all are finally getting a divorce. I'm sure he'll need someone familiar to ease his broken heart." Laura sneered.

Finn moved at lightning speed, catching Charli's fist before she did something she couldn't take back. He wrapped his free hand around Charli's head and pulled her into a kiss that they usually saved for behind closed doors. Charli squeaked with surprise before she melded into him, the tension draining from her limbs as she relaxed against his embrace. Finn backed away, staring into her eyes glazed with want. It was gasoline thrown onto the fire that had been building between them during this separation.

Finn spoke to Charli, not bothering to look at Laura. "You are the most beautiful woman I've ever laid eyes on. My goddess. And I'm yours, always and forever."

Charli looked up at him and grinned, gratitude and pure adoration pouring from her. The beauty of the moment was tainted by the knowledge that once he told her what he'd remembered, she might never look at him the same. His hand squeezed the back of her neck, holding on just a little longer.

Laura made a disgusted noise.

Finn turned to her, his rage boiling to the surface. He'd never lay a hand on a woman, but boy did this one test those limits. He pointed towards the door. "Don't ever speak to my wife like that. Don't ever contact me again. Get the fuck out of our bar, and don't even think about coming back."

Laura's mouth dropped open, her eyes widening. "But, Finny. I—"

"Shut your fucking mouth and leave, bitch," Charli snarled, her arm wrapping around Finn's waist.

Finn nodded towards Mason standing by the door. Mason walked over, weaving through the crowd of oblivious patrons.

"Take her outside. Laura, here, isn't allowed to return—ever," Finn directed.

Mason gave a quick jerk of his head in acknowledgement as he reached for Laura's arm.

She pulled away, fury blazing in her expression. "I can manage myself." She tipped her nose in the air and left with Mason trailing behind.

"I'm sorry—I had no idea—"

"You are my hero." Charli's smile widened.

Her statement took him by surprise—almost as much as the kiss she then planted on him. He gripped her tighter as if he could hold on to this moment forever. The truth was this might be the last time he got to have her in his arms like this.

After they rang in the new year and passed out drinks for another two hours, they ushered the last patrons out the door. Charli yawned, sitting on a barstool. The other bartender, Ken, wiped the counter down.

Finn came up behind her, kissing her on the cheek and inhaling her scent. Amber and honey, like rich whiskey. "I have something I need to tell you, but I'd like to wait until tomorrow when we've both had some rest."

Charli's eyebrows drew together. "Is it bad?"

He ran a hand over his face and sighed. "It's a memory."

"Charli?" Mason interrupted.

"Yeah?"

"Found this on the desk in the office while I shut everything down." Mason handed her a small gift box wrapped in ribbon.

She took it from him and inspected it. "There's nothing but the tag with my name on it. I wonder who it could be from." Charli pulled open the red ribbon before lifting the lid.

The color drained from her face. Her body trembled as every muscle grew rigid.

"What is it?" Finn took it from her hands. Inside was one lone, moon-shaped earring and a note.

I haven't earned this yet. See you soon.

"What the fuck?" Finn asked as he wrapped his arms around his wife. "What is this, baby?"

"I thought I lost it in the attack."

His body turned to stone. "What?"

"I was wearing it the night . . . He's back. He was here, Finn!" Charli clawed at his shirt, pulling him closer, clinging to him like she was afraid for her life.

"We need to call Bently," Mason said, whipping out his phone and stepping away.

Finn set the box on the bar and held his wife while she broke apart in his arms, knowing that this was it. This was the end. Even if she pushed him away and hated him after this, he'd make sure she was safe—no matter the cost. He drew in a fortifying breath, summoning the courage. "I think I know who did it."

Charli gasped. "What? How?"

"It's all my fault." He knew it in his bones.

Charli pulled away from him. His heart cinched tighter the farther she got from him. Tears glimmered in her confused gaze.

"When I went out back, I had a memory return. Well, bits and pieces."

Charli swallowed.

"A man approached me about doing something for him. And I turned him down. He threatened you and my parents."

"You . . . did you do something, Finn?" Fear and uncertainty saturated the air between them.

Finn shook his head. "I remember telling him to fuck off, basically."

Her shoulders relaxed some.

"He said something about messing with *mi familia* and then mentioned Carelli."

"Fuck," Mason said, drawing both of their gazes.

"What?" Finn asked.

Mason pursed his lips together and shook his head. "I worked security for a club in the city one time—and it was my last . . . The Carelli family is mafia, and they are trying to extend from Boston up the east coast."

"The mafia? As in the actual mob?" Finn gasped.

"What does that have to do with you and me?" Charli asked, fear tinging her shaky voice.

"They wanted me to do something, and I turned them down. I think your attack was a warning for me to comply."

"But that was more than a year ago. Why wait so long to come back?" Charli asked.

"I don't know."

"I'm gonna go wait outside for Bently. He should be here any minute." Mason excused himself.

Finn turned to Charli. "It's all my fault."

Charli's expression morphed from confusion to anger.

He deserved all her rage. She'd almost died because of him. And now she was in danger. His child was in harm's way. And god—his parents could be too.

"Why would you think that?"

Her question stunned him. "I should have told you and gotten help from the beginning. Maybe if I'd—"

Her hand rested over his heart. "Stop it right now. Don't you go there. Yes, you should have told me and probably Bently too. But you didn't give in to them. That would be even more dangerous. Once you get caught up in that stuff, it's impossible to get out . . . At least, that's what I know from movies." She offered him a small smile.

Was she delusional? She wasn't blaming him?

She must have read his mind, because a look of recognition flashed on her lovely face. "Finn, you thought this would change everything, didn't you? You figured I would blame you?"

He nodded.

"And you still told me." It was more a statement than a question.

"I promised you. And you deserve to know the truth."

She crashed into his arms, hugging him tight. "I love you, Finn. I love you so much."

Stunned, he managed to squeeze her back and lay a kiss on the top of her head. "I love you too." He closed his eyes, relishing her closeness. "I wish I could remember more. Maybe I said something to Bently about it when it happened."

"You didn't." Bently interrupted them.

Finn looked up.

"Mason filled me in." Bently's sympathetic gaze focused on Charli in his arms. "But I think it's best if we get her home to rest. I can follow you and we can talk there, or we can do this in the morning. I'll get this fingerprinted and taken into evidence." Bently lifted the lid of the box with a pen and shook his head. His expression turned to stone.

"What is it? Why would he send this to me?" Charli asked.

Bently squeezed the bridge of his nose before locking his gaze with her. "I believe it's a trophy. The other victims were all missing an item of jewelry. He hasn't earned it, I'm assuming, means he didn't finish the job he set out to do."

Charli gasped, her hand covering her mouth.

Finn squeezed her closer against him. Blood roared in his ears. *Over my fucking dead body will anyone touch her.*

Finn's gaze swept over his wife. The dark circles under her eyes tugged at his heart, knowing he was the cause of her exhaustion—whether it be because of the growing child inside her or the danger that followed her around, stealing her peace of mind like a thief. "Tomorrow." Finn kissed her temple. "I want to get you home, run you a bath, and take care of you. Let's deal with this when we are more rested."

He thought for sure she'd argue, but instead she sagged in his arms as if all her remaining energy had been drained.

"Okay. I'll get this dusted for fingerprints now and be over first thing in the morning. I'll have a car stationed outside your house for extra security tonight.

"Thank you—oh there is a cigarillo in the back. It might be nothing, but it is what brought on the flashback. Could be his. And the door was unlocked."

"Got it," Bently promised.

Once Finn had her in her coat and settled in the car, he waved to Bently as they drove towards their home.

"Do I get a foot massage?" Charli asked, leaning her head on the window, eyes closed.

Finn reached out and held her hand. "You get a full-body massage."

"Mmm."

After another moment of silence, Charli spoke. "Thank you for telling me everything and taking care of me."

He pulled past the cruiser sitting across their driveway and parked at their house. "I will do absolutely anything you need, Charli-baby. That also means that I will not be leaving you alone until we catch this guy."

"And then?" She looked over at him.

"And then it's up to you."

"I don't want you to go anywhere. You belong with me, at home," she said, her voice full of conviction.

He reached across the console, pulling her into a kiss. His lips slid over hers, tasting her love, feeding off her trust. He sucked on her tongue, pulling her worry, absorbing her fear. He'd take it all on himself if it meant even offering her an ounce of reprieve. She was his everything—his guiding light through the darkest of nights. And he had a feeling things were about to get a whole lot darker before they got better.

46

CHARLI

Charli opened the freezer door, searching for her newest craving. She frowned at its absence. "Fuuuuck." She closed the door a little harder than necessary. Her patience was wearing as thin as her nerves these past two weeks since everything had gone down at the bar.

"What's wrong?" Finn asked, sidling up next to her. He was never more than six feet away from her at all times, which was comforting, but it was also starting to get on her nerves. Other than sitting at his parents' while he worked, being stuck in the house was making her feel claustrophobic.

"We're out of peppermint stick ice cream," she whined. The self-pity in her voice made her cringe. As much as she loved the little pumpkin growing inside her, she was itching to get him out. There was hardly any room left, and the stretch marks now covered the sides of her belly.

"We can go get some," Finn offered, wrapping his arms around her middle. His beard tickled the side of her neck. "And maybe stop by the Stardust Café for some tea and treats."

She sighed into his embrace. "You know how to fix everything."

He stiffened. "I wish."

She turned around to face him. "Bently said he'd have an update today."

Finn nodded as his phone rang. Lifting it from his pocket, he said, "Speak of the devil." Finn tapped the speaker button and answered. "Give me some good news."

"Charli there with you?" Bently asked.

"I'm here."

"Well, I didn't tell you that the FBI showed up after I did some more digging on Carelli," Bently said.

Charli cut Finn a questioning glance.

"What do they have to do with this?" Finn asked.

"Agent Mallory informed me that is above my pay grade." Bently's voice was tinged with bitterness. "But don't worry. I'm not backing down. We will figure this out. I've got some connections, and I'm asking around."

"Keep us in the know," Finn said.

"Of course. You two stay safe. I still have a shift taking turns outside your house, but my resources are thin. If there is a bigger emergency in town, they might get called away."

"Thank you, Bent."

"You got it. Keep our girl safe." Bently ended the call.

Finn slipped the phone into his back pocket. His shoulders seemed weighed down by the news.

Charli threaded her hand through his. "Let's go get those treats you promised me."

"Okay." He leaned in and kissed her temple.

It was sweet, but disappointment settled in her belly. He hadn't given her more than a chaste kiss or made a move beyond holding her these last two weeks. *Is he still blaming himself and pulling away? Is he not attracted to me anymore?*

Everything he did screamed that he loved her, from the way he took care of her to the way his eyes lingered. *So why isn't he making a move?* She pulled away, grabbing her coat off the hook and slipping it on.

As he helped her into her boots and zipped them up, the urge to ask him welled within her. She swallowed, holding it at bay. Fear over him rejecting her was stronger. She didn't want him to respond out of pressure, but out of his own desire. *So why does he stop things when I try to go further? I made it clear I was ready . . . didn't I?*

His phone dinged. Finn pulled it out, the corner of his mouth turning up at whatever was on the screen before he slipped it back into his pocket. Opening the door, he motioned her through. "After you."

They went to the grocery store first. Finn added two cartons of peppermint stick ice cream, while Charli waddled by his side. Her back and hips ached. Her belly felt like a watermelon stretched to the max. Everything hurt. She added some fresh produce and the basics they needed along with chocolate chips, because she'd been baking up a storm at the house. Being stuck inside and not working was driving her crazy. She'd needed something to keep herself busy. There was only so much cross-stitch and reading a woman could do.

Finn held up a bag of white chocolate chips. "Next time you feel like baking, can you do a batch of white chocolate macadamia cookies?"

"You like those?" she asked, surprised. Never in the time she'd known him had he asked for those.

He shrugged. "Brynn made them for Christmas, and I may have been the one to eat most of them."

"I'll ask her for the recipe." She smiled.

"Thanks." He kissed her cheek. Finn's phone went off again. He pulled it out. Brow wrinkling in concern, he tipped the screen away from her as he typed out a reply.

What the hell?

"Who was that?"

Finn diverted his attention to the other side of the aisle. "Where would the nuts be?"

She pointed to the spot a little farther along, unease slithering inside her. *What is he hiding now?*

Charli was about to demand an answer when a familiar voice said, "Hey, guys."

She turned, taking in the tall, handsome beekeeper pushing a cart with one hand and holding the hand of his daughter with the other. "Roman, happy New Year."

"You too."

Charli waved to the little girl. "Hi, Ariel."

She tucked closer to her father and offered a shy smile.

Roman's hand rested on her small shoulder protectively, spinning her around so that she'd look up at him. He moved his hands, communicating to his daughter in sign language as he spoke the words aloud. "Can you say hi to Charli and Finn?"

Ariel lifted her hand and gave a small wave to Charli before squeezing closer to her father.

Charli smiled. "You are getting so big. Did you have a good Christmas?"

Ariel nodded, tugging on one of the dark twists in her hair.

"How's your mom?" Charli asked Roman.

"She's doing good," Roman answered.

"You're Ricky's brother," Finn said, as if just putting the pieces together.

Charli turned, studying her husband's face. Was he still angry at Ricky for being with Laura? Wouldn't that mean he still had feelings for her?

Roman chuckled. "Ricardo is indeed my little brother."

"What's he up to these days?" Finn asked.

"He works with me and the bees," Roman replied.

Ariel tugged on her father's hand. He looked down at her as she moved her hands.

"Sure thing, sweet pea," Roman said before turning back to Charli and Finn. "We gotta run, but it was nice seeing you."

"You too," Charli said.

Finn guided the cart towards the checkout. "Anything else we need?"

"No, we're all set."

They got in line behind a mom talking quietly to her toddler while the checkout person rang up her things.

"Did we go to school with Roman Emerson too?" Finn asked.

"He's four years older than Ricky. When you were a freshman, he would have been a senior. So, maybe your first year."

"He has another brother too, right?" he asked.

"Yeah. And a younger sister. Mama Emerson adopted Ricky and her niece within a couple years of each other."

He nodded as his pocket dinged three times with consecutive messages. Finn pulled it out, switching it to vibrate and putting it back into his pocket without reading them.

"Is his daughter deaf?" Finn asked.

"No. But she's mute. She can hear just fine, but she hasn't talked since . . . well, since everything happened with her mom."

He opened his mouth as if to ask, but the cashier grabbed their attention. "How are you today?"

"Great." Finn loaded their things on the conveyer belt.

A flicker of unease coasted through Charli. She turned around, searching the space around them. No one, and nothing out of the ordinary. But something didn't feel right. An invisible weight settled over her. Anxiety stirred in her belly like the ticking of a clock. A bad feeling twisted in her chest— a premonition that time was running out.

47

CHARLI

The earthy scent of roasted coffee beans and sweet pastries wrapped Charli in a warm hug as Finn ushered her inside the Stardust Café.

"Should we get it to go?" she asked.

"Nah, it's cold enough outside to keep the ice cream frozen. We won't be too long. The rest of the groceries should be fine. Why don't you get a table, and I'll get the drinks?"

"I want a peppermint mocha, half-caffeinated."

"But—"

"One cup of coffee a day isn't going to hurt the baby, and I haven't had any in months." She crossed her arms ready for an argument.

"Okay. Anything else?"

She opened her mouth with a retort but quickly closed it again. She smiled. "A mermaid cookie. Oh, and a lavender scone."

"Be right back."

She admired his backside as he walked up to the counter. Remy wasn't working today, but instead, Rae. The young girl had asked for a job at The Shipwreck not too long ago, but she wasn't old enough. *How many jobs does she have?* She was still working for Jasmine at The Lighthouse Inn last Charli knew. There was a story there.

Settling into the chair, Charli tried to get comfortable in the seat, but at thirty-two weeks pregnant, it seemed an impossible task.

"Here you go." Finn set her goodies and drink in front of her.

"Thank you." She wrapped her hands around the steaming cup of minty coffee goodness and inhaled. Something about the smell of peppermint was almost as good as the taste lately. Her mouth watered as her craving intensified. The only thing that would make this better would be some of that ice cream they'd picked up in it.

"Keep staring at that cup like that and I'm likely to get jealous." Finn laughed.

Charli met his amused gaze and shook her head.

"Wanna go over some of the checkup questions?" Finn asked.

Charli took a tentative sip of her drink, moaning from the richness.

Finn's eyes snapped to hers, Adam's apple bobbing as he swallowed.

"Sure. Where'd we leave off?"

He pulled out his phone. She stiffened. *Another message?*

"How satisfied were you with sexual intimacy this week?" Finn read off the device.

So, he'd added the questions to his notes? She breathed a sigh of relief and relaxed into the chair.

Heat rose to her cheeks. She took a bite of the cookie to buy her some time. She wasn't satisfied this week or last week for that matter. But telling him that was . . . scary. Because what if he didn't want her anymore with her growing and changing body? What if Laura was right? What if her mother had been right all along?

You ruined my body. That's why your father left. You just wait. One of these days your whoring ways will get the best of you and you'll see. You'll be all alone.

Her mother's words were like darts of poison creeping in, tainting her joy. She didn't think of the woman often, but boy her mother's vitriol had a way of sneaking in when she least expected it. *I thought I was over this.*

"Sweetheart?" Finn asked, casting her a concerned gaze as his hand enveloped hers.

A rush of calmness settled over her at their connection. "Honestly, not very. It's hard to be satisfied when we are not having any sex—but I understand that you . . . I mean, I know I'm a walking blimp balloon at this point."

His hold tightened a fraction. "Is that what you think?" Finn's voice was tight.

She sighed. "What else am I supposed to assume?"

His jaw clenched as he shook his head. Tipping the cup to his lips, he took a sip before leaning forward. "If you think for one god damned minute that I don't want you, then you are sorely mistaken. I have a constant hard-on around you, and I've jacked off more times than I can count in the shower." His voice was close to a growl.

He reached over, tracing the seam of her lips with his thumb. "You are the most beautiful woman on the face of this planet, and seeing your belly grow with life makes me want to fall to my knees and worship you like the goddess you are."

Charli gasped.

"Obviously I haven't been doing a good enough job at showing you that. But I thought you needed to take it slow, that you weren't ready. I didn't want you to assume I only wanted to come back to you for sex. Because that hasn't ever been a problem for us. This has." He motioned between the two of them. "So, what's something I can do to improve our sexual intimacy this week?" He smirked, asking the next question on the checklist without having to look.

"Make love to your wife. And that whole getting-on-your-knees thing would be nice too." She grinned, unable to hold back the excitement and pure happiness that radiated from every cell.

"Should I praise you with my tongue or my fingers?" He winked, a wicked gleam in his eye that promised wonderfully dirty things in her future.

"Both."

"I will do that and more. But not tonight."

Her heart sunk, her bottom lip sticking out in a pout.

He chuckled and tapped her nose. "I gotta get to work soon and we both know you'll be asleep by the time I get to my parents' to pick you up. Tomorrow evening, I'm all yours."

"First, I don't want to go to your parents' house again. I'll be fine at home. We have the alarm, and I'll be armed. Second, why tomorrow evening and not the morning?"

He sighed and sat back, taking another swig of his coffee. "I don't want you staying home alone. Not until we catch this guy. That's non-negotiable."

His phone buzzed on the table. Her eyes drew to the name that flashed, but she couldn't read it because he picked it up too fast. Anger rose. "Who keeps texting you, Finn?" Every time she felt like they took a step forward, it was two steps back with this guy. "Are you keeping a secret from me?"

He bit his bottom lip as if holding back a smile. "Yes."

Her belly flipped and then turned to stone.

"But not in the way you're thinking. I promise it's a good secret, and to answer your second question, it's why we won't have time tomorrow morning to fulfill those fantasies of yours." He reached his hand out to hers, his eyes locking on her. "Trust me."

Two words that scared her more than anything. But nothing but genuine honesty reflected in those chocolate-brown spheres. Could she? "Fine. Tomorrow, you'll tell me?"

He nodded. "Promise."

"Alright. Take me home so we can eat before you head to work. Then I'm staying home."

"Charli." Finn's voice was a warning.

She crossed her arms over her chest. "You cannot dictate my choices. I will not live in fear of this asshole. He got the drop on me once, but I'll be ready for him this time."

Finn exhaled a frustrated breath. "Sweetheart, I can't focus if I am worried about you. And it's not just you we have to think about. I know you want to feel in control of something in your life right now, but I also want you to be safe. I would never forgive myself if something happened to you again. I don't care if you get mad at me, but there is no way in hell I'm leaving you alone tonight when I go to work."

Is that what this is? Am I grasping for what little control I can have? That's why he didn't put up a fuss about the coffee.

"I'll see if Emma is still in town. I don't think she's heading back on tour until next month." Charli conceded.

Finn stood. Taking her hand, he helped her up before he wrapped his arms around her. Her belly the only thing between them, he spoke low into her ear. "Thank you. I just want you safe, Charli-baby."

She nodded with a sigh. "I know."

Maybe it was the hormones that were making everything seem like a bigger deal than it was. But if anyone had a right to fall apart, it was her.

Her husband had almost died, then woken up in a coma

not remembering her, followed by the bumpiest ride that had ensued afterwards. Now a serial rapist-slash-murderer was after her, all while she was growing a human inside her. Becoming a mother was terrifying in itself after the example she'd had and the childhood she'd survived. But Finn's fresh woodsy scent brought her an instant hit of calm. His touch grounded her, made her relax into the cocoon of safety he offered. If she'd learned anything over the last several months, it was that life was fleeting and you never knew what would happen tomorrow. So, for now, she'd hold on to him a little bit longer. She'd try to memorize the feel, the taste, the smell of him. Because nobody knew what the next day would bring. Today might be all they had left.

48

CHARLI

Charli opened her eyes, cringing against the harsh light coming from the window. Groaning, she turned on her other side, which was a lot more work with a watermelon attached to your middle. Her hips ached as she adjusted herself, tucking the pillow between her thighs for support.

A chuckle came from her side as the clean scent of her husband wafted over her. He tucked a strand of hair behind her ear. "Are you up, sleeping beauty?"

"I am now. Who left the curtain open?" she grumbled.

"I believe I caught you peeking out at the almost full moon on one of your many trips to the bathroom last night."

She sighed, the fuzzy memories coming back.

Hot lips coasted over her cheek, ending on her nose. His breath was sweet and earthy with mint and coffee. "Need you to get up, sweetheart."

"Why?" she whined. *The secret!*

Charli jolted upright, sure she looked like a crazy person

with wild eyes and bed head. Finn's brown gaze swept over her, hungry and amused.

"What is the secret you've been keeping?"

He grinned, a spark of excitement and was that nervousness shining back in his chocolate spheres? "Just a little longer, then I'll show you."

"You said tomorrow. The time is now, Finn."

He placed a warm hand over her thigh, rubbing back and forth with his thumb. Damn, he shouldn't do that when she'd gone weeks without sex. His touch was like a match igniting the desire within her.

"Okay, first part of the surprise is that Remy, Emma, and the girls will be here to help you get ready. So, you might want to shower and brush your teeth before they arrive in the next —" He picked up his phone. "Twenty minutes."

"Finn!"

He laughed. "You're so cute when you're frustrated."

She scowled at him and crossed her arms over her chest.

He crawled over her, making her lean against the headboard. His hands rested against the wooden frame, caging her in. Leaning in, he ran his nose up the side of her face and inhaled. His voice was a gruff whisper. "After you get ready, the girls are gonna take you somewhere. I'll meet you there. Don't go anywhere alone. And I promise, I'll make it worth your while."

She shivered at the soft command.

"And when we get home, I'm gonna show every inch of your body the attention it needs. Gonna make love to you until the sun comes up. I'll bring you to the edge, again and again, until you beg me for release."

"Why not a preview right now?" Her voice cracked with her own need. Dampness leaked into her panties.

"No time, sweetheart." He kissed her cheek before capturing her mouth.

She clung to his shirt, pulling him closer. "Please?"

He pulled away. Her body ached with the loss.

"Take your panties off."

She couldn't hide her smile as she shimmied out of her underwear.

"Spread your legs and play with your breasts," Finn ordered.

"But—"

"Trust me." He pressed her knee to the bed.

She opened for him. His eyes glued to her fingers slowly pinching her brown nipples. His chest heaved as her mouth parted. She pinched and twisted, sending a zing of pleasured pain coursing through her. Finn groaned, his hazy eyes locked on her ministrations. Her pussy ached for his touch. She squeezed her thighs together in response.

Finn's strong hands pressed her legs apart, opening them wide once again. "Keep those spread. Need to see your pussy while you touch yourself."

Fire coated her skin in an icy hot burn.

Finn licked his lips, his gaze darkening. "That's it, baby. Faster."

"Touch me," she begged.

"Not yet."

She swirled her finger, working herself up, eyes locked on to his as he touched every inch of her with his starving gaze.

"That pussy is fucking beautiful. So greedy. Bet you want my cock, don't you, sweetheart?"

"Yes!" Her voice was dripping with need as she approached the edge.

"You want me to fuck that pretty cunt? Make you scream my name?"

"Finn, please!" His dirty talk had her teetering over the edge. "I'm about to—"

Blinding light filled her vision as Finn's tongue delved between her hot, hungry, tight heat. She arched, lifting her hips off the bed. Rough fingers dug into her hips as he devoured her. Her body pulsed, clenched, and rippled with overwhelming pleasure as a tidal wave of ecstasy slammed through her. She was unable to speak from the sheer unrelenting power of rapture. He sucked on her clit, the tinge of pain adding yet another orgasm rocketing through her. Her legs shook as he pulled away. Her breath was labored and raw.

Finn kissed up her thighs before landing on her lips. Tasting her essence on him sent a bolt of possessiveness through her.

He smirked. "You've got five minutes before they get here."

How was she supposed to function after the most powerful orgasm of her life? Surely, he didn't actually expect her to move for at least an hour. Maybe after a little nap . . .

"Charli."

"Hmmm?"

"Shower."

"I just need a minute," she argued.

"Wish I could let you. But if you want the surprise, it's kinda time sensitive."

She opened her eyes. "Fine."

He helped her up, giving her a kiss before his phone dinged. She stepped into the hot spray of the shower as he checked it.

"They're here. I'll let them in and take off. See you in a few hours." He smiled.

"Love you."

"Love you too."

* * *

Once Charli was clean and had brushed her teeth, she wrapped a towel over her hair and tied her bathrobe. Entering her bedroom, she found her friends congregated. "What are you guys doing here?" Charli asked.

Remy stepped forward, clapping her hands together excitedly. "Can I just say you have the most romantic husband in the world! Well, I mean besides Mikel."

Emma rolled her eyes. "You, my dear, have to get ready."

"For what?" Charli asked.

"For your surprise." Brynn motioned to a garment bag on the bed.

Charli walked over and picked it up. "Did you guys bring this?"

"Your husband sent me to pick up the dress. He selected it out of the options I gave him." Mia smiled as Charli unzipped the bag.

Soft champagne chiffon material slipped out. She brushed her hand over the delicate fabric.

"And I brought the shoes." Belle opened a box, showing off the matching ballet flats.

"I picked up the jewelry he had custom made." Jasmine pushed a blue velvet box with the trident of Poseidon's Treasure logo in gold.

Charli set the dress down and opened the lid. She gasped. Oxidized silver in the shape of the North Star and embedded with tiny diamonds hung from a teardrop gem, matching her necklace perfectly.

"What is all this . . . What is he . . ." She was too stunned to finish her question.

Remy stepped forward. "We are here to do your makeup, your hair, and wait on you hand and foot. Then we are to take you to a special location. Finn can explain everything there."

"You guys really aren't gonna tell me?" She searched her friends' faces. Every one of them grinned back at her and shook their heads.

Her stomach rumbled. "Does this surprise include breakfast?"

"Your hubby had me bring some coffee and goodies from the bakery too." Remy winked.

"Of course, he did. That man thinks of everything." Charli laughed, pure joy lighting her up from the inside out. Excitement did somersaults in her belly like butterflies basking in the warm sunshine of elation.

Maybe Finn had known after the rough weeks, or months rather, they'd had, that she needed this.

"So where do we start?"

* * *

Charli stood in front of the full-length mirror on her closet door. Emma had fixed her long, dark hair into a half-updo. Long, black curls kissed her shoulders and flowed down her back. The gorgeous earrings sparkled in the reflection, rivaling the enchantment in her eyes. Mia had done a dark smoky eye and a clean fresh-faced look that somehow accentuated her freckles. Charli ran a hand over the dress. It resembled something a Greek goddess would have worn. Sleeveless, the material wrapped over her chest, dipping into a deep V before it cinched under her breasts with a solid piece of champagne-colored material that tied behind her. The dress flowed out, leaving plenty of room for her growing belly. She didn't even recognize the woman staring back at her. For the first time in months, Charli truly felt beautiful.

"The limo's here." Emma peeked in.

"Limo?" Charli clarified. Just how many more surprises did this man have in store for her?

Emma winked. "You look gorgeous, babe."

"Thanks."

"Let's go. Your husband's waiting," Emma said, grabbing her hand.

* * *

Charli piled into the limo with her friends. They sipped on sparkling cider as the driver drove around town before finally pulling into The Shipwreck.

"What are we doing here?"

"You'll see. Go on in." Remy practically pushed her out of the car.

"Aren't you coming?"

"We'll be in soon."

"Okay." Charli lifted her dress so as not to get it dirty from the snowy slush as she walked to the door. She opened it and gasped. Twinkling lights covered every inch of the ceiling and walls. The tables and chairs had been rearranged to create an aisle lined with white rose petals and flameless candles. Her eyes traveled down the path, catching on the handsome man in a tuxedo staring back at her with a nervous smile.

"Finn?"

"Come here, baby."

She slipped off her coat, setting it on the bar before going to meet him.

His gaze raked over her, eyes wide and his mouth parting in what seemed like awe. "You look . . . like the goddess you are."

"You don't look so bad yourself, Major."

"Is it too much?" He smirked.

"That depends. What exactly is this? It looks like a—"

His smile deepened as he got down on his knee, holding her hand. "Thirteen years ago, I promised to love and protect you till death do us part. I don't remember it. And you've been the best partner a man could ask for. But I'd like to take the next step, to show you just how much I love you. How much I believe in us, and how committed I am to you. Charlotte Amy Reed, will you do me the honor of marrying me—again? Will you renew our vows?"

Tears blurred Charli's vision. Her heart swelled, the well of love and joy overflowing, saturating every cell with warm, golden bliss. "Yes, Finn. I'll marry you again."

He stood, wrapping her in a hug before kissing her on the lips, his tongue sweeping into hers, savoring her. He pulled away, his hands on either side of her cheeks, a grin splitting his face. "She said yes!" he hollered.

She giggled, his excitement matching her own.

Cheers and applause rang out from behind them. Charli turned around as their friends and family filed in from the back room.

"Everyone is here?" Charli clasped a hand over her heart.

Damon stepped forward. "Wouldn't miss this for the world."

She stepped down and hugged her brother. "It's so good to see you."

"You too."

"Are we ready to begin?" Bently asked, slipping past her to stand by Finn.

Charli had never been more ready in her life. Happiness rose like a bubble of sunshine in her belly, popping and saturating every cell with full-on, utter bliss until she glowed from the inside out. The room blurred through her tears of elation.

Floating on clouds of gratitude and awe, she wished everyone could feel one-tenth as happy as she did. This was what she'd wanted more than anything—for Finn to return to her. For them to get their happily ever after. It seemed some wishes came true, after all.

49

CHARLI

Emma handed Charli a bouquet of white roses and boxwood greenery. "Go back there. We want the full effect."

Zeke slipped his arm through hers. "I'd be happy to walk you down the aisle."

Her eyes swept over the dark blue suit he wore for the occasion. "If I wasn't already crying, I'd start all over again." She leaned her head against her father-in-law's shoulder.

"That's why we used waterproof makeup!" Mia teased.

"Okay, places, everyone." Emma clapped.

Finn stood on the stage with Bently under a canopy of twinkling lights. Their friends and family took their seats on both sides of the aisle. Soft music filtered in through the sound system. The beginning notes of "Falling Like the Stars" by James Arthur wrapped around her like a warm hug of incandescent happiness.

Zeke led her slowly down the pathway as affectionate gazes followed her movements. She smiled and nodded to everyone, but her attention was dragged back to the man at the opposite end, waiting for her. Her heart cinched and tugged her towards her husband, her forever.

Zeke leaned down and kissed her cheek. "You are the most beautiful bride and the best daughter a man like me could ever ask for."

She wrapped him in a hug and squeezed tight. "I love you, Dad."

When she pulled away, he was blinking away the emotion in his eyes and clearing his throat. "Love you too," he replied before taking a seat next to Claire.

Finn held out his hand, helping her up the step to the stage. They faced each other with Bently to their side.

Bently cleared his throat. "Friends, family, we're gathered here today to celebrate with our good friends, Charli and Finn, as they renew the vows they took more than a decade ago."

Charli couldn't help but laugh. Who would have thought that the boy she met in high school would be officiating her second wedding to the very man Bently had introduced her to?

"Now, we know these two haven't had an easy go of things. Those of us who are married know that happily ever after takes work. It takes the willingness to make your partner's needs as a priority. It takes communication, trust, and intention. Above all, it takes a willingness to do the hard work, to face your own issues, and deal with them so they won't hold you back." Bently lifted a hand to Finn. "It's a wonder you've made it this long, Finn."

Everyone laughed, including her husband.

"Jackass," Finn mumbled.

Bently smirked. "These two have something special. And I'm honored to be a part of your lives. Now, for the vows. Finn?"

Finn licked his lips. "Charli-baby, I promise to love you until the end of time. I swear I'll work my ass off to be the man you deserve. I will be honest and true, even when it hurts. I'll protect you with my life. I'll be by your side through the good and the difficult. Because at the end of the day, you're my everything. The woman who stole my heart not once, but twice. The woman who I owe my life to. So, sweetheart, I promise to cherish every moment we share. To be your best friend, your lover, your husband, and the father our children deserve. I will support you in any way you need, because I love you more than life itself. I promise to hold you up when things get too heavy, and to lean on you when I need to. No more hiding and pretending I have it all together when I don't. I may not remember much of our past, but I want to build a future with you."

Charli took the tissue Finn offered and wiped under her eyes before she sniffed. "Hormones."

The crowd chuckled.

"I didn't really prepare anything since this was all a surprise." She laughed, her body warm and content with joy. "I love you too, Finn. I promise to be by your side as we enter this new phase of our lives. I promise to try to be patient with you. To love and honor you with my actions. To support you. I promise to do my best to make you feel like the most loved man in the world. And I will do my best to communicate better with you."

Finn's eyes were red and watery. He sniffed and cleared his throat before pulling her into a mind-bending kiss that melted her from the top of her head to the tips of her toes.

"Hey, I'm supposed to say 'now you can kiss the bride.'" Bently huffed.

Finn pulled away. "Couldn't wait. Forever starts right now, baby."

Charli smiled as the music started again. Only this time, Lincoln spoke into a microphone. "You'd better appreciate this, Finnegan."

Charli spun around as their friend sang the opening lyrics of the song "Hard Stuff" by Justin Timberlake. Finn laughed and wrapped his arms around her, pulling her into a slow dance.

Charli's gaze snagged on Emma's as she watched unsurprised as her stepbrother crooned with a deep, sexy voice Charli hadn't known the man possessed.

Finn tucked Charli in closer, bringing her attention back to him.

"Thank you for this, Finn."

"I'm just relieved you said yes."

"You thought I wouldn't?"

He shrugged, his hand dropping to her lower back. "I hoped. But I was nervous as fuck."

She drew his mouth to hers, infusing her kiss with every bit of love and adoration she held for her man. "You are truly the best thing that's ever happened to me. I love you with everything in me."

"I got a little lost on the way, but I finally found my way back to you." He pressed his hand against her rib cage, where the inked promise rested beneath the fabric.

"Promise you won't leave me again." Her voice wavered, knowing she was asking the impossible.

"Never again."

Relief flit through her.

After their dance, Remy revealed a cake she'd made for the occasion. Finn brought out her favorite tubs of ice cream. Everyone enjoyed a hot chocolate bar and appetizers.

The celebration was filled with laughter and love with all their friends and family. As the evening wore on, Charli's belly grumbled. There was only so much cake and finger foods to keep her appetite at bay.

"Charli?" Bently ran up to her, his face splitting into a smile as he waved his phone.

Finn stepped beside her. "What is it?"

"They got him," Bently said.

"Got who?"

"Apparently, someone sent in an anonymous tip with video footage of your attack to the FBI. They got the guy's face and everything. He was picked up just moments ago in Boston."

Her heart stuttered. She held her breath, afraid to believe her luck.

"Who was it?" asked Finn.

"I don't know all the details yet. Agent Mallory gave me a courtesy call letting me know since the case was still open."

"It's really over?" Charli asked.

Bently nodded. "Fingerprints match the gift left at the bar."

Finn crushed her against his chest, the tension leaving his body was palpable. "It's done, sweetheart. You're safe."

"This is an even better wedding present than the earrings," she joked.

Finn chuckled. "Sure as fuck is."

She sagged against him and held on. Nothing could bring down her joy. She was safe. Her baby was safe. And her husband had returned to her an even better man than he was before.

"Let's go home," Finn whispered.

She nodded. "You read my mind."

They said goodbye, as everyone held sparklers above their heads. Finn gripped her hand and led them out the front door to the waiting limo.

"So fancy." She laughed, tucking her dress under her in the leather seat.

"Only the best for my wife."

Her face hurt from smiling so much.

"Did I tell you how beautiful you look tonight?"

"Mmmm, yes, but it's okay, you can tell me as often as you like." She laughed.

When the limo came to a stop in front of their home, Finn helped her out of the car, leading them to the front door before he picked her up. She squealed.

"I've got you. Gotta carry my bride over the threshold." He chuckled, opening the door and bringing her inside, feetfirst.

He set her down on the ground as her stomach rumbled.

"Hungry?" he teased.

She blushed. "Starving."

"What are you in the mood for?"

"Curry. I've been craving it since Brynn mentioned it this afternoon."

"We'll get takeout." He pulled out his phone.

"And then you can make good on every one of those promises you spoke this morning." She gave him what she hoped was a sexy smirk.

"Better order extra. I'm gonna need my energy for tonight." Bringing the phone to his ear, he rattled off an order before ending the call. "Ten minutes. We should leave now. It should be ready by the time we get there," Finn said, reaching for the door handle.

"You go. I'll wait here."

He stopped and turned to face her, worry creasing his brow.

"I'm safe now, remember?"

"Right." Finn sighed.

"Besides, as beautiful as this dress is, I'd like to get out of it. Get into something a little more comfortable." She shrugged out of her coat and hung it up.

"Alright. I'll be back in twenty. Lock up behind me anyways." He kissed her forehead.

"Yes, sir." She gave him a mock salute.

"Save that for the bedroom," he teased before exiting.

Charli shut the door as her phone dinged from her jacket pocket. She turned around and grabbed it.

Damon: *Brunch tomorrow before we head back to Colorado?*

Charli smiled and typed out her response, heading up the stairs.

Charli: *Sounds good. How about 11?*

Damon: *Perfect. See you at High Tide Diner then.*

Charli walked into her bedroom, tugging at the bow tied behind her. She loosened it and breathed a sigh of relief. After slipping out of her flats, she put them back in the box discarded on her bed earlier. The sound of footsteps drew her attention to the doorway.

Shit, I forgot to lock it behind Finn. He's gonna be mad. "Did you forget something?" Charli asked, standing as a man's silhouette took up the space in the doorway. Charli froze, her blood turning to ice. Panic streaked through her as chills skated across her flesh.

"What are you doing here?" she gasped, reaching for her phone.

"I wouldn't do that if I were you." The barrel of a gun pointed at her. She backed up, hitting the side table behind her. The lamp wobbled and crashed to the floor. There was no way she could reach inside for the gun without endangering her and the baby. "What do you want, Stewart?"

"What's owed."

Her eyebrows drew together. "Finn is going to be back any second."

"I'm counting on it, bitch."

Charli pressed a hand to her belly protectively. Just when she thought everything was over—that she and her family were safe and she and Finn had found their happily ever after—fate had come once again to steal the rug out from under her. "Stewart, he's your friend—"

The man laughed, deep and menacing. "Finnegan hasn't been my friend for years. Not since you got in his head and pussy whipped him. You made him weak. Unlike him, I don't have a soft spot. This is business."

"What business? What do you mean?"

"Get on the bed."

"Stew—"

"Don't make me fucking repeat myself!" he yelled, stepping forward as he thrust the gun towards her belly.

She held out her hands. Panic drenched her shaky movements as fear imbedded deep into her marrow. "Okay—okay. I'll do it." Charli swallowed down the bile that rose. Her body trembled with the very real terror that her life, and that of her son's, were in mortal danger. Horror for what this madman planned to do to her and dread that her husband would be walking into a trap lashed her skin like a whip with sharp barbs.

Please save us, Finn.

50

FINN

Finn paid for the takeout and made his way back to the Jeep. He set the food on the floorboard so it wouldn't spill before he started the engine. Light snow drifted from the dark sky. The moon was obscured by the pregnant, grey storm clouds. The temperature seemed to have dropped ten degrees since he'd run into the restaurant.

Shifting the car into gear, his foot pressed the pedal as an unsettling feeling cinched tighter across his chest. He adjusted his posture, clearing his throat, unable to shake the heaviness. He checked the clock. He'd only been gone fifteen minutes. If he called Charli now, she'd laugh at him and tell him he was worrying over nothing. Maybe it would take some time adjusting to the fact that she was safe—that this was over.

Chiming bells interrupted his thoughts. He picked up his phone and answered on speakerphone as he turned into his neighborhood. "Hello?"

"Hey, man, sorry. I figured you'd be busy." Bently chuckled. "Was gonna leave a message. Just got an update. The man who attacked Charli was Angelo Ezzo."

Whatever else Bently said went unheard as all the blood drained from Finn's face. Flashes assaulted him—memories returning without the smoke to distort them. *Angelo. The man from The Pearl Necklace. Stewart's boss. He was the one who'd threatened his family . . . Charli!*

The car jostled, fishtailing as Finn snapped out of it, steering away from the ditch. A plume of snow rained down on the windshield as thick branches cracked the glass. The seat belt pinched his waist as the car careened sideways before skidding to a stop.

"What was that? Are you okay?" Bently demanded.

"Charli's in danger," Finn said, slipping the car into reverse, only to hear the telltale sound of a wheel spinning without traction. "Fuck!" Panic seized his breath as he unbuckled, grabbing his phone. He pushed the weight of the door open and escaped.

"What—"

"Stewart works for Angelo. He— Listen, I'm almost home, but I have a bad feeling. Please, send help." Finn ended the call and dialed Charli as he ran as fast as his limbs would take him. The cold wind did nothing to his already numb body. Adrenaline fueled his sprint as the phone rang and rang with no answer before her voicemail picked up.

Am I too late?

I never should have left her.

"Ahhhh!" he screamed, expelling precious air as tears of fear and rage and hopelessness blurred his vision. *If only I could have remembered. I let that piece of shit in my house. I put her in danger.*

The lights of his home came into view. Nothing looked amiss. But the anxious unease that twisted his belly into a thousand intricate knots and the tiny hairs standing on end all over his body told him different. No, he knew it in his soul—

his wife was in danger. She needed him to protect her. And he would, even if it was the last thing he ever did.

"I'm coming, baby."

Finn jogged up to the front door. Common sense told him to wait for Bently or search the windows first to assess the situation. But none of that could stop his hand reaching for the door handle or stepping in blindly. His wife and his son were in danger. Creeping inside, he quickly entering the code before the alarm sounded and sending out an SOS. He tucked himself against the wall as his ears perked up, his vision darting around the space. Muffled voices came from upstairs.

Finn surveyed the area before making his way to the kitchen, silently grabbing a knife and slipping it up his sleeve before padding quietly up the stairs. Instincts kicked in, most likely from his Army training.

The bedroom door was cracked open, and the sight before him sucked the air from his lungs. His stomach lurched, knees wobbling and threatening to give out.

Stewart smiled at him, holding a gun to his wife's head. Charli's tear-filled gaze flashed with relief only a moment before the fear returned.

"Nice to see ya, buddy," Stew said.

"What the fuck are you doing?" Finn's voice was low and deadly.

Stew straightened, pulling Charli off the bed and beside him. She winced as he pulled her hair tighter. "Cleaning up the mess my former general made so I can prove to the actual boss I'm ready for a promotion. It's just business, Finnegan. Nothing personal."

"Get your hands off her!" he roared.

Stew chuckled. "I told you this woman would be your ultimate downfall. Thought maybe with the whole memory problem we could make everything right." Stew sighed. "But as usual, you fell for her pussy. What happened to bros over hoes, huh?"

Finn grit his teeth and clenched his fists, the weight of the knife against his arm only a small comfort. It would do him no good with that gun against his wife's head. Finn needed to draw Stewart's attention and rage towards him.

"Cops are on their way. Why don't you put the gun down now, and I'll only beat you to a pulp instead of killing you for putting your hands on my wife?" Finn threatened.

Charli squeaked, her eyes motioning to her side as her hand rested against the top drawer of the nightstand.

The gun.

Stewart smirked, his beady eyes narrowing. "Or I can put a bullet through the both of you and tell them how I walked in after a call from my delusional friend who killed his wife before taking his own life. After that head injury, things just weren't right with you."

The gun swung towards Finn. Staring down the barrel should have brought him overwhelming fear, but relief was the only thing that washed over him. Finn looked to Charli, trying to memorize the soft curves of her terrified face. There was no way they could both make it out of this alive. He'd wondered why he would survive just to have his memories stolen from him. Maybe this was why. Maybe he came back just so she and his son could live.

"You should have taken the deal and smuggled in the drugs for distribution in the bar. Angelo never would have had to use her to send a message. We could have shared laughs, extra cash lining our pockets, and celebrated with a lap dance at The Pearl Necklace. Instead, you've forced my hand," Stew snarled.

"Why do they want anything to do with me?" Finn asked, keeping the attention on himself.

"They're expanding up the seacoast from Boston. Your bar happens to be a key distribution center for the area and a great way to launder money. You could have made a killing. We could have been rich together. But no, you had to be all high and mighty as usual. Nobody turns down the Carelli family." Stew's laugh was dark and evil.

Finn's eyes darted to his wife's. "I love you, Charli-baby." He gave her a slight nod, hoping to god she could do what she needed to.

"Finn—"

"Safety first," he said, hoping she'd understand his message.

"You two are disgusting," Stew said, pulling her hair down so she had to bow at her waist.

She gasped and groaned in pain as the top drawer behind her opened. Finn needed to distract Stew so she could reach in.

"Hey, motherfucker, are you deaf as well as a dumb shit? Take your fucking hands off her!"

Stewart cocked the gun, sneering with a twisted smile. "Maybe I'll see just how good this pussy is that's got you so wound up. Make you watch."

Fury blanketed Finn like he'd never known. Pure, unadulterated rage boiled his veins as Stewart's fist wound around his wife's pillow-soft hair. His knees wanted to buckle under the hopelessness of the situation. Every cell screamed at him to attack. But the chance that Charli could get injured if he flew off the handle like he'd done in the past held him back. This was life or death. He wasn't willing to risk her.

The flash of blue and red reflected in the window as if still in the distance.

A glint of metal drew his attention to the weapon easing

up to Stewart's crotch, bringing a smug flash of glee. *Shoot his dick off, sweetheart.*

"Do it!" Finn yelled.

The small click of the safety being turned off was the last sound Finn heard before pain like he'd never known crashed over him, knocking him down. Red blossomed over his vision before darkness swallowed him whole.

51

CHARLI

*B*ang!
A warm spray of blood shot over her face as she crumpled to the floor, ears ringing. Stewart writhed, his hand dropping the gun to cup his mutilated genitals. Charli grabbed his weapon and crawled through the pooling blood to her husband. Blindly, she reached out to his leg. "Finn!"

But his arms didn't surround her. He didn't move at all. Charli's gaze darted up his legs, past his torso, and her heart stopped.

"No!" Dropping both weapons beside her, she reached out to his face and stopped. The side of his head oozed with blood. A piece of his skin hung there. Sirens blared, coming closer as Stewart screamed in pain. But nothing could compare to the deafening silence of her husband lying there in a pool of his own blood. Charli clamped her hand over the gaping wound. *That's what you're supposed to do with injuries like this, right?* A sob broke free. A violent sickness made her stomach lurch.

"No, baby. No. You can't leave me. Not like this. Not after everything. You promised. You promised you'd never leave me. Finn!"

His closed eyes sliced through her like a knife.

"Charli?" Bently called from down the stairs.

"Help! Bently! Help! Finn—he's—"

Bently rushed upstairs, gun drawn and aimed at Stewart as he entered the room, sweeping it like he was assessing the situation. He picked up his radio. "Vargas, I need a bus ASAP! Send Owens up here with the kit."

Bently pressed his fingers to Finn's neck. "He still has a pulse. It's faint, but it's there."

Charli sucked in a ragged breath. Hope flickered. Leaning down, she begged him one last time, ignoring the tears that streamed over her face. "Don't leave me, Finn. We still need to have our second honeymoon. You have to meet your son. Come back to me. You promised you'd always come back." She kissed his limp mouth, tasting the bitterness of copper, the wreckage of her grief, and emptiness of dreams lost.

The next moments were a blur, moving too slowly and at warp speed all at once.

The next thing Charli knew, she was standing in the cold, sterile hospital waiting room. Numb with shock, each inhale was a new torture as if she were inhaling shards of glass. The agony of not knowing if her husband was dead or alive on a table in a room down the hall was all-consuming. Voices spoke around her, sounding muddled as if she were underwater.

A warm palm covered her bloodstained hands. Charli's focus sharpened, the dark melanin reminding her of Finn's. Would she ever get to have his hands on her again?

"Charli?" Belle's voice grew clearer.

Charli lifted her chin, staring into two dark pools of

sympathy. Belle knew how this felt. But it didn't make it any easier. *Is she going to tell me he's gone?*

"Why don't we get you cleaned up?" Belle lifted a pair of Charli's clothes. Had her friend retrieved them from her house?

"Claire and Zeke are on their way," Belle said.

Charli obliged. She wanted to wash the blood off her, but she didn't want to miss Finn when he was out of surgery. What if he didn't make it? It could be the last chance she'd have to see him before he was gone forever.

"We'll be quick," Belle assured her as if she could read Charli's thoughts.

Charli stood, blindly following Belle into a patient room. She moved through the steps like a zombie as Belle brought the warm washcloth over her skin. Charli stared at the crimson-stained water as it washed down the drain with what was left of her hope. She closed her eyes as they burned with a fire she'd never known. *The chances of surviving a shot to the head are astronomically low.* Finn already got his miracle. Fate wouldn't be so kind a second time.

Belle pulled Charli's hair up, out of her face, before leading her back to the waiting room. The tender tug on her still-sore scalp reminded her of Stewart's greasy hands yanking on her hair.

Two pairs of arms encircled her, holding her tight.

"I'm so sorry——" She hiccupped.

"You have nothing to be sorry about," Claire assured her.

"Finn's a fighter. He'll—— He'll make it through this." Zeke's voice broke.

They released her, and Claire asked, "When is the last time you ate something? You're shaking."

Charli shook her head. "I can't——"

"I'll go grab you some tea and crackers," Belle said before leaving the small room.

"Bently said he's in surgery. Probably be awhile before we hear anything. Why don't you rest, dear?" Zeke ushered her to a chair.

They didn't get it. It was Charli's fault Finn was dying. If she hadn't shot Stewart, the man wouldn't have pulled the trigger, probably a reflex. Maybe if she'd waited, they could have ended things differently.

What's done is done. Now her husband lay in one operating room and the man who'd stolen the other piece of her soul in the other.

Bently sat across from her, his expression grim. He wouldn't even look at her. Belle walked in, followed by a doctor with a surgical cap. Bently shot to his feet, approaching the surgeon as Belle handed Charli the crackers. Charli stood, eyes glued to the doorway where the men spoke in hushed tones. Bently shook his head, shoulders dropping. The words "I'm sorry" formed on the surgeon's face before he flicked a pitying glance towards Charli.

She staggered back, her knees giving out. She reached for the arm of the chair, steadying herself. *No. Nonononononono.* Her lungs stuttered as violent pain raged through her, incinerating everything left in its path until all that was left was a hollow shell of devastation.

"Nooooo!" Charli screamed as a flood of water burst from her, trickling down her legs and pooling on the floor.

Her hands went instinctively to her belly, panic once again swallowing her whole. "No. It's too early. Not my baby too!"

"How far along are you, Charli?" Belle asked, immediately coming to her aid.

"Thirty-two weeks," she grit out as a wave of pressure barreled through her.

Belle snapped orders. Charli was put in a wheelchair and rushed into a room. The bright lights made her wince. Pain tore through her. Her chest ached. More commands were shouted as her clothes were cut off. Cold oxygen pushed up her nose from a plastic tube. Sweat beaded her brow as she screamed, unable to do anything but survive in that moment as wave after wave of pain sliced through her.

"Heart rate dropping."

"Cord prolapse."

"Prep the OR."

Voices of nurses and doctors and whoever else was in the room pulsed through the fog of pain.

"Do you have any allergies, Charli?" Belle asked, tone urgent.

Charli shook her head. "No."

"Charli, I'm Doctor Stanley. Your baby is in distress, so we're going to need to get him out. Okay?"

"But it's too early." She grit her teeth through another contraction. The bars on the bed lifted beside her as she was wheeled out of the room and down a hallway.

"We have the pediatrician ready and are equipped to handle a preemie. We promise we're gonna do everything we can, but we need to get the baby out *now*." The doctor's tone was kind but firm.

The surety that her baby was coming whether she was ready or not encompassed her. There was nothing else she could do at this point but hope and pray to a god she wasn't sure existed that her child would make it. "Okay."

"I'm going to gown up and be right back, Charli," Belle said before dropping her hand.

The double doors to the operating room opened for her. Several masked people already stood by machines and trays of operating instruments.

A woman appeared to her side, placing a mask over her face. "We don't have time to give you a spinal. We need to get the baby out because he's in distress. Do you understand?"

A wave of grogginess blurred the room as Charli echoed her husband's last words. "Do it."

Don't take my baby too.

Then her world went black.

52

CHARLI

Beep. Beep. Beep.

Charli moaned. Pushing her eyes open took so much effort, like her lids were made of lead. The dim light still seemed too bright. She opened her mouth to speak and promptly closed it. Had someone stuffed it with cotton balls?

"Charli?" a deep voice next to her said, before her hand was swallowed up by another's.

Finn? *No.* Pain lashed across her chest, memories flooding back to her. No. Finn was dead.

She turned her head. Zeke's brows were drawn together in concern.

"Water?" she croaked.

He nodded, grabbing a cup with a straw she hadn't noticed beside him. Charli took a sip and nodded. Zeke set it back down as she asked, "The baby? Is he—"

She couldn't finish the sentence. Had everything been taken from her today?

"Oh, he's doing just fine. Claire's with him in the NICU." Zeke patted her hand.

Charli's heart stuttered as relief flooded her body like warm sunshine. Her son was alive. He was going to survive. "I want to see him."

Zeke pressed the call button beside her seeming to know better than to argue with her.

After a heated discussion with the doctor, Charli's bed was wheeled into the NICU by Belle and a couple of orderlies. Her friend had helped convince the doctor that these were extenuating circumstances. Charli slipped a mask over her face, ignoring the throb from her incision site. She wanted to lay eyes on her son—see that he was okay for herself. He was all she had left of Finn.

Claire slipped out, giving Charli a gentle hug. "He's perfect."

Charli nodded as Belle pushed her inside the isolated room to what looked like a glassed-in case with two holes on the side. The light brown infant was impossibly small. He looked like a sleeping doll. So fragile.

"I know he doesn't look it, but he's a strong little guy," Belle said.

"Can I touch him?"

"You can hold him. Skin to skin would be really good for him." Belle lifted the tiny infant, careful of all the tubes and cords attached to his body before she set him against Charli's bare chest.

Charli pressed her hand gently to his back, holding him close. It was as if a piece of her heart now lived outside her body in this small human. His hand kneaded the flesh of her breast. It was so tiny, just big enough to wrap around the pad of her finger.

"Have you picked out a name?" Belle asked.

Charli bit back the bittersweet tears. "Finn wanted to name him Jamison. I think we'll go with that. Jamison Finnegan Reed."

"Strong name. Suits him." Belle squeezed her shoulder. "He's really quite healthy. The concerns when they're born this early are his fragile immune system and the potential of infection. With the lack of fat stores, he isn't quite able to regulate his body temperature yet. And his ability to suck, swallow, and breathe will take some time."

"But he's okay?"

"Yes. Five pounds four ounces of perfection."

Charli leaned closer, trying to memorize his little, pink rosebud lips and the dark swirls of hair matted to the top of his head. She inhaled his sweet scent—a complete contrast to the sterile hospital room. This moment was supposed to be so different. Finn was going to hold her hand and they were going to greet this tiny human together. But that isn't what happened. Not even close.

Belle's phone buzzed in her pocket. She pulled it out as Charli ran her thumb over her son's arm.

"I'm here, buddy. You're doing so amazing. You're a fighter, just like your daddy." Saltwater pain leaked down her face. Surely by now she'd have run dry of tears. But that wasn't the case.

"Bently is outside. He'd like to talk to you about Finn."

Charli shook her head. *No.* If he said the words, it would be the last nail in the coffin. She wasn't ready for her loss to be so final.

"Okay. Take as long as you need," Belle said.

* * *

An hour later, Charli shifted in the bed and winced. Belle placed her hand over her shoulder. "You should get some rest. You won't be any good to Jamison if you don't take care of yourself. He won't be alone. We'll all make sure of it."

Charli nodded, knowing her friend was right. Belle had her bed pushed back down the hall.

Bently was waiting outside her room, leaning against the wall with dark circles under his bloodshot eyes. His head snapped to them as she was wheeled into the room. Sharp stabbing pains flashed through her abdomen. She hissed.

"I'll give you a little more pain medication if the doctor okays it." Belle situated her IV bags.

"Finn—" Bently started.

"I don't—please don't say the words. Don't tell me he's gone. I can't take it right now." Charli squeezed her eyes shut as if that would close out the pain that engulfed her physically, and emotionally saturated every cell. Grief-stricken and raw, she just wanted to escape for a little while. Go somewhere where she didn't have to feel anything.

"But he's alive," Bently argued.

"I said—what?" Her eyes snapped open.

"Finn's alive, Charli. He's in the ICU. That metal plate from his accident? It saved his life."

Chills skated across her skin as she shook her head in disbelief—afraid to hope, to believe that Finn was truly still here. "He's alive?"

"You thought he died?" Belle asked, shock clear in her voice.

"The surgeon came into the waiting room and . . ."

"Stewart died on the table," Bently clarified.

"Oh my god." She clasped a hand to her mouth as a sob broke free. Tears streamed freely down her face as sweet, golden hope swept over her like a tidal wave. She couldn't catch her breath, each burst of oxygen tugging on her incision brutally. *But Finn is alive!*

Belle wrapped her arms around her. "Oh, sweetheart. Deep breaths."

"I want to see him."

"You just got back in here. Rest, and then we'll make it happen," Bently promised her.

"The doctor wanted to talk to you about his condition. And they won't let us wheel you into the ICU. You'll have to have the catheter removed and be able to walk before we put you in a wheelchair," Belle said.

Three hours later, after Charli threatened the doctor that she would leave against medical advice so she could visit her husband, he caved. Charli was wheeled into the cold room. Finn lay on his back with a bandage on his head and wires all over him. His mouth was open with a tube sticking out. The steady whoosh of air coming from a machine to his right puffed his lungs with air.

The nurse wheeled her to his side.

She reached out, taking his cool hand in hers.

"If you need anything, just holler."

"Thank you," Charli said, not looking away from her husband. "You saved us, Finn. Jamison is so tiny. He looks like his daddy." She rubbed her thumb over the soft flesh of his hand. "He's strong—just like you. Please hold on. You have to meet your son." She brought his hand to her mouth and kissed it. "Come back to us. I'll be right here . . . Please come back to me, baby."

Charli's head swam with the rundown of what the doctor had said about Finn's condition. Head injuries were no cut-

and-dry situations. Finn was once again in a coma. Would he wake up? Would his brain function be impaired? Would he recover?

She'd been down this road with him before. And like last time, she chose to believe that fate wouldn't be so cruel. Whatever they had to face, she'd be by his side. If only he'd wake up.

53

FINN

Finn's body felt as if it was floating in the middle of the ocean, drifting in the middle of nowhere. Flashes lit up the sky above him. Charli sneaking into his window as a teenager. The first time he'd climbed in bed with her because she was scared. Their first kiss. The nerves when he'd asked her to marry him the first time. Their wedding. Their honeymoon. Every memory washed over him, filling his consciousness until it all came back to him. He remembered everything. He tried to sit up, searching for her. But something held him down. The more he fought it, the stronger the pulsing pain in his head grew.

He opened his mouth to scream her name, but nothing came out. Turning his head, he found her glowing like the brightest star off in the distance. She gave him a sad smile. "You saved us, Finn. Jamison is so tiny. He looks like his daddy."

What? His son was born? No. It wasn't time yet. Did Charli die? Was this the afterlife?

A jolt of energy buzzed over his hand.

"He's strong—just like you. Please hold on. You have to meet your son."

He opened his mouth to scream, to say something. Still his voice was held captive. *I'm coming.* Each moment that passed, Finn drifted further away until Charli was nothing but a bright light in the distance, his North Star.

Vibrations tingled over his arm closest to her voice.

"Come back to us. I'll be right here . . . Please come back to me, baby."

He fought with all his might to get up, but it was no use. Whatever weight held him down was immoveable. He thrashed wildly, reaching towards her. The pounding in his head grew, excruciating pain rendering him spent.

I'm coming. Wait for me. I'm coming, Charli-baby.

54

CHARLI

Charli spent the next two weeks switching between her newborn in the NICU and her husband in the ICU. Her stitches were healing, but every step took effort. Claire and Zeke helped her take turns so that neither of her guys were alone for very long. Belle, Brynn, and the girls all popped in to check on her, bringing her food and reminding her that she was healing too. The family she'd created dropped everything to support her and Finn. Gratitude didn't come close to what she felt for them. Mason had the bar under control. Damon even offered to fly out to stay with her. But she couldn't bear to go home without at least one of her guys. She wanted to be here when Finn woke up. And he would. She knew it in her bones.

Charli walked to the cafeteria with Brynn. They picked out a sandwich and cup of tea. Charli was still limiting her caffeine now that Jamison could breastfeed as long as she used the nipple guard. She smiled. He was growing in leaps and bounds, and they'd promised her just that morning that he could go home with her in a few days as long as he kept his body temp regulated because he was eating so well.

She sat and surveyed the room, her gaze catching on a familiar face with blonde hair. "Emma?"

Emma's expression was grim, her eyes blank.

Charli moved closer and repeated herself. "Emma?"

Her friend looked up as if not really seeing her. "Dad had a heart attack. And Link—I've never seen him this . . . distraught. I need to find him." Emma stood.

"Oh my god!" Charli wrapped her arms around the young woman as Remy ran into the cafeteria, her head swiveling around as if searching.

Her eyes locked on them and she rushed over. "I'm here. Emma, sweetheart. I'm so sorry."

Charli backed away so Remy's arms could replace hers.

"He's gone." Emma's voice sounded so hollow.

Charli stepped away, giving them a moment of privacy. Brynn offered Remy a tissue for their friend.

The phone in Charli's pocket rang loudly. She scooped it out, not bothering to see who it was before she answered, stepping away. "Hello?"

"He's awake!"

Charli sprinted out of the lunchroom and along the hallway towards her husband's room, ignoring the pain in her waist. She caught her breath as she waited for the elevator. There was no way she was taking the stairs, not unless she wanted to end up back in a hospital bed herself. The doors opened and she pressed the button repeatedly for Finn's floor.

Moments later, she rushed into his room. Finn's gaze snapped to hers. It was like déjà vu.

"Finn?"

His eyebrows drew together in confusion.

"Do—do you know who I am?"

He shook his head.

Her heart sunk. *Not again.*

A wide smile broke out on his face. "Shit. I'm sorry. Thought it would be funny this time."

Realization spread over her like the sun moving out from behind storm clouds. "You asshole!" She stepped to his side, tears of joy, of grief, of relief pouring from her eyes.

His hand reached up to cup her face. "I'm sorry, sweetheart. Don't cry. I can't take it." His lips coasted over hers. He slid to the side, making room for her on the bed. "Lie with me."

"Won't I hurt you?"

"Need you." His voice shook.

She carefully climbed in as Claire excused herself.

His hand rested gently on her flatter stomach. "Is he . . ."

"He's perfect. And he can't wait to meet his daddy. He's a fighter like you."

Finn sighed with what she assumed to be relief. "I'd say more like his mommy."

She filled him in on the birth and the last couple weeks.

"You named him Jamison?"

"I thought I'd lost you. I wanted to hold on to whatever pieces I could. So, I went with Jamison Finnegan Reed."

He traced his finger over the side of her face, his eyes growing watery. "I love you."

"I love you too. So much." She kissed him.

"When I saw Stewart's hands on you—"

"Shhhh. He's gone. It's all over," she assured him.

"But it's all my fault you were put in danger."

She locked eyes with him. "And it's my fault you were shot in the head and almost died."

Anger flashed in his expression. "The fuck it is."

"We can go back and forth over what was whose fault, or

we can both be grateful for our second, or third, or whatever chance we're on now. You're alive. Our baby is safe and healthy. I'm okay. Let's just move forward together. Leave the past where it belongs. And trust that we both did what we thought we had to in that moment."

He nodded and then winced. "Okay."

"Are you in pain?"

"Just a headache. How about you?"

She rested her hand over his on her abdomen. "I'm much better now that you're here."

He leaned down, touching his forehead to hers. "I knew I loved you since the first time I saw you."

She gasped. "What?"

"I didn't touch Laura after I met you. It just didn't feel right. That's why she turned to Ricky. I just didn't know what to do with how I felt. Didn't know what it meant."

"You—you remember?" she asked, stunned.

"All of it. I remember everything." He kissed her, sucking her bottom lip into his mouth. His tongue melded with hers, as she melted against him.

All the grief, all the pain they'd been through only made this moment that much sweeter. Joy burned inside her chest like the sun, incinerating the remnants of the shadows that had taken up residence these past months. Her husband held her, cherishing her with his lips, with his gentle, possessive touch reaching her soul.

EPILOGUE

EIGHT MONTHS LATER - CHARLI

Charli leaned against the doorframe of the nursery. The sight of Finn rocking their eight-month-old to sleep made Charli's ovaries ache. If she wasn't already completely head over heels in love with the man, this would have surely done her in.

He kissed his son's forehead before he set Jamison in his crib. Turning towards her, he gave her a wink and a smirk as if he knew what he did to her. Finn grabbed her hand and tugged her towards their bedroom. She followed, taking one last glance towards their slumbering babe.

"Zack called while you were putting Jamison to sleep," Charli whispered.

Finn stopped and turned to face her as they entered the bedroom. "How is he doing?"

She shrugged. "He sounded okay. He said they're doing a memorial barbeque with the rest of the guys from your unit for Smithson on the anniversary of his death next month. Wanted me to let you know we're invited."

Finn nodded, concern lines marring his features. "I wish I

could have been there for him when everything happened. Eric fucking loved him with everything in him. Because of the amnesia, I abandoned him too."

Charli lifted her hand to his cheek. "Hey. Zack knows why you couldn't be there. The other guys from your unit were. He was surrounded by both his own and Eric's family. And now you can go to the memorial too."

Finn sighed. "You're right. I can't control the past. But I can be there for him now."

"So we're going to Washington next month?"

"Yup."

She smiled, leaning up on her tippy-toes to kiss his cheek. He pulled her against his chest and kicked the bedroom door shut before turning the baby monitor on. His lips crashed over hers, hungry yet gentle, pressing her to the door.

Finn stepped back, breathing hard. Each rise and fall of his chest brushed against her sensitive nipples, pebbling under his desire-filled gaze. "You're so beautiful. Every day, I just can't believe you're mine."

She traced her finger over the jagged scar on the side of his head—a reminder of what she'd almost lost, of everything she'd gained.

His palm enclosed around hers, dragging it to his heart. "How satisfied is my wife this week sexually?" One corner of his mouth curved up.

She looked at the ceiling, pretending to think. "Hmm. Well, I'd say it's an eight out of ten."

"I see." He pressed his lips to her neck, to the sensitive patch of skin right below her ear.

Chills skated down her arms and legs. Desire pooled in her center, flames lapping the edges.

"What can we do to change that eight to a ten?" His voice deepened, heavy with lust.

"Make love to me." Her plea came out breathy.

He trailed kisses over her neck as he lifted the T-shirt over her head. Warm, hot lips danced and caressed over her collarbone, between her breasts, across her soft belly, not missing a single stretch mark. He pulled her leggings off as he got on his knees, kissing the red scar over her pubis. His hands kneaded her ass and upper thighs.

She threaded her fingers through his hair, gripping tighter. He tipped his head so their gazes locked. Licking between her already wet pussy lips, he teased her. Her nipples puckered and hardened under his hungry stare. Her body combusted into white-hot fire. Hot and cold. Need and want. Hope and awe. A million emotions swarmed inside her like a storm. Her body shuddered from the intensity brewing between them. It had never been this intense. Trust was a powerful thing, propelling them into new planes of pleasure.

He licked again, reaching her clit, stoking the flames.

"Finn?"

"Yeah, baby? What do you need?"

"Make me come."

Calloused hands pressed her thighs apart, hooking one of her legs over his shoulder as he steadied her with one hand, holding her against the door for support. He dove down, sucking and licking through her sex, lapping her juices. He thrust two fingers inside her as he fluttered his tongue over her clit, up and down, flicking the soft muscle across her throbbing nub in a fast rhythm. Finn curled the pads of his fingers until they hit that sensitive spot inside her. His hands and mouth worked in tandem, building the pleasured pressure until she cried out, clenching her muscles around him.

Her orgasm crashed through her, upending like a tidal wave. Her limbs grew heavy. Finn stood, scooping her up in his arms before he laid her on the bed. The sound of fabric dropping to the floor preceded him climbing on top of her. His mouth immediately latched on to her nipple while he massaged the other. Liquid sprayed from one, dousing the side of his face.

The first time her milk had let down during sex she'd been embarrassed. But Finn only seemed to get even more turned on. He hardened to steel against her thighs.

"I need you inside me." She writhed under him, wrapping her legs around him. Open and pliant. Empty and aching for his cock.

His kiss swallowed her moan as he teased the tip of his dick up and down over her clit. Her stomach muscles clenched, taut with need. Lust spiraled. Fierce love and the overpowering greed of her pussy to have him buried inside her had her digging her nails into this back. "Please!" she begged.

"You want my cock, sweetheart?"

"Yes! Oh, god, yes." She pulled him closer, rocking her hips so that he slipped inside her slick channel.

A growl emanated from his chest. "It's all yours." He thrust, root to tip, stealing her breath as he stretched her to perfection. His eyes locked on hers.

"You." He pulled out. "Own." He thrust back in hard in exquisite torture, repeating the motions with every word. "Every. Fucking. Part. Of. Me."

She cried out, clinging to him as he rocked her higher towards the peak. Her legs shook, heels dug into his firm ass, urging him on.

She closed her eyes. It was all too much. She writhed as if she could escape the damning pleasure. He only gripped her tighter, melding his lips to hers as the sound of slapping flesh echoed in the room.

His teeth raked over her bottom lip before he pulled away.

"Open your eyes, baby."

She obeyed.

"Want to see you leave your body. Need to see that flash of your soul as I make you reach the stars."

"I love you," she cried, her orgasm spinning her up. Overwhelming ecstasy rippled through her as she was thrust into delirium-inducing divinity.

"You. Are. Everything," he grunted. His body clenched, the veins in the side of his neck pulsed. Dark brown eyes burned with the fire of a thousand suns as he commanded, "Come with me, baby."

Everything fell away until nothing existed but the two of them somewhere high in the universe—a duality of souls joining until they burst into something bigger and brighter than they ever would have been alone. A sun. A star. A supernova. Burning hot and bright with enough energy to light up a solar system inside her.

Somewhere in the haze, Charli was aware of Finn growling her name as he emptied himself inside her.

He lay on top of Charli, seeming as spent as she felt. He was still connected to her, his hot release leaking down her thigh. Finn kissed her, long and slow, tasting of promises kept and a whole future of tomorrows.

When he pulled away from her, his thumb caressed her cheek, wiping away the tears she hadn't realized were falling.

"What's wrong?" he whispered.

"You came back to me."

His gaze softened, eyes crinkling at the edges as he kissed her once more. "Promised I would. I'll always find my way back to you, baby. You're my true north."

The End

Thank you! We hope you enjoyed reading *His True North*.

Now, turn the page for a sneak peek of Chapter One in the next book, **In The Grey**, (Book 6, featuring Emma and Link's story).

Or visit the website below to order Book 6 in the Shattered Cove series right now.

WWW.AMKUSI.COM/INTHEGREY

SNEAK PEEK OF IN THE GREY
CHAPTER 1 - EMMA

Emma wiped the sweat from her brow. Her hair stuck to her neck under the hot spotlights. Her chest heaved as adrenaline coursed through her veins. The cheers from the crowd were deafening. Closing her eyes, she relished the high—every atom buzzing and alive. Moments of happiness were fleeting in her life. But the stage was one place Emma didn't doubt she belonged. Here she was, Emma Sterling, rock goddess and lead singer of The Sirens.

She lifted the microphone to her lips as the last notes of the electric guitar ended. "Thank you, Nashville, and goodnight!"

Screams erupted and chants for a second encore echoed as she exited the stage, her bandmates at her heels. *Yes! What a goddamn high.*

"Here." Callie, their band manager, handed her a bottle of water as she sunk onto the couch in the green room.

"Thanks." Emma twisted the top before guzzling half the bottle.

"Taking care of you is my job." Callie winked. "And I'd be more than happy to meet *all* your needs. Just say the word."

Emma let her eyes wander over the gorgeous woman's body. It wasn't the first time Callie had offered. But Emma didn't mix business and pleasure anymore. That was the deal they'd made as a group after Asher had stirred up trouble with the last manager by sleeping with him.

"Fuck, that was rough without Geo," Asher said, sliding in next to her, beer in hand. His dark eyes clouded over as an invisible weight descended upon the room.

She reached out and took his palm in hers. His long fingers wrapped around hers and squeezed.

"Geo will be back. He'll get through this. We have a lawyer working on an appeal." She offered him what she hoped was a comforting smile.

"He turned the suit down," Nicky said, blowing out a cloud of smoke before passing the blunt to Leo.

"Why would he do that?" Emma gasped.

"Because he thinks he deserves prison," Ravi grumbled.

"It was an accident. He didn't mean to—"

Leo held his hands up. "We know that. Tell it to Geo."

Emma shook her head and swallowed the lump in her throat. Just when they'd hit it big, achieved the dreams they'd fought so hard for as a team, Geo had been ripped out of their lives—all for a drunken mistake.

They'd lost their second guitarist, their best friend, and brother. *This can't get any worse.*

Missing Geo only added to the ache in her soul. She took another sip of water, trying to quell the nerves. The hollow pain increased as the high from performing wore off. No one cared about her dark family history on stage. Or her long string of ex-boyfriends and girlfriends, who never came close to filling the hole in the center of her heart. Reality slammed into her. Numbness sunk inside her bones like gravity. Wanting reared its ugly head once again. She was homesick for a place she'd never known, yearning for someone she'd never had.

Why wasn't she happier? Even before Geo had been taken away, a grey had settled over her life. Shadows had followed her ever since she could remember. She'd thought for sure making her dreams come true would chase them away for good and thrust her into the light. But this was like climbing Mount Kilimanjaro and the view being just *okay*.

Maybe there is something wrong with me. Why couldn't she feel anything unless it came with an adrenaline rush or endorphins?

Giggles filtered into the room as Callie let in the few VIPs and groupies.

"Oh my God! It's her!" someone screamed.

Emma braced herself for the onslaught of questions and pictures.

"Em? Your phone's been blowing up." Callie handed it to her.

Emma glanced at the screen and her heart stuttered.

Link.

Why would he be calling her? Her belly flipped and tumbled with nerves. He never called her, much less spoke to her when they were in the same room—as rare as that was. He put up with her for her stepdad's sake.

Her phone rang again.

Something isn't right.

She swiped the screen and answered, "Hello?"

"Emma—" His voice caught, fear bleeding into the space between them.

"What's wrong? Is Dad okay?"

Silence was her only answer.

No, no, no, no, no, no.

Emma stepped away from the noise.

A fan thrust a pad of paper and Sharpie in front of her face. "Can I get your autograph?"

Emma shook her head and pushed past her, finding a storage closet as dark as the cloud looming over her. "Link?" She choked back her rising panic.

His voice was gruff, haggard, like he was barely holding it together. She'd never heard him like this. "His heart . . . You need to come home."

"I'm coming." Emma pulled the phone away, ending the call with a shaky hand as her body trembled. Her lungs squeezed tight as she opened the door and walked back into the lounge. Laughs and squeals faded into the hum of background noise as the world around Emma darkened. The blackness of despair lapped at her feet.

"Em? Are you okay?" Callie sounded like she was in a wind tunnel.

Emma shook her head. "I have to get home. My dad—"

She swallowed. A new surge of adrenaline rocked through her body, sharpening her senses.

"I need a flight to Shattered Cove five minutes ago."

Callie nodded, seemingly understanding the importance. "Let's get you to the airport, then."

Dad is going to be okay. He had to be. He was the only one who'd ever really loved and cared for Emma, even though they weren't blood related. He was the only one who'd ever chosen her.

"There's a flight to Boston leaving in forty-five minutes," Callie offered.

"Book it." Emma ducked into the SUV, not bothering with her seat belt.

The driver broke the speed limits to get them to the

airport. But something told her that—even with the fastest jet plane—it would be too late.

To continue reading Emma and Link's story, visit the website below to get your copy of *In The Grey* today.

WWW.AMKUSI.COM/INTHEGREY

JOIN OUR NEWSLETTER

The best way to get updates about new releases, sneak peeks, pre-orders, giveaways, and more is by joining our newsletter.

You'll also receive a FREE short novel that's not available on any retailer to read.

Visit the website below to join now.

WWW.AMKUSI.COM/NEWSLETTER

THANK YOU

Thank you for reading *His True North*. We hope you are emotionally satisfied with Charli and Finn's love story. If you enjoyed this novel, please consider leaving a review on your favorite retailer and sharing it with your friends and family.

Also, you can start reading the other books in The Shattered Cove Series right now!

Remy and Mikel in ***A Fallen Star (Book 1).*** The eBook version is FREE on all retailers.

Andre and Mia in ***Glass Secrets (Book 2).***

Belle and Bently in ***Defying Gravity (Book 3).***

Jasmine and Atlas in ***The Lighthouse Inn (Book 4).***

Link and Emma in ***In The Grey (Book 6).***

Lastly, if you haven't read our first complete series, ***The Orchard Inn Romance Series***, make sure you get your copy so you don't miss out on three wonderful love stories.

Thank you again for reading *His True North!*

Cheers,

Ash & Marcus.

ABOUT A. M KUSI

A. M. Kusi is the pen name of a wife-and-husband author team, Ash and Marcus Kusi. We enjoy writing romance novels that are inspired by our experiences as an interracial/multicultural couple.

Our novels are about strong women and the sexy heroes they fall in love with, are emotionally satisfying, and always have a happy ending.

Discover more about us at:

WWW.AMKUSI.COM

To receive updates about new releases, giveaways, sneak peeks, pre-orders, and more, visit the website below to join our newsletter today:

WWW.AMKUSI.COM/NEWSLETTER

After you join the newsletter, we will send you a FREE novella to read.

To contact us, use this email address amkusinovels@gmail.com.

Happy reading!

facebook.com/amkusi
instagram.com/amkusinovels

ALSO BY A. M. KUSI

A Fallen Star (eBook FREE on all retailers)

(Book 1 in The Shattered Cove Series)

Glass Secrets

(Book 2 in The Shattered Cove Series)

Defying Gravity

(Book 3 in The Shattered Cove Series)

The Lighthouse Inn

(Book 4 in The Shattered Cove series)

In The Grey

(Book 6 in The Shattered Cove series)

The Orchard Inn (eBook FREE on all retailers)

(Book 1 in The Orchard Inn Romance Series)

Conflict of Interest

(Book 2 in The Orchard Inn Romance Series)

Her Perfect Storm

(Book 3 in The Orchard Inn Romance Series)

For a complete list of all our books, visit:

WWW.AMKUSI.COM/BOOKS